I0593399

GRUnGE.001

Licence to Die

GRUnGE.001

Licence to Die

Mazzy Adams

Zest N Zenith
Creative & Academic Group
(ABN 93 714 288 498)
PO Box 9219 Wilsonton QLD 4350 Australia
znz@zestnzenith.com.au

First published 2022
Text © Mazzy Adams 2022
Interior images, layout, and cover design © Catherine J Sercombe

Scriptures referred to and/or quoted are taken from the NEW INTERNATIONAL VERSION (NIV): Scripture taken from THE HOLY BIBLE, NEW INTERNATIONAL VERSION ®. Copyright© 1973, 1978, 1984, 2011 by Biblica, Inc.™. Used by permission of Zondervan.

A catalogue record for this book is available from the National Library of Australia

ISBN: 978-0-6489726-0-0 (paperback)
ISBN: 978-0-6489726-1-7 (ebook)

All rights reserved. No part of this publication may be reproduced, stored in, or introduced into a retrieval system, or transmitted, in any form, or by any means, electronic, mechanical, photocopying, recording or otherwise, except for brief quotations for printed reviews, without the prior written permission of the publisher, unless specifically permitted under the Australian Copyright Act 1968 as amended.

This is a work of fiction. Names, characters, businesses, institutions, organisations, agencies, places, events, localities, and incidents mentioned in this novel are either the products of the author's imagination or used in a fictitious manner. Any resemblance to actual persons, living or dead, or actual events, is purely coincidental.

Dedication

For Grace
who gave me life and showed me how to love
and be loved sacrificially

And Gary
my beloved husband and hero,
who is happy to eat tinned tuna
when I'm lost in the creative process.

—◦—

Welcome to Aussie Style!

Dear Reader

I've used our distinctive Down Under approach to spelling,
language, punctuation, and style conventions to reflect
the Australian characters and setting within.
We love our quirky Aussie-ness.
I hope you'll love it too.

Mazzy

UP FRONT

Easter 6 April 2012

Canberra, Australia

LOUD BANGS demolished Ben's Good Friday sleep in. He surrendered his fractured dream without regret. His pillow? Not so much. It had been a rough night. The reek of stale sweat wafting from his t-shirt agreed.

A bell from the local parish church chimed in, clanging its solemn call to worship on the offbeat.

'Bah! They're in cahoots!' He buried his head under the pillow. *Sleep wreckers.*

The bell fell silent. The unrepentant clatter morphed into a belligerent knock.

Ben grunted, hauling himself up and his t-shirt off in one fluid movement. Clad in boxer shorts and a mood as rank as the shirt he'd tossed, he stumbled downstairs and opened the front door to a tardy autumn—

And two uniformed police officers.

'Benjamin Ail Jandro?' The spokesman—one Marsden Vaig—tapped his name badge by way of introduction.

'Close. It's pronounced Alee-handro. J is soft. No beer up front.'

The female officer's bemused expression mirrored his own.

Constable Vaig-of-the-nametag aborted his tepid smile and barrelled on. 'Your father is Patricia?'

'Patri-ar-ca. It's Spanish. Most people call him Pat. He's away this week. Work gig. Europe or thereabouts.' Ben failed to stifle a bone-shuddering yawn. 'Sorry. Scuse me. You were saying?'

'Mother home? Imee, is it?'

Ben raked his scalp. 'She cleared off months ago.' He rubbed the sleep, if not the strain, from his eyes.

Several pedestrians, church-goers most likely, had paused to stare. Ben hitched his shorts up a smidgen. Their rubbery waist elastic snagged a hair. His manoeuvre snagged the female officer's attention.

She scanned his upper torso before flipping her focus to his ear. 'Nice stud.' She smiled. 'Black opal?'

Ben offered a subtle nod. Leading *Senior* Constable Torino was observant. Few people noticed his helix piercings. Fewer commented.

'Gift from a friend?' she asked.

'Family heirloom.'

'Seventh generation, no doubt.'

'At least.'

Her smile was stunning.

Vaig cleared his throat, gaining her attention. He pointed to his notepad. 'What about this one? Next of ki—?'

'You took the call.' Authority weighted the dress-down in her tone and her glare.

Vaig's expression soured. 'Sorry, mate.' He snapped the pad shut. 'Public holiday info-train's caught us short of a carriage or two. Does the name Christopher Darnell mean anything to you?'

'Why? What's—?' A whisper-thin breeze scraped its splintery edge across Ben's skin. He shivered.

LSC Elspeth Torino stepped forward. 'I am sorry, Benjamin. I'm afraid we have difficult news for you.'

PART ONE

Burned
and
Bereaved

1. BURNED

Six years earlier ... (25 March 2006)

Northern Beaches, Sydney, Australia

'USE MUM'S paradise routine.'

Christian Maxwell smiled at his kid sister's conspiratorial smirk. She'd signed in Auslan then zipped her lips.

Silent discussion. Perfect. He signed back. 'You think?' He could hear their mother clinking dishes in the kitchen.

Amy nodded. 'Works every time. Bet you five.' She rubbed her thumb and forefinger together.

Chris grimaced. He needed to borrow money, not bet with it. He spread his fingers and rocked his hand. 'Maybe.'

'Won't know if you don't try. Just go for it, bro.'

'I dunno,' Chris mumbled.

'Chicken!' Amy repeated the sign till Chris raised his hands in surrender. She narrowed her eyes. 'You do remember how it goes?'

Chris nodded. Mum's paradise routine—a replay of how she'd engineered the family's relocation to Sydney—was legendary, a sure-fire way to prep Dad for his pitch.

'If it works, I call first dibs on play.' Amy scrunched her nose. So cute.

'If it works, Dad'll call first dibs.' Chris mimicked her nose scrunch, cuteness excluded.

Amy sighed. 'This is true.' Her face lit up. 'Second dibs?'

'We'll see.'

Amy pushed back from the breakfast table and stood. 'Wait up. I have to pee.' She spun around and collided with their dad.

'Whoa!' he said, hugging her by default. Dad tucked a finger under

Amy's chin and raised her face towards his own. 'Do I detect a whiff of mischief in the air?'

'I dunno, Da. Did you break wind too? Godda go!' Amy wriggled free and took off. She was quick, that one, in more ways than one.

'Signing instead of speaking, Christian? Come on. 'fess up. What dastardly game is afoot?' Dad brandished his parental superpower spill-your-guts laser stare.

Chris parried with a cheesy grin.

'Amy's hearing is fine now. You know that. It's her diction that needs work.' Dad wielded the eyebrow lift.

'Mum reckons signing's good spelling practice.'

'For you, maybe. Amy has no trouble spelling.' Amusement tweaked his father's expression. 'Perhaps you should spell, "Good morning, honoured pater. It's Saturday. Sit down and relax while I bring you breakfast."'

Chris's optimism soared as he headed to the kitchen to enlist his mother's help.

BREAKFAST DELIVERED, Chris dropped to his knees to invoke their tried-and-tested family ritual. 'We *have* to buy it, Alastair! Pretty pleeease?'

'Hey, cheeky. That's my line.' His mother flicked him with her tea towel. 'Our son says we *have* to buy it, Alastair. Pretty pleeease?' She tossed the tea towel onto the breakfast table with a dramatic flourish.

Chris grinned. So far so good.

Dad played along, straight-faced. 'But we haven't even seen it, Zoe.'

'Oh, Alastair, it sounds divine. A dream come true. Please say yes.' She linked her fingers under her chin and fluttered her eyelashes.

Chris slapped his arms across his chest, threw his head back, and laid it on. 'It's the ultimate investment for our personal patch of paradise. With lake views to die for.' That's how the real estate agent had described their house.

'A performance sung with perfect sales pitch.' Dad sucked in a grin.

Mum curtsied. 'With or without hindsight, we all agree it was meant for us. Arianna Trace? Arianna Lakes? The name alone—'

'I know, I know. Arianna was your mother's name.' Dad rolled his eyes.

'Grrrrandmother's name.' Mum rolled her r's like an opera singer.

'Grrrrrrandmother's name.' Dad upped the ante.

Chris drew a huge breath. 'Grrrrrrrrrrrrrrandma Arianna!' He stood and high-fived his mother.

Dad gave a slow clap. 'Okay. Pantomime's over. What are we buying this time?'

'This.' Chris grinned and pulled a folded catalogue page from his back pocket.

'You mean I get to see it before I pay for it?' Dad winked.

Back in the day, Mum had pushed their 'personal patch of paradise' purchase, sight unseen. The real estate agent hadn't mentioned the eight-metre cliff that split their allotment in two, or the marijuana crop being cultivated in their 'extensive elevated garden' by a neighbour. Dad had gone ballistic. Mum had laughed, reported the crop, and instigated a clean-up. 'Some days you gotta roll with the punches,' she'd said.

Chris tried to avoid punches. Thankfully, his computer gaming rep deflected most of them at school. And helping his dad build a chair-and-rope-pulley system to scale the cliff had been fun.

'So, my son and heir, you want the latest Xbox and you need how much?'

'Thirty dollars. I've saved the rest.'

Amy picked that moment to re-enter the room. 'Did it work? Did he say yes?' she signed to Chris.

'Aha! So it is a conspiracy.' Dad waved the page. 'I will fight, but never surrender-errrrr.'

Chris offered a sheepish grin. 'Please, Dad?'

'Oh, alright. But I call dibs on first play!'

'You've got it!' Chris hugged his dad, kissed the surrendered cash, and scrambled to leave the room.

'Isn't it your turn to stack the dishwasher, Chris?' Mum dangled the tea towel. 'I emptied.'

Chris's shoulders slumped. He tipped his head towards Amy. 'Swap, sis? I'll do double duty tomoz?' Unsigned.

'Double duty. Promise? And second dibs!'

Chris nodded. 'Cross my heart and hope to die.'

'Okay, I s'pose. Then can I go up to the cubby to read, Mum?'

'Use the harness. Take your phone and text me if you need me.'

'Always do.' Amy's book lay open on the table. She flipped it shut. Dad smiled. 'Good book, toots?'

'Complicated. But it's the kind of book I want to write one day.' Amy picked up her empty breakfast bowl.

'Well, never let it be said I stopped my children reaching their full potential. You'd better get reading, tout de suite! I'll do the dishes this time.'

'Thanks, Da.' Amy dumped her bowl, grabbed her book, and scurried out the back door.

Chris wheeled his bike out of the garage minutes later.

'Warriewood Square only,' Mum yelled from the upstairs veranda. 'Then straight home, okay? Wear your helmet or—'

'I'll have a terrible accident and split my head open—'

'And the ambulance will go to the wrong suburb—'

'And I'll bleed to death! I know! Will you shut the garage door, please?'

'Who killed your last slave? Go on.' She waved.

'Love you, Mum.' Chris secured his helmet and eased his bike down the steep driveway.

The little boy from next door called out. 'Hey, 'rischen, where ya goin'?'

'Shopping. For a new Xbox.'

'Cool! Can I play?'

'If your mum says yes. I gotta go now, matey.'

'You better wait till the ambla-lance goes past.'

An ambulance was indeed cruising up the street. 'No lights or sirens. There's no emergency,' Chris said.

'Don't they do 'mergencies?'

'They're probably taking Mr Spinnaze for dialysis.' Chris spun his peddles to push off.

'What's dalsis?'

'I'll explain later, Timbo. See ya.' As he cycled past the ambulance, his thoughts returned to the Xbox.

CHRIS COUNTED twenty-seven flat-screen TVs in the Warringah Mall electrical store. And fifty million people in the checkout queue. But he had scored the latest and greatest Xbox on the first day of its Australian release. Sweet!

He shuffled his feet and rechecked his watch. Mum'd be miffed he'd cycled to the mall, but the Warriewood store had sold out. *A man's gotta do what a man's gotta do.* At least, that was the excuse he'd offer. One day, he'd be the world's best computer game designer and make his parents proud. Chris blew a raspberry. It was tough being the ordinary Maxwell.

'A fiver says she'll cinch it.' A loose button on the wannabe prophet's tweed golfing cap caught Chris's eye.

'I beg your pardon?'

Tweed pointed towards the televisions, all synced to the same channel. 'Commonwealth Games. Chantell Newberry. She'll get the gold.'

'Oh.' Chris watched twenty-seven identical swan dives, uncertain what the fuss was about. When it came to on-screen action, if it moved without a hand-held game controller, he couldn't care less, unless—

Twenty-seven splashes froze as Chantell Newberry hit the water.

Christian stared as 'Breaking News' hauled twenty-seven massive fireballs into view, followed by twenty-seven silent fire engines drag-racing in an epileptic storm of blue and red flashes.

A retail assistant increased the volume.

'—amateur footage of the carnage as we cross live to Arianna Lakes where an explosion has destroyed a house in Arianna Trace. The fire—'

'Hey! That's—' Chris dropped the Xbox, tore through the store's anti-theft entrance scanners and sprinted for the car park. His feet pounded fear and fire.

Run, Christian, run!

He mounted his ten-speed bicycle and assaulted the traffic. Horns blared. Drivers yelled.

Chris pumped the pedals for ten endless kilometres, cursing his killer calves, burning lungs and stinging sweat. His retro racer lugged like an overloaded Kombi van. 'Come on, you old clunker!'

A low-hanging tree branch caught and ripped his hair. 'Screamin' piglets! Forgot my helmet!'

A thunderous crack and whoosh pushed out a pungent burst of smoke. Chris copped a lungful and coughed. He was close.

He swerved into Wakehurst Parkway's merging traffic lane and flinched as a grinding squawk augured his error.

The truck driver burned brake pads.

The smell burned Christian's senses.

And the bitumen burned him.

2. ERASED

April 2006

New South Wales Police Forensic Services Group, Sydney

'RETURNING AN evidence sample which detoured via my desk. No point killing a newbie's career over an honest mistake. I know the way.' Sinbled patted his badge with presumed authority and strode past the fresh-faced probationer attending the section desk.

'Excuse me, sir,' she called. 'I need to sight your ID. Please.'

'Of course you do.' He turned back.

She scrutinised his credentials. 'Agent Horon Sinballidh?'

'I say it quickly: Ron Sinbled. Less trouble with airport security that way. Three Australian-born generations diluted our Assyrian bloodlines but not our good looks.' He winked and flashed a roguish grin. 'I see FSG security is in capable and beautiful hands today.'

She blushed. His source had been correct about the best time to come. He cruised down the corridor and entered Callahan's windowless room without knocking, locking the door behind him.

Callahan looked up from his computer console. 'You realise the boss will have my guts for garters for breeching protocol, right?'

'Nonsense. I'm lightening his load.' Sinbled pulled up a chair. 'On with it, man. I haven't got all day. Let's see what you've got.'

'Precious little. The explosion and fire destroyed most of the security system and video footage. I've enhanced the devil out of this shred.' Callahan clicked play. Title typography identified the video as *Maxwell Residence Security Footage, Saturday, 25 March 2006.*

Sinbled frowned. 'You weren't kidding about the quality. That paramedic—' He tapped the screen. 'Has he been identified?'

'Bogus. Triple 0 Emergency Control Centre dispatched fire, police and ambulance crews to Arianna Trace *after* the explosion, not before. Although, the ambos do have a regular weekday booking for a dialysis patient who lives four doors up. The uniform looks legit but—'

'Back it up and zoom in ... Again, on slow mo?'

Callahan obliged.

'Stop there.' Sinbled pointed. 'Tattoo on his neck. Axe and snake.'

'Crudely drawn.' Callahan shivered. 'That snake looks like it's moving, pulsing with his carotid artery perhaps?'

'Could be the Snakeman.' Sinbled clicked his tongue. 'He's on our watch list. Big boys' jurisdiction.'

'What's he done? Before this, that is.'

'He's a drug syndicate enforcer with an appetite for blood. The tattoo harks back to his days as a bomb-maker for ETA.'

Callahan shrugged. 'Never heard of 'em.'

'Basque separatists who evolved into terrorists. Snakeman slithered into Sydney with an offsider around 1980.'

'So, was this explosion a terrorist attack?'

'Doubt it. I'd say tit for tat pay back. Those two lowlifes dispatched a mid-level Northern Beaches drug-dealer way back when. The mate got twenty-five years without parole courtesy of an eye-witness. Snakeman disappeared into the underworld abyss. He hasn't left a living witness since, just a trail of gruesome remains. Who else has seen this footage?'

'No one, yet.'

'Keep it that way. Give me the enhanced digital copy and original VHS. Tell your boss the tape disintegrated when you tried to resurrect it and you passed useless dregs to our experts. He can't fault you for that. Destroy every trace on your system and forget what you've seen.'

Callahan hesitated. 'And you'll make that other thing go away?'

'I can't fix your predilection—'

'I was set up!'

'Aren't we all? Of course, I could contain the evidence of your indiscretion ...'

'If I destroy all evidence of your intrusion and interest in this video.'

Sinbled returned to his SUV, amused by Callahan's misplaced trust in the notion of mutually assured destruction. With the evidence safely ensconced in the vehicle's discreet customised lockable compartment, he gunned the engine and gratefully escaped Sydney's western suburbs, driving east, then north towards the Central Coast.

3. CRUSHED

April 2006

Private Medical Facility, North of Sydney

RAW, SERRATED sensation scoured Christian's skin and pricked his nose. What was that horrible smell? Public toilet? Men's room potpourri? Only more antiseptic, with notes of car park stairwell.

'Urgh!' Chris lurched and dry retched.

'Hang on, sailor. Tube's out. Welcome back. You've been in a coma.' An indistinct face hovered over his.

Chris willed his eyes to focus. Another wave of nausea hit. This time he threw up for real, into a kidney dish supplied by a quick-thinking nurse.

'Blame the morphine,' she said. 'You good now?'

Chris flopped back onto a pillow. Antiseptic, stale toilet and vomit. Bad.

'How's your pain level, Christopher?'

'Chrishn.'

'Crushing? You have crushing pain? Where's the pain, Christopher?'

'Nuh Chrishphr. Chrishn.'

'I'm putting morphine through your cannula. For the pain.'

Chris grunted and coughed. 'Ow!'

'It's okay, pet. The worst is over.'

Chris frowned. Didn't he have to get somewhere? Fast? His leaden eyelids didn't think so.

He woke to the incessant beep of an IV drip machine. He'd have hurled the wretched thing if not for the unrelenting pain crushing his chest.

Someone had delivered a meal on a tray. Chris eyed its dubious contents. *Blerk!* Nothing worth moving for.

Blip. Blip. Blip.

For cryin' out loud. Nurse? Someone? Anyone, come and shut this blipping drip up.

The nurse was slow to silence the machine but quick to shut the conversation down when Chris asked her where he was and what had happened. She moved his meal tray closer and said, 'Brain food. Eat up.'

A medico eventually explained his injuries, not his situation. 'Give it time. Temporary memory loss is understandable following a traumatic incident.'

Incident! A plaster cast encased his left leg. Broad bandages strapped his cracked ribs. Multiple stitches pulled and itched, and ugly bruises mocked the stupid nurse who said, 'No helmet and no permanent brain injury. You must be the luckiest boy on God's green earth.'

No helmet. An avalanche of fiery images compounded his chest crush.

———◦○◦———

THE ROUTINE rudeness of medical care and cleaners' clatter announced another lonely morning. The smell of antiseptic was particularly noxious today. What he'd give for a breath of fresh air. And some honest answers.

'Good morning, Christopher. How are we today?' Nurse Pippa, being painfully pleasant as usual.

You're perky. I'm lousy, and my name's Christian, not Christopher. The staff had ignored his correction so many times, he'd given up. According to his medical wristband and chart, he was Christopher Darnell.

Pippa stretched his bunched-up bottom sheet back over the top end of the plastic-coated mattress and fluffed his pillow. 'Better straighten you up. You have a visitor!'

'Who?'

'Who, indeed? He reminds me of that sexy Spanish matador—what's his name? Ordo-something? Ordóñez.' She licked her finger and touched it to her bottom, making a sizzling sound as she connected.

Chris wasn't sure where to look. Awkward! Pippa gave a cheeky wink and moved on.

His visitor entered with a squidge of leather soles on polished floors and a concerned smile. 'Awake at last, but not sure you want to be?'

'It only hurts when I breathe in. Or out.' Chris evaluated Pippa's 'matador'. Dark, wavy, grey-flecked hair, prominent cheek bones, designer stubble. Bullfighter? Chris conjured Antonio Vargas upstaging Mercurio's paso doble in *Strictly Ballroom*.

Matador offered his right hand. 'My name's Pat. Pat Alejandro. I've had the pleasure of working with your father on and off since our university days.'

Chris stared at Pat's signet ring, a fiery opal inlaid with a golden anchor. Its shape was familiar. Had he met Pat before today? He scanned his peripheral memory for a hint of recognition. Nope. Nothing.

'Too sore to shake? It's Chris, isn't it?'

Chris nodded. 'Christian M—'

'Chris will do. Although the staff will be discreet, it's safer to conceal your identity.'

'How come?'

The man with the golden anchor sighed. 'It's not a happy story.'

A vice squeezed Chris's heart. 'They're all dead, aren't they?'

Pat touched his arm. 'I'm so very sorry. Would you like a moment to yourself?'

Chris turned away. The effort to nod was more than he could manage.

⸺◦⸺

CHRIS WILLED his tear-burnt eyes to focus on the foil 'Get Well' balloon dangling from the ceiling. It was pink. And dusty. And utterly pathetic.

Like him. He swallowed hard.

Pat returned with a chair. He retrieved a tissue box for Chris before he sat.

'The fire ...' Chris blew his nose. 'Was it an accident?'

'The investigation's ongoing but I understand they found explosive residue which suggests criminal intent.'

'Explosives! Who'd want to bomb our house? Or us? Why? What for?'

'Those are good questions.' Pat's expression was intense. 'Chris, what do you remember about that morning?'

'Not much. My memory's fuzzy. I remember cycling to Warringah Mall. I wanted to buy—'

To buy! We have to buy it, Alastair.

The memory of his father's bemused expression and tender smile overwhelmed him with the bittersweet agony of loss and love.

4. LEVERAGED

April 2006

Canberra, Australia

Regret HAS many faces. Sinbled's wasn't one of them. Not anymore. He zipped into his parking space, buoyed by the success of his mission, revitalised by the drive back from Sydney … drifting through the curves, letting loose on the open stretches … disdaining the saintly ideologues who always cruised the national-security-and-law-enforcement highway in a straight line.

Not him. He'd seen the light after his brother-in-law's sure-fire short cut to wealth had rendered him shirtless, pantless and penniless. He'd have lost his jocks too, if not for Deabrua, the man with the snake tattoo.

The enforcer's network needed a 'dry cleaner' to remove stains from high-profile 'suits'. Sinbled signed up after his brother-in-law's body surfaced in a sludge pond at the Lower Molonglo sewerage treatment plant, an ironic end for the bum who'd flushed his bank balance.

Sinbled gathered his concealed stash and strutted towards the building, activating the jaunty beep of his car lock as he went. He parked his car like he'd parked his regrets—no looking back. No need. Dry-cleaning had proved surprisingly palatable. He and Deabrua had cleaned up financially.

As their latest venture required the ongoing favour of the network's boss, Sinbled had supplied Deabrua with a shirt-button video camera to obtain protective leverage. He'd collected that footage as well while he'd been in Sydney.

Interesting city. Geographically stunning. Still, he preferred his own domain where he could shut the door on prying eyes and the judgment of others, if not his own conscience.

He grabbed a coffee from the lunch room before settling in his office to watch Deabrua's video. It had been doctored, judging by the abrupt start, but there was no mistaking the ire or the identity of the network's boss, Tighearnach Ulvelaik, a criminal heavyweight whose dramatic facial scar augmented his left cheek like a metallic tangle of tree roots.

'Neolithique! Lunatique!' Ulvelaik waved a dismissive hand. 'Your methods and mindset are *médiévales, mon frère aîné*. In an age of technology, you build a trebuchet.'

'The son of a French whore presumes too much from his bastardy. You betrayed your Basque bloodline by adopting her tongue, and the name she gave you.' Deabrua's voice.

'Our *origine mutuelle* is the only reason I let you live, Mozorrotua. You should leave before I shoot your Stone Age *cerveau*.' Ulvelaik aimed a gun at Deabrua's head. The video stayed steady as Stonehenge.

'Business before pleasure, Titanium Lavalake.'

Sinbled smirked. The nickname fit the face like a photoshopped meme.

'You hope to offend me because that *sordide* Basque bestowed this scar by his own hand?' Ulvelaik's silken accent failed to cloak his obvious vitriol. He caressed his damaged cheek. 'I wear both scar and title with pride, hallmarks of my strength, and volatility! Beware *Le Volcan, mon frère.*'

The Volcano? A tired B-grade movie cliché? Sinbled snorted his disdain. Between the scar, the accent, and Ulvelaik's French-for-English substitutions, Deabrua's video parodied burlesque.

Deabrua hawked phlegm—and spat by the sound of it. 'Tell someone who cares, Tig. We both danced on the old man's grave.'

'As I will on yours.' Ulvelaik cocked the pistol.

'Always the headshot. Not my style. Too quick. Anticipation always increases the pleasure.'

Ulvelaik lowered the gun. *'Vive le libertinage*. State your business before I grow impatient and change my mind.'

Deabrua obliged. 'The original prototype is keyed to the software, yes? I could slice it from the recipient's head and deliver it to you, for the right price.'

'*Imbécile!* It would no longer transmit data. Besides, *le génie* will create a dozen implants *pour moi.*'

'Only because you threatened his family.'

'He rejected my generous offer. And he insulted me by suggesting my contribution was tainted with blood. I merely accommodated his belief to improve his attitude. Soon, the ears of my loyal volunteers will sprout implants.' Ulvelaik worked his jaw, twisting his metal-embedded scar like a grotesque sideshow stunt. 'All of them useless! Worthless without the software! Do you have that?'

'Development proceeds, slowly.' Deabrua's laboured bronchial wheeze filled a pause that rivalled human gestation. 'I could, perhaps, hasten progress ...'

Ulvelaik scowled. 'Speak.'

'Power speaks. Pleasure speaks. Profit speaks.' Deabrua. Smug.

'As always, this is what your ears itch to hear. Mine wish to hear the voice of *honneur*, respect, *fidélité*. Perhaps, when I hear these things in your voice, we will speak the same language.' Ulvelaik toyed with the gun again. 'After all, how will it profit a man if he gains the world, but loses his soul?' His eyes chilled and his skin turned a bluish-grey, as if he'd overdosed on colloidal silver.

'You would know.' The angle and view of the camera shifted as Deabrua rose from his seat. 'I tell you this. Technology types hate giving up. Their pride and obsession goads them. The programmer will persist. Eventually, his software will respond to the signals. Then I will have both, and you will have nothing.'

'*Rhétorique vide.* You forget, I already own the world.' Ulvelaik swept the air as if tracing a globe. 'I could give it to you.'

'Would you, brother?'

'*Mais oui mon frère.* You see, I want far more than this world.'

5. PROTECTED

May–June 2006

Private Medical Facility, North of Sydney

CHRIS SLOTTED the one-thousandth piece into yet another picture-perfect jigsaw puzzle. This one showed a rugged mountain view, unlike his windowless hospital room. Both dead opposites of the amazing view from his home, before it had been—

'Blown to smitherEEEEEENS!' Chris swept the jigsaw to the floor, scattering a thousand fractured dreams with its pieces. He shoved the table and kicked it.

'Why?' Kick. 'Them?' Kick. 'Not!' Kick. 'Me?' Kick. Kick. 'I'm the useless one!'

'Chris! Calm down!' Pat Alejandro strode through the door.

Kick. Kick. Kick.

'Chris! Stop!' Pat grappled the table and pushed it aside. Chris's kick connected full force with his shin. 'Christian!'

Chris froze. Christian? Pat had called him by name. His real name. Christian. 'Pat! I didn't mean—I'm so sorry!'

Pat enfolded Chris in a hug. 'It's okay, son. I understand. I'm okay. You're okay.'

'Me? Okay? No way. I'm … worse than useless.' A hopeless gravity overwhelmed him. His body had healed, but his soul was imploding.

FOR SEVERAL weeks, Chris contemplated the notion of his soul imploding. He played mind games with the idea, assigning images and manipulating them like characters in a computer game. Oddly enough, it made his new identity easier to accept. He pictured 'Christopher Darnell' as a satellite of intellectual consent orbiting the black hole of his inner space. One by one, he tucked the luminaries of his old life, his past life, his once-upon-a-time-in-a-far-flung-universe life, into its depths. Through it all, Pat maintained his stabilising gravitational pull.

'Hey, Chris, how's it going?' Pat placed a briefcase on the floor and a clothing store bag on the bed. 'What's up?'

'The sky, maybe, unless it fell since I saw it last. It's been a while.'

'High time we rectified that.' Pat patted the bag. 'These are for you. My wife picked them out. Hope they're okay. I figured you were about the same size as our son, Ben.'

Chris peered into the bag. 'Diesel! Jeans, jacket and T-shirts. Nooice!'

'Don't blame Imee for the generic brand jocks and socks though. I bought them.'

'Still a step up from hospital pyjamas.'

'And they won't let you loose in those.'

'Especially with no home or family to go to.' Chris slumped onto his bed and squeezed his eyes shut. Stupid tear ducts. He swiped his nose and sat up again. 'Sorry, Pat. Thanks for the clothes.'

Pat nodded. 'About a home—'

'I know—care facility. Foster family if I'm lucky.'

Pat removed a document wallet from his briefcase and offered it. 'Letters and documents.'

'Uh-huh.' Chris didn't want to touch them.

Pat put them on the stainless steel bedside unit. 'I think I mentioned Alastair and I were at university together.'

Chris nodded.

'We were … close. I was Alastair's *padrino*. His best man.'

Chris frowned. 'My parents eloped. Mum said that's why they had no wedding photos.'

'Eloping was Zoe's spur-of-the-moment idea. They still needed witnesses. I joined them at the registry office.'

That's where Chris had seen Pat's anchor—pressed into wax on his parents' wedding certificate, and on his own dedication certificate.

Pat continued. 'Zoe wore a garland of mock orange blossoms. The marriage celebrant was allergic to them. Alastair, as solemn as a parsnip, promised to have and to hold for better or worse, for richer or poorer, to love and to sneeze forever. Without batting an eyelid, Zoe promised to love him and ensure an endless supply of tissues.'

Chris grinned. 'Dad loved Mum's spontaneity. Said it kept their relationship lively and the world guessing. He reckoned I was like her.'

'Your father was a remarkable man—and surgeon—and enormously proud of you and Amy. He told me so before ...' Pat swallowed hard. 'He said your gaming intuition and ability to jump one level after another amazed him. Such focus and passion. He marvelled at his children's intensity and creativity.'

'Amy's, you mean. My little sister was brilliant. She could have changed the world if those mongrels hadn't—' Chris snarled. 'I hate them! Every night, I blow their faceless carcasses to smithereens in my dreams. Eye for an eye, you know?'

Pat sighed. 'I can't undo the hurt you've suffered. But I can help with what comes next. And I can provide some insight into why, though it may shock you.'

'How earth-shattering can it be? I've already lost everything.'

'Were you aware that your mother lived under an assumed identity as a protected witness?'

Richter scale six! Chris stared, incredulous, as Pat explained how she had seen a pawn-shop-owner-cum-drug-cartel-lackey murdered. An unfortunate wrong-place-wrong-time scenario.

'Your mother was sixteen, and incredibly brave. Her testimony and the killer's plea bargain helped police bust part of the Mr Asia drug syndicate.'

Richter scale seven!

'The cartel tried to kill her. They missed, on that occasion.'

Richter scale eight! Chris was stunned. 'Who? Wait. The bomb. Was it them? How'd they find her?' Chris pounded the mattress with his fist. 'That stupid MP! Blowing his trumpet about crime reduction in his electorate. When Mum reported the marijuana crop, he rocked up with his promo people. They put a photo of Mum in his campaign newsletter without telling her. She was livid.'

'With good reason. That's the hell of it.' Pat slowly shook his head. 'Chris, your parents appointed me as your legal guardian in the event of their deaths. Their estate will easily support your enrolment in a boarding school of your choice.'

'Wow.' Chris grabbed the sides of the bed to steady himself.

'I've discussed this at length with Imee. We'd both prefer to maintain the estate in its entirety for you, till you're eighteen. In fact, Imee, Ben and I would love you to live with us, as a member of our family, in Canberra.'

Chris blinked rapidly.

'Think about it. Let me know tomorrow.'

Chris nodded. 'Family versus boarding school? Sounds like a no-brainer.'

'Either way, it's imperative you grasp the significance of your own protected identity.'

'Why? Mum's dead. They got what they wanted.'

'After waiting two decades. Vengeance has long arms and a careless grasp. Evil like that will kill again.'

Not if I get to them first.

'Chris, you cannot discuss your former life with anyone—not Imee, not Ben, no one—for your safety, and theirs. Do you understand?'

Chris thought about the long arms and careless grasp of vengeance. When the time was right, his revenge would be careful and deliberate.

But right now, all he had was Pat.

He gripped Pat's hand and shook it.

6. COMPARED

15 July 2006

Canberra, Australia

CANBERRA. THE nation's capital. Chris had never even visited the place. Why on earth had he agreed to live here, with two people he'd never met, and a guardian he barely knew? No-brainer or not, the choice he'd made bounced and banged against his ribs and intestines like a boulder rolling down a cliff.

Today's four-and-a-half-hour drive to get here had been way too short to psyche himself up, even with the extra toilet stops.

Remember, Chris, you're happy about this.

Remember, Chris, you're happy about this.

He internalised the mantra as Pat opted for a scenic entry, pointing out the 'planned' city's landmarks along the way. His guardian's helpful-not-helpful detour via the circuits surrounding Parliament House sent his sense of direction spinning like a renegade compass.

Remember, Chris, you're—

'… just ahead on the left. It was originally built in Sydney as a railway station. The local parish purchased the building—or what was left of it—in the nineteen-fifties and moved it here, stone by stone.'

'Uh-huh.' *Remember, Chris, you're happy about—*

'… adding stained glass windows and repositioning the bell tower.' *Ding dong dell. Remember, Chris, you're—oh, forget it.*

'It's a handy landmark to remember because,' Pat made a right turn into a leafy street, 'it's close to home. Are you ready to meet the family?'

What? Now? Nooooo! He managed to utter a sort-of-positive grunt nonetheless.

He was, after all, *supposed* to be happy about this.

The tyres made a crunching sound as Pat pulled into a gravelled driveway.

'Wow! Your house is different.' Chris's cheeks flushed. 'In a good way, I mean. It looks Mediterranean, but the wattle trees shout Aussie, Aussie, Aussie. Kind of foreign and domestic.'

'That's us. A little different, but easy going.'

'My fam—' Chris stopped short. He'd been about to say, his family was far from normal. *Don't go there. Don't compare. Pigeonhole memories. Avoid pain. Bluff past it.* 'I'm boring and ordinary.'

'I suspect you're extraordinary. One day you'll figure out how.'

'Yeah. April first. Before lunch.'

'April Fools' Day? No way! Besides, that's too far away. We'll aim for September nineteenth.'

'September nineteenth?'

'International Talk Like a Pirate Day. Aharrrr, me hearty!' Pat's reassuring good humour etherised Chris's raw edges as they crossed the front lawn. Pat shoved the front door open. It grabbed and squawked on the floorboards.

Screamin' piglets! Chris gaped at the huge ship's anchor standing floor to ceiling in the vestibule.

'Second Mate Christopher Darnell, welcome aboard the Good Ship Alejandro. My wife, Imee, and our son, Ben.'

Imee stepped forward and touched his arm. 'Please call me Mim. Ben does.'

———◇———

IT WAS hard not to compare mothers. At least Chris didn't have to call Mim 'Mum'. That'd feel wrong. Granted, Mim knew how to decorate. His new bedroom was epic, as were the clothes she bought. Her cooking was palatable, just. But her efforts to connect—overworking conversations, animating awkward gaps with small talk—drove him crazy. Worse than a Yiddish yenta, Mum would've said. Mim needed to chill.

Like Ben. He took things easy. Gave Chris companionship when he wanted it. Space when he needed it. Having a same age 'sibling' was okay. Bro and Dro. Brothers and best mates. Even if the Alejan'Dro' was a hard act to follow. At least Ben understood personal space. He wasn't needy, like Mim. Thank God.

7. HEATED

Saturday 11 November 2006

Canberra, Australia

'GAH! WHY do drive-through restaurants always hand you the cold stuff first?' Ben squirmed and rearranged the hot takeaway chicken and chips searing his lap. He'd tucked the coleslaw, Coke and Fanta between his feet. The ice-cold drink bottles toppled against his legs each time his father turned a corner.

'Sorry, Ben-man. Burnt knees or frozen ankles?'

'Both. But at least we won't have to eat Mim's burnt offerings tonight.' She'd blackened dinner three nights in a row this week.

'Her cooking's still better than mine.'

'You said it, not me. Chris reckons he and I should take cooking lessons.'

'That bad, huh?'

'We may be forced to choose Food Technologies over Computer Studies next year.'

Pat grinned. 'I'm glad you and Chris have hit it off.'

'Yeah. Me too.'

'Does he talk much about his past?'

'Nope.'

'Have you asked?'

'Nope. You said not to. You and Dr Phil.'

'Dr Phil?'

'Philippa Hargreaves. The foster care counsellor Mim and I saw before Chris arrived.'

'Pippa. Of course.'

'She warned us about triggering repressed memories, like his blow-out about camping at Great Lakes this Christmas.'

Pat nodded. 'Sorry about that. Mim's looking for a bush cabin at Barrington Tops instead.'

'Bye-bye Bulahdelah, Boolambayte, Booti Booti and Boomerang Beach.' Ben helped himself to a chip to mask his disappointment.

'If your curiosity about Chris gets the better of you—'

'Dad. We're guys. We're fifteen. We talk about food and video games.'

'Which reminds me, any requests for your birthday?'

'A restaurant dinner with an all-you-can-eat buffet. Please.'

'I'd better Google options at Barrington Tops.' Pat pulled the car into the garage and relieved Ben of the hot food. Ben gathered the drinks and coleslaw and followed Pat through the side door into their kitchen-diner—smack bang into a grilling, with Chris on Mim's menu.

'Yep? Nup? I dunno? What is it with you, Chris?' She'd cornered him, literally, where the breakfast bar met the wall. 'I asked about your day because I'm interested in you and your wellbeing. I'm not the Spanish Inquisition.'

Who was kidding who? Mim's glare could have burned Chris at the stake.

'At least try to engage me in decent conversation.' Mim put her hands on her hips. Not good.

'About what?' Chris raised both hands.

'People. Places. Politics, if you have an opinion.'

'You want to discuss politics? Gutless gamers who destroy people then ask for your vote? No thanks.' Chris folded his arms. 'At least computer games give you a fighting chance.'

Mim huffed. 'Life's not a computer game, which you'd realise if you played less and read more.'

'Like Ben, you mean? Why don't you ask him about politics?'

Ben froze.

'Go on. Ask him. He *is* your real son. I'm just the useless add-on. Maybe you should get rid of me, before I wreck your happy family.'

Mim blanched. Her face downloaded a defensive shield.

'That is not going to happen, Chris.' Pat placed the hot food on the bench. 'While we enjoyed a lazy Saturday, Mim worked back-to-back shifts in the emergency ward. She's entitled to put her feet up, don't you think?'

Chris lowered his eyes and nodded.

'Then please help Ben set the table. I'll carve the hot chicken, before it gets cold, so we can all enjoy dinner together, as a family.'

Ben offloaded the drinks and coleslaw and gave Chris a sympathetic shrug. Of late, the family's temperature fluctuations were worse than the food's.

8. DUMPED

Two and a half years later ... (June 2009)

Secondary School, Canberra, Australia

'"**A**MBULANCE DRIVERS fog lights hit jumping kangaroos." What has this to do with maths?'

Chris stiffened.

Ms Cranshaw, Ruler Supreme of Senior Mathematics, glared at the note he'd passed to Ben.

'Benjamin? You're supposed to be plotting algebraic functions, not playing silly games with lettered gibberish.'

'Sounds like algebra to me.' Chris's cheeky remark intensified Cranshaw's corrosive stare.

'It's a code for a game we're designing, Miss,' Ben said. 'It uses Sudoku puzzles. Number logic.'

'Which may be maths, but is it the maths you're supposed to be doing?'

'No, Miss.' Ben's contrition sounded real.

'Not exactly.' Chris feigned his.

'Not exactly, Chris? I'd say not even remotely.'

Class chatter volume increased from radio static to mosh pit. Ruler Supreme glared at her restless dominion. 'Quiet down, you lot! Unless you all want to join me at lunchtime?'

'You shouting pizza, Miss?'

Ruler Supreme's ability to command respect had plummeted during a first term geometry practicum when students discovered that her height plus the diagonal of a McCain's Supreme Pizza box measured exactly two metres. Chris had coined the moniker.

'It's not like you to be off task in my lesson, Ben.'

Chris squirmed. He'd dumped Dro in it again. Ben said nothing.

Ms Cranshaw folded her arms. 'Algebra. Now! Design your game during lunchtime detention. Or vice versa. Your choice. So long as your actual maths problems are done before you go home today.'

Some choice. Though working on the code, even in detention, was cool.

'I'm sorry, Miss, but could we do double detention tomorrow, instead?'

Chris's jaw dropped. Was Dro nuts?

'Chris and I have a Careers and Tertiary Information excursion. We leave at morning tea.'

Oh, yeah. That.

'If you wish to bargain, I'll accept three lunch hours this week in lieu of today's. Does that seem reasonable?'

Ben nodded.

'Christopher?'

'S'pose so.' Chris thought it was grossly unfair. Next time he passed a note to Ben, he'd be way more discreet.

Ms Cranshaw examined the confiscated page. 'I suggest you add an apostrophe after the s in 'drivers' to show plural possession or you'll piss off your English teacher too.' She returned the note and turned to the whiteboard.

───◌───

'WE COULD'VE searched career options online, Dro. This excursion thingy better be worth it. I hate surrendering lunch hours.' Chris burped for emphasis.

'Whose fault is that?' Ben's friendly nudge propelled Chris onto the bus.

The seat beside MPeg was free. Woo-hoo! Chris claimed it and winked at Ben who sat beside Cokecan, their gaming crew's fourth— or opposition depending on whether it was practice or competition.

Chris was proud of his protégé. When he'd moved in with the Alejandros, Ben had been a gaming virgin. Chris soon fixed that, but MPeg and Cokecan had won every game for months. Exasperated, Chris had yelled at Ben. 'You're so busy strategising, you miss your cue to act. Trust your instincts. Just go for it, Dro!' They'd won that day, and soon busted their friends' winning monopoly.

'Bit of shush for roll-call, please?' The school's librarian leaned against the driver's partition, clearly unhappy about leaving his comfort zone. The students knew the drill well enough—quiet down or wait forever to get underway. 'Thank you. Benjamin … Ail Jandro?'

'Alee-handro, Sir! J is soft. No beer up front. He's right there.' Chris pointed smugly.

Sir relinquished his leaning post and braced, feet apart, for a challenge. 'And you are?'

'Here too. Ready and raring to go.' Chris grinned.

'Hail St Christopher! Patron saint of travellers!' Cokecan saluted.

Sir sniffed. 'As in Christopher Darnell?'

'One and the same, Sir.'

Sir tapped his pen on the roll. 'The ne'er-do-well who infected the library's computer network with subversive Pac-Man clones.'

A dozen stares warmed the back of Chris's neck.

'And yet you're still enrolled, thanks to your influential guardian. It must be nice to have friends in high places, Saint Christopher.' Sir dripped sarcasm.

Chris dropped his eyes. 'Yes, Sir. Sorry, Sir. It won't happen again, Sir.'

'Not on my watch, that's for sure.'

Chris was acutely aware that Pat had saved his bacon, in more ways than one.

Sir consulted the roll again. 'M Peregrine Blythe?'

'Here, Sir.' MPeg rapped Chris's knee with her knuckle.

Sweet!

9. BINNED

June–September 2009

Canberra, Australia

'HOW ABOUT this one? Roles in ICT, Intelligence Analysis and Linguistics.' Ben's career search had unearthed ASIO's website. '"The Australian Security Intelligence Organisation offers a brief window of opportunity for school leavers interested in an IT Traineeship Program. A time of unique expansion."' Ben's skin tingled, a weird, excited shiver triggering goose bumps. 'What do you think, Chris? Should we go for it?'

Chris hovered, reading the laptop's screen. 'You can't ask me. All applications are handled in strictest confidence. Discussing it with others may adversely affect your application. We'd have to kill each other, Dro.'

'Dad joke, Bro. Seriously, we should both consider it. They usually recruit graduates. This says we can apply now, start straight from year twelve. It's on-the-job training. Study with a regular pay cheque.'

'I plan to make my fortune in computer games. This ASIO gig sounds more like your thing.'

'But this way, we'd create cyber games with real world applications— training simulations, software to operate drones, robots, satellite communications and stuff. Thwart international criminals and terrorists and protect our own home turf. We could be Bro and Dro, Spy Duo! Saving lives and money.'

'Games to take out real-life criminals.' Chris's expression darkened. 'That I'd like to see.'

FRIDAY AFTERNOON. Finally. Ben's exaggerated sigh of relief whooshed over the ship's anchor as he walked through the vestibule. Chris's shenanigans had made for a harrowing week. He headed for the kitchen, almost colliding with his dad on the way.

'Hi, Dad. You're home early. Has our ship sprung a leak?'

'No. Company's sprung another field trip on me next week, so I took an early mark.'

Ben knew better than to ask details. His father's research and development gig was strictly hush-hush, discussed in vague terms only. Killer confidentiality clauses applied. Pat's company was currently negotiating several international contracts, which meant his regular overseas business trips had increased in frequency and length, much to Mim's annoyance.

She was so touchy these days.

'Got your laptop handy, Ben-man?'

'Right here.' Ben slipped his school bag off his shoulder.

'Great. I want to install a new program I've designed. It looks and behaves like a recycle bin, but it maintains a hidden data storage space, accessed via a code-locked grid. You can keep your ASIO application in there, so no one sees it by accident. Confidentiality is intrinsic to that job. Might as well adopt the habit now.'

'Won't you get into trouble for sharing this?' Ben handed his laptop over.

'I developed it for me, not for work. Besides, I used one of your ingenious puzzle ideas. It's only fair I share it with you. We're the only two people in the world aware of its existence.'

Ben was chuffed. 'Hang on. What about Chris? Won't he need it for his application?'

'You mean the one he hasn't started yet?'

'He might need your help.'

'Which I'll give when he shows inclination and initiative. Grab a snack for us while I set this up?' Pat took Ben's laptop into the study.

Ben raided the fridge for a six-pack of chocolate-iced donuts, hugged his mum, and joined his father.

'Ha! You used my Sudoku Scrabble Scramble.'

'For the grid lock, yes.'

'What's the alpha-code?'

'It's variable so you can set your own. I use Bible verses and disguise the reference as a phone number. I'll show you.' Pat demonstrated his access method and the program's capabilities.

'Cool. What's it called?'

'Haven't named it yet. Any clever ideas?'

They demolished donuts while they brainstormed names. No joy.

Ben wiped his sticky fingers on a scrap of paper, balled it and lobbed it towards the overflowing rubbish bin. 'Missed.'

'Must be time for a cuppa.'

'And a KitKat?' Mim poked her head in. 'Ben, any idea where Chris is?'

'He and Cokecan went to MPeg's place after school.'

'No way José! I told him no gaming till his English assignment was done. Tell Chris he's grounded for the weekend. Pat?'

'Yo?'

'You need to back me up this time.'

Pat nodded. 'Chris grounded for English.'

'For disobeying my instructions. He fritters his time away playing computer games with that girl while his schoolwork suffers. She's a right royal screw-up if you ask me.'

'Chris grounded for screw-up. Got it.' Pat gave her a thumbs up.

'I mean it, Pat. Chris has played the poor orphan card for three years. Enough is enough. You don't let our son get away with Chris's nonsense.'

Ben's ears tingled.

'I'll speak to Chris, Imee. I promise.'

'Not before time. Have you remembered I'm working the graveyard this weekend?'

'Night shift, already? I thought you had two weeks on day shift.'

'I did.' Mim's where-have-you-been-all-week glare made Ben squirm even if Pat missed it. 'Remind Chris. And don't wake me for lunch tomorrow. I'll love you all when I'm back on day shift. Toodles.'

Ben waved. 'Bye, Mim. Have fun.'

Her 'Not!' accompanied the noise of the front door scraping and scoring the floorboards as she left.

'I must fix that door.' Pat scratched the back of his head. 'Is it my turn to cook, or yours?'

'Chris's. He's springing for pizza.'

'Great. I'll percolate coffee while you empty the rubbish bin.'

'Ugh! It's full of grunge.'

'So?'

Ben grimaced. He picked up the overflowing bin and headed for the door. 'That's it!' Ben spun around. Scrunched paper avalanched. 'Grunge! Sticks to the bottom of the bin.'

'Only when you're too lazy to clean it.'

'Dad! The program's a digital recycle bin with guaranteed retention. Files stick to the bottom, just like grunge. It's perfect!' Ben grinned like Goofy.

Pat grabbed a sheet of paper and wrote something. 'How's that?' Ben scrutinised Pat's scribble.

GRUnGE.OO1
Guaranteed Retention Under Gridlocked Encryption

Pat had concocted an acronym. 'Name, description and version number—double-oh-one—in honour of your anticipated licence to kill software bugs.'

Ben face-palmed.

Pat grinned and saluted. 'Now, go empty the real bin.'

———

'YES! WAY to go.' Ben tossed his phone in the air and caught it behind his back.

Pat peered over his breakfast cereal and raised an eyebrow. 'Good news?'

'I've got a security interview after school with a Mr Chassic. That means they're considering my application, doesn't it?'

'Considering, yes. But don't get too excited. And for heaven's sake, don't blab to your mates. Remember, your ability to maintain confidentiality is crucial.' Pat scooped a soggy spoonful of Weet-Bix into his mouth.

'I know.' Ben pocketed his phone. 'It's still epic.'

'What's epic?' The sixties-style swinging bar doors clattered as Chris entered. Pat surreptitiously shook his head while Chris fetched Coco Pops and a bowl from the cupboard.

'I had an idea for my physics investigation, Bro. Motion studies. I want to see if GPS tracking of pedestrian movement is a feasible option. Thought I'd do some preliminary research after school today.' Ben retrieved a bottle of milk from the fridge.

'Dro, we need to discuss what constitutes epic. Unless you're talking PPU's and game engines, physics investigations are not epic.' Chris plonked himself at the breakfast bar and tipped Coco Pops into his bowl. A few escapees scattered across the bench. He swept them up and popped them straight into his mouth. 'What about the gaming challenge this arvo?'

'Man, I forgot. Get MPeg to fill in for me, alright?'

Chris launched a death stare. 'Seriously? We set this comp up weeks ago. You're piking out for a physics assignment?'

'I'll make it up to you. Besides, MPeg'll go ballistic! Ga-ga!'

'MPeg ga-ga. Gee, ta. That's all I need. It'll cost you, Dro. And stop hogging the milk.'

Ben passed the milk to Chris before helping himself to a bowl of Coco Pops.

———

BEN'S ASIO interview rocked. Mr Chassic headed a special project team. He wanted fresh, raw talent to mould. He'd earmarked Ben's application accordingly. Provided nothing untoward surfaced during the remaining security checks—or Ben stuffed his final exams—he was in.

'If you sign on the dotted line, all things being equal, you can kick off with our orientation program on November thirtieth.'

'You bet, Mr Chassic! Your pen or mine?' Benjamin Alejandro was bound for the fast-track.

10. SMASHED

October 2009

Canberra, Australia

'**W**HOOPEE! YAHOO! Epic!' Chris burst into the kitchen, tossed his phone in the air, fumbled the catch, stumbled over the rubbish bin and landed in its scattered contents.

'On your bum in garbage. Yep. That's epic.' Ben chuckled, offered Chris a hand up then let go as Chris pulled.

Chris landed on his rump again. 'Screamin' piglets!' Chris laughed too. He fished his phone out of a junk mail crumple, then hauled himself up. Without Dro's assistance, thank you very much.

'Screamin' piglets? Where'd that come from?'

Chris baulked. His mother had coined the phrase when he and Amy broke her best china teapot while acting out their own version of *Babe: Pig in the City,* but he couldn't tell Ben that. 'Repeating it will cost you.'

'I'm broke,' Ben said. 'So I guess your secret's safe. What's so epic?'

'We've got Mpeg's cousin's place in Queensland for Schoolies. A whole week with a state-of-the-art gaming system. While the rabble get smashed on surf and beer, we'll rock digital smash, crash and burn, 24/7. It'll be awesome.'

'When do we sleep?'

'Sleep when you're dead, Dro. It's Schoolies.' Chris set his laptop on the kitchen bench. 'I wrote Mpeg's bank account details on my arm. I promised to transfer our share of the rent this arvo. I'll pay you back next week.'

Ben looked as twitchy as a tourist entering drop bear territory.

'What's up, Dro? I'm good for the money. Promise.'

'It's not that. It's just … I can't do Schoolies. I've got a job. Start straight from school.'

'A holiday job before uni next year?'

'A traineeship. Full-time. I'll get my IT quals on the job.'

'Wow. Where?'

'I, it's, I can't …' Ben squatted and retied his shoelace.

Chris twigged. 'You got in, didn't you? You can't tell me, but I know. We both applied. You got in. I didn't. End of story.' Chris dropped the lid of his laptop shut with way more force than he intended.

'Chris—'

'Forget it, Dro. I get it. Your secret's safe with me.' Chris tucked the laptop under his arm and headed for his bedroom. He paused midway through the swinging doors. 'I'll tell MPeg you're piking. Again.' The bar doors flapped shut as he left.

Little Benjamin Perfect could pick up the rubbish.

II. STRETCHED

Two years later ... (Thursday 29 Sept 2011)

Canberra, Australia

'THIS IS not a restaurant, Benjamin.'

'I'm sorry I missed dinner, Mim.' Ben shaped an apologetic smile.

'It's ten o'clock at night.' Mim glared at two uneaten plates of food on the table.

Leathered gravy skin. Yuck. 'I said I was sorry. I had a critical work deadline to meet. I wasn't hanging with mates.'

'No. That's Chris's specialty.'

'That's Chris's choice. I don't have a choice. Work is intense right now. Top priority.'

'And there's your father's usual excuse, always for someone else's benefit. One workaholic in the family is bad enough.'

'Imee, you knew it would be like this for Ben. It comes with the territory. I'm sure he's doing important work. And Chris aced his Game Studio internship despite our reservations. They're men with responsibilities now.' Pat smiled.

He'd waved a red flag at a bull.

Mim charged with full-blown bellow. 'Men! Your work and your friends are so-oo important. What am I? Dregs in the backwash?' They heard her bedroom door slam loud and clear, even from downstairs.

Ben shrugged his commiserations. Tension between his parents was already stretching the integrity of their tungsten-carbide wedding rings. Ben's ASIO fast-track—squeezing three years training into eighteen months—hadn't helped. Advanced IT, academic and psychological indoctrination, parallel training regimes in physical fitness and defensive weapons management, intelligence rules, regulations and responses

39

dominated his life, leaving little time or energy for relationships. Or socialising. His friends had given up inviting him to GTA and pizza nights. Or Chris no longer relayed the invite. Lately, their conversations amounted to 'pass the Vegemite' or 'coffee's on' at breakfast time.

The next morning, Ben found Pat reassembling the sofa bed in the study. Mim didn't speak. At seven-thirty that night, Ben received a cryptic text message from her.

Dinner is served. House specialty: burnt offerings and bridges.

He scurried home to find Pat and Chris wrestling the front door. It had jammed. They entered through the back.

'Imee?'

'Mim?'

'Imee love? We're all home now. Lover?'

She'd gone, along with her suitcase. Other personal belongings were strewn across the bedroom floor. Pat scooped up a silk blouse and buried his face in it. His shoulders wobbled.

'She's only packed for a day or two, by the looks.' Ben pushed as much hope into his voice as he dared. 'Maybe she went to Brian and Sylvia's.'

Pat scrunched the blouse into a ball. 'They're overseas till the end of October.'

'Did she offer to house sit while they're away?' Chris asked.

'She never has before.'

Ben called her mobile. 'Number not available. That's weird.'

'Or she's removed the SIM card.' Chris shrugged. 'I'll boil the jug. We can work out who to call over a cuppa.'

Ben nodded. 'Come on, Dad.'

Mim had dumped a pile of charcoaled food on the dining table. Pat sat, head in hands. Chris scooped up the mess and binned it. They drank tea in silence.

Ben and Pat called and messaged Mim's friends and colleagues until it was too late to disturb them. No one knew where she was.

Ben called the bus transit centre. They weren't answering.

Chris handed him a fresh cup of coffee. 'Has Pat called the police, yet?' he whispered.

'He's checking airline passenger lists at the moment.'

'This morning? That can't be right.' Pat listened, eyes closed. 'No, that's all. Thank you.' Pat discarded his phone and kneaded his eyes.

'Dad?'

'She boarded a flight to Barcelona, via Melbourne and Beijing.'

'Spain. For a holiday?' Chris asked.

'To see her parents, I'd say.' Ben had never met his only living grandparents. In their eyes, his father was persona non grata. 'It won't be an easy call for Dad.'

That was an understatement. Ben's grandfather roared through the phone.

'Why should I help you, Patriarca?' Pat winced and moved the handset away from his ear. 'You stole my daughter from me! Kept her from me nineteen long, lonely years! You gallivant around the globe like a schmancy salesman, but cannot bring our daughter and grandson to Spain even once? Use your fancy software to find her!'

Ben whispered to Chris. 'That's cruel. When Mum married Dad, *Abuelo* said he never wanted to see her again. He forbade us to visit.'

Pat's efforts to appease his father-in-law failed.

About ten minutes later, Ben's mobile rang.

'*Benjamín?* This *Abuelita,* your grandmother. Your mother text me your *teléfono.* She say she contact you when she ready. She need time and space. Tell Patriarca to … not to call.' Though her tone sounded conciliatory, *Abuelita's* voice, shaky with age, was unfamiliar to Ben, and far from affectionate. Then again, he hardly knew his grandmother.

Pat spent the weekend fixing the front door.

Three weeks later, Chris announced he was moving out. 'MPeg and Cokecan need a third for their share house. My bonus from the release of *Blackstone: Galaxy Slayer* will cover bond. I'll be closer to work and the boss wants me to go full-time now.'

'How will you manage that and uni, Chris?'

'I'll defer. Game development's what I love. And I'm good at it. Besides, I should've given you guys space to be a family long ago.'

'Chris, you are family. You always will be.'

'Maybe. Right now, I need space.'

Ben followed his father's example, or default position, by keeping too busy to dwell.

Maundy Thursday 5 April 2012

'MORE OF the same, I'm afraid.'

'Lucky me.' Ben grimaced as his supervisor added a stack of folders to the tray he'd just cleared. Six months of self-imposed busyness had sucked his ASIO fast-track into a cyber tech slough. His enthusiasm for all things spydified—a term Mim had coined—was stagnating in swampy algorithms and boggy boredom.

Geoffrey Fletcher shrugged. 'Serves you right for—'

Ben's computer chimed as an email notification slid across the screen.

My office in five? Zèf Kayif.

'A summons from on high. Lucky you.' Fletcher hovered.

Ben frowned. 'Any idea what it's about?'

'Specifics, no—above my pay grade. But they say trouble and opportunity knock on the doors of fools and faithful alike. Either way, Zèf has the contacts to sort you out.'

'Great pep talk, Fletch.'

'Ha! Droll.' He cracked a reassuring grin. 'Don't worry. Zèf keeps his eyes on the future; he can spot potential at fifty paces.' Fletcher picked up the pile of files again. 'These can wait for next week, if not for you.'

Zèf Kayif's reputation for being both influential and accessible was no secret, but would his summons provoke positive change? Ben's optimism hovered as he approached Zèf's open door.

'Ben, do come in. I believe you've met the venerable HS Chassic?'

The man who had conducted his ASIO interview stood and offered his hand.

Ben shook it. 'Mr Chassic. It's been a while. I'm delighted to see you again.'

'Likewise, Ben, and my colleagues call me HS.'

'Though none of us know what it stands for,' Zèf added. 'Chassic reveres his secrets.'

HS offered Ben a conspiratorial wink. 'Even the fool who keeps his mouth shut is esteemed as wise.'

Ben nodded. 'Point taken, HS.'

'Good.' He resumed his seat. 'Your supervisor claims you've a particular knack for sniffing out bugs in code. How'd he put it, Zèf?'

'Something about a bloodhound on a scent trail, though Fletcher would have us believe your senior colleagues wear nose plugs. Right or wrong, you've been touted as the best of his current team.' Zèf leaned towards HS. 'From my perspective, Ben's young and malleable. If you want him, I can make him available.'

'How about it, Ben? Want to stick your nose into my business?'

Fool or faithful, opportunity knocked and Chassic's expression prescribed an immediate response.

Ben took a deep breath. 'Whatever's needed, I guess.'

'Good. I need you.' HS rose and handed him a business card. 'Address is on the back. Sign Zèf's paperwork and come straight over.'

Ben swallowed a sandwich of excitement and vulnerability.

Zèf signalled Ben to sit as HS left. 'Any questions for me before I fill out this Asspit shi—, ah, secondment paperwork?'

'Asspit? Sounds unfortunate. Somewhere between a donkey pen and an outhouse.'

'Chassic claims it discourages employees spruiking about who they work for.'

'I can see why. Are they 'Attorney-General's Department' or private enterprise?'

'Chassic runs ASPT which stands for Associated Special Projects Team. Their exact relationship to ASIO proper wallows in 'Associated' legalese. They're a mystery unto themselves. I can tell you ASPT secondments are only offered to best-in-fields. And it's a Four G.'

'A what?'

'Four G: God-awful Gig that Guarantees Glory, if you succeed. Your reputation and commitment suggest you will. So, what's it to be?'

Ben drummed his fingers on the desk. Why had he joined ASIO? His father's ambiguous work-related absences for project installation, strategic networking, market negotiations and implementation of business protocols had long fuelled his imagination. Undoubtedly his heroic pater daily saved the world. As a child, he had aspired to that ideal. Mim's disdain for computer gaming had made real spy-games even more enticing. ASIO's recruitment drive had dangled that carrot.

What did software tech-head Ben want? The thrill of covert intrigue! Chassic's offer was covert, and intriguing.

'Where do I sign, Zèf?' Fletcher's muddy algorithms had just become someone else's quagmire.

12. TEMPERED

Maundy Thursday 5 April 2012

Canberra, Australia

THE BUILDING which housed ASPT was a red brick and Zincalume steel hybrid which reflected Fyshwick's suburban mishmash of light industry and retail enterprise.

A mature-aged receptionist—Veronica, according to her name tag—passed Ben's satchel through a scanning device before she ushered him into a manicured suite of offices.

'How many people work here, Veronica?' Ben asked.

'HS calls me Veronica.' She paused and sized him up. 'You can call me Von. Or Ron. Take your pick.' She walked on. 'Everyone works on individual, unrelated projects. HS doesn't let his left hand know what his right is doing. This'll be your office.' Von knocked on the door.

Chassic opened it. 'Glad to see you found us, Ben.'

'Your new boy's a bit of a stud, Chas. You'd better play nice with him or I'll steal him from you.' Von growled like a cougar and departed with a cheeky smile.

Ben blushed.

Chassic shook his head. 'Don't worry. Veronica's harmless.'

Ben's new office was equipped with quality furniture, a state-of-the-art computer set-up and top-notch security.

'Top Secret protocols apply throughout. Keep your door locked at all times, even when you're in here.' HS handed Ben a small device on a neck chain. 'Look familiar?'

Ben turned it over in his hand. 'Biometric door key?'

'And more. PIN, thumb and iris combinations control your door lock and your wall safe.' Chassic took Ben through the biometric scanning process. 'After I've exited, close the door and enter your own eight-digit PIN. Then you, and only you, can unlock the wall safe. Veronica and I have master key access for the door locks, but the safe override requires complex simultaneous input from multiple sources.' Chassic locked eyes with Ben. 'And you have to be dead.'

'Sounds a bit extreme.'

'We try to avoid it.' Chassic broke the eye-lock. 'You'll find your project outline in the top draw. Lock the file in your safe before you leave tonight.'

Ben nodded.

'We'll talk office routine and big picture stuff after the weekend. I'll expect to see you bright-eyed and bushy-tailed Tuesday morning, so take it easy over Easter.' HS gave the door an emphatic tap as he left.

CODE SET, door locked, Ben sat and retrieved the file. It was labelled TOP SECRET, titled LIES. Ben opened the file.

Language Impulse Enhancement and Synthesis
Sound and Thought Impulse Reader (STIR)
Parallel Development Initiative

The stated aim of the project was to improve communication for the hearing and speech impaired. As Ben ploughed through the file, his excitement grew at the harvest of possibilities in its pages. The STIR implant utilised a biosynthetic neuroweb to capture impulses from the brain's language centres, and a prototype cochlear implant to convert, amplify, and transmit the data via satellite. LIES software—his project—would transform that data into text, for conversion to audio or other languages, providing a literal voice for the voiceless.

Or a long-distance mind-reader. Now that would create a stir.

Because of the highly speculative nature of the STIR implant's brain to computer interface, he'd be using simulated signals to develop and perfect the LIES software. If he succeeded, the medical technology would enter the clinical trial stage.

As Ben closed the folder, two things dawned on him. He'd agreed to develop lies for an asspit. How could he admit that with a straight face?

And … it was knock-off time. Long weekend! Time to tune out work and tune in freedom. And that ain't no lie. He cringed at his own pun.

With a minor sense of awe at being lord of his domain, he unlocked the wall safe. It contained a single envelope, addressed '*Ben-man*' in his father's familiar scrawl. The implications were—

The phone on his desk beeped. He answered the internal call.

'Von here, Ben. It's knock off time. I need to close up shop and notify security as per protocol.'

'No worries.'

He locked the LIES file in the safe, slipped Pat's letter into his satchel, locked the door behind him, and bid Von a Happy Easter on his way out.

Ben synced the upbeat music on his smartphone to his car's sound system, an after-market add-on, and one of the few things about his car that worked well. Buoyed with anticipation over LIES and possibilities, he drummed the tom-tom out of his steering wheel all the way home.

———◦◦———

THE HOUSE was dark when Ben arrived, but the shadows tempered his elation only slightly, even if he did have to cook and eat alone. Again.

'Not sure when I'll be back,' Pat had said. 'Could be several weeks. Sorry I can't elucidate. I imagine you'll encounter the same problem one day, given your chosen field and employer, whoever that is.' He'd offered an exaggerated double wink.

Ben had parried. 'I know, Dad. You could tell me where you're going, and I could tell you who I work for, but—'

'We'd have to kill each other.' Camaraderie had synchronised their voices.

Ben flipped on the vestibule light, placed his keys on the hallstand and smiled at the anchor. He caressed the nautical piece as if the essence of his father dwelt in its rough and rusted form.

'Fair weather and crimson sunsets, Dad. The home port misses you.' Ben's words rippled through to the kitchen. He followed them into it, set a brew of Torrefacto Mixed Roast percolating, and sat down to read the letter.

Hey Ben-man,

Congrats on the ASPT promo! You do me proud, son. I'm well pleased with you.

Love, Dad.

PS Don't forget to clean out the GRUnGE in your bedroom bin.

Pat had pressed his signet ring into wax at the bottom of the page. Mim had suggested a matching ring would be perfect to mark Ben's high school graduation. 'You're kidding,' he'd said. 'Signet rings are so middle ages. No offence, Dad.'

He'd taken none, then given Ben a complementary pair of studs—a black opal and a titanium anchor—styled in homage to the ring, for his eighteenth birthday. Ben had opted for double helix piercings. He fingered his ear studs, anchored in cartilage, separate yet belonging together.

Ben ran his fingers over Pat's signature seal, positioned within an embossed circle of words:

Anclajes ~ Seguridad ~ Protección ~ Transformación

Anchors ~ Security ~ Protection ~ Transformation

The same acronym as ASPT, with an entirely different meaning.

SLEEP CAME slowly that night. Ben's head buzzed with coding ideas. He dozed a restless few hours short of dawn, dreaming of beautiful senoritas clamouring to have their thoughts transformed into languages of love and desire. His code produced chattering Minion mumble. The dream devolved into chaos as the ghost of Felonious Gru burst through his bedroom door, demanding—

Hang on. If Gru's inside, who's banging on the front door?

Sleep sodden, sullied and soured by the stupid dream, Ben staggered down the stairs.

'Benjamin Ail Jandro?'

Alejandro. J is soft. No beer up front …

13. DISCONNECTED

Good Friday 6 April 2012

Canberra, Australia

'I AM sorry, Benjamin. I'm afraid we have difficult news for you.' Unlike Vaig-of-the-nametag, LSC Elspeth Torino introduced herself by rank *and* first name. 'Perhaps we should continue this conversation inside. May we come in, please?'

Torino's (extremely attractive!) face projected genuine concern.

Ben's heart skittered. He stepped back, closer to the anchor.

'Thank you.' Her tone was gentle. 'I suggest we sit. Lounge to the left?'

He pointed mutely to his right. Torino's confident advance only underscored her physical appeal.

Vaig sniffed and followed her.

Ben closed the front door and joined them in the lounge room.

He sat. They didn't.

Through a muffled wash of words, he heard, 'plane crash ... inaccurate passenger manifest ... multiple fatalities ... DNA identification ... Patriarca Alejandro.'

'No! God, no. Please.' Ben's prayer bounced off Vaig's bland expression, the floor, the walls, the ceiling and heaven itself.

'Would you like me to call a relative or friend, so you're not alone?' Torino's voice sounded distant. Disconnected.

Like him.

'That won't be necessary.' He stood mechanically. 'If there's nothing else? I'll see you out.'

He watched the reversing police car disrupt the flow of churchgoers. Some aimed curious stares before heading on to worship.

Ben retreated into the empty, anchored space behind him, overwhelmed and drowning. Why, Father? Why? Why have you forsaken me? His own heart bled words from a lifetime of Good Friday sermons. He shrank into a knot beside the anchor and let the full tide of his sorrow drench it until exhaustion forced an ebb. Then he slept, right there on the bare floor.

Another knock, gentle but insistent, roused him. He could have ripped the door from its hinges so no one would ever knock on it again.

'Hello Benjamin.'

'Mr ... HS.'

'I'm so very sorry for your loss, son. May I come in?'

Ben nodded and stepped back from the threshold. 'I, um ...'

'Need a cuppa? I boil water like a Japanese Iron Chef. Show me the kitchen and I'll brew a winner. Tea or coffee?' HS pressed a paternal hand against Ben's shoulder, eased him toward a seat at the breakfast bar, and made tea without conversation or fuss. Only the teaspoon's clink broke the silence. Ben was midway through a refill before HS spoke.

'Do you need help with funeral arrangements?'

Ben shook his head wistfully. 'There's no need. No body to bury.'

'Won't family and friends want to remember and celebrate Pat's life with you?'

'There's only me. My mother's beyond reach.' Ben thought about Chris's aversion to funerals. Understandable for someone who'd lost both parents. Ben's sense of kinship surged. 'I'd rather say goodbye privately. My ... brother would feel the same.'

HS finished his tea in silence. He rose and rinsed his cup then used it to water the wilting anthurium on the window sill. Ben had bought the plant for Mim because of its heart-shaped spathes and leaves. Those hearts had languished since her departure. Ben sighed.

'I'll arrange compassionate leave for you, of course,' HS said. 'The project will wait while you honour your father as you see fit.'

'I'd like to work. That's how I'll honour his life and memory. Moping around here won't help anyone. The project will.' Ben stood, pulled his shoulders back and held out his right hand.

HS gripped it and nodded. 'Tuesday morning, then. I'll see myself out.'

'I've lost my father, Mr Chassic. Not my manners.'

50

Ben walked his employer to the door. 'Thank you, sir.'

'For what, Ben?'

A quiver of uncertainty tested Ben's stoic smile. 'For, um, the tea. For coming.' Ben extended his hand again.

HS used it to pull him into a firm hug.

Ben's tears fell freely.

***

AFTER TWO cups of tea, Ben's stomach rumbled, and his bladder demanded action. He obliged the latter, but his stomach rejected Vegemite toast after three mouthfuls. He dumped the remaining slice and a half into the swing-top kitchen tidy, leaving a black smear on the lid. As he reached for spray-cleaner, he remembered his father's written exhortation.

PS: Don't forget to clean out the GRUnGE in your bedroom bin.

Only he didn't have a bin in the bedroom. Ben frowned. Dad knew that. Why would he write—?

GRUnGE. Guaranteed Retention Under Gridlocked Encryption.

Of course! Comprehension propelled him to the old turnkey wardrobe in his room. In his haste, he fumbled and dropped the key which bounced under the bed. He belted the door with the heel of his hand. The mangy door sprang open and whacked him back. Stunned by the blow, he sat on the bed to calm down.

Once his breathing settled, he retrieved a chunky Dell laptop—his first—from the bottom of the wardrobe. He'd have tossed the outdated technology if not for sentimentality. The battery was flat but the machine powered up when he connected the charger. He'd forgotten how sluggish it was, but not how to access the GRUnGE. It contained a recently added file: FromDad20120330.

Hey Ben-man,

Sorry about the cloak-and-dagger stuff with the GRUnGE. The etiquettes of confidentiality etch their habits deeply. I knew you'd catch on. It's rotten timing, my being away now. You deserve more than the usual 'business trip' tripe. This trip is different. I couldn't explain when it was need to know and you didn't. Now you do.

You will have seen the LIES documentation, background information omitted. Private enterprise funded the original project. My friend and colleague, Dr Alastair Maxwell, developed the STIR implant prototype. Satellite interface and software development was my domain. When ASIO offered us ongoing protection and safety, Alastair refused, concerned that their proposal (or ulterior motives) could restrict STIR access for those in genuine need.

Was ASIO aware of specific threats to our safety? I don't know. It appears their concerns were justified. Alastair and his family were killed when their house exploded. Authorities blamed an unidentified drug syndicate for the blast, supposed retaliation for reporting a neighbour's criminal activity, but no one was indicted. After that, HS Chassic and I negotiated ASPT's responsibility for the project's development via an arrangement that satisfied ASIO's interest.

A few months ago, I discovered a possible bungle, or worse, a cover-up over the explosion. While DNA evidence was found for Alastair's wife and daughter, Alastair's body was not conclusively identified. Recent scuttlebutt from Europe suggests Alastair was drugged before the explosion, kidnapped, detained in France or Spain, and coerced into making more prototypes to protect the family he believes is still alive. True or not, such leverage would be impossible to ignore. I can't ignore it either. I keep thinking, what if you or Mim were held captive? I know where you are, safe and sound. I must ensure she's okay too.

When I told HS I was suspending work on the LIES software to search for Alastair and Imee, he suggested bringing you in to work on the software during my absence. I gave my blessing. If you apply your wisdom and experience you'll keep the project on track. The STIR has so much potential to counteract disability. Even save lives. It would be wrong to see that good destroyed by evil intent.

Study my techniques and methods. Follow my example. Please use LIES MS simulated monologue samples to test the software. I'll tackle MXP2 mixed source samples when I return.

Now for the tough part. I'll be under deep cover in Europe. That limits my ability to communicate with HS, or you, without endangering us all. In Australia, HS is my eyes and ears. I'm relying on you to be the hands, brains and heart of the development program. I'm confident you'll soar through cyberspace like an eagle on an updraft. I miss you already, my son. I'll return as soon as I can. With Imee, God willing.

Love always, Dad.

PS It should go without saying, but I'll say it anyway. Powerful enemies will kill for this technology. Be wise as a serpent and careful who you trust.

―――∞――――

BEN STARED at his father's missive. Confusion buzzed his brain like insects at a barbecue, droning words like greed, corruption, cruel, unfair, and useless as an empty can of fly spray. Which he could have hurled.

He kneaded his eyelids.

Buzz, buzz, buzz. Brain-battering fuzz.

He shut the laptop, stretched and slumped.

Buzz, buzz, buzz. Maybe a shower would shift it.

He peppered his face with hot water.

Buzz, buzz, buzz. His head static sizzled.

He tried cold water shock treatment.

The static hissed and fizzed like spit on a hotplate.

Questions bombarded his head till it pounded from the pummelling. He raided the medicine cabinet for painkillers and shuffled to the kitchen.

He boiled the jug.

Stared at the rising steam.

Bent his head into it as he poured water over a teabag.

Closed his eyes.

Breathed the soothing, moist heat. It was easing if not appeasing. He sweetened his tea and swallowed two paracetamol capsules.

What if ...

The plane crash was a smokescreen! An undercover ruse to cover Dad's absence?

The teacup hit the sink and smashed. Ben bolted for the desktop computer in the study. What if, what if, *what if?* Oh Lord, if only ...

His fingers shook as he entered 'plane crash April 2012' into Google search. Please be a myth. Be a mistake. Be—

>>> ATR-72 Turbo-prop crashes: 31 dead <<<

The headline shot holes in Ben's hope. His body drooped but his thoughts kept moving, seething, swirling, rising.

Fight this, Ben. Rise above it. Soar like an eagle above the storm.

Ben could almost hear his father's voice.

Soar like an eagle? He was a fledgling, falling fast.

You're an Alejandro. Called by name to be a helper and defender of mankind. You were born to it as an eagle is to flight. Find your wings, Ben.

Wings! After a plane crash obliterated the person he loved most?

Trust me, son, even as you know me. We know that in all things God works for the good of those who love him, who have been called according to his purpose.

The quote was biblical. His father's favourite.

Believe it! Believe in your God-given purpose.

Could he? Could Benjamin Jaime Alejandro believe *he* existed for a divine purpose?

It was a mighty big ask.

14. SHAKEN

Tuesday 10 April 2012

Canberra, Australia

WHILE THE sunlit shimmer of ASPT's Zincalume did little to brighten Ben's spirits, knowing he walked where his father had walked before him brought some comfort.

'Good morning, Von. Pleasant Easter?'

Von stood. 'Ben, I—' Her eyes were red and teary. 'I spent most of it at the vet. My cat choked on a furball.'

'Oh, I'm sorry.'

'Cat's fine. HS wants to see you. Come through.' She grabbed a tissue and hurried ahead. Chassic's lock clicked open at her knock. 'You go on in, love.' Von seized Ben in a brief-but-motherly hug, and left, blowing her nose as she went.

Ben took a deep breath, and entered.

The decor in Chassic's office was an eclectic mix of executive stress and ocean breeze. The desk bore the charts and compasses of leadership, while a superb collection of seascapes filled the walls.

Should my approach reflect professional savvy or Great Barrier Reef? He settled for enthusiastic newcomer moderated by subdued admiration.

'Ah! Benjamin. Take a seat.' Chassic launched into his captain's spiel, providing Ben with essential information. He also explained that Ben's colleagues were 2PD's—Secondary Project Developers. Their purpose was to deflect attention from Ben's exclusive domain, the LIES project. 'Of course, I've not told them that, and neither must you. Strict confidentiality and separation of information applies throughout. Always keep your office door shut and locked. Don't leave files open on your desk or computer unless you're physically working with them. Discuss your progress or concerns with me only, in my office or yours, behind closed doors. Nowhere else. Not the lunchroom, bathroom, hallway, foyer, or outside.' Chassic handed Ben a file of additional security protocols. 'Study these. Follow them to the letter.'

Ben nodded.

'If you're good with all that, I expect we'll enjoy smooth sailing. Have you any questions, shipmate?'

Ben smiled and saluted. 'Aye, Cap'n, there be one or two things I be wonderin' about. My father, for example?'

Chassic leaned back in his chair. 'Pat was highly respected within ASPT, Ben. Losing him is more than a setback. We all grieve with you. In fact, we've planned a small memorial in his honour. I know you didn't want a formal ceremony, but we'd love you to join us.'

'I appreciate the invitation, Sir.'

'HS will suffice.'

Ben nodded. 'HS it is. I have to ask. Is my father really lost to us? Or ... temporarily misplaced?'

HS pursed his lips. 'Ben, I'd love to tell you Pat was not on that plane. The evidence says he was. Your father believed his exploration was warranted. I trusted his judgement. The plane crash—' HS reached for a handkerchief.

Ben dropped his eyes, respecting Chassic's obvious grief, and battling his own.

'We share a great loss, Ben. We'll make good, in spite of it. Pat's project will live on through you.'

'So I'm Plan B.'

'Let's say Plan A, Dot Point 2.'

'And what if I get killed?'

'I can't guarantee you won't.' The intensity in Chassic's eyes provoked Ben's resolve.

'Then you should arrange a backup for me. Dot Point 3.' Ben folded his arms.

'Do you have someone in mind?'

'I do. You're aware that my brother applied to ASIO at the same time I did?'

'I considered his application. I did not feel he met our requirements at that time.'

'What about now?'

HS straightened the desk blotter. 'What makes you think he's suitable for this job?'

'Chris is tech-savvy, competitive, driven to win, beats the odds, goes for it, manages the consequences.'

'So he leaps before he looks.'

'I'd say he's not easily intimidated and persists under pressure. Mr Chas—, HS, I don't know what happened to Chris before he came to live with us. He wouldn't, or couldn't, discuss it, but his scars, physical and emotional, spoke loudly. Chris suffered a lot. I think he lost everything, including himself. His time with us wasn't exactly perfect. Despite that, he's hot property in the gaming tech development market. He's very good at what he does.'

'I've heard. But is that enough?'

'He can also keep a secret, no matter what.'

'Which is crucial, I agree but—'

'There's one more thing.' Ben straightened his back and shoulders.

'Only one?' Amusement danced in Chassic's eyes.

Ben blushed contrition. 'They boil down to one. Chris is a survivor. If I don't, he will.'

'Perhaps I'll invite Chris to the memorial. It will be a sad and difficult time for us all, but I'd like to see if he's comfortable with me, and you, before I decide.'

———○———

May ... June ... July ... August ...

ASPT'S MEMORIAL homage to Pat had been thoughtful and respectful—before the booze-up—but Chris's absence had buffeted Ben. Had Chris made his choice, or had HS not invited him?

The residue of Ben's grief swilled like brine in a dirty martini, but he imbibed the LIES project with the dedication of 007. That's about where the Bond analogies ended, apart from Pat's licence-to-kill-software-bugs, for which Ben needed the ingenuity of Q.

Pat had concealed LIES project records, software and sample STIR signals in a GRUnGE. Ben was surprised. He'd expected to find sophisticated in-house encryption protecting such sensitive material. The

GRUnGE's access procedure shouted spoof, not hi-tech genius. Its multi-phase entry system had once earned him a multi-phase detention—fun, games and misadventure motivated by the mock spy games he and his father played. A reminder on Pat's email dashboard—Phone Jeremías Viejo (New) Int +34 912 310126—was the only clue Ben needed to extrapolate and apply Pat's personal access codes.

Although Ben appreciated the complexities and communicability of Pat's system, he set up his own GRUnGE with an alpha-code he knew by heart—three silly sentences which used all the letters of the alphabet in sequence.

Then he bought a six-pack of choc-iced donuts for lunch.

Over time, Ben refined the LIES software and tested it against the signal samples stored in Pat's GRUnGE. Weeks became months.

Then it happened. The first stirrings of success. A STIR sample responded to the software. Actual text spattered the screen. Those first heavy droplets shook and stirred Ben's equilibrium more than any martini could.

PART TWO

Binned and Blocked

15. DEVOURED

Friday 20 July 2012

Landsborough, Queensland, Australia

DEVOURING TIME, *blunt thou the—*
  'Stop tapping, Mac. It's annoying.'
And make the earth devour her own sweet brood. Pluck the keen teeth—
  'Mac. Stop it.'
  'I'm being framed by a tin roof, Liss. It's pinging from the heat.' Aidan MacGreggor highlighted the metric anomaly in line three.
  Liss placed a jug of liquid fizz on the table. 'Li said to expect guests. Want some?'
  'Devouring humans is illegal, Liss.'
  'Smart alec. Do you want some ginger beer, or not?'
  'No, thanks.' Mac swapped the highlighter for a pen.
And burn the long-liv'd Phoenix in—
  'You're tapping again.'
  'I am now because I'm counting poetic meter. It's called scansion.'
  'Can you scan without tapping?'
And do whate'er thou wilt. Hullo, doorbell. 'Want me to get it?'
  'Don't be stupid, Mac.'
  'Thou dost forbid me one most heinous crime.'
  'I beg your pardon?'
  'I'm quoting Shakespeare. Sonnet nineteen. Line eight. Sort of. Should I disappear?'
  'No. This concerns you.'
  Li emerged from the hallway with two men.

Oh, no. Pinstripe. Whoa, his offsider's an ugly bloke. Saggy jowls, bloated bowels, jaundiced eyes. Alcoholic?

Li ushered them towards the table. 'It'll be cooler in here. The lounge room's hot and stuffy this time of day.'

'I miss Queensland's heat, especially in winter. Canberra can be a cold hole.' Pinstripe faked a shiver.

'You should have stayed local.'

The lush speaks.

'The Queensland Crime Commission persuaded me otherwise, Bosworth, though you weathered it well. Brock's a Bundy man, Li. He can handle the heat. And how are you doing, Mac? You've become a fine-looking lad since I saw you last.'

'But you're still wearing the navy pinstripe, I see. Minus the chartreuse shirt with spaghetti sauce on the cuff—a gift from your mother. The shirt that is, not the spaghetti sauce. Did your Labrador recover?'

'My Labrador?'

'Sunny-girl. Having her teeth cleaned by the vet. Mouth infection. You raced off to collect her before closing time.' *Fake excuse. Yeah, you remember. Eye tick's a dead giveaway. You should squirm. What happened to your promised explanations, assistance and follow-up visits?*

'You've impressive recall, Mac. Are Li and Liss keeping you well?'

'I'm defecating regularly, if that's what you mean.'

Liss glared a warning. 'Please have a seat, gentlemen. There's homemade ginger beer.' Liss strained her smile through thinned lips.

'Thank you, Mrs—'

'First names only, Bosworth. Never know who might be listening.'

'Everyone within cooee knows Liss's surname.' Mac ran a thumb around the rim of the jug to make it squawk. 'Shall I pour, Mr Bozo? Brothel? Rotwell?'

'Mac!' Liss frowned.

'Pleash pardon my shpeech impairment, Mishter Boshwart.' *Shmooth as Sean Connery.* 'With or without ice?'

'I'll save the ice for the hard stuff, mate.'

'Pleasure after business, eh Brock? Thanks, Mac. Cheers.' Pinstripe raised his glass and downed its contents. 'Nice drop, Liss. Just the right edge.'

It's usually crap.

'You mentioned business?'

'That I did, Li. Generally speaking, our protection program provides one identity change per customer, unless a serious new threat is detected. We have reason to believe the security of Mac's identity has been compromised, necessitating another change.'

'Are we all in danger?' Liss's cheek twitched.

'It's Mac we're concerned about.'

'Why now? I didn't see anything. I can't identify anyone. Besides, I died. Remember?'

Pinstripe pulled a photo from his pocket. 'Do you recognise this face, Mac?'

'That's Jake Leicester. BSDE student. We chat online through iConnect.'

'Mac! You're not supposed to use social media.'

'I'm not supposed to be breathing either, Liss, but hey, call me a rebel. iConnect's for school, not social media. I block the webcam. Never post photos or identifying info other than my fake name.'

'You should stop interacting with this Jake. He may be a plant.' Pinstripe pocketed the photo.

'We've interacted for nearly two years. If Jake's a Stinking Roger, won't cutting him off tip him off?'

'It's precautionary. Brock will take you to see our photographic specialist who'll prepare your new identity portfolio and documentation. It'll mean a train trip into Brisbane.'

'Can I check out Queensland Uni and QUT's Garden Point campus while we're there?'

'Not this time. The photo session will be after hours. Midnight jaunt. You'll be back in Landsborough for breakfast. The actual changeover will occur during Schoolies Week. I hope you haven't made plans.'

'I don't make those sorts of plans. My social life is non-existent. Apart from Jake, who lives in Toowoomba.'

'He may be closer than you think.' Pinstripe tapped the pocket that held Jake's photo. 'Close and dangerous. Which is why Brock will remain here to provide you with round-the-clock protection.'

Twenty-four-seven ugly fugly. 'Great.'

'You and he will share a mobile phone communication setup in case you're separated.'

'I get my own phone? Finally.'

'Yes and no. It's a purpose-built smartphone designed with your cochlear implant in mind, however, your outgoing communications will be restricted—'

'Let me guess—to meet the budget's bottom line?'

'To keep you out of the morgue. You'd be surprised how many protected witnesses end up there after chancing a phone call. You'll only be able to communicate with Brock's phone and com set.'

'So if I want pizza delivered, I sweet talk Brock. Got it! Can I have music on my phone?'

'Brock can help with that.'

'And a decent Australian dictionary and thesaurus app?'

'Sounds reasonable.'

'What about my tertiary admission application?'

'Can't you use your computer for that?'

'Duh! I meant, how will I link my results and preferences to my new identity?'

'We'll sort that.' Pinstripe raised his empty glass. 'Any more ginger beer left, Liss?'

'Mac, check the fridge for our guest, please?'

More icky fizz, coming up.

'Will we have to relocate? Mac's bound to receive a university course offer and move into student accommodation. But after traipsing the fruit picking circuit all those years, Li and I would rather stay put.'

'Don't worry, Liss. We'll take care of you all. I promise.'

That'd be a change. If we dropped off the edge of the world, you'd probably appreciate the fiscal savings. 'Ice with your refill, Mr Pinstripe?'

'Thanks, Mac. Ice would be great.'

Figures. Hope you choke on it.

16. NEEDED

Thursday 9 August 2012

Canberra, Australia

'SCREAMIN' PIG—' Chris braked hard to avoid a collision. The boxed pizzas beside him hit the floor.

'Use mirrors and blinkers, ijit!' He aimed a rude gesture at the offending driver, wishing it was his boss.

The whinger. Threatening to cut his hours, complaining that he, Christopher Darnell, their best and hottest designer, had been 'off the boil' since Easter.

According to Grumblebum, morbid and miserable was for emos and undertakers, not cashed-up game buyers. 'Dark and intriguing sells,' he'd said. 'Not this lukewarm mush. Fix it or find a new job.'

Idiot bosses and idiot drivers; a perfect end to a lousy day.

Mangled pizza aside, a night of buttered popcorn and binge-watching anime with MPeg would be a welcome relief.

Or not.

He found her, head down, bum up, shuffling through one of four large cardboard packing boxes she'd lined up against the wall.

'Whatcha doing, MPeg?'

She straightened up and used an envelope to point to the boxes in turn. 'Trash, Lifeline, Melbourne and please explain!' She flapped the envelope in his face. Her face was an angry red.

'Explain what?'

'Why I found Ben's condolence card buried in a box?'

Chris jiggled the pizza boxes. 'Hot and fresh.'

'You promised me you'd give Ben the card, in person, at Pat's memorial.'

Chris shrugged. 'Pizza's slightly mangled but I avoided a prang.'

'You didn't go, did you?'

Chris drew his lips apart like a half-baked Apple emoji.

'You promised me! You lied to me! And you disrespected the man who raised you. To top it off, you neglected Ben, your very best friend, when he needed you most.'

'Ben? Need me? That's a joke. For cryin' out loud, Peg, I wrecked his family. I'm sorry Pat's dead. But nothing I did or didn't do can change that. I only wish ... bah!' Chris tossed the pizza into MPeg's 'Trash' box. 'Who cares what I wish?'

'Your friends care. Friends who happen to think your backbone is stronger than your wishbone. Friends who need you, like Ben and me.'

'Is that why you're moving to Melbourne?' He gestured towards the carton.

'Melbourne's wishful thinking.'

'Don't let me stop you. I'm sure any place would be better than here, with me.' His words tasted as bitter as they sounded.

'Only when you trash hot pizza.' MPeg retrieved the box and checked its contents.

'It's too messed up. Like me.'

She helped herself to a piece and took a bite, her expression defiant.

'I'm truly sorry about the card, MPeg, but there's no way I could've faced Pat's funeral.'

'Why not?'

Why couldn't she let it go? 'Because I wish it had been my funeral, not his. There. I've said it. Are you happy now?'

She put the pizza down. The gentle sadness in her eyes cut him. 'Is that why you constantly dig your own grave?'

Those eyes. He turned away. He didn't deserve her compassion.

She sighed. 'I've primed the anime DVD. If you want butter popcorn, you'll have to nuke it yourself. I'm going out to post Ben's card. Better still, I'll deliver it in person. Don't wait up.'

17. DUSTED

Friday 10 August 2012

Canberra, Australia

BEN SCRATCHED his neck, irritated by stubble and stupidity. MPeg's surprise visit—and her revelation that Chris had chosen to avoid Pat's Memorial—had played havoc with his concentration. He'd made a dozen silly errors, derailing his planned attempt at an actual STIR transcription. Till now.

Here goes nothing. He selected a sample file and activated LIES. A colour-shifting box with a countdown appeared.

MXP2 Engaged. Data Active. Transcription in Progress.
Estimated time to completion: 00:09:14

MXP2. Ben facepalmed. He'd selected a mixed source file by mistake, jumping the gun on his father's instructions. Oh well. Too late now. Transcription was already in progress.

In progress! Woo-hoo! HS would want to see this. He phoned Chassic's extension. No response. He phoned Von. No response. Ben checked his watch. 7:15pm. Past knock-off time.

File at 100% Capacity. Transcription Paused.
Select: View Text. New File. Exit.

Ben selected 'View Text'.

Text dusted the screen like cinnamon on blancmange, one of the few desserts Mim made well. But if his first thought had been sweet, his second was sour. The transcript contained a conglomeration of run-on sentences devoid of syntax and punctuation. It was a reader's nightmare. He'd have to modify the code, again, to produce legible text.

Maybe ASPT should hire a bunch of editors. He pictured several spectacle-clad bibliophiles trussed up like a flower posy and pondered potential collective nouns for editors. He decided bouquet was the best of a bad bunch, groaning at his Pat-like pun. His father's face, mischievous and smiling superseded the editorial posy. Ben's lips smiled, but his heart ached.

I wish you could see your STIR-baby born and breathing, Dad. I wonder what its future holds?

Ben checked his watch. Coding the changes would take eons, but he could manually format and punctuate a short section using common conventions like quote marks for dialogue and italics for thoughts.

Besides, he was way too pumped to go home. The only real objection came from his stomach. He was alone in the building, security wise. Risk it for a biscuit? He locked his door, trotted to the coffee maker, press-buttoned a caramel latte and raided the biscuit barrel while the machine spat out the automated brew. With coffee in one hand, two Arnott's Monte Carlos and a couple of Delta Creams in the other, Ben munched his way back to his office, a trail of crumbs and coffee drips marking the journey.

He sent the screen saver to its hidey-hole.

An hour later, he'd transformed letter soup into his first LIES transcript—a thought-based sample which ended in a brief verbal exchange.

LIES/MXP2/20120810pm73882

AND SEND. Yay! English assignment done and dusted. Hullo. Leicester's online. Hey Jake.

Yo Mac. Sup?

Just subbed my Hamlet eulogy. Where for art it is done to death. Glad to see the rear of Shakespeare. You?

Killing graphics. Btw I got a part-time job carting bricks.

That what you want?

No choice. My old man says he'll kick me to Bourke and back if I'm not OTJ day after my last exam.

At least you'll get dough, bro.

Peanuts! You going to the formal?

Not really my thing.

Same here.

What happened to Jake Leicester, chick magnet?

Too busy charming the local talent. BSDE chicks live too far away. Wouldn't mind getting it on with Tracie Baker though. She's hot.

Enough to burn you, bro. I think she's taken.

Pity. What about you, Mac?

Li'l ol' me? I'm free as a bird in a cage. Why? Got a bromance going on for me, Jake?

Hell no! I meant are you going to the formal?

I just told you, brick-head. Not really my thing, remember?

Sorry. Brain fart. Gotta go, mate. This brick-head's brain dead.

...

Really Jake? Hell no to a bromance? My best friend—my only friend— tells it like it is. My life sucks.

'Mac! What are you doing online?'

'Chuck-a-duster, Brock! Don't sneak up on me like that.'

'Well?'

'I lodged my Shakespeare assignment. That's all.'

'I hope you took my advice.'

'What? Stuff it up so I don't draw attention to my unique attributes? You were kidding, right? Messing with me?'

'I was deadly serious. You need to chop the tall poppy off your head. Stick with your gay options. You don't need straight A's for a Hairdressing or Salon Management Certificate.'

'That's such a stereotype, Brock.' *Moron.* 'Being gay doesn't dictate career choice.'

'No, but avoiding killers does.'

———

BEN STARED at the text. OTT drama for a test sample script. He was about to hit print when a door shoofed open and shut, somewhere in the building. Conscious of confidentiality, he set a rapid secure shutdown and went to investigate.

He found HS in the reception area. 'You're working late, Ben. Everything alright?'

'I—' An alarm bell interrupted Ben's reply. HS turned and pressed numbers on the security key pad. Ben's internal alarm sounded as well, rousing an inexplicable reluctance to share his success with his boss. 'Lost track of time. Engrossed in a process.'

'Security called me. The building should have been empty this time of night. Veronica warns them if someone is working overtime. Were you in the men's room when she left?'

'Must've been. Sorry. I didn't think to phone security. My bad.'

'I wonder why the alarm didn't trigger earlier. I'll have the movement sensors checked. Can't have intruders pinching our loo paper. Call it a day, Ben.'

Ben obliged without delay. He had a bigger problem to process—that transcript was no mere sample. It was an actual conversation. Somewhere, somehow, a STIR implant was transmitting signals from a real live human being.

Whose name was Mac.

BEN DROVE home, disturbed not by traffic, but by an ethical dilemma. He'd eavesdropped on Mac's thoughts. Hypothetical had become actual. The moral cyclone twisted and turned his stomach so much, he skipped supper and went to bed.

All night long, he dreamed of winged gremlins swooping and clawing his thoughts and pallid green witches pelting him with jumbled syntax. 'You stole-ole my brain-ain you wicked-icked-icked boy aisle isle I'll get you!'

The tumultuous dream whipped and tossed his questions high, then hailed icy question marks that pierced and ripped his skin. Ben ducked and ran as the wind jeered and mocked, 'Run to find the wisdom, the wonderful wisdom of—'

Who? Dear God, who?

The dream did not answer.

18. TANGLED

Saturday 11 August 2012

Canberra, Australia

BEN WOKE in a tangle of bedsheets, thoughts scattered like storm debris. He couldn't clear this mess alone. So why had he hesitated to share his discovery with HS? In the light of day, he found no rational justification beyond his feelings of guilt for invading Mac's privacy. He called Chassic's mobile phone number.

'Benjamin. What's so important it can't wait till Monday?'

'Something I failed to explain last night. I had a breakthrough with the software and got more than I bargained for. Should we meet at the office or can I give you the gist by phone?'

'I'll come to you. We can talk in my vehicle without being overheard. Leave your phone inside the house.'

Half an hour later, while HS calmly sipped coffee from an insulated travel mug, Ben broke down his breakthrough, broke up his technical conundrum, then broke out with his ethical one.

'Clearly this thing's upset you, Ben. It's an age-old quandary encountered by every inquiring mind from Adam to Zeppelin; new discoveries have potential for good and evil. We choose our responses.'

'I don't know how to respond. I'd feel better if we contacted the STIR recipient immediately. Confirm he's on board with the project and has a master switch to limit transmission unless it's a controlled test.'

'Is that not the case?'

'I don't know. The small section I decoded is mostly harmless chatter, but some bits sounded private. I wouldn't want my private thoughts recorded. I can't imagine this Mac would either.'

'They were definitely thoughts? Not a verbal conversation?'

71

'STIR delineates the signal source. These were thought-based impulses, apart from a brief verbal exchange at the end. I think our STIR recipient was chatting online.'

'Only he isn't ours.'

'Isn't he?' Ben scratched his head. 'I assumed you'd know who he is.'

'The STIR prototype's creator died before the software was anywhere near completion. Given the risks associated with implant surgery, ASPT planned to recruit recipients after the software proved viable. Which you've just done.'

'Surely someone from the original research program must know?'

'There is no one from the original program, not since—' HS took a breath and sighed.

'Not since Dad died.' The reality reinforced Ben's sense of isolation.

'I'm afraid we're it. There is one thing I can do. Have done, actually. One of our 2PD's has requested a transfer. I've hired a suitable replacement. He took some persuading I might add.'

'Working for Australia's intelligence agency, in an asspit, is not everyone's dream job. Some people are smarter than us.'

'Benjamin Alejandro! Do you disparage your employer?'

'Sorry, boss. I had a heavy night. Just trying to lighten the mood. How will employing a new 2PD colleague help my project, or quandary?'

'He's coming as your assistant. I had to twist his arm. He's got history. With you.'

'It's not—? Chris? You're kidding me.'

'Christopher won't have agent status like you, but he commenced the short induction course yesterday. He'll be non-contactable till the end of September. You might have to build a few bridges.'

'I'll be glad to, HS. Really glad.'

'Good. We'll talk more on Monday, okay? Make it an early start. Seven?'

'Monday, seven am. And HS? Thanks.'

Monday 13 August 2012

BEN'S SOFTWARE triumph was a perfect high dive, but he no longer stood high and dry on the platform. The Eureka moment had filled him with elation. The emotional storm had drenched him with dilemmas. He was over overthinking. He sat in Chassic's office, wanting answers and action.

'HS, we must locate Mac so I can work with him. Establish boundaries like an on-off switch. Recipients must be in control.'

HS linked his fingers together. 'Our legitimate recipients, yes, but we don't have any. This recipient is not our concern. Especially if, as you suggest, he's not aware of the hardware.'

'Invading his privacy makes him our concern. What if he's in danger from unscrupulous elements? Isn't that why ASPT acquired the project in the first place?'

'Our reasons were more complex than that. Our mandate covers multiple aspects of national security.'

'Finding this recipient, this person, is the least we should do. National security includes the wellbeing of individuals.' Ben folded his arms. 'My father died pursuing that ideal.'

Chassic frowned. 'Pat's death was a tragic accident, but you're letting emotion skew your focus. You can't hijack the LIES program with a wild goose chase. You were hired to ensure the software functions. Need I remind you of your legal and contractual obligations as an ASPT employee?' HS folded his arms too.

'My obligations? Surely this breaches privacy regulations? I can't work in an ethical void. What about ASPT's legal obligations to Mac?'

'They lack precedent. Thoughts have never been transmitted and translated this way before. The legalities require arbitration. That's my concern, not yours.' HS spread his hands. 'However, utilising transmissions as an intermediary resource seems expedient. It could take months to enlist volunteer recipients.'

Ben pursed his lips. He'd unwittingly forced Mac's enlistment by testing a second phase file.

Chassic relaxed, his expression conciliatory. 'We're damned-if-we-do, damned-if-we-don't. Either way, we've insufficient information to act upon. Can you identify and locate the recipient from this transcript?'

'Not yet.'

'But you think future transcripts might identify him.'

'Or past ones.'

'If so, I'll bring him in. Sound reasonable?'

Ben nodded. What else could he do? He knew so little about Mac.

But he'd discover more. He'd find Mac with or without Chassic's blessing.

As Ben returned to his office, he glimpsed an unfamiliar figure in the hallway, without Von or a 2PD in tow, an unacceptable lapse in protocol. He called out, 'Can I help you?'

The stranger kept moving. Ben issued a challenge. 'Stop! This is a secure area. Who are you and what are you doing here?'

The man paused and drew himself full height. 'Federal Agent Talbot Locke. NWPP.' He flashed his badge and identification card.

Ben perused them. 'National Witness Protection Program Liaison. What brings the federal police here so early in the day, Agent Locke?'

'Nothing serious. I was nearby and thought I'd surprise HS at his new HQ. We go way back.'

'Mr Chassic's office is this way.' Ben raised his arm to usher the visitor.

'I need to take a rain check. Urgent office text. Work before pleasure, right?'

Ben frowned. Locke's demeanour was more thief-caught-red-handed than federal agent. 'Mr Chassic's a busy man. You could make an appointment. If you give me your card, I'll pass it on. After I see you out, that is.'

'I should have one in my wallet. Fiddly things. Stick together. Here you go. One for HS and one for you. I didn't catch your name?'

'I didn't throw it. The exit is this way, Agent Locke.' Ben walked him out and watched Locke drive away.

Ben went back to Chassic's office and knocked.

'Yes?'

'Sorry to disturb you again. I just had an odd encounter with an Agent Locke who claimed he wanted to catch up with you at another time. I requested his card.'

HS scrutinised the business card. 'Talbot Locke. National Witness Protection Program. Card looks genuine. Name doesn't ring a bell. He'll call again if it's important. Thanks for the intercept, Ben. Was there anything else?'

'No. All good.' In truth, Ben felt anything but. The morning's conversation had clarified one thing; when it came to identifying Mac, he was on his own.

19. LOCKED

Monday 13 August 2012

Canberra, Australia

AUSTRALIAN FEDERAL Police Agent Talbot 'Bud' Locke sat on the grass under the fickle shade of a casuarina tree. He slurped the dregs from his thickshake and tossed the cup towards the river bank.

'Write yourself a ticket for littering, you naughty boy.' Judy Callahan slapped his thigh playfully.

He grabbed her wrist and yanked her across his lap. 'Watch it, sweetheart. Exacting punishment is my job, not yours.' He patted her lightly and released her.

Judy brushed a few bits of dried grass off his lap. 'You could have picked a nicer spot to eat our lunch.'

'What's to complain about? We have shade trees above us, the nuanced rippling of the Molonglo River before us—'

'Crass commercialism to the rear and ants biting our behinds. Ow!' Judy swept one off her ankle.

'But you won't run late for work, unlike this morning.'

'Sorry about that. I got caught in a traffic snarl. Grrr!' Judy pounced on Locke like a cat. He grabbed her hair like a cat's scruff, pulled her head back and bit her chin. 'Ow!' She pulled away. 'What was that for? It hurt.'

'Because you were late, I got caught in the hallway and had to bluff my way out.'

'In the hallway! How'd you get past Von?'

'Lots of practice. Don't be late again. Chassic might sack you.'

'Doubt he'd notice. He ignores me and my project. The newbie's got his attention though. You might be right about Chassic's preference for boys.' Judy stood up. 'Time to go, Locky-jock. Carry me back to asspit. Take me kicking and screaming if you must.' Her tone oozed sexual innuendo.

Locke ushered her to the car and opened her door. 'I'd like to have ears in the new boy's office.' He raised an eyebrow.

'Don't look at me. It was hard enough bugging Chassic's room.'

'You said he loved the oil painting. Hung it straight away. How's that difficult? Commissioning the piece with the bug embedded was the tricky part. What's the new kid's decor like?'

'I dunno. Each PD's office is their exclusive domain. Locked door policy, remember?' Judy buckled her seatbelt.

Locke closed her door and settled himself in the driver's seat. 'What about out-of-office discussions? Perhaps you should cultivate a relationship with—what's his name?'

'Benjamin Alejandro. Pat's son.'

'Same office?'

Judy nodded. 'He's as zealous as his old man when it comes to security.'

'I noticed.' Locke kicked over the engine and eased the vehicle back along the dirt track towards the road. 'Could you do him?'

'Hmph! Bite me.' Judy pulled a packet of Warheads sour lollies from her handbag. 'Ben's a good boy. Not my type at all.' She popped a lolly into her mouth and offered the pack to Locke. 'Want one? They bite too.'

20. MYSTIFIED

Monday 13 August 2012

Canberra, Australia

BEN BEGAN his quest to identify and locate Mac by re-reading Pat's letter.

Study my techniques and methods. Follow my example. Please use LIES/MS simulated monologue samples to test the software. I'll tackle MXP2 mixed source samples when I return.

Return. If only he had.

Ben dug deeper and discovered that the existing MXP2 files contained seven weeks' worth of raw transmission data. Pat's default setting automatically deleted older data. Pat had activated live signal retrieval in March. Ben worked out how to engage and pause LIES transcription and save the resulting files to increase their longevity.

Over fifty thousand minutes of content existed, increasing with every second. Days evaporated while Ben transcribed, saved, edited, digested, searched for patterns and information, and tried to understand the Sound and Thought Impulse Reader and its wearer.

The STIR transmitted Mac's internal contemplations, anything he read, silently or aloud, and any verbal conversations. These were held almost exclusively with 'Liss', 'Li', or 'Brock'. No familial endearments were used.

There were gaps, periods of time devoid of content. Maybe Mac did have a switch? Doh! The diagrams showed the cochlear implant's external speech processor clipped onto a bone-anchored abutment. Mac probably detached it to shower and sleep.

Ben soon had a handle on transmission mechanics. Coming to

grips with their content was a whole other challenge. From mundane to urbane, Ben gleaned facts, gained impressions, and experienced the déjà vu of Year Twelve study, minus the social life—Jake Leicester being the exception.

Mac dispersed goodwill sparingly and shed rancour like a moulting moggie. Acrimony, bravado, candour, cynicism, and yet ...

The roiling magma of his turmoil pushed uncut diamonds to the surface.

Mac's thoughts.

Ben was mystified. Who was this curious fusion of poet and prat? Mac could ink the air with profanity one moment, then eulogise a seventeenth century poet and preacher the next, and not just for school assignments.

"Batter my heart, three-personed God, for you as yet but knock, breathe, shine, and seek to mend that I may rise and stand. I am betrothed unto your enemy. Take me to you ... for I, except you enthral me, never shall be free, nor ever chaste, except you ravish me."
From your heart to my hell, John Donne.

Ben had met some weird people in his life, in school and out, but never one so vehemently attracted to words. Mac pursued them, mining literature for the meaning of life itself. Was it coincidence that Ben's own connection to Mac existed purely through words? Discarnate, metaphysical words.

"We in us find the eagle and the dove. The phoenix riddle hath more wit by us: we two being one, are it. We die and rise the same, and prove mysterious ... and if unfit for tombs and hearse our legend be, it will be fit for verse."

Ben stared at the words on the screen.

Unfit for tombs and hearse our legend be.

Poetry wasn't Ben's forte but, weren't suicides denied proper burials back in Donne's time? Had he sensed something in Mac's undercurrent?

And we in us find the eagle.

Ben recalled his father's exhortation to soar through cyberspace like an eagle on an updraft.

The phoenix riddle—we two, being one, are it.

The phoenix was a mythical bird that rose from the ashes of its own destruction.

We two, being one … die and rise the same.

The words reached through time and space and pierced Ben's heart with unexpected ferocity. It skipped a beat, or three.

Ben swallowed the lump in his throat. What did it all mean? Why did those particular words project such power? Such presence?

Did they speak of things past?

Or things to come?

Wednesday 22 August 2012

AS BEN studied Mac's transcripts, his fascination with the mind behind them grew. So did his conviction that Mac was in peril.

He told HS as much. 'This guy's suffering psychological and emotional trauma. He's on the edge. Surely we should intervene?'

'What do you mean, "on the edge"? Is he self-harming? Suicidal?'

'The latest transcript says, "My life is pointless. I want the pain to go away." Doesn't sound too good.'

'Let me see.' HS read a few of Mac's transcripts. 'You're seeing trouble to justify your desire to intervene with guns blazing. I see no evidence of neglect, physical violence or sexual abuse. Mac gets three square meals a day, whatever he needs to complete his schoolwork, books to read and various other entertainments. His social life's dull as a home-schooler, but he chats online with school friends. In my honest opinion, Mac's negativity is typical teenage hype and boundary testing. What adolescent doesn't think the world is conspiring against them? I bet you had your moments. This kid's blowing off steam.'

Ben's insistence the threat was subtle but implicit fell on deaf ears. He retreated to his office and slammed the door.

How could HS brush him off like that? Imply he was indulging a hero complex? Ben's scalp tingled with guilt for that grain of truth. Even so, Chassic's resistance galvanised his resolve to exploit every means possible to find Mac, covert or otherwise.

He searched Brisbane School of Distance Education records for year twelve students whose given or surnames could be shortened to Mac. Aidan MacGreggor was the most likely candidate because all identifying information was 'withheld due to custody issues.' Aidan enrolled as a 'Traveller' in 2007, starting with year four lessons, though he was old enough for year seven. Progress disrupted by a transient lifestyle? But he was no slouch. Within two years he'd surpassed his age peers. Ben found frequent references to extension materials posted to multiple Queensland locations, usually c/- a post office. Aidan had transferred to the 'Special' category in 2011. After that, lesson materials went to a post office box in Landsborough, Queensland. Ben found no records of a Li or Liss MacGreggor living nearby. Different surname, perhaps?

Ben identified Aidan's birth parents from his Queensland birth certificate. They died on the sixteenth of July, 1994, nine days after Aidan was born. Ben could find no official records between then and Aidan's registration with BSDE—no care facility records, no foster or adoption records, no immunisation, education or family assistance records. No records at all. If they existed, an information black hole had swallowed them and no amount of creative throat-tickling by Ben regurgitated them.

Although Mac was eighteen, he didn't have a driver's licence. Perhaps his unusual domestic situation made that problematic. So, what personal facts did Ben know about Mac? He developed a profile based on several transcripts.

- Intelligent
- Opinionated
- Attitude! Bit immature.
- Angry, bitter, cynical.
- Contemplative
- Mature vocab, passion for words, literature.
- Reads a lot, mostly fiction. Escapist?
- Special memory? Mac thinks so.
- Gay?
- Lonely, feels isolated. Limits on socialisation ref schooling.
- STIR recipient. Cochlear implant. Medical records!

Despite exhaustive and slightly questionable search tactics, Ben found no trace of Aidan MacGreggor's surgery, or even a Medicare number.

Talk about spooky. Either Mac was an illegal immigrant, or his records had been deliberately obscured.

Thursday 30 August 2012

BEN'S SEARCHES devoured time, time needed to refine the software to edit intuitively. Complex software development, such as LIES, demanded extensive collaboration and teamwork. Ben was it. He wished he had a clone. Or ten.

Von habitually shunted him out of the building well past knock-off time. 'You need a lady love to entice you home each night. I'd volunteer, but my cat's very possessive.' She puckered up and threw a kiss.

Ben pretended to catch it and smiled. 'I'm nearly done, mum. Please don't worry. I'm a big boy now. I can ring security all by myself.'

Von rolled her eyes. 'Find a sweetheart, Braveheart!'

Find a sweetheart? He couldn't even find a sourpuss. Ben glared at his computer screen. Should he call it a day? He was beyond thinking. He reached for his lukewarm coffee and knocked it over.

'Bum!' He shifted papers to mop up the mess, and uncovered Talbot Locke's NWPP liaison card. Could witness protection explain Mac's mystery? It was too late to ring Locke today. First thing tomorrow.

Ben tried one more avenue of enquiry before he left—a search for Mac's online school buddy, Jake Leicester.

Jake Leicester's iConnect profile shouted hacker.

Whoa! Ben stared in disbelief.

Jake's profile pic used the portrait photo Ben had supplied with his ASIO employment application.

His own confidential file had been hacked.

21. STYMIED
Friday 31 August 2012

Canberra, Australia

FRACTURED SLEEP had stretched Ben's patience tissue thin. It was 10am and still no sign of HS.

'Sorry, Ben. HS won't be in today. Didn't he tell you?' Von offered a mechanical smile.

Ben called Talbot Locke. Also unavailable, though his assistant noted the particulars and urgency of his enquiry.

Stymied again. Ben glared at his screen saver and prayed for revelation. None came. Perhaps God was out of his office as well. Taking a tour down under, joy-riding the thermals.

His father's voice sounded in his head. *Fight this, Ben. Rise above it. Soar like an eagle above the storm.* If only the voice was real. Dispirited, Ben opened the file containing Pat's final letter.

It's rotten timing, my being away now ...

What an understatement!

Dr Alastair Maxwell developed the STIR prototype ...

Ben couldn't quiz HS or Locke right now, but he could query information on Alastair Maxwell, both his scientific research and the explosion. He had better-than-average access to official records—forensic and otherwise. As for media reports, if he shook enough logs, blogs and posts, perhaps information about Mac would fall from the woodwork. With any luck, the walls were jerry-built.

Ben stored everything—from nebulous debates about the nefarious returns investors could expect from experimental research to Alastair

Maxwell's doctoral thesis and employment records—in the GRUnGE. The Maxwell family's social media presence was noteworthy for its total absence! Ben filed news reports about the explosion, a speculative piece connecting it to an earlier police drug bust, and a video interview with the Maxwell's neighbour, recorded shortly after the explosion— the woman's preoccupation with herself only increased the GRUnGE's growing collection of unhelpful leads, none of which revealed Mac's identity.

Ben jumped as his phone rang. 'Hello? Ben here.'

'Talbot Locke, returning your call.'

'Agent Locke. Excellent. I'm trying to locate one Aidan MacGreggor from Landsborough, Queensland. He may be in witness protection. I suspect he's in danger. If NWPP could provide me with his whereabouts and situation, I could ensure his wellbeing.'

'So my assistant explained. We have no Aidan MacGreggor in our program. I've checked the records inside and out.'

'You're absolutely certain?' Ben sounded as disappointed as he felt.

'Stake my reputation on it. What have you got on him?'

'I can't elaborate, at least, not without the boss's approval. When I have that, I'll be in touch.'

'As you wish. Good luck with your search.'

'Thanks. I need it.' That wasn't all he needed. It was well past lunchtime and he needed to stretch his legs.

<hr>

BEN SAT in a sun-drenched corner of the café, sipping his ice-cold Bundy Brewed Guava drink through a straw. Rivulets of condensation drizzled down the outside of the glass bottle leaving tiny puddles on the table. Several old fishing magazine photos were positioned underneath its clear plastic cover. Ben scanned the nostalgic collection while he waited for his takeaway ham, cheese and pineapple sandwich to toast. Walking to the Fish and Chips shop had cleared his cobwebs, but not his reluctance to buy deep-fried fish there. He had a thing about Canberra being too far from the coast to buy fish. Chris had dissed him about it.

'Dro,' he'd said, 'Fish is snap frozen on the boat. It's as fresh in Canberra as any sea port. Don't be a piker.'

Ah Bro, the day I buy fish in Canberra, it'll be off for sure. Besides, nothing could match the smell of the sea, the flap of tent canvas, the grand adventure of dusk to dawn fishing—depending on the tide—the whoosh and sizzle of a portable gas cooker. Fish caught at midnight, pan-fried in butter in the wee hours, eaten as the moon opened or closed a silver zipper across the waves ... that was the food of kings.

The memory misted Ben's mood with salt-laden melancholy. The year Chris arrived, Mim had organised a brilliant camping spot near Booti Booti, between the beach and a lake.

'The Great Lakes have views to die for,' she'd said. 'We can relax in paradise.'

Chris had freaked. Yelled, bawled, begged to go anywhere but ...

Ben could still see Pat's face, pained but gentling. 'Don't worry, Chris. I'm sure Imee can find us a fantastic mountain retreat. We'll go bushwalking and the like.' Pat and Mim had exchanged meaningful glances.

'Mountains are good,' she'd said. 'Should I ... find a cabin?'

'Camping's fine.' Chris had wandered off to watch TV as if nothing had happened.

Mim's dumbfounded expression had said it all. Chris's blow-out sank family fishing trips for good.

Back then, Ben had been willing to trade life's simple pleasures for the sake of relationship—for all the good it had done him. Right now, he was more alone than a homeless possum.

For cryin' out loud—as Chris'd say—how could anyone hate the beach? Even the mercurial Mac liked the beach. He grumbled to Liss because they never went.

I wonder what else we have in common, Mac?

'There you go, hun.' The girl who'd taken his order broke his reverie. 'Ham, cheese and pineapple toasted to perfection.'

Ben smiled. 'Thanks. I could have picked it up. Saved you the walk.'

'No worries. You can pick me up next time.' She flashed an alluring come-hither smile and flounced back to the counter.

Ben smiled. He enjoyed attention. He just wasn't ready to act on it yet. Not seriously. Not that he wasn't interested, he was ... what? Too busy? Too cautious? Too particular?

Of the two genuinely, attractive women he did know—Elspeth Torino and MPeg—both had arrived on his doorstep bearing bad news. What did that say about them? Or him?

22. COMPROMISED

Monday 3 September 2012

Canberra, Australia

WHEN BEN greeted Von Monday morning, she announced that HS was still away. 'Also, Talbot Locke is waiting to see you.'

'I told him I'd have to clear our discussion with HS first.'

'He came to see Judy Callahan about something. She must have forgotten because she took a flexi-day. Locke said he'd wait for you, so his trip wasn't wasted.'

Ben found Locke pacing outside his office door. 'I'm sorry to keep you waiting Agent Locke. If I'd known—'

'No worries. It was a spur of the moment thing.' Locke offered his right hand.

Ben shook it. 'Come on in.' He unlocked the door and scanned his desk to confirm he'd left it clear of confidential documents. It was, of course. Something about Locke's manner piqued Ben's caution sensors.

'Please, have a seat. Were you able to identify Aidan MacGreggor after all?'

'No. As I said, not one of ours.' Locke remained standing.

Ben sat, hoping Locke would relax his guard. 'You mentioned you knew HS the other day.'

'By reputation and acquaintance. Did he acknowledge our history?'

'Not to me.'

Locked shrugged. 'Men of Chassic's calibre indulge certain blind spots. Tell me, Ben, has he ever told you what the HS stands for?'

'Is that relevant, Agent Locke?'

'You were one of ASIO's year twelve recruitment finds, yes?'

'I understood ASIO's application process was confidential.'

'It is. But I am federal police. There's some overlap—security checks and such.'

'I'd assumed it was done in-house.'

'Enthusiastic youth assumes many things that aren't so.' Locke pointed to the picture on Ben's wall calendar. 'Cityscapes look so clean and elegant in the photos. No rough edges or dark underbellies.'

'Agent Locke, is there something specific you wish to discuss?'

'I need to offer a word of caution, especially if you search outside your terms of reference. You may bite off more than you can chew.'

Ben raised an eyebrow. 'Are you offering dietary advice or selling dental insurance?'

'Perhaps both. May I be frank?'

'Please.'

Locke took the seat Ben had offered earlier. 'HS Chassic spearheaded a vocal minority that pushed the intake of young blood. We suspect some pushers had unpleasant ulterior motives.'

'Such as?'

'Apart from exploiting an undergraduate intake to reduce wage costs, there are rumours—unsubstantiated mind you, or we'd have acted on them—that a paedophile ring appropriated photos and information from those applicants and created fake online profiles to groom younger boys and girls.'

Ben drew in a sharp breath. Should he mention Jake Leicester? If he didn't, and his photo had been used by a paedophile ring, could he be implicated? His discovery had been incidental to his software development, so his knowledge of Jake could hardly be considered confidential.

'May I show you something, Agent Locke?'

A smile slid across Locke's face.

———◦———

BEN WANTED any suggestion he'd embraced impropriety, willingly or otherwise, eradicated. Yesterday. 'What should I do about Leicester, Agent Locke?'

'Nothing for now. I'll have the Jake Leicester profile investigated, discreetly, and dismantled. You may need to testify at some stage, but these things move slowly.'

'Whatever it takes to bring down a paedophile ring.' Ben shuddered. 'You've implied HS was complicit. What evidence do you have?'

'I can't elaborate. The investigation's ongoing.'

'I work for the man. I want to know what I'm up against.'

Locke pulled a USB from his pocket and toyed with it. 'If I show you this, you must keep it to yourself. One careless word could undermine our entire case.'

'I understand security protocols, Agent Locke.'

'As did the proverbial dead man before he told his tale. I'm not here to play games, Ben. We've been monitoring a darknet chat room for Ancient Assyrian Fantasy Explorers. A Horon Sinballidh caught our attention. With those initials ... HS?'

'Initials? That's all you've got?' Ben shook his head.

'Read the intercepts. I'll wait.' Locke passed the USB to Ben.

Interception 21 01 2011 18:44

> The mosquitoes are bad this time of year. You don't want to get bitten.
> We stay indoors to minimise the risk of infection—by mosquito-borne viruses that is. We need more funds for research.
> My entrepreneurial friend may increase his contribution, but he'll demand a substantial return for his investment. I'll get back to you.

Interception 18 02 2011 18:51

> You received my friend's additional contribution?
> It will be put to good use.
> I hope so. He has several friends he's impatient to oblige.
> I thought the local population was the priority?
> For you and me, yes. My friend's panorama is broad. But there is greater profit for us if the local product shines. I suggest you make it so. Soon!

Interception 13 04 2012 18:23

> Why have the funds dried up?
> Perhaps the wind that blows the rain clouds favours a more lucrative landscape.
> That's absurd. This is an exclusive crop.
> I'd like to observe the farmer's methodologies in person.

Interception 21 08 2012 18:37

> Has the farmer found a wife? Are they making hay?
> Good Lord, man. These conversations are so corny, I could add salt and butter and sell them at the cinema.
> Better corny and cautious than compromised. I repeat; are they making hay?

Locke removed the USB. 'Not enough to build our case. But cause for concern. And caution. Remember, Ben, mum's the word.'

FAR OUT! Or far-fetched. Locke's intercepts were gobbledygook. Then again, the Leicester hack was real. And Chassic's identity records—personnel file, driver's licence, passport and other documents Ben 'accidentally' stumbled across—all listed Chassic's given name as HS. In short, Locke's long shot left Ben feeling ... relieved when Von announced HS had extended his absence yet again. It gave Ben thinking space.

Be wise as a serpent and careful who you trust. Once again, Pat's words came to mind. *What did you not say in your letter, Dad?*

Ben set about creating a deeply layered GRUnGE system for all the LIES records and software. He saved it on an external hard drive which he locked in his office safe when he wasn't working on the files. He maintained a decoy filing system on the main drive.

Paranoid or not, he couldn't risk unauthorised access to this stuff. Bad enough having his identity info pinched.

His identity. They'd touched such a personal thing. Ben's indignation and sense of betrayal fed his growing empathy for Mac. He searched Mac's earlier transmissions for relevant statements and began another list:

- Protection program provides one identity change per customer, unless a serious new threat is detected.
- Mac's identity compromised ... necessitating change.
- Stop interacting with Jake. He may be a plant.
- Interacted two years. Cutting Jake off tip him off?
- Brock Bosworth organising Brisbane train trip, photographs, documentation.
- Changeover Schoolies Week.

Ben explored the connections. Brock Bosworth was another false ID. Who were these people? If Mac wasn't officially protected, who was protecting him? And from whom?

What had triggered the new threat? The Leicester online fiasco? Or Ben's discovery of the hack? Or had Pat instigated trouble when he'd activated live STIR transmissions in March? If so, how could Ben reassure Mac's people he posed no threat? He had no clue who they were.

Please, Mac, think things that will let me find you.

Tuesday 11 September 2012

AS BEN worked through the transmission backlog, LIES gradually lifted a shroud, bringing Mac to life before his eyes. He even named the transcripts—for organisational convenience, he told himself.

He labelled Mac's communications with Jake Leicester, *Done and Dusted*. Hopefully Locke would ensure the Leicester threat was also done and dusted. He dubbed others for Mac's mood: *Lonely; Cranky; Buoyant*. Some reflected attitude, activity or subject: *Salute to Shakespeare; Calculus Optimisation Sucks; Hair Dye Stinks; Why Me?* He labelled a philosophical reflection, *It's All Greek to Me*, and another, *Beautiful Ashes*.

The titles reflected the substance of each transcript and gave them personality, like their owner. Date and time stamp seemed too sterile, too dispassionate, too detached for the compelling vitality of Mac's paradoxical musings. How could one person be so bereft and cynical, yet remain so blithe and spirited? Ben was intrigued.

As a man thinks, so is he. Did the proverb ring true? By divulging Mac's esoteric contemplations, could LIES reveal—

Ben's hands recoiled from the keyboard as from a searing hot-plate. He shot out of his chair, backed into the closed door and leaned against it, hands tucked under his armpits. His heart raced, and his breath could not keep pace.

Dear God, what have I done!

He'd stripped something sacred, that's what! Mac's face and body may be obscured, but—

He'd gazed at Mac's naked soul! Unannounced! Uninvited!

No man, short of Christ himself, had done such a thing before.

Ben gazed at the ceiling, the walls, the floor. His sense of decency
urged him to look anywhere but—

at his computer screen,

where Mac's innermost thoughts danced,

backlit and brilliant in liquid crystal elegance,

tempting him to linger …

to explore …

to unveil, touch, experience …

this curious, alluring dynamic.

23. ARRESTED

Wednesday 12 September 2012

Canberra, Australia

'YOU WANT out, just like that?' Locke followed Judy into her bedroom, slamming the door behind him.

She spun round and flattened her palm against his chest, arresting his stride. 'I don't want out. But Mum can't cope with Dad's deteriorating condition. They need me, Bud.'

'I need you more.' It wasn't total spin. He drew her hands around his waist.

She slid them lower and pulled him against her. 'Me? Or this?'

'You're a wicked, wanton woman.'

'But totally irresistible, yes?' She began to loosen his belt buckle.

He stopped her by stepping back. 'Your brother could care for them. He's got less to lose.'

'He can't go back there. Too risky. It has to be me.' Judy flopped on the bed and pouted.

'Ah. So that's where his indiscretion took place.' Locke sat beside her and toyed with her hair. 'I'd assumed Sydney.'

'If only.'

'How big is Beerburrum, eh?'

'Not big enough.' Judy turned her head and kissed his hand.

He stroked her cheek with his thumb. 'What about us?'

'Is there an us?' Her smile was wistful.

'There could be.'

Judy shook her head. 'Be honest, Bud. It's been fun. Good fun. But this is a game we play. It's all about the adventure, the tension, the risk of being caught. What we have is role play, not relationship.'

'And you want the game to end. Is that it?' Locke grabbed Judy's throat and squeezed.

She clawed his hand away. 'Only when you play mean.'

'If you want the game to end well, you'll get me that package before you leave town.'

'Ooh, is that a threat or a promise?'

'I'm serious, Judy. My best tech people can't crack Chassic's online peddy network. He's got some super software mojo happening at ASPT. Whether Pat's boy knows it or not, he's aiding and abetting a criminal syndicate. That's where the real game's being played. I need everything on Alejandro's computer.'

Judy sighed. 'And if I get it for you?'

'I'll do everything in my power to help you get home to your folks. I'll speak with the right people and make sure you get your position of choice.'

Judy giggled. 'And?' She walked her fingers across his thigh.

'I'll make sure my farewell is something you'll never forget.' He bent and kissed her. He wasn't quick about it.

'Mmm,' she said as they drew apart, 'wicked or not, Bud, I will miss this. And you.'

'Then I'll have to visit you in Queensland, won't I? To check on your behaviour.'

24. DITCHED
Friday 14 September 2012

Northbound, Brisbane Suburban Rail,
Queensland, Australia

LIES/MXP2/20120914am20857

'**H**ERE'S OUR train, Mac. Stay close.'

'Aww, Brock'ms. You still love me.'

'Don't push it, sunshine. You whinged non-stop for two hours.'

'Felt like three.'

'For a one hour identity fit and kit. We'd be home by now if you'd cooperated. Pick a double seat. I'll sit aisle side.'

'I've got an essay to plan. I'll sit by myself.'

'Have it your own way. But keep your com on.'

'Phony phone earbuds in and on. Don't kill the music. Or the muse.'

'The what?'

'Move it, blockhead. You're blocking the aisle.' *Stupid minder. Wasn't my fault his flippin' fit 'n' kit took forever.*

Pick a name, he says. Any name. You tell me, train, what's wrong with Adrian Arianna? Nothing. Exactly. So good it could be a stage name. What's he choose? Ash MacDonald.

Sounds like a burnt hamburger. Hi. I'm Ash MacDonald. My future's fried. Or it will be if Bozo has his way.

'Stand clear. Doors closing.'

In more ways than one. Ugh! Come on, Green Day. Take my miserable muse out of this tunnel of darkness into the glorious light as dawn reveals ...

Sheesh! Scintillating views of the industrial backside of Brisbane, the bums of shops and the private parts of houses, places you're not supposed to see, full of junk, debris and dirty secrets.

Hey! Urbanites! What have you got to hide? Come on. Fess up. Tell me your lies!

I bet my lie is better. It's been carefully constructed by experts to keep me alive.

What a joke. It's already destroyed most of me. I breathe. I eat. I regularly excrete. Everything else is totally screwed.

...

"You will know the tries and—" What? Oh, that's ironic. Some graffiti artist's changed truth into lies on the church's billboard. The truth will set me free, eh? Fat chance.

My truth's been erased. Annihilated. Replaced by an impenetrable edifice of deception.

Edifice. I like that word. Just like the mirror glass surface of a city high-rise, the shiny, bright façade hides the murky mysteries within.

'Mac, can you—?'

'Wow-ow!' *Bust my eardrums, Bozo! My implant has limitations you know.*

'Sorry about the squeal, Mac.'

Screeching banshee, more like.

'Listen, we'll change trains at Wooloowin to be on the safe side, okay? Did you hear me?'

Loud as a fart and twice as obnoxious.

'Mac?'

You want fries with that?

'Mac? Nod twice if you heard me.'

I'm nodding already. Quit interrupting the music, Bozo.

Cast me adrift,

a mindless tourist,

lost and tossed by haunting refrains,

floating along my own Boulevard of Broken Dreams.

'Bowen Hills Station.'

'Not yet, Mac. Wooloowin's the second station after this.'

Not yet, Mac. Nod your head, Mac. Stay close, Mac.

Kiss my butt, Bozo. Look at him, gawking at that chick's cleavage. Pervert. Eeuw! He's salivating.

I bet Brock Bosworth's a fake name. Wonder what it means? Aha! Phony phone search to the rescue. Five four ... Can't call an ambulance to save my scrawny rump, but I can look up the meaning of ...

Being? Hmph. Predictive text being absurdly optimistic. Delete.

Meaning of Brock. A badger. Suits him. He's bald as.

*What about Bozo? Huh? Gonzo? Where'd that come from? Flippin'
autocorrect. Neat fit though. Gonzo the Gawker. Big beak, birdbrained,
looks to match. Nose and mouth like a proboscis monkey. Eyes and jowls
of a Titicaca Scrotum frog. God help Australia if he's all the Feds can dish
up. Bozo-the-beer-bellied-bodyguard. They should retire him.*

*Hmm. Maybe I can hasten his retirement. Instead of swapping trains
at Wooloowin, what if—*

'Albion Station. Train continues to Doomben. Passengers for Shorncliffe
and Caboolture lines change at Eagle Junction. This is Albion Station.'

Albion. And Bozo's still got his eyes glued to that woman's chest.

*Disgusting. Serves him right if I ditch him. I could do with a bit of beach
time. Bad luck, Bozo. I'm taking a detour. To Shorncliffe. Catch me if you can.*

'Dammit Mac. Mac! Get your ar—, carcass back on this train.'

Too late, mate. Com's out and I am not lip-reading.

WOO-HOO! I ditched the frog.

*No earbuds. No interruptions. And no music. Oh well. It's just you and
me, train, so do your thing. Play your secret lullaby. Fake a rocking baby
moment. Play pretend and let me dream my life is going somewhere.*

*Trains are reassuring. Predictable. Always following the tracks laid out for
them. Linear journeys. Start. Travel. Stop. Repeat. Passengers get on or off
along the way. But the train doesn't deviate from the tracks. You know where
it will go, where the terminus is, when you'll reach it. No nasty surprises.*

*Then again, there's no mystery either. Just the same old same old. Only
the travellers have unique stories. What are you all doing, heading out of
town this early on a weekday? Skipping work?*

*I bet Grandma's off to babysit. Nana's day-care, safe and reliable. Good
on her. Must be cool to have grandparents living nearby.*

'Hang on, Ma. You dropped your bunny.'

'Gracious! Thank you very much. It's my granddaughter's favourite.
There'd be a kafuffle if I'd lost it. What a lovely young man you are.'

Did she wink at me? Cheeky!

'Northgate Station. Change here for Caboolture-Nambour line. This
train continues to Shorncliffe.'

Yup. Linear and predictable. A well-ordered essay on wheels. Definitive start, loaded with topical body paragraphs, wrapped up by a neat conclusion.

I'll give them a well-ordered essay. Behind the Edifice, a Building Crumbles: The Inherent Shortcomings of the National Witness Protection Program.

Introduction: Be in the wrong place at the right time to piss off somebody powerful.

Paragraph one: Disappear or die. Preferably both.

Paragraph two: Bury relationships, hope, independence. Suffocate your soul.

Paragraph three: Let the man with the plan and the money in hand resurrect you, redesign you.

Paragraph four: Discover your new identity has been compromised and complicated by some stranger who may not exist.

Conclusion: Repeat whole ridiculous charade.

Story of my life. Well-ordered if not predictable.

. . .

Stories don't have to be linear. Or predictable. You can start down the track and flash back. That's the kind of story I want to write. Start where I am, not where I've been. Forget the hell behind me. Get to where it's better.

I want to transcend time.

Manipulate the order of things.

Fracture the fabric of the universe.

Heck, I want to become a story that can jump tracks without derailing!

So what if I cause a shemozzle. Better than being stuck on a track I don't want to ride. Even a derailment would be ...

better than this.

25. WRECKED

Friday 14 September 2012

Canberra, Australia

FRIDAY MORNING, Ben hit the seat running, his enthusiasm for LIES renewed despite its challenges. Mac's STIR signals were flowing with a frequency and intensity he'd not seen before. Finally!

LIES/MXP2/20120914am20857

TAKE MY miserable muse out of this tunnel of darkness into the glorious light as dawn reveals ...
  Sheesh! Scintillating views of the industrial backside of Brisbane.

Ben's excitement uncorked a rush of endorphins. He rubbed his palms and drummed his thighs. Before, he'd justified transcribing STIR signals as necessary for Mac's wellbeing. Now, he acknowledged another motive—his personal need to know and be known by Mac. He zealously fine-tuned transcripts, highlighting each potential clue.

Pick a name, he says. Any name.
  ...
What's he choose? Ash MacDonald.

Ben face-palmed. Not another fake name to search for. That was as good as a mirror to a blind alley cat.
  He needed a face. Mac's face!
  Of course! Mac's face might show up on railway security surveillance video. But which train?
  Come on, Mac. Give me a clue. Please. Ben's hope was a kid on a trampoline.

Instead of swapping trains at Wooloowin, what if—
'Albion Station.'
Serves him right if I ditch him.
Bad luck, Bozo. I'm taking a detour. To Shorncliffe.

Yes! He'd search for teenage males who boarded a Shorncliffe train at Albion Station during the STIR signal's time frame.

I'll give them a well-ordered essay. Behind the Edifice, a Building Crumbles: The Inherent Shortcomings of the National Witness Protection Program.
Discover your new identity has been compromised and complicated by some stranger ...
Repeat whole ridiculous charade.

Ben frowned. Despite the NWPP's imperfections, Mac clearly believed they'd organised his protection package. Yet Locke had sworn otherwise. Had he been too preoccupied with paedophiles infiltrating high-level organisations to check?

An unpleasant knot squeezed Ben's sternum. If only his thoughts could direct Mac's actions. *Please help me find you, Mac. Do something unpredictable. Stand out from the crowd.*

Transcend time.
Manipulate the order of things.
Fracture the fabric of the universe.
Become a story that can jump tracks without derailing!

Go for it, Mac! Do it your way. Don't let dodos clip your wings. Ben smiled in spite of himself and kept reading.

How far to Shorncliffe? Where's the schematic? I think my new identity needs glasses. Or coloured contact lenses so I don't have to hide behind sunglasses. Sunnies suck indoors.
Bindha, Banyo, Nudgee, Boondall, Deagon, Sandgate, Shorncliffe. Or bus from Sandgate to Redcliffe. Better beach. Better not press my luck. Bozo'll be—
'Banyo Station.'
What the hell? No! God no! What's—

The STIR signals quit. Abruptly. Ben sucked a breath to steady his heart rate. He checked the equipment, hardware and soft. Nothing explained the sudden break.

Was the problem at Mac's end? Ben's stomach clenched as his mind veered towards the unthinkable. Had the signals stopped because Mac could no longer produce them?

Don't go there, Dro. It's a signal glitch. An internet hiccup, satellite stuff-up or broken sea cable. Focus. What next?

Surveillance footage!

He had two options. Hack, a risky tactic, or—

HS was in today. With Mac in imminent or actual danger, would he authorise an official search? It was worth a try. Ben hoped HS was feeling receptive.

⚬

BEN GLARED at Chassic's paperweight, a miniature *Mary Celeste* entombed in a glass ball. According to HS, the American merchant brigantine had been found abandoned and drifting in 1872. Ben could have hurled the glass ball through the window.

'I don't get it, HS. You agreed to deploy a field operative if I could locate Mac, yet you won't let me access railway surveillance on privacy grounds? That's beyond ironic. Mac's in trouble. He needs us, and we need him. He's a living, breathing STIR recipient, or he was! It's in ASPT's interest to locate this kid, pronto, whether you care about his wellbeing or not.'

'And you think I don't care.'

Ben stood and paced the wall of sailing ships. He didn't know what to think. What about Jake Leicester? Locke's paedophile theory? Should he challenge HS about that? Hounding and pounding wasn't working. But how do you accuse your boss of something so heinous without proof?

You catch more flies with honey than vinegar. The thought stopped Ben short in front of an oil painting, *The Wreck of the SS Dicky*. The sand-bound ribs of the ship's perishing hull stretched impotently skyward, straining to touch a glorious twilight. Ben swallowed. Was he chasing an elusive sun or a dying day? Was he willing to beach his career, his future, for the sake of ... a mystery?

HS came and stood beside Ben. 'That's Dicky Beach. The only recreational beach in the world named after a shipwreck. It's up north, on Queensland's Sunshine Coast. Ever been there?'

'Sunshine Coast was on our family's camping list. We never got there.'

'It's worth a visit. Just been there myself. Had to brief and debrief a field agent. A cafe at Moffat Beach sells the work of local artists.' HS tapped his finger on the picture. 'That's where I picked up this beauty.'

Ben couldn't care less about local artists but—*use honey*. 'Dicky Beach? Moffat Beach? I've heard of Noosa.'

'That's at the northern end of the Sunshine Coast. The southern end starts on Pumicestone Passage, near the tip of Bribie Island. The beaches stretch north beyond the Caloundra headland—Kings Beach, Shelly, Moffat, Dicky—'

'Where this wreck rests. What happened?'

'They hit cyclonic weather as they tried to clear Caloundra Head. The captain beached the ship to avoid hitting rocks off Moffat Beach.'

'Bet that was a tough decision.' Ben folded his arms.

'That's what leaders do. Make tough decisions. And answer for the consequences—a lesson to be learned from *SS Dicky*. The captain preserved the ship and all aboard it, but the marine authorities blamed him for negligent navigation, and for his earlier decision to proceed across the Wide Bay Bar in threatening weather.'

Ben sensed Chassic's scrutiny. He riveted his own on the painting. 'If he preserved the ship, how come it's a wreck?'

'They refloated it twice. It beached each time. So they cut their losses, stripped the boat of everything saleable, and left the hull to rot. The price of iron was too low to make salvage worthwhile.'

'Is that your approach to Mac?' Ben turned to look his boss in the eye.

Chassic met his stare. 'Do you think I'm cutting my losses? Or leaving the hull to rot?'

Ben blinked but held his gaze. 'Perhaps you're distancing yourself from the responsibility. Or limiting your liability.'

HS did not offer an answer. Ben turned, took a step and opened the door.

'Do you have plans for the weekend, Benjamin?'

Ben paused but didn't turn. 'I'll work through, in case Mac finally drops something conclusive about his identity or location.'

'I've a better idea but you'll need to close the door to hear it.'

———◦———

BEN'S JAW ached from grinding his teeth. HS hadn't offered one reasonable answer. He'd prattled on about the field agent he'd sent to the Northern Hemisphere to 'develop his winter survival skills as much as he'd developed his surfing prowess'.

What did that have to do with Ben's problem? It had solved his boss's problem. Instead of flying back to Canberra, HS had driven Agent Karey's previously assigned work vehicle back from Queensland—to become Ben's problem, because he was now driving said vehicle, at Chassic's request, to get it washed, detailed and refuelled.

'Take the rest of the day if you need to,' HS had said. 'You're too caught up in this Mac thing. You need a breather, away from the office, to regain perspective.' HS's expression had precluded argument. 'I've assigned the vehicle to you, Ben. You'll need it for field work eventually. Personal use is approved. Keep a mileage log. That may alleviate one of your current dilemmas.'

That had stung. His car habitually broke down. He'd been late for work or stuck in the car park too often. He'd come by taxi that morning, all because of his stubborn refusal to use his father's car.

He didn't want to use Pat's car—beyond ticking it over to charge the battery. It would be moving on from his father's death too soon. It had only been five months and twelve days. He'd told himself a dozen times it was a car, not a memorial. And he was thankful for the work car. It meant Pat's car would be there when—

'Aargh!' He'd done it again. Scratched a niggling splinter of doubt about Pat's death. Tweezed the hope that he'd turn up in all his strength and glory with some reasonable explanation for dropping off the face of the planet, apologetically offering some outstandingly understandable and utterly forgivable excuse for—

'Breaking my heart, Dad!' Ben startled himself with the vehemence of his outburst. Maybe HS was right. Maybe he did need time out to adjust his perspective.

Ben turned the radio on while he waited for the traffic lights to change.

'A truck driver is in hospital with serious injuries after his semi-trailer and a passenger train collided in Brisbane this morning. The loaded truck bottomed-out on a level crossing near Banyo station at 6:30am.'

'Was it still dark, Frank?'

'I don't think so. Why would it be?'

'Don't the good folks up north avoid Daylight Saving because the extra sunshine confuses their dairy cows?'

Ben smiled at the old joke.

'I think you're confused, Danno. Daylight Saving starts in October.'

'Sounds like somebody was confused. A stuck truck blocks the line and nobody informs the train driver?'

'Maybe they were busy feeding their cows.'

'Now we're milking it. Fortunately folks, there were very few injuries. Disrupted peak hour travellers—'

The lights turned green. Ben moved his silver SUV forward and turned into an automatic car wash facility. He killed the radio and relaxed, letting his mind wander as water, suds and rollers swished the vehicle.

Banyo ... whoosh ... train crash ... whoosh ...

The sudden halt in Mac's transmission!

Ben's seatbelt grabbed as he bolted upright.

He had to get back to his desk, pronto.

———◦◦◦———

IN HIS haste, Ben parked the SUV across two spaces, jogged through the office door, and collided with HS in the foyer.

'I didn't hear the fire alarm, Ben. Didn't I give you the afternoon off?'

'I know what's happened to Mac. The Banyo train crash. He was on that train. I've gotta check the—'

Chassic's hand signalled stop. He shook his head, tilting it towards the receptionist. Ben had almost committed a cardinal sin, talking about LIES outside the confines of his or Chassic's office. HS turned and walked that way. Ben followed in silence until they were behind closed doors.

HS pointed to the chair. 'Sit.'

Good dog, Fido. Ben sat.

'What train crash?'

'A derailment at Banyo. Mac's train was on that line when his STIR signals stopped abruptly, hence my request for railway surveillance access, which you refused.' If Ben floated hope of an apology, Chassic's expression sank it. 'I came back to check online media reports, videos, photos. There should be a stack by now. If Mac wasn't hurt, there may be new STIR transmissions.'

'And if he was hurt?'

'That might show up in the news reports.' Ben bounced and drummed his knees to dissipate his surging adrenaline.

'Then you'd better get to it. And Ben?' HS waited as Ben curtailed his attempt to rise. 'I will set your surveillance access in motion, but—'

'Awesome!'

'It could take a few days. If, and I do say if, you acquire sufficient information to make a field trip viable, I'll assign a fully trained field operator to support you. Ben?'

Ben took a deep breath. 'I'm sure I can—'

'You're sure of things you cannot possibly be sure of. Temper your zeal with wisdom and caution. Your responsibilities and value to this program are too important for you to race off half-cocked on a wild goose chase. I have to consider the big picture. I'm responsible for the program, and for you. Your safety is my priority. I gave your father my pledge of honour on that before he—'

'Raced off half-cocked?' Impatience had dulled Ben's caution.

'Left with my full approval and blessing on a mission for which he was fully trained, well informed and well equipped.'

The floor suddenly demanded Ben's full attention. 'I spoke out of turn. My comment showed as much disrespect for my father's commitment as it did for yours.'

'I've no doubt your father would be immensely proud of everything you've done and become. Your inclination towards ... let's call it decisive action rather than brashness, is not entirely unique. You are, after all, his son. His capacity to put others first lives large in you. That's why you can justify finding Mac as your top priority. I concede Mac has relevance to our program. But how and when we attempt contact must be my decision. *Usted comprende eso, amigo mío?*'

HS spoke Spanish? Ben nodded. He understood.

'Good. Collate any and all information you can. We'll discuss a course of action on Monday.' HS checked his schedule. 'Monday at 1:30pm. I'll be away till then. Yes, you can work the weekend if you must. I'll notify security. You must appreciate that numerous authorities will want the crash footage. We'll have to wait in line. That won't matter, because I want you here when Chris arrives. He starts Monday week, the twenty-second. Spend a few days getting him up to speed so he can monitor the transcripts while you and a supporting field agent go after Mac. Is that acceptable?'

Ben nodded again.

HS pulled a business card from his draw and gave it to Ben. 'These people are our automotive specialists. Deliver your SUV to them first thing Monday for a field-ready service. They'll provide a courtesy car. You can collect your SUV after our meeting Monday afternoon.'

Ben was itching to move, but HS continued to thumb through business cards. He pulled another and tapped it on the desk.

'Did this Locke fellow try to see me again?'

'Not exactly. He did drop by to see me.'

HS raised an eyebrow.

'He's our witness protection liaison. I telephoned Agent Locke to see if Mac was one of theirs.'

'And is he? One of theirs?'

'No. Locke was adamant.'

'What else did Agent Locke have to say?'

'Not much. Locke's full of himself, puffed up with his own importance. You know the type—always trying to maintain an air of mystery to discourage the minions from questioning their methods.'

'Yes. I do know Locke's type.'

Ben hoped his smile didn't look as contrived as it felt.

'Oh, go on. Check your precious Mac survived.'

Ben needed no second bidding.

26. NOTICED
Friday 14 September 2012

Brisbane, Queensland, Australia

LIES/MXP2/20120914am26113

THE UNIVERSE *hates me. There's no other reasonable conclusion. One lousy chance in a million to please myself and a truck gets stuck on the level crossing. Grrr!*

And now my bum hurts. This seat's more like a glorified garden planter than a—

Hullo, what's he saying?

'While wreckage is cleared and line damage assessed. Translink Authorities will arrange additional bus connections for inbound and outbound passengers. Expect extended delays. Taxi services will prioritise return to station. Please register your details at the ticket office to streamline cab sharing.'

Batpoo! Bye-bye beach. Uh-oh! Photographer! Double batpoo! Last thing I need is my mugshot in the news. Now I'll have to call Bosworth.

Five four . . .

'Mac?'

'Yeah, it's me.'

'What on earth were you thinking?'

'I wasn't, what with being up all night. I thought we'd reached Wooloowin. Then I caught the wrong train. My bad. I'm stuck at Banyo. You heard about the crash?'

'Are you hurt?'

'Nah. Bumped my processor loose, that's all. Look, Brock, there are news crews everywhere. I think a photographer caught me on camera. I can get a taxi, but I'll need to give them a booking name and destination.'

'No Mac. I'll bring a taxi to you. Are you okay to walk a bit?'

'Yeah.'

'Walk a couple of blocks so you're clear of photographers. Hang on. Let me check maps … You there?'

'Where else would I be?'

'Where you shouldn't be. Head down Tufnel Road. It's the stem of the T intersection outside the station. Can you see it?'

'I'm standing in it.'

'Good. Walk to Earnshaw and turn left. Then third right into Approach Road. You'll see the Catholic University Campus. You should blend right in.'

'Oh, yeah, right in.'

'There should be a bus shelter. Need I repeat directions?'

'Duh! Like I'll forget.'

'First time for everything. I'll meet you there asap.'

'Whatever. Walking.'

I'd rather be walking on the beach. Love that soft, squishy squeak of sand underfoot. Nobody'd notice me in oversize boardies and hoodie. Li's such a stick-in-the-mud.

Oh wow! Mango trees in the school yard. I wonder if they attract flying foxes like Liss's pawpaw trees. Beware the dreaded fruit-poop bombing raids.

Earnshaw. Left.

Poinciana trees like the ones in Bundy. I miss the farm picking circuit. The great outdoors. Almost made all those freaky dreams about alien strangler beans and monster pumpkins bowling me over worth it. Floating effortlessly above the cane fields just because I thought of it—that was a good dream. Fantastic. Till ash from the burn-off choked my eyes and ears and nose and I couldn't breathe, and the ground seethed with a million black snakes so I couldn't land, and they were under the bed and under the dining table and—screeching banshees, Mac! Get a grip! Focus.

. . .

Jacaranda trees. Cool. Raining purple flowers all over the place. Kinda poetic.

Purple rain, on path,
in drain, spring showers causing
hayfever havoc.

A hack-cidental haiku. Go me! Purple rain, on path—

Approach Road. Right turn. Row of rectangular buildings—they look like coffins lined up after a massacre. Yup. I'd fit right in.

Five four …

'Hi, Brock. I'm at the bus shelter. Can't chat. People coming. See ya.'

'Sim's logic. It's moronic. I can't follow it. Between that and her psycho prejudices, I have no idea how I'll pass the subject. Her chaotic brain is completely at odds with mine.'

'Your brain is odd, Jo.'

'You'll keep, Rigs. Hey, mate? Has the three-oh-seven been through yet?'

'Don't think so, but I've only been here a few minutes.'

'No worries. Day off school?'

'I'm—'

'Playing hooky, right? I used to do that. Sneak down from Earnshaw, catch the bus into town, window-shop and bus it back before pickup time. You can get away with it at your age, but you better give it up before senior if you've aspirations of coming to this place.'

'Aspirations is it, Josephine? Use a few highfalutin words like that in your logic essay and you might pass after all. Here's the bus.'

'You catching this one, mate?'

'No. I'm waiting for someone.'

'Watch out for Larsen's larks. They dobbed me in once.'

'Give it a rest, Jo. He's not one of theirs. He's wearing mufti. Armani Jeans t-shirt which is like, two hundred bucks a pop. Your old man must be loaded, bro!'

'eBay knock-off. Ten bucks.'

'Way to go.'

'C'mon Rigsby.'

'See ya, mate. Have a good one.'

Hmph. Is that ironic or what? Me playing hooky. Tried and failed. I guess I'm just a hooky rookie. Oh God, save me from my brain. Get Bozo here before it gets any worse.

…

Finally. Look at that—Bozo's opening the door for me. Proper gentleman, ain't he?

'Nice ride, Brock! Chauffeur driven.'

'Don't push it, Mac. Driver, can you take us to Landsborough?'

'For a price. Surcharge to cover return.'

'Will four hundred cash cover it?'

'Landsborough it is.'

'Expensive stunt of yours, Mac.'

'Just like my t-shirt? It got noticed, by the way. I told you it was a bad idea. I thought you wanted me low-key.'

'If they noticed your clothes, they weren't looking at your face.'

27. BOMBED

Friday 14 September 2012

Canberra, Australia

BEN GRINNED. Mac had survived, audacity intact. And the latest LIES transcripts dovetailed with the news reports. Ben searched, listed and cross-referenced every potential identifier.

- Banyo Station/online images/Google Street View
- Garden planter/seat
- News reports/Photographer/Social Media.
- Witnesses: Rigsby/Josephine/Catholic University/ Earnshaw College truancy records/Social media
- Mac short/small build? (mistaken for younger high school student)
- Armani Jeans t-shirt—logo?
- 307 bus driver
- Taxi driver/Landsborough destination address.

Ben downed his umpteenth cup of coffee. Despite his advanced ICT skills and specialist training, the search was time-consuming and tedious, filled with wasted detours and dead ends. Every link he explored, even useless ones, demanded far more than the half-dozen rapid-fire key taps that Hollywood's cyber-analysts, fraudsters, hackers and would-be terrorists used to save or destroy the universe in fifty minutes or less.

What Ben did have was patience, persistence, and weekend overtime to find and file his research in the GRUnGE. And hope for a breakthrough.

By midnight, his neck hurt, his head hurt, and he was seeing double. *Sorry Mac. I'll have to start fresh tomorrow.*

He telephoned security.

'Are you last out? Apparently, Callahan's working through.'

'I'll check.' He could see a strip of light beneath Judy's door. 'Looks like she's still here. If not, I'll call you back in five.'

'No worries, mate.'

Ben knocked on Judy's door …

'Hi, Ben. Everything okay?'

'Security guy said you're pulling an all-nighter?'

'Tying up loose ends. You heading home now?'

Ben nodded. 'See you, Jude.' He turned to leave.

'Ben?'

'Yup?' He turned back.

'It's my last … I'm leaving ASPT.'

Ben smiled. 'So I heard. I'm sure you'll be missed.'

'Not by Chassic. But there you go. We can't all be favourites. Goodnight, Ben.'

Ben hesitated, but Judy moved to close her door. 'Night, Jude.'

She paused. 'Look Ben. You seem like a nice kid. Maybe you should know. There's more to Chassic than meets the eye. Watch your back, okay?' She shut her door before Ben could respond.

He slept badly that night.

⎯⎯◦⎯⎯

16 – 17 September 2012

BEN'S BREAKTHROUGH came Sunday. He found an image of stranded commuters outside Banyo Railway Station. Several stood. Four sat on glorified planters, including a slight young man wearing a visored cap, classy hi-end jeans, Chuck Taylors, and a grey long-sleeved over-shirt with chest-sized logo: Armani Jeans Quality Goods.

'Got you!'

Ben high-fived the wall, then zoomed in on the image which showed Mac partly side-on, biting on a pair of sunglasses and thumbing a smartphone. His cap was pulled low over his face, exposing crew-cut red hair at the back.

'The elusive Aidan MacGreggor, in the flesh. Hallelujah!' Ben studied the image and printed hard copies. Good job Mac wasn't wearing the sunnies, though the way he clenched them with his teeth accentuated his grim expression—one to which he was entitled, no doubt. Hopefully, Ben could remedy that, provided HS made good on his promise.

He thought again of Judy's cryptic comment. Stuff it. Benjamin Alejandro wasn't some vulnerable kid. He was a man, called and destined to help and defend, if he believed his father's words. Chassic himself had acknowledged that Ben, like his father, held the capacity within him to put others first, and to take decisive action.

Whether he felt ready for it or not, the opportunity to step up had arrived, especially now that Chris was on board. Ben grinned as he imagined Chris's response: 'Just go for it, Dro!'

He would indeed. The moment he'd confirmed Mac's location, the Alejandro would mount a rescue, with or without Chassic's blessing.

BEN SPENT Monday morning establishing a secure remote access system—intuitive to Chris, but hack-proof to an outsider—so they could communicate privately online. He could send Chris instructions that way.

He was careful to make all the right noises at his meeting with Chassic but, by the time he collected his SUV from the service depot Monday afternoon, Ben wore his savings, in cash, in a body belt. He headed for the Majura Park Shopping Centre to purchase non-perishable food and a swag so he could sleep in the SUV if necessary.

He gave a bone-shuddering yawn as he parked. Swag or bed, he'd sleep the sleep of the dead tonight. He felt totally bombed.

PART THREE

Beached and Bloodied

28. BLASTED

Monday 17 September 2012

Canberra, Australia

CHRISTOPHER DARNELL'S teammates were slicked with mud. He was Teflon-coated—until they threw him into the pond.

Screamin' piglets! Six hands pulled him onto dry land again.

'Way to go, Darnell!' Ellis slapped his back.

'Now we're a proper team.' Reikan gave a muddy thumbs up.

'Gee, ta!' Chris flicked a soggy leaf back into the pond.

'I've got to admit, your super-tech mojo worked just like you said it would.' O'Grady shrugged.

'Thanks fellas, but we won because you three got down and dirty.' Chris knew he'd fluked a position of advantage.

'You each demonstrated good judgement and great teamwork.' Their supervisor rarely offered praise. 'You have four days left on this training course. Use them to glean from each other's expertise, as you did today.'

Chris and his teammates nodded deferentially.

The super scanned their faces before she cracked a smile. 'Reckon you've all earned an early mark. See you at dawn.'

They grinned and relaxed into conversation.

'I vote Darnell teaches us strategy. You up for it, D?'

'I'll give it my best shot. Speaking of which, I could use your help delivering real shots. My weapons management score is embarrassing. That's the difference between taking a game shot and firing an actual handgun.'

'Don't sweat it. Under current regulations, we won't have to carry. Later, lads.' O'Grady turned off towards his quarters.

Chris entered his own quarters, eager for a hot shower and dry clothes, and grateful his odd-man-out feeling had begun to thaw.

Despite the challenges, he'd flourished during basic training and found good mates in his team members. Pity they were headed in four different directions assignment-wise. As much as he hated to admit it, he was basking in warm fuzzies. He'd missed the team spirit buzz, like when he and Dro had slaughtered MPeg and Cokecan twenty-two games in a row back in year twelve. He and Ben had been a team like no other. Before the rift—chasm—Mariana Trench—where he'd wallowed and floundered in self-pity.

And whose fault was that? He'd cultivated his emotional rut. Mpeg had challenged him to stop digging and start living.

'If you're not happy where you're at, make a change. Quit comparing yourself to Ben. You act like you missed out on some magic mojo. Is that what you think?' MPeg had stood, her full 155cm in high heels, toe-tapping the floorboards.

'Reckon so.' Stonewall Jackson.

'Listen here, buster, the only magic in this world is attitude. It makes you great or it kneecaps you. I should know. Attitude lets short people run in high heels while giants crawl barefoot.' MPeg had clumped across the room, snagged her platform-enhanced stilettos on the rug, and landed, sprawling, on the sofa.

'That's what I call attitude! Smooth as.'

She'd reassembled herself before challenging, 'Are you cruisin' for a bruisin'?'

'No, Peg. My pride's already taken a well-deserved hit.'

'Pride is not your problem! Your self-respect is stunted. Stand tall. Change your perspective. Stop navel-gazing and start star-gazing. Do that and when I make it big in Melbourne, I'll buy you a telescope.'

'So you've made up your mind? You're moving to Melbourne?'

'Buying my ticket tomorrow. Look me up when you've bought your first pair of high heels. Metaphorically speaking.'

Stop digging and start living? He'd wanted to, with her. He suspected she'd wanted it too, but he'd clamped shut when the topic arose. She'd bumped into his protective shell, the one he used to stop people getting too close. Stonewall Darnell. No wonder she'd opted for her cosmopolitan sea change.

Lovely, lively and lithe Margaret Peregrine Blythe—words he'd often thought, but never spoken. She'd whooped with delight the first time he'd cheekily called her MPeg. She'd endured so much of his nonsense. He'd no right to begrudge her desire to move on. Who knows, maybe he'd check Melbourne out for himself one day.

Or Adelaide. Or Perth. Come to think of it, there was a whole lot of Australia he hadn't seen. He'd been too busy creating fake landscapes for gamers, desperately trying to—,

'Justify my existence.' There. He'd said it aloud. Given voice to its terrifying, ugly—

Porthos. Athos? A picture of his kid sister trying to read *The Three Musketeers* materialised. Chris face-palmed. *Pathos*. A word Amy had discovered, the day before the valuable members of his family had—

Burned. The one word he couldn't say out loud. What was the point? Nothing could change his—

'Failure to prevent it!' Chris thumped his left arm with his right fist. Again, the physical pain failed to mask the emotional one. Nothing ever had. Not even his efforts to legitimise his passion for gaming by becoming best-in-field, good enough to—

Justify his existence. He'd looped the loop again, back to the past, to regret. It was old, familiar territory.

It was a decrepit, debilitating shack. And he was sick of squatting in it. MPeg had kicked enough dirt into his rut to create a ramp up. That's why he'd stepped up when Chassic's headhunter had called. His stomach still mimicked Dreamworld's Giant Drop whenever he anticipated working with Ben, but he had seven days to overcome his elevator belly.

As Chris showered, he imagined his negative habits riding the soap suds down the drain. Refreshed, he towelled off, donned clean jeans and t-shirt, flopped on the bed and switched on the TV news.

Politicians were prattling on again.

He yawned and shifted position.

'… drama outside the Majura Park Shopping Centre when a silver four-wheel-drive mounted a traffic island and exploded. Police are yet to determine if the accident caused the explosion or vice versa.'

Car bombs in the capital? Near the airport? Bit of a worry.

'… suggested the incident was a daredevil stunt gone wrong. Eyewitness—'

Chris's eyelids drooped.

Monday 24 September 2012

'STUPID STUNT! *Trying to revive the push for a new dragway at Fairbairn.'*

'*Took off up Spitfire Avenue like a bat outta hell. Cut through the vacant lot … wedged on the traffic island … wild antics, spinning wheels, smoke everywhere.'*

'*Massive area, charred as black as a plane crash. Police cordoned the area—'*

'*Kablooey! Man, what a blast!'*

'*Massive fireball. Screamin' piglets! Did you see that crazy kid on a bike? Driver swerved to avoid him.'*

'*Kid's a pariah. Burns everybody who gets too close. Truss him up! Bury him beside his best mate.'*

'*Light him up, boys! Let's see this kid burn.'*

'No!' Chris screamed himself awake from the unspeakable horror of a recurring nightmare—one that burned everyone and everything he loved—that had reinvented itself nightly since the fatal explosion at Majura Park.

The explosion that had killed Ben.

For the umpteenth time, Chris's anguished tears mingled with the sweat of his night terrors, a Molotov cocktail of memories mangling his soul with their twisted menace.

'I loved you, Dro. More than I ever showed you. If only I'd been there for you, with you. I wouldn't have to face today, without you.'

THE PERFECT start to a new job! His predecessor's memorial service. Funereal agony.

Chris's expression tightened. It had been six years since he'd missed his own funeral, and those of his real family. He'd imagined that ritual time and again; constructed a million eulogies—all inadequate—each futile attempt compounding his anger, confirming his impotence.

His failure.

His contribution to Ben's memorial—a pseudo-funeral to say

goodbye while the powers-that-be resolved a suspicious death—felt equally absurd and empty. There'd been nothing tangible to farewell. No urn filled with ashes. No coffin for the flowers. Nothing tactile to kneel beside, feel the loss ... *beg forgiveness from.*

Chris slumped into the passenger seat of his new boss's SUV and yanked the door shut. He wanted to hit something. Punch a door, kick a wall, break things, scream, throw a tantrum like a tennis player. But he couldn't do any of that right now. He was angry, yes, but not with Chassic. He was angry with the universe. With fate. With God. But mostly, with himself because he'd let jealousy trash his relationship with Ben.

He wouldn't make that mistake again. Oh sure, he'd interact with people when he had to, but he'd never let himself truly care—for anybody.

Chris opened the car door just so he could slam it shut again. Anger powered his resolution at an atomic level, a split and spent nuclear force with a shock wave strong enough to blast every potential relationship to Bourke.

Or Maralinga. From now on, Christopher Darnell would exist at the centre of his own exclusion zone.

29. FOXED

September 2012

Canberra, Australia

'**W**HAT THE hell were you thinking, Deabrua, taking him out so publicly?' Sinbled pressed as much anger into his voice as he dared while still moderating its volume. He couldn't risk his phone call being overheard.

'Me? Wasn't that your stupid stunt? You had access to the vehicle. I figured you'd secured the software and eliminated future competition.

'You're the bomb maker. Isn't that how you earned your pathetic axe and snake?'

'Don't disrespect—'

'Your use by date?'

'Not when yours has expired. The Volcano is ready to blow his top if you don't give me that software, now.'

'Give it to a messenger boy? In your dreams, Moz. With prototype and software in my possession, I can offer Ulvelaik a package deal. Should ease tensions. Though he may be less halcyon towards you.'

'That's absurd. You're insane.'

'Insanity is your department. What I am, my friend, is in control. Now, buzz off to your metal-faced boss. Tell him what an annoying little mosquito you've been. If you're as significant as you claim, he won't swat you down, as I will, if you don't deliver my message.'

Horon Sinballidh disconnected the call and opened his laptop to observe the aftermath of their conversation, in comfortable anonymity, thanks to the hidden video camera he'd installed in Deabrua's hotel room.

He watched Deabrua shake his fist, hurl an electric kettle at the wall, and rant about the exquisitely painful demise he'd inflict. The exertion triggered a coughing fit which left Deabrua wheezing. He fished an asthma puffer from a knapsack, inhaled three puffs, and sat on the bed till his chest and shoulders stopped heaving.

'Didn't see that coming! Flea-bitten fox outfoxed me. Stinking mongrel cur! Self-interested manipulating—' Deabrua coughed again. 'Musta learned something from the old devil.'

Sinbled indulged himself with smug satisfaction at Deabrua's grudging admiration. Deabrua had treated him as protégé. But Sinbled was a visionary, moving way beyond Deabrua's coercion by cesspool methodology. When Deabrua had pressed him, back in 2006, to hide Amy Maxwell and track the LIES program to the point of maximum profit, Sinbled had prophesied an eventual shift in power, not that he'd told Deabrua. He'd nurtured Deabrua's belief that Amy was the perfect bargaining chip to extract a down payment, and higher profit, from Ulvelaik.

While Sinbled waited for the software, funds flowing from Deabrua's criminal conduit had bankrolled his preferred lifestyle. Amy was expendable now. Deabrua would see to that. Revenge already wrote its script on Mozzie's twisted brow. Sinbled smirked. What a patsy! Deabrua would kill the girl to spite him; clean up the loose ends. Pity the old devil had only a vague idea where the kid was.

Never mind, Moz. I'll make sure you find your trophy on cue. My cue.

As if predestined, Deabrua picked up the telephone, booked and paid for a flight to Brisbane, with a rental car waiting at the other end.

Sinbled flipped his laptop shut and inhaled his predicted triumph.

30. PUZZLED

September 2012

Canberra, Australia

FUNERAL FALLOUT—that lingering mix of grief, regret, confusion and survivor's guilt. Chris had nourished his negativity with it for years. If death had wrecked his first family, negativity had wrecked his second, despite regular doses of MPeg's positivity. He could use a dose of her now, but she'd become Melbourne's medicine.

Her voice filled his head. 'If you hate funerals so much, Chris, why constantly dig your own grave? Rutter, Rutter, Rutter! Ditch your downer shovel and get a life.'

He was a sucker for MPeg's directives—imagined or otherwise—and he was trying. He'd started a new job. Wasn't that worth brownie points?

Chris contemplated the high-tech computer console in his new private office. At his previous job, he'd occupied one of fifty freezing cubicles. The industrial warehouse featured frigid air-conditioning which kept the servers running cool and staff complaints running hot. Here, eerie silence and the empty strangeness of space that had held and empowered Ben surrounded him.

Images of his friend oozed unbidden through cracks in his memory casket, that internal mausoleum where Mum, Dad, Amy—and now Ben—dwelt. Ben had never known the memories in that space. Chris had ached to share them, but he'd promised Pat he'd never disclose his past.

He'd kept that promise. Cold metallic irony now put his teeth on edge; he'd never intended to cause the Alejandros harm but, ultimately, Ben and Pat had paid for his shortcomings through Mim.

He'd been the bane of her existence as she'd juggled the demands of a brat who undermined her other relationships. Her departure had devastated Ben and Pat, but they hadn't blamed him. He never understood why. He wished they had blamed him. Gotten rid of him, before he'd fattened his green-eyed monster with envy at Ben's success. No, not his success—Ben had earned that. He'd begrudged Ben's opportunity, one they'd both reached for, but only Ben had grasped.

Until now.

Chris fingered the keyboard. Computers were his friends. More than tools of trade, they were extensions of himself, a technological link to vivacity. He could animate worlds through keys and code. He stroked the raised dash on the f and the j. Not every keyboard had them. This one did. Without giving thought to any words in particular, he typed.

Ambulance drivers' fog lights hit jumping kangaroos. Log mad nerds on proper quests. Rats soon trip up vegans with xray vizors.

Apostrophe included. Hmph! *That* troublemaking sentence. His memory was pathetic. Dumped what he longed to remember. Hoarded what he longed to forget. It had failed him even before his accident.

Unlike Amy's. Her mind had been wired like a video recorder. She could replay her life with one hundred per cent accuracy. His little sister had been born with a gift. What a difference she could have made to the world if she'd grown up.

Toad-licking, butt-sniffing thugs. *Why God? Why'd you let them kill her? Tell me that, if you can!*

'Got a moment to chat, Chris?'

Chris nearly peed himself. He'd not expected a response.

Chassic stood in the doorway. 'If you're up to it?'

Chris gulped and swiped a salty splotch from his cheek. 'Mr Chassic—'

'Don't stand on ceremony. Call me HS. Want a coffee?'

Chris nodded.

'Good. White with one for me, stirred anti-clockwise. My office in five.' Chassic rapped on the door. 'Locked door policy, remember?'

Like a corrupted hard drive.

Chris washed his face and hands in the men's room, then located the automatic coffee machine in the lunchroom. A few minutes later, he handed fresh coffee to Chassic.

'Thanks, Chris. Have a seat. Enjoy your drink then we'll get into it.' Chassic sipped, preoccupied with something on his laptop.

Chris fought his urge to shoulder hover. His boss's expression was … Ha! Niggling! Because it sat between nebulous and non-existent in the dictionary, which is how Chris's senior English teacher had once described his efforts. Cokecan had muttered, 'If she wants sympathy, she'll find it after sin, but not after syphilis.' Chris swallowed a grin with his coffee.

'Not bad. Coffee the way I like it. You're off to a good start.' Chassic set his cup down.

Chris nodded deferentially.

'So, Christopher, I've had my eye on you for several years, long before your original application to ASIO. I knew your father well.'

Father? Chris quashed his urge to correct HS. 'I wondered if Pat worked for ASIO, especially when …' He bit his tongue.

'When ASIO hired Ben? Pat worked for ASPT, not ASIO. Ben earned both positions on merit, but my word won't convince you, will it?'

Chris opened his mouth, shut it, raised his empty cup to his lips, and slurped air. Heat stung his cheeks.

'In fact, Ben urged me to hire you, even during his ASIO interview. Almost blew his own chance. I thought that degree of affection and loyalty made him vulnerable to manipulation. I need agents whose heads rule their hearts—most of the time. The more Ben pressed, the more reluctant I was to consider either of you.'

Great. Stick the boot in. 'I'm sorry, Mr Chassic. I'm not sure where you're going with this.'

Chassic drummed his fingers on the desk and his scrutiny onto Chris. 'Towards the truth, I hope.'

'Which is?'

'That Ben loves you, Chris. With a pure love. The love of a true friend. The love of a brother. I want to know if you feel the same way about him.'

Uninvited tears threatened to gatecrash the conversation. Chris blocked them with a scowl. 'I felt that way about Ben. But that won't bring him back. My feelings won't interfere with my work.' Chris almost choked. His declaration would be easier said than done.

Chassic gave a single nod. 'Actually, I hope they'll enable you to do what I'm about to ask.'

'And that is?'

'Help me work out where Ben is.'

'I don't understand, Mr Chassic. What do you mean?' Chris's thoughts freewheeled. 'Do you want to know my religious beliefs?'

'I do wish you'd call me HS.' Chassic's eyes sparkled. 'Ben does.'

'You mean did.'

'I never say things I don't mean.'

'You mean ... Ben's still alive?' Chris fought an outrageous urge to hug his boss.

'According to the shopping centre's security video. Have a look.' HS pressed a few keys on his laptop.

Chris leapt to his side. The video showed Ben pushing a shopping trolley to his vehicle and unlocking the driver's door manually with the key.

HS paused and pointed. 'Key-in-door was probably habit, Ben's own car being older.' HS resumed play.

Ben lifted the rear tail gate, turned to unload his trolley, shoved it aside instead, and dashed off leaving his keys dangling in the driver's door. A hoodie-clad delinquent nicked the SUV in a flash, accelerating towards Spitfire Avenue.

HS stopped the video. 'We've no idea what prompted Ben's lapse in concentration, or his sudden dash. Some security cameras were down. A trolley collector pushed Ben's trolley towards the building. Presumably, Ben collected his bags from it.'

'Either way, he wasn't in his vehicle when it exploded.'

'No.'

'Where'd he go?'

'I'm hoping you can find out.'

'Me? Where do I start? How do I start?'

'By doing what you do best. I do my homework before I headhunt, Chris. You're among the hottest gaming players and developers in the market. You're flexible and adaptable, which makes you ideal for this job. Ben's progress with the LIES software is superb, but he's filed the stuff so creatively, no one here can access it, let alone understand it.'

'What makes you think I can?'

'You know Ben. Better than anyone else I know. Get inside his head. How does he think? What would he do? Think of it as a game, a search and rescue mission, a puzzle to solve, a race to the finish line. Think strategies, outsmarting the opposition, exploring unknown terrain. Ben's advantage was his capacity to hide his tracks. Your advantage is that you've seen him in action. Anticipate his moves as you would a gaming competitor. Ben's a puzzle maker. How does he create them? Work that out and you'll be in. The info is there. Find the files, and you'll find Ben.'

31. FAKED

September 2012

Canberra, Australia

SCREAMIN' PIGLETS! Ben was alive! Chris rode elation to his office where his doubt devils bucked him off.

HS must be desperate trusting him to find Ben. Chris knew how Ben thought before he went all spook. He could kick Ben's gaming butt any time. But by year twelve, Ben was whipping his. Combine that with Ben's specialist training and—

'*Quit your bellyaching, Christian. Make a difference.*'

Whoa! Where did that voice come from? Not MPeg. Not this time. He hadn't heard *that* voice since … twenty-seven flat screen televisions destroyed everything. Not since the heavens iced over like an Antarctic winter. Not since he'd given up on … God?

'*Jumping kangaroos. Just go for it, Bro! I'll help.*' That was Ben's voice. Chris had no idea how.

'Get inside Ben's head,' HS had said. Seemed like Ben was inside his.

Chris hammered the keyboard and opened the Games folder looking for Sudoku.

Yes! He double-clicked.

Username: Benjamin Alejandro

Nope.

Username: Ben-man

Nope.

Username: GrandTheftAuto

Not that either.

Username: Lost&Damned

We will be if I don't get this.

Username:

What about Ben's sass-phrase—the one he used when people mispronounced his surname? Chris tried it.

Username: NoBeerUpFront

Bingo!

Now for the password. Trying regular methods to crack it was pointless. Ben would have anticipated them for sure. Chris tried to remember other sayings or idioms Ben used. One of Mim's came to mind.

NoWayJose

NowayHozay

N0wAH0zA

Chris worked through the Alejandros' idiomatic repertoire. He gained frustration in spades. But access?

Not on your Nelly. Which also failed.

What was he missing?

'Just go for it, Bro.' Ben's voice again, which was weird because that had been Chris's line, carelessly thrown whenever Ben had baulked at his harebrained schemes.

Could it be? Going AWOL was pretty harebrained. Chris held his breath and tried it.

Unbelievable!

He was in. Chris solved the Sudoku like a pro. When the box for the alpha-code appeared, he entered:

Ambulance drivers' fog lights hit jumping kangaroos. Log mad nerds on proper quests. Rats soon trip up vegans with xray vizors.

The computer applied the sequence, flashed 'Access Approved' and opened a letter from Ben.

Yo, Chris!

Figured they'd hustle you if I went AWOL. Welcome to my GRUnGE! Click here (later) to learn how it works. I've set it up so I can access it remotely to communicate with you. Throw up a flag so I know you're here.

A word to the wise: Don't trust anyone else, not even at ASPT.

I expect HS has outlined the LIES project which is active and functioning courtesy of one Aidan (Mac) MacGreggor whose STIR implant is transmitting data. I haven't located him yet, but you'll find his decoded transcripts <u>here</u>.

I'm convinced Mac is in danger, hence the need to find him pronto, hopefully with your help. HS said he'd have another field operative join me eventually. If you're reading this, I've jumped the gun and plan to keep a low profile. I won't risk Chassic pulling me in before I've found Mac.

Don't stress if you don't hear from me soonish. I won't contact you unless I have to. That way, you won't have to account for my actions.

Chris, I know we hit a rough patch but we're still Dro and Bro, brothers and best mates. We've never been anything else. I may not deserve your help, Bro, but I sure need it. I need you now.

Ben needed him—exactly what MPeg had said.
Only this time, it felt good.

—◦—

CHRIS BROWSED feasibility studies, technological suppositions, software development outlines, progress reports on software functionality ... and pinched himself. The logic of Ben's GRUnGE mocked its bizarre contents. The LIES concept and STIR implant shouted science fiction—as had all bionic implants once—and yet, his sister's hearing had been transformed by one, for a few short years.

He clicked the link to the software program. A GRUnGE Sudoku and a telephone number appeared: Lukas Nuevo (New) Int +34 912 223157. When 'Jumping Kangaroos' wouldn't unlock it, Chris moved on. The software worked. That was good enough. He was more interested in Ben's research links and Mac's transcripts.

Chris opened the next folder. The first file crash-tackled him.

>>> Bomb Obliterates Arianna Lakes Home <<<

Bile rising, he grabbed the waste bin, expecting to vomit. Regret was so undignified. He swallowed back and set the bin down. Yesterday, he'd have thrown up, howled, and raged himself into a week-long funk. Today, he had a job to do.

File by painful file, he sifted through media reports and interviews, suppressing every raw, reactive impulse that threatened his resolve until he found a flimsy glimmer of hope—an unfinished sentence that begged a question: Had his family's deaths been faked?

>>> News Footage: Sydney, March 25 2006 <<<

Woman: We felt it even though we were upstairs. The whole bloomin' house shook.

Reporter: Did you know your neighbours well?

Woman: Well enough. Their lad was good to my son, kind, like a big brother.

Reporter: Did you notice anything unusual before the explosion?

Woman: Not a thing. Just boom and smoke and sirens and me screaming. I swear my house has shifted.

Reporter: That must have been distressing.

Woman: They nearly had to cart me off in the ambulance. Seeing it go off empty was terrible. No survivors. Emergency services arrived real quick too. So sad.

Timbo: Ma, the ambla-lance was here before the 'splosion. They took a—

Woman: Am-buew-lance, Timothy. Now hush, Mummy's talking to the nice reporter lady.

Chris remembered the ambulance. It had been driving up Arianna Trace presumably to collect Elias Spinnaze.

'What's dalsis?' Chris could still see the disappointment on Timbo's face when he'd brushed him off. Some big brother he'd been.

Chris sighed and replayed the video.

The ambla-lance was here before the 'splosion. They took a—

Chris frowned. Took what? He listened again.

They took ay—

Long ay. Not short. And Timbo's tone was contradictory. Chris rewound for context.

'Emergency services arrived real quick too. So sad.'
'Ma, the ambla-lance was here before ... They took ay—'

Ages? Or ...

'Amy!' Chris slapped his hand over his mouth. He'd promised Pat he would never mention her name out loud. Ever.

He glanced to make sure his door was shut, got up, opened it, checked the corridor was empty, then locked himself inside again. Good thing the office was air-conditioned. He dripped sweat.

If, by some incredible fluke, Elias's ambulance was still there, had they rescued Amy? Taken her to a hospital? Had Amy survived? Like he had? Had Amy been given a new identity? Like he had? Had Pat known? Surely he would have reunited them. Unless Mim had objected.

Too late to ask now. Even if Pat had known, he was dead. Chris frowned as he thought about Pat. Something in his peripheral memory dangled beyond reach as it had when he'd woken up six years ago to—

Hospital smells. A few months before the explosion, Amy'd had surgery to fix a problem with her cochlear implant. Had Chris glimpsed *Spanish Matador* at that hospital? Had Amy received a STIR implant? Could Mac be Amy?

Chris jumped up, intending to—

Do what? Ask HS? Surely he'd have said if he knew.

Chris paced and jitterbugged. What could he do? Ask Ben via the GRUnGE?

No way. Ben didn't—couldn't—know Chris was a Maxwell.

What if he left a private message in the GRUnGE for Mac with hints only Amy would recognise? Would Ben pass it on without probing? Probably. Then again …

Scouring Mac's transcripts for references to shared childhood experiences was the obvious place to start. Chris sat and opened the first transcript.

32. STRIPPED

September – November 2012

New South Wales and Queensland, Australia

BEN HAD breezed through the shopping part of his Majura Park stop having purchased everything from a battery backup for his computer to ring-pull tins of tuna and baked beans. The twist occurred when a familiar figure caught his peripheral vision and disappeared into Costco.

'Dad!' Ben dropped his bags and ran, heart and feet pounding. There. Near a stock pallet. 'Dad. You're alive.' Ben grabbed his father's shoulder.

A total stranger turned and smiled good-naturedly. 'I should hope so. They object to zombies shopping here.'

Ben's hope plummeted with his face. 'Sorry. I thought you were someone else.'

'No worries, mate. Have a good one.'

Ben shuffled dejectedly to the store's exit in time to see a fireball devour his SUV.

STRANGE HOW soothing the ordered layout of a route map could be. Ben rode the Route 10 bus and stared at the coloured diagram. He'd need Route 7 to get home. Inconvenient, having to change buses with bags of shopping.

Inconvenient! Ben grunted. His autopilot had kicked in. His reactions were mechanical and methodical, but hardly rational. He should have been stark raving mad! His car had just exploded in front of him.

But not around him, thank God.

How? Why? Sabotage? A bomb? A terrorist with a grudge against government employees? Someone at the service centre HS had sent him to? Locke had virtually accused HS of being a criminal. Ben shuddered.

When he got home, he retrieved spare house keys from a backyard hidey-hole then instigated a simple plan. His parents had once owned a small campervan which they'd given to friends who operated Anchors Retreat, a Bed & Breakfast at Lake Macquarie. Brian and Sylvia had painted a wild floral motif on the van that screamed 'tourist'. They rented it out, but always free of charge to the Alejandros. Playing tourist could be a useful cover story. A quick phone call confirmed the van would be available in a week.

'Why not spend a few days with us till it's ready? Our shout.'

'If it's not too much trouble?'

'An Alejandro? Too much trouble? Never. Sylv and I used to give your dad heaps though, back in the day. We've mellowed since then.'

'He loved visiting you guys. Declared it almost rivalled fishing.'

'Almost? Cheeky blighter.'

'Would it be too soon if I come tomorrow? An early start would get me there by lunchtime.'

'I'll have spuds and snags ready for a barbecue. Hang on … Sylvia wants to know if you prefer coleslaw or pasta salad?'

'Both. I'll bring dessert.' Food was the least of Ben's worries, but keeping up appearances would avoid awkward questions.

'Goodo. See you tomorrow.'

Ben loaded his father's car, checked the glove box for roadmaps, removed the GPS navigator, drove through the night, parked in a quiet Central Coast location near Tuggerah Lake and snoozed till sun-up. He kept a discreet profile until mid-morning and arrived at Anchors Retreat armed with a chocolate mud cake and a profiterole torte just as the sausages joined the foil-wrapped potatoes on the barbecue.

———◦○◦———

A WEEK and a half later, Ben drove the colourful campervan to Queensland via every minor country road he could find, overthinking conspiracy theories, contemplating doppelgangers, remembering the spy games and 'what if' scenarios he'd played with Pat, the red rope 'laser' maze Mim had rigged for his sixth birthday party, the cake she'd shaped and iced like a cartoon bomb.

He stopped to stretch his legs, eat cold tuna from a tin, second guess his decision to go it alone …

And kept driving anyway.

Along Thunderbolts Way, his ASIO indoctrination played his thoughts like an iPod Shuffle. According to one trainer, a field agent's greatest asset was a 'bility'—flexibility, adaptability, unflappability—the list had been extensive. 'Neglect those and you'll be a liability. Or dead.'

Being invincible and infallible wouldn't hurt either, but would God work for ASIO?

Somewhere between Walcha and Queensland, Ben entered the spy zone where his training and instinct merged. For several days he stayed flexible, adaptable, unpredictable, untraceable—and unsuccessful. Showing Mac's photo to random people in small-town Landsborough and asking where the MacGreggors lived had elicited quizzical looks and umpteen suggestions he google White Pages, but no information.

Ben was out of options. He needed help. Which meant leaving an untraceable message in the GRUnGE and hoping like crazy Chris had hacked his way into it.

The untraceable aspect was problematic considering his laptop and broadband dongle had disintegrated with the SUV. Thankfully, he'd backed up to USB. *Shoulda been a Boy Scout.* After considering the risk versus convenience of using a 'dead' man's phone, he'd intentionally destroyed that too.

Only now he had no phone. Also problematic. Australian telco rules required proof of identity to purchase or activate a prepaid replacement. His real identity dusted the stratosphere.

He'd have to embrace his Field Agent alter ego ID, courtesy of ASIO, and hope for the best. Good thing he'd stashed it with his cash.

Being stripped of technology sucked. Feeling very old school, Ben searched the Post Office's hard-copy Yellow Pages for an electronics store and dog-eared its location on the Queensland UBD street directory he'd purchased.

At the store, he weighed the odds, calculated costs, and emptied eighty percent of his cash stash on the best discreet mobile and data tech combo he could figure.

It's only money. Can't take it with me when I die. Oh wait. I did that already.

Ben was no fan of dark humour. He hoped his dalliance with it would be short-lived.

33. CEMENTED

November 2012

Canberra, Australia

'WHAT DO you want?'

'Tsk tsk. So abrupt today! How's the weather in sunny Queensland?' Sinbled coughed artificially into the phone.

'How would I know?'

'Come now. You've been buzzing around the South East corner since our last conversation. Taking in the sunshine, no doubt.'

'It's none of your business where I am.'

'You made it my business when you offered the head of our security to Ulvelaik to cement your relationship with him. That cement is showing a few cracks. I'm willing to help you into his good books again.'

'What makes you think I'm not?'

'I don't think. I know.'

'Want to know what a short stay holiday at Lower Molonglo feels like? I can organise a package deal. The swimming is to die for.'

'An overwhelming experience, no doubt, but I must decline. I've spent my holiday budget on you—an all-expenses-paid trip to Spain, if you successfully collect and deliver our valuable investment.'

'Sounds like fun.'

'I'll text the address. And Deabrua?'

'What?'

'Don't leave a mess.'

34. WRANGLED

November 2012

Canberra, Australia

*U*H-OH! PHOTOGRAPHER! *Double batpoo! Last thing I need is my mugshot in the news.*

A photo of Mac? How had he missed that? Chris scrambled through the records, picturing Amy as he remembered her, face awash with sunshine, chocolate and roses, engrossed in her favourite book, *A Wrinkle in Time*. What would she look like now?

Photo, photo, photo.

Blurry!

He enhanced the image, his heart drumming impatience as the photo's finer details emerged.

Wow. What a sourpuss.

Was there any hint of the four-year-old princess he'd carried on his shoulders at the Brisbane Exhibition the year before they'd moved to Sydney? One block later, she'd begged a better view from Dad's shoulders. She'd signed, 'I love you brother,' from on high. As she'd rubbed her knuckles together for 'brother', she'd toppled backwards and grabbed Dad's head with both arms, covering his eyes—he'd gently tucked her hands round his neck.

Tears welled as Chris relived the moment. He'd always fallen short.

Flawed, that's me. Always—

'Aargh!' Always the sad sack! Why couldn't he be stoic? Amy had been, responding to pain with a plaintive, puzzled expression, unless it was intense, or shocking. Then she'd vomit.

Chris stared at his reflection in the computer screen as the screensaver's lines swirled and snaked around his head and shoulders. Negativity wasn't just his excuse; it was a noose he tied for himself. The rope-like lines encircled his neck, tightening as their trajectory contracted.

Whoa! He restored Mac's image to the screen.

Although the photo was inconclusive, Chris's conviction intensified as he read each transcript. He rode Mac's revelations like a roller coaster, from soul-squeezing lows to sky-touching highs where Mac's thoughts were the sun of Amy's hopes—and idiosyncrasies.

Like her hyperthymesia and brilliance. Her outrageous passion for discovering words, crazy big words for a little kid. She'd sign them, letter by letter, then write them into a story. And the way she mimicked their mother's lexicon. Amy had taught him the word.

Mac's sayings were so familiar. Was that coincidence?

Then came the clincher:

Pick a name, he says … Arianna.

After Grandma Arianna—the reason the Maxwells had bought into Arianna Trace, next door to a drug dealer.

How could she possibly choose that name? That name had doomed his family. Ruined his life. Chris punched the wall beside his desk.

He left a dent.

⸺∘⸺

Friday 9 November 2012

'DID I include building renovations in your job description, Chris?'

'I'm sorry, HS. I'll pay for the damage.'

'Start an art display. I find seascapes relax me.' HS winked.

Chris turtled his head into his shoulders. 'Or I could resist punching the wall.'

'Preserve the knuckles. Good idea.' HS sat on the edge of Chris's desk. 'Apart from redecorating, how's the work going? You've accessed Ben's files. Any clues on our prodigal's progress?'

'Mac's or Ben's?'

'Mac is not our prodigal.'

Chris almost snorted his frustration. 'I cracked Ben's filing system. It's smooth as, but I can't crack the software protection code. Not that I need to. The software's fully functional.'

'Don't tell me you're giving up?'

'Prioritising. I've been scanning Mac's transcripts to see if Ben's made contact. I understand why he believes she's in trouble. Is there nothing else you can do to locate her?'

Chassic's face was granite. Uncrushed.

Chris changed tactics. 'From a developmental perspective, we're effectively running the LIES tests blind. With Mac on board, we could advance to the next phase. Assess her physical attributes. See how her brain functions with real-time imaging. Use that knowledge to enlist more STIR recipients to broaden the testing platform.'

'Sound, analytic, reasoned argument.' HS nodded. 'Truth be told, I'd hoped we'd all be together on this by now. I'm concerned about Ben running solo. That's a tough place to be.'

'Ain't that the truth?' Chris leaned his elbows on the desk and massaged his eyes.

HS clicked his tongue. 'You said "her" brain. Ben thought Mac was male.'

Chris swallowed hard. Had he blown it, again? 'I possibly misinterpreted.'

'If Mac is a miss it might complicate Ben's options. Either way, I'll need authorisation to send reinforcements. I'm in conference with the big guns next week.' HS picked up a desk calendar and turned its pages. 'We've had what? Ten weeks of consistent positive results now? If that doesn't validate the LIES program, I don't know what will.'

Chris sat back. 'Whoever tried to take Ben out seemed convinced of its capabilities.'

'Are you suggesting we have a mole?' HS shook his head. 'Ben was scrupulous about security. The police haven't indicated a sinister cause for the explosion, nor attributed criminal intent, beyond the joyrider. Not much joy there.'

'Yeah. That deserves another wall dent.'

'Lucid thought would be more constructive.' HS stood. 'Take an early mark, get your calm on, start fresh on Monday.'

Chris shook his head. 'I'll monitor incoming transcripts through the weekend.'

'Go home. Revitalise. I need you at your optimum next week while I'm away.'

'But I—'

'Scoot! Or I'll snap at your heels till you do.' The way HS tipped his head precluded argument.

Sunday 11 November 2012

CHRIS WRANGLED his three-cheese lunch toastie from grill to plate, punched the tab of a cold Coke, settled on the sofa again and pressed play. Five minutes later, his plate dripped melted mozzarella onto a cushion and his snores competed with the velociraptors in *Jurassic Park*.

Chris dreamed he, Mac and Ben were the 'Cheeze Kings' world champion gaming team: Mozzarella Chris, mild-mannered hero who goes gooey under heat; Parmigiana Mac, the hard, sharp whiz-kid with kick; and Tasty Ben, the people's man. Fans cheer as they shred their opposition onto pizzas. The Cheeze Kings take a victory lap. The crowd roars, 'Cheeze Kings! Cheeze Kings!' Suddenly, a giant salivating jaw bears down, teeth chomping. They slip and slide in a slobbering slaver of drool as—

Chris woke, a river of cold Coke drenching his lap. 'Bummer.'

'Not quite the welcome I'd hoped for.' MPeg stood before him.

'Hey! MPeg! Wow! How—?'

'Flying visit to placate the parentals. I let myself in. Did you miss me? Or—' MPeg glanced at Chris's trousers.

'I—'

'Let me guess. Market research for Napisan? You're animating their new ad campaign.'

'Fell asleep. Spilled my Coke.'

'Sounds like you. Want some pizza? Three cheese and sweet chilli?'

CHRIS APPRECIATED MPeg's visit. However brief, her timing was perfect. Her feisty wit and genuine friendship always perked him up. He even dared to feel slightly more deserving of her company since he'd embraced a career change. He couldn't help but mention it.

'Double woot, mate. That's quite a leap. Designer hotshot to—what exactly does a "SPIT" guru do? I've never heard of them before.'

'Better pretend you still haven't or I'll be out on my ear.'

'Ah! My lips are sealed. Do you love it?'

'Like shovelling elephant poop.'

'Maybe I should throw you in elephant poop, Darnacle.'

Chris cringed. MPeg applied the nickname—her blend of Darnell and barnacle—whenever he clung to his old gripes. He contemplated tackling and tickling her for dredging it up, then opted for noble concession. 'You know me. Cheerful as ever.'

'No longer wearing your miseries like a pair of smelly socks?'

'You did tell me to wash them.'

'Sorry about that.'

'Why should you be sorry? I'm the stinker.'

MPeg shrugged. 'I've no right to judge. Walk a mile, eh?'

'God forbid, Peg. I hope you never have to walk a mile in my shoes.'

'I dunno. I once suggested you try walking in mine.' MPeg blinked in slow motion.

Chris swallowed. Had he detected subtext? 'I'm … not sure I'm ready for high heels yet. Although—'

'You could fake it till you make it.' Her eyes were warm and inviting and a smile teased her lips.

Or he could hold her close and kiss her delirious.

'Time to go.' She stood, abruptly.

Too slow. He sighed.

'Sorry. Flight to catch.'

'Melbourne mojo calling? Do you … love it, Peg?'

'It has its attractions. Perhaps you should check them out.' She took a step towards the door.

'What attractions?' Chris rose to intercept her and gently touched her arm.

She slipped, unabashed, into his personal space, tilted her head, and searched his face. The puff of her breath brushed his chin and her cheeks acquired a distinct flush. 'My apartment's a good place to start. You could stay with me. My décor is minimalistic and charmingly seductive.' Her voice was husky.

'Is it?'

'Mm-hmm. You could say it's almost naked.'

Chris cleared his throat to camouflage a growl of arousal. 'It sounds … irresistible.'

MPeg looked decidedly pleased with herself. 'So you'll visit?'

'You bet I will. Just as soon as I find—' *Shut it, Darnell. You can't tell her that.*

'Find what?' She no longer looked pleased.

He'd done it again. Broken the moment. Worse. He'd dropped one barrier only to raise another. Good old Stonewall Darnell. 'I will come. I promise. Just not sure when.'

She eased back. 'Suit yourself. But be warned—if you take too long, I'll sublet the spare room.' She glanced at her wristwatch. 'I really do have to go.'

'So soon?'

She stepped in and kissed him. Quickly.

Too quickly. Should he—?

'Be good okay?' She was already opening the door.

'And if I can't be good?'

'Be careful.'

---

12 November 2012

HIS SPIRITS buoyed by MPeg's visit, Chris arrived at work early on Monday morning.

'Christopher Darnell, are you a workaholic?'

Chris jumped as Von bounced up behind the reception counter.

'Wow!' she said. 'You're on edge. Have a fight with the cat and she threw you out?'

'I don't have a cat, Von.'

'It's a joke, Chris.'

'Oh.'

'Darnell is not a morning person. No worms for your breakfast.'

'Guess not. Just a stack of work without maple syrup.'

'And a message from a Fed to get your juices going. Talbot Locke called by Friday afternoon. He left a note on your desk.'

'You let him into my office?'

'No. You did, by leaving your door unlocked. I thought you'd gone to the loo when you didn't answer my knock. I left Locke waiting in the hall.'

'HS gave me an early mark.'

'You always lock your work up before you go, don't you?'

'Home, yes. Loo, no.'

'Good thing you weren't in the loo.' Von wagged a finger. 'Always lock up, loo trips too, alright? Or you'll get us both sacked.'

Chris offered a sheepish grin. He headed to his office and located Locke's message:

I have info re your predecessor's Aidan MacGreggor enquiry. See me asap?

Chris lifted the phone and punched in Locke's number.

'Liaison.'

'Could I speak with Talbot Locke, please? Christopher Darnell. ASPT.'

'Agent Locke is away until Thursday.'

'He wanted to see me urgently.'

'I can make an appointment for one pm Thursday.'

'If that's the earliest.'

'At your office, Mr Darnell?'

'Thank you, yes.' Chris dropped the phone into its cradle, logged on to his computer and tapped into the GRUnGE.

35. SQUASHED

Thursday 15 November 2012

Canberra, Australia

BUD LOCKE leaned against the railing, trying to decide whether the Telstra Tower at the top of Black Mountain Drive was ugly enough to merit its iconic status. Judy Callahan had thought so, when they'd met here for coffee then wandered into the bush. She'd dared him to frisk her for the USB drive containing copies of Alejandro's computer files, not that they'd helped much.

She was a minx, that one.

Not at all like his ex-wife, although they'd both admitted to falling for his police blues. For his ex, the novelty had faded as fast as his ability to support her preferred lifestyle on a constable's salary. Judy preferred to strip his uniform off him rather than understand the man who wore it. Bud sighed and traipsed into the bush again to make a private phone call.

'Bosworth here.'

'Bud Locke, Brock. I trust you're enjoying your post-retirement gig?'

'Passable. My charge can be a cantankerous little git. She calls me Bozo, like I'm clowning around instead of saving her butt.'

'Then you'll be glad it's time to implement the changeover.' Locke swished a fly.

'Mac'll love that like a hole in the head.'

'A familiar experience in her case.'

'You can be a mean SOB, Locke.'

'Sentimentality is an expensive luxury. I'm a pragmatist. Can you handle the changeover on Wednesday?'

'I can. I'll test run the scuba gear on location tomorrow and refill the tanks.'

Locke swished the fly again. 'Skip the test run. Keep her secluded until Wednesday.'

'The test run is for me. It's been years since I worked the police diving squad. The currents in Pumicestone Passage are tricky, not to mention sand shifts. I'd rather not drown Mac or myself by accident.'

'Normally I'd agree. But threat level is red. You need to stay put. Scuba diving is like bike riding. Once you know how and all that. You've kept your certification up to date. You'll be fine.'

'I don't know.'

'There's no debate, Brock. You and Mac stay put.'

'I still don't like it.'

'You're not paid to like it. You're paid to do it. I can drop you from the payroll. I have younger men who would—'

'Stuff the whole thing up through inexperience. Point taken. Lock-up it is, until Wednesday.'

Locke slapped the fly which had landed on the back of his neck. He squashed it.

36. FLUSHED

Sunday 18 November 2012

Landsborough, Queensland, Australia

LIES/MXP2/20121118pm47942

'**M**AC. ARE you with me?'

'Like gum on your shoe.'

'I need you to focus. Remember every detail.'

That's the least of my worries. Surviving them—that's the challenge.

'Go for it, Bo-rocko. I'm on your page.'

'I need you on the same letter of the same word or this goes belly-up, yours and mine.'

'Schoolies. Pumicestone Passage. Throw myself, fully clothed, into a capricious current at midnight. What could possibly go wrong?'

'You can tread water, can't you?'

'In theory. Not for long. Swimming lessons weren't high on Li's agenda.'

'I'll be there with scuba tanks.'

'Scuba! We're going under water? Aren't you forgetting the screw in my head?'

'God forbid! I'm told you have a super-duper prototype which is mostly inside your skull. We won't go deep, just out of sight. Your aqua-kit will protect the external processor. They've sent me a bumbag protection pouch for your backup processor and battery pack.'

'Why? It'll be safer at home.'

'Mac, we relocate immediately to a new safe house.'

'What about my belongings?'

'You'll get new stuff. Should make you happy.'

Oh goody goody. Fix my miserable existence with clothes and presents. I'm so lucky.

'I still don't get why I have to drown. Can't I disappear like a normal missing person?'

'Not with a photo of you in circulation, thanks to your train switching stunt.'

Ouch. Low blow. Bring on the guilt trip. Blame the kid.

'We must persuade everyone you're dead.'

'I will be if you don't get to me tout de suite.'

'I'll get to you. Takes me minutes to tank up and get underwater. When I grab your feet, let yourself sink. I'll have air. We'll swim underwater until we're out of sight. Now, look at the map. You go in here, beside The Esplanade, at the point closest to the tip of Bribie Island. I go in— no, that's too open—here, under the boardwalk to the north. I'll swim around the point. I'll give you a 'go' time to make sure I'm in position when you take your dip. It'll be dark. Crowd should be drunk by then. Just make sure their attention is on you, not me. Make a fuss about swimming across to Bribie.'

'What if some brainiac decides to save me from my own stupidity?'

One can hope.

'Be demonstrative. Your death must be convincing. Your life depends on it.'

'Do you have any idea how absurd that sounds?'

'Trust me, Mac.'

Trust Gonzo the Gawker? This drown plan is foul.

Monday 19 November 2012

LIES/MXP2/20121119pm57319

'YOU DID what? What hellish demonic brain fart possessed you to do such an idiotic, abusive, insensitive, despicable, moronic—'

'It's for the best, Mac.'

'Crapping out a gastro bug is for the best but it still stinks. You flushed my exams and essays. Gutted my results. Shattered my chance at uni. I could kill you!'

'Mac—'

'Don't you Mac me. Don't you … aargh! Don't even speak.'

'What's done is done, Mac.'

'Shut it, Liss. It's your fault too. You nominated this bozo as my exam supervisor.'

'The threat sounded legitimate. A perfect exam result would've branded you with a bullseye.'

'And you'd never risk getting yourself or Li caught in the crossfire on account of the kid, right?'

'Keeping your identity under wraps hasn't been easy for any of us. Our survival means hiding your light under our bushel.'

'Great. Misquote King James at me. You know what? Go right ahead. Quote chapter and verse for all I care, because even the honest-to-God quotes don't do it for me.'

'It makes little difference either way.'

'It does to me, Brock! You subvert my smarts? The only thing not hobbled by the past. You stole the one freedom I had. You might as well drown me for real.'

'Mac.'

'Shut up! I'm going out.'

'You can't. It's not safe.'

'Look on the bright side. If I die taking a walk, you won't have to drown me. Save taxpayers money.'

'Mac.'

'Let it go, Liss. Mac needs to blow off steam.'

'Don't slam the—'

GOD! HOW could you let them do that? Haven't I suffered enough?

Stalking Bozos! I can't even walk down the street without a lapfrog in tow. It's humiliating. Isolated, alone, but never on my own.

Ow! Bloodsucking Culicinae. Got him! One less breeding Scotch Grey. Sheesh. Swarming mosquitoes, stalking Bozos and—Whoa! Swooping plovers! Screeching banshees! Maybe this was a bad idea.

'Oi! Shoo!'

Freaky birdbrains. But you still protect your own, don't you? With your kick-ass cries and never-say-die fly-bys. Alright. I know. You belong here, and I don't. Well, I'll be gone soon enough. Maybe for good. You can have your putrid tea-tree swamp all to yourselves.

At least the swamp can't suck you into its misery. You've got wings. You own earth and sky. You can fly wherever you like.

Are you mocking me? Prattling over your good life? Itch-ay itch-ay hitch-a-ride-and-run-away. If only I could. Go heckle the trains that rumble your turf, burring bass lines rocking out rhythms to a world of choices, places, freedom.

'Shoo!' Guano. Poo. Stupid plovers. 'Shove off!'

Mean old birds. What did I ever do to you? What did I ever do to anybody? 'Shoo!' Phew. They've gone. Feathered fanatics.

Ha. Your turn, Bozo. Serves you right. Karma.

Jake says life is karma. Reap what you sow. Well, I didn't plant bombs, did I God? Hey? No!

Chuck-a-duster, I didn't even swear back then.

Other kids swore You didn't kill their families. Flush their futures. Toss them into the sea to drown them.

Well, except for Jonah, but you saved him.

And Paul, when he got shipwrecked. I remember the picture in Mum's old story book. Paul was always in trouble. Was that payback for hurting Christians, you know, when he was still called Saul? Bet he was glad to shed his old name. Far out. It's years since I read Bible stories.

Ha. What about the dead girl Jesus revived? Jairus's daughter. No mention of her name. Witness protection, old school. You wanna try that one again, God? Might come in handy if Bozo's too slow. Just sayin'.

The Good Shepherd. I liked that one. Stupid sheep wanders off. His minder finds him and carries him home. Hey Bozo, piggyback?

Talk about lost. I'm so lost, I'll never be found. They've obliterated so much, I can't even find me. And you couldn't care less, could you God? I'd smack your face if my arm was long enough.

"Don't fight me, Mac. Trust me. I will rescue you. I will bring you back. I know the plans I have for you, plans to bring about the future you hope for."

Whoa! Where did that come from?

37. LACERATED

Monday 19 November 2012

Landsborough, Queensland, Australia

BEN FOUND a quiet parking spot, configured his new technology, and logged in to the GRUnGE. Yes! Chris's flag was flying.

The potential for an armistice had skyrocketed. Ben uploaded a message: Need your help, Bro. Please phone me asap. He added his new phone number and signed off.

Time for a quick restock of baked beans and tuna. The IGA near the post office sold hot chicken and offered an excuse for small talk at the checkout concerning his 'second cousin', Liss.

'I haven't seen Liss since I was a kid. She and Li moved here about two years ago. I'd look them up if I knew their surname.'

'I know a Liz Applebee.' The checkout operator scanned a tin of beans twice.

'Lizzy Applebee was born and bred here. She's one of the Shore girls.' The lady serving the chicken-and-deli counter nearby offered the information. 'There's a Liss and Li Li on our delivery run. Older couple. Look Asian. Don't sound it. Your cousin, you said?'

'Second cousin. By marriage.' More than humidity made Ben sweat. He found deception uncomfortable, good cause or not.

'Liss phones in her order. Young lad answers the door sometimes.' The lady held up a small hot chicken. 'He's a bantamweight, but not Asian. Did they adopt?'

'Our family's into foster care.' Close to the truth.

'The Li's house is tucked in behind trees on Gatla Street near Winslow, I think.'

The checkout operator unhooked Ben's bag of groceries. 'Forty-two seventy-eight. Cash or card?'

'Cash. Thanks.' Ben paid and scooted.

———◦———

WHEN BEN'S phone finally rang, its tremor and jangle mirrored the state of his nerves. 'Yup?'

'Dro? It's me. Thank God you're still alive.'

'Chris! You cracked my GRUnGE. Legend. Good to hear your voice. I've missed you, Bro.'

'Yeah, me too. Sorry about that. And everything else. I—'

'Don't sweat it. You're here for me now. I have what you might call a situation.'

'No kidding. Have you found Mac?'

'I wish. I've run up more dead ends than a cemetery, trying to dig up an address.'

'I can help with that,' Chris said. 'Between Mac's transcripts and other—let's call them hypothetical—searches, I've narrowed it down to—'

'Are you using the work phone?'

'My personal smartphone. Thought it would be safer.'

'Hope so. Give me the lowdown, Bro.'

'It's in the GRUnGE. Can you download?'

'Give me a minute … done.'

'Dro, this drowning ruse they've concocted.' Chris outlined the latest. 'You've got to stop them. It's crazy stupid. They've bullied Mac into it.'

'Don't worry. I'm right on it, thanks to you.'

'I'll compile transcripts as they arrive. Let's hope Mac's feeling communicative. Dro, I … I'm glad we're cool. Again.'

'Me too. Let me digest what you've sent. I'll call you back.'

———◦———

BEN SCANNED the download. Chris had been meticulous, including everything from 'house with pawpaw trees' to weather forecasts, tide times, and images of the beach and Pumicestone Passage marked 'drowning location'.

He'd tracked Mac's September fourteenth taxicab journey from Banyo to Landsborough. The drop-off address was a vacant block. Chris had scanned the area using Google Street View, and 'hypothetically' connected the post-office box listed on BSDE records to a house.

Or rather, to an overgrown jumble of plants that obscured everything behind it. The location dovetailed with the chicken-lady's info.

Definitely plausible.

———⋈———

BEN NOSED his campervan under a copse of trees and walked east in search of Chris's thicket-and-pawpaw-patch mystery house. He'd wrestled a hundred druthers over the best approach, then locked on to the obvious—ring the doorbell. What came next was less obvious. He could hardly say, 'Hi. I'm Ben, your friendly neighbourhood spy, here to rescue Mac.'

Thankfully, the post office's prepaid satchel display had inspired a solution. He now carried a parcel of books addressed, A MacGreggor, Gatla Street, Landsborough. He'd knock and say, 'Hi. I've just moved in down the street. I think I received your parcel by mistake.' Then he'd wing it.

Ben frowned at the bushy anti-personnel barrier that fortified both gate and house. Pity he couldn't wing it over that. He grappled with a laceration of spiny palms, spiky citrus, hostile bougainvillea, and St Andrew's Cross Spiders, to locate the front door. Which stood ajar. Odd, given their stranger-danger mindset and jungle-like deterrent.

Ben knocked. No response. 'Hello? Anybody home?' He listened for movement. Only heard his heart thump.

'Cooee? Anybody home?' Apparently not. 'Shall I come in then?' Did silence constitute affirmation?

He could try the back door. Ben negotiated the side yard. A white four-wheel-drive utility occupied a cave of branches. Their soft foliage draped the bonnet. The natural arbour led him to a sliding glass door, also open. He raised his hand to knock. And froze.

Dear Lord. No!

Security cameras hummed as Ben blundered in, compelled by the horrifying carnage of two prone and bloodied bodies cameoed in gruesome relief on the kitchen floor.

Male and female. Asian. Middle-aged. Slashed and gashed. Beyond help.

Not Mac.

'Mac? Can you hear me? Mac! Call out!' Ben scoured the house, fearing the worst, but assessing carefully. Family, dining, lounge rooms, clear. Twin bed master with ensuite, clear. Walk-in robe—clothes would fit the bodies. Bathroom, toilet, laundry, clear. Back door, deadlocked. Study nook—with an assignment folder labelled 'Aidan MacGreggor'. Definitely Mac's home but—

This was nuts. Beyond two dead bodies, the house was absurdly normal, if too pristine for a family.

Ah! Not this room. Boswell's? The smell of old man, stale grog, sweat and dirty bed linen fit Mac's assessment of the lush.

Ben opened the remaining bedroom door, revealing Spartan décor and a mobile clothing rack that smacked of impermanence. Woah! Double take. The rack held menswear, but the bed was stockpiled with fluffy toys. Tokens of Mac's brain/behaviour age disparity perhaps?

Ben's teeth ached. Still no sign of Mac or Bozo, nor clarity re their appearance or whereabouts.

The security cameras! With footage of Mac? Bozo? The murderer? And himself! Explaining his presence to police would be complicated. Best avoided, for now.

Ben pressed his tongue to his teeth while he tracked down the security system's recording equipment. Its portable DVR, similar to those used with hidden body cameras, was small enough to fit in a pocket.

Or post to Chris—whose home address escaped him. Work address? What if Von intercepted the package? She opened mail automatically, overlooking words like private and confidential. HS? Not after the bombing incident.

He'd post it to himself, c/- Anchors Retreat—after he'd watched it for a good look at Mac and Bozo.

Ben mentally photographed the bodies, retrieved his parcel of books from the kitchen bench and skedaddled back to the campervan.

38. RIGOR MORTISED

Monday 19 November 2012

Sunshine Coast, Queensland, Australia

LIES/MXP2/20121119pm59228

'HOLD UP, Mac. The plovers are worse than magpies. That last swoop bloodied my bald spot. Are you okay?'

'Like you care.'

'Mac.'

'I needed some air, okay? Wow! They got you good, didn't they?'

'Looks worse than it is. Head wounds bleed a lot. You wouldn't notice if I had hair there.'

'Shoulda worn your hat.'

'I left in a hurry.'

'Coulda let me be. I'm not a kid. I know where I live.'

'You're no longer a child, that's for sure. Being a kid? That's a different freedom. Even adults need to be kids sometimes.'

'Sorry, mate. Musta missed the memo.'

'Nevertheless, we need to get back indoors. Boss reckons trouble's close. A passing car could deliver it.'

'Like that cruisin' flower-power campervan? Truckin' terrorists for sure!'

'Mac.'

'Keep your hair on. The air's already redolent with guano. I'm merely following suit.'

'The air is what?'

'Redolent. You know. Stinks. Redolent.'

'You really are one smart cookie, Mac. I agree the exam substitution wasn't fair.'

'It stank.'
'Redolently?'
'Like a dead carcass.'
'Better than becoming one.'
'Not funny, Brock.'
'It had to be done, Mac. I had no choice.'
'Welcome to my world.'
'Well, at least we have one thing in common.'
'You think? Sheesh!'

'BANSHEES, BROCK. You did leave in a hurry. Left the front door open.'

'Wait up, Mac. Let me go first.'

'Why. It's just—'

'Mac. Stop! I did not leave the door open. Li wouldn't either. Something's wrong. Wait here. Quietly, please. Let me check it's safe.'

'Whoa! Since when did you carry a gun?'

'I always carry a gun. I'm just not obvious about it.'

'I know that. See what you've done? I'm so upset about the exam thing I mm mm—'

'Forgodsake, shush! Now, if I take my hand off your mouth, will you please zip it? Good. Stay.'

This is spooky.

Ouch. Rotten mozzies, eating me alive.

Stupid shrubbery.

'Psst! Brock! I'm being devoured by blood-sucking disease carriers. Can I come in?'

. . .

Now I'm getting the silent treatment?

Tough bikkies. I'm going in.

'Brock? What's going—aargh! Liss! Li!'

'Mac! I told you to stay put.'

'They've been st-st-stabbed! Are they dead?'

'Murdered. Thank God it was them—'

'Thank God! Are you insane? Li and Liss are swimming in blood and you thank God?'

'No! I meant thank God you took off or—'

'I'd be dead too-ooo-ooo!'

'It's okay, Mac.'

'It is not.'

'It's okay to cry, I mean. It's a shock. It's—'

'Not okay-ay. Howling duddn' fix stuffn'. I should know-oh-oh. Crap!'

'Tissues?'

'Ugh! Ta.'

'You should probably drink some water.'

'What! I can't go into the kitchen!'

'No. Nor past it to the bathroom.'

'I'll—laundry. Wash my face.'

'I'll come with.'

'I'm not a baby.'

'I need to check the camera feed.'

'Oh. Course. And call the police.'

'I did. Before you came in.'

'So they'll be here soon?'

'Not the local police. I called the boss. I suspect it's an organised hit.'

'So messy. Horrible.'

'Hopefully the security cameras have … [censored] DVR's gone. These people are pros.'

'What about the nan-hic-cam?'

'The what?'

'Nanny-cam. Giraffe in my bedroom.'

'Let's check it.'

...

'Got you! Wow. He looks young for a pro. What? You look like you've seen a ghost.'

'That's no ghost. That's Jake Leicester.'

'Your online mate? Mac? Oi! Mac? You with me? Crumbs, the way your face froze I thought I'd pressed your pause button, not the nanny-cam's.'

'Huh! My blood caught the chill.'

'The boss nailed it. Jake's no friend.'

'He's a stalker who walked over my grave.'

'Here, wrap this around you. You're shivering. Could be shock.'

'Could be shock? Brock Bosworth, master of understatement.'

'Well, you could just be cold. I never assume anything with you.'

'Are you saying I'm contrary?'

'If the shoe fits.'

'That is so sad. True. But sad. They say truth is a dynamic compound of opposites, savage contraries for a moment conjoined.'

'Which 'they'?'

'A Bartlett Giamatti. Free dictionary quote for the word "contrary".'

'You're the dynamic compound, Mac. You and your memory. Contrary is fine if the word helps you focus. Balances your equilibrium.'

'That's redundant.'

'Good.'

'No, it's not. It's like saying stabilise your stability. It's repetitious.'

'So sue me. It's better than riding a see-saw. Okay?'

'Okay.'

'Good. We're both equiliberaliserated.'

'That's not even a word, Brock.'

'It is now.'

'If you say so. What next?'

'We go ahead with the identity change.'

'Now?'

'We're ready to go. Schoolies started Saturday. It'll soon be dusk.'

'So I die tonight. Just like that.'

'Jake can't murder a corpse. We've got to convince him and his cronies you're already stone cold. Rigor mortised.'

'Great. I really need that picture in my head right now. Perfect match for Li and Liss. The ultimate family portrait. Screeching banshees, you can be an insensitive prat.'

'Sensitivity is not my priority. Protecting your life is. And making your death a plausible ruse. People don't hound the dead. Well, the sane ones don't.'

'Sane people don't pretend to drown themselves either.'

'BROCK! SLOW down! You're way over the speed limit.'

'Only slightly.'

'You'll get us pulled over.'

'I will not.'

'You might if you don't slow down.'

'I want to put that scene behind us asap. Don't you?'

'You think? I get it. Slow down anyway.'

'I'm not speeding, dammit. Who's driving? You or me?'

'You know full well I can't. Look Brock, I'm not trying to be a pain. It's—'

'Habitual.'

'Aargh! When I'm stressed it takes over, alright?'

'Like prickly pear.'

'What?'

'There. Beside the road. Invasive cactus. Covered in sharp thorns. But you can still make sweet jam with its fruit.'

'And you should—' *Hang on. Bozo's smiling?* 'You should probably smile more, Brock. Improves your—'

'Butt-ugly face? You're probably right, Mac. Maybe we should both smile more.'

What a day that'll be. 'So, when you mentioned prickly pear before, you meant me. Metaphorically.'

'Compare you to a thorny transplant that's survived outside its natural habitat? I must be living dangerously.'

'You think? My thorns stop people asking me pointless questions. Or questions I'm not allowed to answer. Usually.'

'So it's not because you're having an off day.'

'Yeah, well, murder exacerbates an off day. Most discommodious.'

'Discommodious? The words you come out with, Mac.'

'What's wrong with them?'

'Nothing. They're just not what you'd expect from the average teenager.'

'Who says I'm average? Apart from the teacher who marked my final English exam.'

'Mac, I'm truly sorry about the whole exam thing. You really are one smart cookie. You deserve to enjoy the fruits of your incredible mind.'

'Yeah, well, hairdressers should be geniuses, right?'

'I think you'll succeed at whatever you set your mind to. And Lord help anyone who tries to stop you.'

'I could be a hairdresser by day and a genius by night. Hang on, that didn't come out right. I meant like, you know, not, um.'

'Good gravy! The word whiz is wost for words! Did I miss the apocawipse?'

'Ha-ha. Stop looking so smug.'

'Who me? Never. I've no doubt you could be a hairdresser by day and a genius by—writing in your spare time. Hypothetically speaking.'

Nice save, Bozo. Creds for that. 'Yeah, well make sure you reach me in time tonight or my options won't even be hypothetical.'

'I'll get to you, Mac. Trust me. I will rescue you.'

Trust Bozo? Some choice.

"Don't fight me, Mac. Trust me."

Whoa! Déjà vu! How weird is that?

"Trust me."

Who? What? I trusted Jake. Look what that got me. Dead carers. Carers—that's a misnomer. Li and Liss cared about support money, not me.

Truth or dare? They had scant reason to care. Mac, the brat. No wonder they hated me. I hate me. It'd be better all round if I drown for real. Guzzle the beer, not just pretend. Go out smashed.

'Penny for your thoughts?'

'Cheapskate. Make it twenty bucks and I'll consider it.'

'Ten. And for that I expect fancy words.'

'You can have pictures if I draw a mind map.'

'What? You're an artist too?'

'Mac-el-angelo Buonarroti.'

'Prove it. Draw your thoughts. Pad and pencil in the glove box.'

'For ten bucks?'

'Mac-el-money-grubber. Okay.'

...

Knife-wielding murderer. Wiggly waves. Swim little fishies over my head. Bozo in scuba gear. Stick figure sinking. Bunch of beer cans under my feet. Waving hand. Goodbye cruel world. Nice knowing you kid. Finito!

'How's that? Artistic perfection. Ten bucks worth. Pay up, Brocko.'

'Hmph. Don't quit your day job, Mac.'

'Cheeky. This is pure artistic genius. You wait. One day, this little sketch will fetch millions. History will prove it.'

'History is but mystery, invented, rearranged and recorded to convince us existence makes sense.'

'Wow! That's actually profound, Brock.'

'You think so? I thought that one up myself. After I read *Homicidal Psycho Jungle Cat*.'

'Sounds like my kind of book.'

'Calvin and Hobbes comics. You've captured the homicidal part in your, um, art.'

'Why, thank you.'

'Ten bucks for another episode? Or better still, words to complement your artwork?'

'Wow. Never knew my thoughts were worth so much.'

'Maybe they're not. I won't know till you give 'em up.'

'Okay … there.'

'Read it to me, Mac. I'm driving.'

'Mac's artwork is fantastic. Complimentary words. Ten bucks. Pay up.'

'I'm broke.'

In more ways than one. 'Your quote, the history is invented one? I don't have to invent mine. I remember it all.'

'Not everything, surely.'

'I have eidetic hyperthymesia. It's like a biographical video camera. Didn't they tell you?'

'They told me to keep your tuchas out of trouble. So, you have a secret power charging your brilliance?'

'I guess. Although I still have to see or read or hear things or think them before they get recorded and filed.'

'And your whole life is stored in your retrieval system?'

'Almost. My baby memories are scratchy, but pretty much everything else is there since I was about three. Except for the flash gap.'

'Ah! The flash gap. Every good story needs one.'

'It's more like my memory disk was corrupted, so it didn't record details in my brain. I have flashes, but the images don't make sense.'

'Such as?'

'The lady in the cubby.'

'She sounds ominous.'

'She's—I don't know. I thought maybe it was Liss, but that doesn't make sense.'

'Why not?'

'Because the cubby was at my real home. I met Liss later.'

'Tell me about your real home.'

'It blew up.'

'And you were all killed. But aliens intercepted your flying body and use it to spy on earthlings. That's why you're so weird. Got it. What? Mac, no. I didn't mean to make you cry. I was playing along, you know. Creative story telling.'

'It's n-not a st-story, Brock. It's real. My parents and brother were killed.'

'Gravy Mac, you're serious! No one told me. I would never—'

'No one told anyone. That's why I'm in witness protection. My mum dobbed in a drug syndicate. They killed my whole family in revenge.'

'That's deplorable! You poor kid. No wonder you're so—'

'Screwed?'

'I was going to say angry. Who wouldn't be? I'm guessing you survived because you were in the cubby?'

'Our yard occupied two levels with a cliff in the middle. The cubby was in the top yard.'

'Being knocked unconscious could explain your memory gap.'

'But I wasn't. That's the thing. I clearly remember seeing a lady run towards me from the neighbour's house which was also on the top level. Then nothing. Nothing more till I woke up in a strange bed in a caravan with Li and Liss. Then your boss turned up in pinstripes and spaghetti sauce.

'But?'

'But what?'

'That's what I'm asking you, Mac. I sensed a "but" in your voice. What? What's so funny all of a sudden?'

'I dunno. Ha-ha! The way you said—'

'What?'

'I got this, ha-ha, crazy, ha-ha, craxy—'

'Craxy?'

'Gah! No! Crazy mental picture of a butt in my—hic!'

'Oh yeah. I see where you went with that. What can I say? I'm a funny guy.'

'You were right. My hic— Gah! My "but" was the strange feeling it was Liss.'

'Who? The cubby lady?'

'Yes. But when I asked Liss about it she said my memory was playing tricks.'

'Not unusual after a concussion.'

'I guess.'

'But the "but" is still there.'

'Because the cubby lady signed my name in Auslan. How would a stranger know to do that? Liss knew Auslan.'

'That I didn't know.'

'Why would you? Liss stopped me signing years ago. She said it increased my risk of discovery. With my cochlear implant I didn't need to, so I stopped.'

'That's a pity. It's a useful skill, like having a second language. *Une autre langue invite le monde dans votre vie.*'

'You speak French!'

'*Oui, mon ami.* Another language invites the world into your life.'

'Wow! That's so incongruous.'

'I'll take that as a compliment. My wife was Canadian-born, and bilingual. We wanted our children to learn both languages.'

'Well knock me down with a feather and call me Cupid! You have a family, Brock?'

'Had a family. They died in a boating accident.'

'Oh Brock, I'm so sorry.'

'I was thrown clear. I tried to save them, but the boat sank too deep too fast. They were trapped under the hull. If they'd found an air bubble, if I'd been able to swim deeper, hold my breath longer.'

'Ifs. They're the worst.'

'The infernal ifs haunt me.'

'Time doesn't heal nearly as well as people say it does.'

'You're right about that, Mac. Time just walks the pain down the road a bit.'

'Where it waits for you, and trips you up when you least expect it.'

'That it does. You know, the pain, the ifs, are the reason I signed on for the police diving squad. And kept my diving certification after I retired from the force.'

'You gave up retirement for this gig? Crazy is as crazy does.'

'The boss was there for me after the accident. Helped me weather the storm and its consequences.'

'Somehow, I can't picture him as the compassionate type.'

'People change. Especially when life throws out a curve ball. He was good to me. I owed him. When he asked me to see you through this lunacy, well …'

'Lucky me, hey?'

'It's also the reason why I will be there to save you tonight, Mac. Okay?'

'I know, Brock.'

'And Mac? I'm really, truly sorry about the exam thing.'

'Oh, I forgive you!'

39. LOADED

Monday 19 November 2012

Canberra, Australia

CHRIS SHOOK his head in disbelief. With one phone conversation, he and Ben had leapfrogged the awkwardness of the past and landed side by side. Well, almost. He'd stifled his urge to tell Ben he suspected Mac was Amy. His promise to Pat still held. He'd literally bitten his tongue over it during the phone call. Drawn blood. And triggered a new worry—would withholding information put Ben or Mac in greater danger?

As the afternoon progressed, Chris's relief at hearing from Ben dissipated with each successive LIES revelation. Mac's transcripts were loaded with death. And Ben's phone was out of service.

Chris felt like a fly in a spider's web, oscillating between speculation and dread.

'Chris. Time to—'

'Chuck-a-duster, Von! I'm on a deadline. Literally.'

'No need to shoot the messenger. All souls save ours have departed for the night and I'm leaving now. I need to call security if you're staying back. How much longer will you be?'

'All night if I have to. Things are—'

'Don't get snarky. I'll tell security you're pulling an all-nighter. If you leave sooner, ring them. Okay?'

'On it. I gotta make a phone call, Von.'

'Then make it, grumpy-bum. And shut your door.' Von left in a huff as Chris's smartphone pinged an incoming SMS.

A missed call message from Ben. Chris punched the call back.

40. DRIVEN

Monday 19 November 2012

Sunshine Coast, Queensland, Australia

'Bum! No reception.' The plover walking down the middle of the road took flight at Ben's outburst, ki-ki-kicking its own complaint.

In the rear of his van, Ben viewed the brutal security footage—a balaclava-clad figure forcing entry, backing Li into the kitchen, dropping him with a flurry of arms and fists, Liss cowering in a corner. The intruder unsheathed a knife and—the images churned Ben's stomach. Mac wasn't in them, thank God.

The external camera had captured the murderer undoing the utility's tray cover and meddling with a scuba tank.

Not good.

Ben checked his phone. Still no reception. He climbed through to the driver's seat. His phone and the DVR rode shotgun as he drove to the post office. He arrived moments before closing time, selected an Express Post Pack and sent the incriminating video on its way.

Ben tried phoning Chris again.

'The number you have dialled is currently unavailable. Press hash to send your number as a text message.'

Ben hashed as the street lights turned on. His phone rang as he reached the campervan again. 'Chris! Things are getting—'

'Murderous. I know. Mac's LIES. Are you—?'

'I got there after it happened. No sign of Mac or Bosworth. Security cameras recorded the murder. I took the DVR and posted it somewhere safe.'

'Mac identified Jake Leicester from the nanny-cam footage.'

'No. That's all I need.'

'That's good isn't it? Shows he's the murderer.'

'Jake Leicester's a fake ID. Some hacker stole my photo from my ASIO file.'

'You're kidding.'

'I wish. I searched room to room. That's my mug on nanny-cam. Have you any clue where Mac is now?'

'With Boswell. They're on the road. I'm scanning the incoming transmission now which says ... slow down ... prickly-pear ... discom-domdidom—?'

'What?'

'Beats me. Um ... Don't fight me, Mac. Trust me. Better all round if I drowned for real.'

'Aargh. I told Chassic Mac was suicidal.'

'Homicidal psycho. Lady in the cubby. Home blew up. Parents, brother killed. Drug syndicate. Two levels with a cliff. Ben, I know who—'

'I've got to move now if they're driving. Where are they?'

'Schoolies. Pumicestone Passage. Must be headed for Bullcock Beach to carry out their fake drowning ruse. Guzzling beer and Bozo scuba diving.'

'The murderer tampered with the scuba tanks.'

'No! Go, Ben. Now! Get there in time. You can't let her drown. I'm begging you.'

'I'm going, Bro. I'll switch to Bluetooth and pocket my phone. No GPS so call me back.'

BEN HOICKED his camper into gear, bounced it over the railway line and raced for the coast. Twilight's serenity mocked his desperate urgency as he skirted the lily-clad reaches of Ewen Maddock Dam and sped through a darkening tunnel of sub-tropical forest. He flew across the M1 overpass and burned the black ribbon that snaked through coastal scrub. And prickly pear.

The engine growled as the van climbed Little Mountain's rising prelude to ...

A dusk-clad panorama of oceanic ink.

And a 'Welcome to Caloundra' sign. Any other day!

Chris urged him towards a coastal stand of Norfolk Island Pines. Rainbow lorikeets trilled and screeched overhead; their volume matched Chris's as he yelled, 'Where are you now?' in Ben's ear, via Bluetooth.

'Crawling past Beachview Seafoods on The Esplanade. Schoolies are everywhere, stampeding the road.' The raucous crowd spilled over the boardwalk; their tension and excitement mirrored his own.

'Bozo parked at Happy Valley. Mac pondered the irony.'

'Sounds like Mac.'

Chris directed Ben to the parking area. 'Look for location markers on the beach. Bozo's getting his scuba gear on near 293.'

'I see it.' Ben galloped down the steps at the end of the boardwalk. 'Pile of clothes and shoes here. Bozo's already diving. Where's Mac going in?'

'I don't know. Transmissions are disjointed. Crowd's too much. She can't stay in the zone.'

'Crowd? Back near The Esplanade. Gotta run.'

'Drive. I'll direct you.'

Ben followed Chris's directions: 'Left into Lower Gay, take the dogleg, next left into—'

'Can't. Barricade.'

'Keep going straight ahead.'

'Can't. All blocked off. Right turn only. I shoulda run.'

'Then run.'

'Nowhere to park. I've taken a left into— Gah! Otranto's blocked too.'

'Next street sweeps back onto The Esplanade.'

'Got it.'

'Ben! Mac's going in. Where Bribie Island is closest. Near 298.'

Ben revved onto a grassy footpath, fled the van and ran. He battered through the block of bodies and bounded onto the boardwalk.

'Mac's drowning! Where the hell is Bozo? Where the hell are you?'

Ben couldn't answer. He was too busy ditching shoes, dashing down stairs and diving into the water.

41. DROWNED

Monday 19 November 2012

Sunshine Coast, Queensland, Australia

LIES/MXP2/20121119pm66777

BANSHEES, THE water's cold. Ease in, Mac. Slowly does it. Give the bozo lots and lots and lots of swimming time.

Who'd have thought Bozo had a family? Those poor kids.

This is insane. You better be round that sandbank, Brocko. You promised me. Used real words and everything. Stitched onto my soul, they are. Banked in my memory like an IOU. I expect to collect.

'Brrrrr!' Sooner rather than later, pleeeeeeease?

'Hack! Yuck!' Sea spit. Blerk. Come on Brock, you promised. Time to cough up.

'Cahough! Yuck!' You, not me.

Hey, remember our convo! I can. Verbatim. "Can't lose you now, Mac, even if you are a pain." That's what you said.

And I said, "What else would you do if you didn't have me to mind?" And you said you'd be a miserable cruddy drunk and that minding me had pushed you to get a life and for that, I'm a peach.

Sweet! I'm a sufferin' soggy peach right now. Come on, Brock. Hurry the truck up.

Whoa, current's dragging my shoes. I can't—

'Hack! Cahough!' Dragging dumb Chucks! Shoulda ditched the flippin'—

'Yacks! Shoes! Yikes!' Before—'Hack! Yuck!'—drimming drunk in, swimming punk in punka pumma ...

'What-the-hexit?' Floaty rock stuff. Pumma, pumma—

'Pumicestone Passage! Brock! F-hoc! Cahough! Yuck!'

Why'd I drink that vile beer? Salt sea and wombat pee. Vile as blerk'n—

'Brock. Help! Brock! Cohough!' *Air! Gah! Gotta get …*

…

Air … I'm …

…

Such an idiot trusting …

…

Pinstripe … Brock … Jake …

…

'No! Jake! Hock! Brock! Help! Cohack! Jake! Don't! Liss n blerk n blood n—aargh!'

'Don't fight me, Mac! Trust me!'

Must fight! 'Blerk n blood!' *Too much … too hard …*

Don't … fight … too … hard … just write …

Epi-taph …

Life … lousy … while it … lasted.

…

Drown dudn hurt …

…

Much.

…

Bludn Chucks.

…

NO SIGNAL DETECTED.

…

42. SHATTERED

19–20 November 2012

Canberra, Australia

'No! WHERE are you, Dro?' Chris gripped the computer monitor as if he could squeeze Mac's thoughts from it through sheer willpower.

NO SIGNAL DETECTED.

Silent red letters screamed from a mute screen, portents of disaster flashing on and off, like emergency lights on a fire truck—

Arriving too late!

Like Bozo.

Arriving too late!

Like Ben.

Arriving too late!

Like him.

NO SIGNAL DETECTED.

Nothing. Zip. Nada. Transmission had ceased.

Was Mac—? No! Please God, no. *I've just found her!* Could he be so cruel?

Chris tried phoning Ben again. 'Come on, Dro! Answer your phone!'

Bip-bip-bip-beeeeeeeeeeeeeep.

Chris's phone battery was dead. Dead as ... Ben? Mac?

'Amy-e-ee!' Anguish ripped her name from Chris's throat as he slammed his phone down. Its screen shattered.

Like its owner.

Chris implored, cajoled and screamed at the universe.

NO SIGNAL DETECTED.

What was the point! All this mind-boggling technology and they still couldn't save her.

Chris's fury craved direction. At who? Ben, for being too late? Chassic, for being too reluctant? Himself, for not pressing the point? His mother, for provoking the cartel's revenge? His father, for using Amy as a guinea pig? Why couldn't she have been normal?

How could he even think that? Chris punched his self-recriminations into the desk until the pain penetrated deep enough to smash his tear ducts. He sobbed and howled his grief until merciful exhaustion overtook him.

The jangle of the desk phone woke him. 'Huh?'

'Are you okay? I've been knocking on your door. Did you pull an all-nighter?'

'Sorry, Von.' He clicked his door open for her. 'I fell asleep.'

'Bad dreams?' She examined his bruised and bloodied fists and grimaced. 'You look as bad as your breath smells. Go home. Surely your project can wait a day.'

'It could wait a lifetime and never be fixed.'

'That's fatigue talking. I'll get you a coffee. That should wake you up enough to drive home safely.'

'I have to talk to HS.'

'He's in Spain, eight hours behind us. Wait till three to phone, if you must. Even then, he may be in conference. I'll get that coffee while you freshen up.'

Chris returned from the bathroom to find a tube of antiseptic cream, a box of Elastoplast flexible dressing strips and a hot coffee waiting on the floor outside his door.

He dressed his knuckles then imbibed online news with his coffee.

>>> Schoolies Prank Backfires <<<

Chris's heart sank. What did the report say?

Police quiz Schoolies over prank emergency calls. Local youths claimed they'd witnessed a drowning last night when an inebriated schoolie attempted to swim from Bullcock Beach to Bribie Island. No one could identify the alleged swimmer. Despite an extensive search and rescue effort, Emergency Services found no body. Police may fine the nuisance callers.

Chris also found a Police Seeking Information bulletin concerning suspicious deaths in Landsborough that had 'ruptured the tranquillity of the historic hinterland village'. Caloundra police had located a campervan on Tay Avenue that matched the description of one seen in the vicinity of the alleged crime. They urged the driver of the vehicle to contact them.

Other Sunshine Coast news reported the death of a mature-aged scuba-diver, presumably from a heart attack.

So Bosworth was dead, but there was nothing about finding Mac and Ben's bodies. Just the van. Surely Ben would have moved it if they were still alive. Unless they'd reached the long spit of sand and nature reserve at the northern tip of Bribie Island. Were they hiking for help? Chris chided himself for daring to hope. He should knock some sense into himself.

His throbbing knuckles disagreed.

Instead, he opened the GRUnGE. The words, 'No signal detected' flashed twice, and the screen went blank. A moment later, a new message took its place:

SIGNAL STRENGTH INSUFFICIENT TO TRANSMIT DATA.

PART FOUR

Beguiled
and
Betrayed

43. ACQUIRED

Monday 19 November 2012

Sunshine Coast, Queensland, Australia

FROM THE first cold shock to the last swim stroke between Ben's entry point and Mac's sinking point, Ben's mind chanted, save Mac, save Mac, save Mac. When he grabbed Mac's shirt, he did not expect a cat fight.

Mac scratched and gouged and flailed and howled like an underdog alley-cat.

'Oi! Don't fight me, Mac. Trust me.'

'Blood n blerk!' Mac squirmed, twisted loose and sank again.

Ben gulped air and dived. This time, he grabbed the back of Mac's jeans at the waist, and hauled for the surface. Both gasped for air.

'Quit struggling, mate. You'll drown us both.'

'I ... who ... I—' Mac passed out and floated face down.

Ben applied a vice grip turn and trawled for the shore. The current swept them towards a wooden dinghy trailing from a boardwalk pylon. Ben latched on to it as Mac came to. 'You're okay. I've got you. Just breathe, okay?'

'Jake?'

'Ben. Jake's a fake, a hack.'

'You killed—'

'No, Mac. I found them dead. Trust me. I'm trying to keep you alive.'

Mac slurped a breath and coughed it back.

Ben held tight. 'Easy, Mac. Relax. Breathe.'

'How? Who? You ... Why?'

'Long story. Later. Right now, don't drown.'

'Be easier in the boat.'

'It would.' Ben's attempt to boost Mac over the gunwale and into the dinghy failed. They both went under again.

'Not working, Ja— Ben. You get in and pull me up. My Chucks are anchors. What idiot swims in boots, right?'

Ben cracked a smile. He couldn't help it.

'Well, I'm glad you think I'm funny.'

'Just feisty.'

'Freezing, mostly. Can we get on with it?'

'Sure. Hold on here.' Ben pointed to the gunwale.

Mac obeyed.

Ben pulled himself and then Mac into the boat.

'Thanks.' She threw up all over him.

'YOU LOOKING for the shower blocks, mate? Wash off the spew? Hope's courtesy bus goes that way. I'm Nate. Red frog?'

Ben eyed the stranger cautiously, then realised he was a Red Frog Volunteer. 'Courtesy bus? I thought you guys walked schoolies back to their digs.'

'We do, but the Sunny Coast is spread out. Bert Adler, chaplain from Nambour, organised a free bus service here and back tonight.' Nate pointed to a Toyota Coaster with 'HOPE' painted on the side in big letters.

'Thanks, Nate. Sounds good. Come on, Mac.' Ben urged his new charge forward with a gentle hand to her upper arm. She obliged him only until they'd moved beyond Nate's earshot.

'What are you doing? I can't catch a bus with a stranger.'

'The driver's a chaplain, Mac. He'll have a Working with Children Blue Card.

'I meant you, not him.' Mac folded her arms.

Ben glanced toward his campervan, currently under police scrutiny. 'Mac, I need you to trust me on this. I'm ... Brock Bosworth's back up.'

Mac's eyes went wide. 'Really? He didn't mention you.'

'I can't help that. We should get to a safe house.' Ben was thinking on the fly. 'We're not safe out in the open.'

'The police are just there. We could—'

'Make a huge mistake trusting the wrong people.' Ben propelled

Mac towards the bus. 'I know what I'm doing. I rescued you, remember? I'll explain later. When you're safe.'

———◦———

BEN WAS glad Mac's transcripts had given him sufficient insight to sound like he knew the drill. She was cooperative but far from trusting.

Her appearance, albeit bedraggled, had totally thrown him. Far cry from the photo; her cap had covered audacious red curls, complemented by a cheeky net of freckles that could land a boat-load of admirers. If her eyes didn't drown them first … indigo-ringed, oceanic, beautiful, restless, immersive … Ben needed to surface, fast.

He went to chat with Bert.

By the time they'd reached Nambour, Ben had established an easy rapport with the driver who invited them back to the church hall where a small group of young adults reclined on swags. Most were asleep despite the fluorescent light illuminating the diehards chatting in the corner.

Bert had explained they formed the Hypotenuse Outreach Puppet Ensemble. HOPE's repertoire included educational and arts programs for schools and indigenous communities. They were leaving in the morning for a new Christmas tour. Bert's wife, Cassie, was the team's creative director, writer, and organiser. Bert wore several hats, including team chaplain and chief puppeteer. His favourite puppet, Potsherd Pavarotti, had been riding the bus's centre console.

'Cass? Cassie! Are you awake?' Bert tossed Pots, the puppet, in her direction.

Cassie snorted, opened one eye, bleared across Potsherd's bald spot and sighed. 'Pots, please tell Uncle Bert I am sound asleep and snoring.' She sat up anyway, hugging Pots.

'Told you she'd still be awake. Come on.' Bert advanced at a clip. 'Sorry to wake you, m'love, but I've acquired a pair of lost souls who need to ride with the tribe for a week or two or five. Mac? Ben?' Bert waved them closer. 'Meet HOPE's intrepid leader, my wonderful wife, Cassie Adler.'

Cassie fumbled for her glasses.

'They're brothers, backpacking out of Canberra. Had a slight mishap and need a hand. I figured we've got spare seats on the bus.

And spare swags.' Bert tilted his head and fielded a Good Samaritan face. 'Decent lads, I reckon.'

Ben had a feeling they stood beside a master of persuasion. Cassie's considered smile suggested her husband had done this sort of thing before.

She tutted. 'You look rather damp and bedraggled, poor things. Did it rain?'

'No, ma'am.' Ben dipped his head in salute. 'We scored an illicit dunking in a Schoolies Week prank. The current swept us south. We hitched a ride on the courtesy bus.'

'They lost all their gear, Cassie. Pretty lousy thing to happen on a holiday. I suggested they join the team for a bit.' Bert tipped his head towards a poster on the wall that said, "Truly I tell you, whatever you did for one of the least of these brothers and sisters of mine, you did for me. Matthew 25:40."

Cassie looked from Ben to Mac and back to Ben again. Her gaze was penetrating. Ben held his ground under her scrutiny, hoping she couldn't hear his thumping heart.

'We could use extra manpower shifting luggage.' Bert grinned. 'Seeing as you women outnumber us two to one.'

Cassie narrowed her gaze. 'Have you two *brothers* let your parents know what happened?'

Oops! Ben had overlooked his Mediterranean genetics. The contrast with Mac—

'They're dead,' Mac said. Blunt force trauma.

Ben gentled a protective hand onto Mac's shoulder. Unexpectedly, she leaned into him. 'We're on our own these days and more than happy to pull our weight.'

Mac nodded. 'What Ben said.'

Whether or not Cassie believed their story, she threw Pots back to Bert and found her feet. While Bert unrolled two extra swags, Cassie unearthed two pairs of pyjamas for them from the church's charity clothing stash—checks and stripes.

44. SPRUNG

Tuesday 20 November 2012

Queensland, Australia

'WHAT DO you mean, all the way? Wasn't this just a bed for last night?' Mac aimed a withering death stare at her unlikely saviour—who seemed to be winging it. 'What about your so called safe house, Ben-who's-not-the-fake-Jake? Is it fake too?'

'Brock's plan was compromised. I have to improvise. Travelling with these people makes sense.'

'To Central Australia? For six weeks? When I don't know them from a bar of soap?'

'If soap is your acid test, I must be Solvol. Last night you thought I was a murderer.'

'Well da-a-ah.' Mac folded her arms. 'You could be a cold-blooded sadist, perniciously delaying my demise to satisfy your warped ego.'

'By dragging you onto a bus full of potential witnesses?'

'I admit, that is a dumb move for a killer, although ... I don't know—'

'I'm not a killer, Mac.'

'I was going to say, I don't know how smart you are.'

'I'm beginning to wonder. Maybe I should've let you drown.'

'Maybe you should've talked to me *before* you agreed to go with them.'

'We're talking now.'

'And they're leaving in fifteen minutes. We could get a taxi back to your campervan.'

'The police were all over my van last night. Probably towed it. Besides, it's thirty kilometres away. Do you have that kind of cab fare on you?'

'No. I thought I could drown for free.'

Ben pressed his lips together as if biting back a retort.

Hmph. Gotcha.

'I'm sorry, Mac, but what's left of my soggy cash stash won't cut it either.'

'Great! The man with the plan is broke. I'm screwed.' *If it's sympathy he wants, I'm fresh out.*

'These people have offered us a free ride to Canberra—'

'Via Winton and Alice Springs.'

'With a team of young adults. We'll blend right in. Safety in numbers. It's our best option, Mac.'

'For you, maybe.'

'I promise I'll organise a permanent safe house for you when we reach Canberra. Till then, you'll just have to trust my judgement.'

'Sure. Like a two-legged stool.'

'I've heard those things are great for toning butt muscles.' Ben winked.

'Gah!' *And I thought Brock was infuriating.*

'Remember to fasten your seatbelt and you'll be fine. You're welcome.' Ben saluted and headed towards the growing collection of suitcases.

Fine? Hitching a ride with a bunch of churchy dudes and a dead-ringer for a murderer? Sheesh.

He's probably a serial killer. Or a lunatic.

Pity.

He's actually kind of cute.

In a rugged toreador sort of way.

Especially with that chin dimple.

Just sayin'.

———◦◦———

THE BUZZ of activity hassled Mac like a plague of Christmas beetles, trounced only by Tully and Sarah, in character as The Impatient Twins, Milly Nilly and Rilly Truly Reddy.

If they weren't rilly nilly outta there soon, she'd rilly truly rip their heads off. *The puppets, that is, not the girls, although—*

Judging by her expression, Cassie felt likewise.

'Oi, team! Heads up.' Bert's shout drew everyone's attention as he held his phone aloft. 'Our Tennant Creek contact's plugging for extra gigs Thursday night and Friday lunchtime. Our ETA was Friday night, but if we skip tourist breaks, we could get there Thursday morning. Whatcha think? I need to ring him back.'

There was a positive murmur.

'So who's happy to make a beeline for Tennant Creek?' Most hands went up. 'What's up, Eli?'

'It's too much for one bus driver, Bert.'

'Don't forget, I drive the bus too, when I have to,' Cassie said.

'Our Cass is definitely a driving force, amen?' Bert blew her a kiss. 'We'll share and catnap. Reach Barcaldine by midnight. Sleep at Barkly Homestead Wednesday night.'

'Still an exhausting schedule, even for two drivers.' Eli glanced around as if gauging support.

Ben raised his hand. 'My licence is MR heavy vehicle class. And it survived my dunking.'

Bert nodded. 'Thanks, Ben. That makes three drivers. Eli?' Bert held his palms open.

'I was mainly thinking of you and Cassie, Bert. Most of us only have regular vehicle licences.'

'I have a motorcycle licence.'

'Go, Sarah!' Eli offered a high-five. 'Not enough wheels for a bus though, even with trainers.' He ducked when her returned high-five went wild.

She poked her tongue at him. He winked. 'If Ben's happy to drive, I'm good to go.'

'Okay then.' Bert double-clapped his hands. 'Let's get this show on the road.'

While Ben pitched in with the pack-up, Mac hovered, live-chook-in-a-plucking-shed awkward till Cassie offered an out.

'Could you pop my handbag onto a bus seat for me, please?'

'Sure thing.' Mac grabbed the bag. 'Anything else I can do to help?'

'Nah.' Cassie shook her head. 'We're old hands at this. Pick a spot you like, and we'll sit together. Don't worry. I only bite when the moon is full.'

Mac needed no second bidding.

MAC SAT behind Bert, secretly hoping Ben would sit with her. Her dagger stare missed its mark as he settled beside Bert, oblivious. Cassie boarded last.

'Want the window, Cass?'

'Aisle's fine, so I can subdue the rabble in a hurry. Speaking of which—' Cassie turned. 'Seatbelts on, everybody?'

'Yes, Miss Cassie!' A good-humoured chorus replied.

'If not,' Bert yelled, 'don't forget to wave as you—'

'Fly through the windscreen!' A dozen voices synced.

Bert honked the horn. The Coaster leapt forward.

Mac stared out the window, courting paranoia over Cassie's apparent concern. Or scrutiny. 'Do your puppets teach maths stuff to kids?' Mac jumped at the sound of her own voice. She hadn't planned to talk.

'Teach, yes. Maths, no. We use fun and music to promote hope, positivity and a love for literature through our school programs. This trip is a Christian outreach tour, so our sketches will express our faith.' Cassie's smile seemed oddly familiar.

That's weird, considering we've never met.

Cassie tilted her head and mirrored Mac's quizzical expression.

Sprung! Mac dropped her eyes. 'Isn't hypotenuse a geometrical term?' Her glance caught Cassie's nod, and another smile. *Phew!*

'It's part of the right-angled triangle which symbolises HOPE's purpose.'

'How?'

'The vertical axis represents our link with God, our hope in him as Christians.'

'My mum was a Christian.' *That's it! Cassie smiles just like Mum did.* 'You remind me of her. Not to look at. More your voice and the way you talk. You do this quick laugh thing, like she did. As if your happy bursts out just because it can.'

'How about that?' Cassie tilted her head. 'Similar backgrounds perhaps? My family moved to Sydney when I was eight. People pegged us as Queenslanders by our idioms and easy interaction with neighbours and strangers. Although, it might have been a polite way to call us country bumpkins.' Cassie winked. 'Cocktail frankfurts vs. cheerios.'

'As long as they're dipped in tomato sauce, not ketchup, who cares?'

'Exactly.' Cassie was a natural at easy interaction.

Mac relaxed a notch. 'We lived in a couple of states, but I can't say where my mum was born. She was murdered when I was a kid.'

'Mac, I'm so sorry.'

'Why? You weren't to blame. My foster parents were murdered too. I can't tell you about that either. It's safer if you don't know. I wouldn't want to jinx you. Might mess up your happy.'

'Like it's messed up yours?' Cassie's smile had vanished. Or been banished.

'Happy is overrated.' Prickly pear.

'Do you think so?' Cassie's expression was inscrutable, but her eyes were soft.

'I wish I knew.' Mac sighed. 'About hypotenuse, you were saying?'

'I was, wasn't I?' Amusement tickled the corners of Cassie's eyes. 'I rarely finish a sentence, let alone an explanation, when this mob's on the hop.'

Mac grinned and raised her hands to mimic a kangaroo. 'I'm all ears, listening and twitching.'

Cassie saluted. 'Vertical axis—hope in God. The horizontal axis represents our desire to reach and teach positive life skills. The hypotenuse links the hope we have in God with the hope we offer people.'

'Clever. Wordplay and mission statement combined. Do you have a logo?'

'Yup. Eli designed it.' Milly Nilly's puppeteer appeared beside them. 'Hi, I'm Tully. Mac, isn't it?'

Mac nodded. 'You're with Sarah, right?'

'When we're being the Impatient Twins. We mix and match it up a bit. Except for Egermeier. He's Eli's alter ego. And Bert is Pots.'

'That's the bearded bald one, right? Bert introduced us last night.'

'Yeah. Pots is cool. Ever operated a puppet, Mac? You're welcome to try. We can always use extras when the gang is singing.'

'Me? Sing? I have enough trouble talking. Late developer, after I got my cochlear implant.'

'Wow! That's awesome!' Tully had increased her volume. 'I would never have guessed you were deaf! Tongue-tied, maybe.'

'I can hear you fine.' Mac grinned and tapped behind her ear. 'Processor attached.'

'And I'm shouting!' Tully face-palmed. 'My bad. But you don't have to sing. We use recorded music. Even if you suck at moving mouths, you can jig and dance a puppet. It's loads of fun.'

'I'll think about it.'

Tully tapped a fingered hashtag. 'Don't strain your brain! Hey, Cass, when's our first break? Will my bladder survive another can of Coke?'

'If you're desperate for a pit stop, Gympie in fifteen minutes. We'll stop at Gin Gin for lunch around one.'

Tully turned and yelled, 'Who else needs a pee-break at Gympie?'

—◦—

TYRES PLY *the highway,*
  Radial banded hymns skim
  the blacktop, singing revolutionary odes to—

'Choices, places, freedom.' Mac pointed to Cassie's notebook. 'Sorry. That's rude of me, reading over your shoulder.'

'Not at all. That's a great line. Would you like to collaborate?'

'Love to.' Mac grinned. Time evaporated while she and Cassie created a kaleidoscope of word pictures together.

Cows play chess on green and gold chequerboards.
Farmers sow crops into earthy eiderdowns.
Vistas whisper—

'This is fun, Cass, collaborating, I mean. Reminds me of the Christmas my brother gave me a Prismacolor pencil set so I could draw characters for him to animate on the computer.'

'You're an artist too? You're certainly a gifted poet.'

'I dabble. Words are my preferred medium.'

'Me too. Want to hang on to these?' Cassie moved to tear the pages out.

Mac touched her arm. 'You keep them, please. I'm content to remember the experience.' Not to mention the surprising affinity she felt for someone she'd just met. 'Thanks, Cass. This was ... special.'

Cass covered Mac's hand with her own. 'It was.'

'Ta-da! Gin Gin, folks.' Bert pulled the bus into a parking area. 'Famous for being halfway between Brisbane and Rockhampton. And for growing sugar cane.'

184

'Thereby contributing to an appalling obesity epidemic.' Sarah stood in the aisle, hands on hips.

'Give a hand to our fix-the-world-with-a-whim-and-a-prayer Sarah as she takes the podium, folks.' Eli clapped. Sarah curtsied magnanimously.

'No doubt the farmers are too busy making ends meet to overthrow the world's dubious consumption habits,' Ben said.

Sarah offered Ben an exaggerated bow replete with opulent hand flourishes. *Mais oui, Monsieur.* On zat point, *mon ami*, I will 'appily concede defeat.'

'Good,' said Tully. 'Because de rest of us want to put de feet off de bus to eat de food at de local cafe, okay sweet-ay?' She wrapped her arms around Sarah from behind and penguin-walked her to the stairs.

A supermarket across the street caught Mac's eye. 'Cassie?'

'That's me.'

Mac pointed to the supermarket. 'I'd like to get a toothbrush and stuff.'

'Sure, if you're quick.' Cassie made to stand up.

'Um, could I borrow some money for that?'

Cassie sat back again. 'I'm sure our budget can cover a few toiletries for you and Ben.'

'And maybe another change of clothes if there's an op shop open? We'll pay you back.' The church charity shelf had been well stocked with clothes in Ben's size, but not extra-small men's.

'Our contact in Tennant Creek runs an op shop. We don't have time to shop for clothes here, but I'll talk to Sarah. She's about your size and shape and always packs more clothes than she needs.'

'Girls clothes?'

'Really, Mac? Are you going to argue with me about that?'

Should she?

'Come and eat first, then you and Ben can purchase toiletries.'

Mac shared an outdoor table with Ben and Cassie, listening to their small talk and banter as she ate. The cafe burger was delicious. She licked the barbecue sauce that dribbled between her ring finger and pinkie.

'Sounds like you've had a rough trot, Ben, since your mum passed away. It's difficult to lose a loved one, especially a mother.'

'She's not dead. She walked out on us. It's my father that's—'

Uh-oh. Mac glared at Ben.

Cassie smiled innocently. 'Would you two *brothers* like a moment to compare your recollections?'

Ben studied the crumbs on the table. Cassie excused herself to go to the bathroom.

———◦◦◦———

'SHE'S RIGHT about one thing, Mac. We do need to talk.' Ben raised an eyebrow.

'Well, duh! I told you that this morning, but you were too busy throwing me on the bus with this mob.'

'At least I didn't throw you under it. Don't tempt me now.'

'We could've hitchhiked to your van.'

Ben sighed. 'How old are you, Mac?'

'Old as my tongue. Older than my teeth. What of it?'

'I was led to believe Aidan MacGreggor was eighteen. But that's not your real identity any more than Jake Leicester is mine.'

'So you say. Technically, Aidan drowned last night.'

'But you didn't. You might be a year twelve graduate—'

'How do you know that?'

'Schoolies? After an accelerated home-school study program perhaps?'

'Maybe.'

'So you're a smart cookie, but not yet eighteen.'

'It's none of your business how old I am.'

'Typical no-go area for women over twenty-four and girls approaching sixteen. My guess: you're fourteen. Ow! Punching me confirms it. Ow! Stop it, kiddo.'

'Don't call me kiddo.'

'Fifteen then.'

'Wrong again, smarty-pants. I'm sixteen. Oh, batpoo! I'm not supposed to tell!'

'Don't worry Mac. Your secret's safe with me.'

'I don't know that. I hardly know you.'

'Well I turn twenty-two next month, which is a very good reason for not taking an attractive sixteen-year-old girl with me to Canberra in a campervan.'

'Oh. I didn't think of that. Been channelling teenage boy too long. But Jake Leicester would know that.'

'I'm not Jake Leicester.'

'Then how'd you know my name? How'd you know where to find me? Do you work for Talbot Locke?'

'You know Locke?'

'I've met him. Twice. He's federal police—'

'Witness protection liaison. I met him through my work.'

'If Locke sent you after me, why didn't we talk to the police at Caloundra?'

'I don't work for Agent Locke, Mac. I work for a Government-sanctioned special projects team, or I did. Technically I'm AWOL. And Locke denied any knowledge of you.'

'Then how could you possibly know—?'

'Like I said, it's a long story.'

'Don't give me that claptrap again. If you want me to trust you, 'fess up, big brother. Now!'

'I'd like to hear that confession too, Ben.'

'Bert!'

'Tell me, Ben. This newspaper photo, is it you?'

45. DERAILED

Tuesday 20 November 2012

Queensland, Australia

BEN READ the headline:

>>> Double Homicide at Landsborough <<<

The nanny-cam had captured his grim expression brilliantly.

Bert and Cassie's expressions were equally grim.

'Well?' said Bert. 'The picture quality might be poor, but the resemblance is obvious. Give me one good reason why I shouldn't escort you to the local police station immediately.'

They're closed for lunch? One could hope. 'Honestly, Bert, I'd take myself there if not for Mac. She's in grave danger and I'm responsible for her safety.'

Cassie frowned. 'Isn't that more reason to involve the police?'

'Normally, yes,' Ben replied. 'But our situation is far from normal. Please, sit down.' They didn't. 'I won't run. If I may?' He removed his body belt and retrieved his ASIO identity card, both of his driver's licences, and three damp newspaper clippings. He placed them on the table. 'My identity documents. Benjamin Jaime Alejandro on one licence. ASIO employee Benson James King on the others.'

'You're a spy? Wow! That's awesome!' Mac face-palmed. 'That's why you know stuff about me.'

'So much for being siblings.' Cassie glared censure.

Mac closed one eye sheepishly.

'Two different IDs? If anything, that's more worrying.' Bert huffed.

Cassie sat and leaned in for a closer look. 'Which one's legitimate, if any?'

'They're both legitimate,' Ben said, 'except officially, Benjamin Alejandro is dead.'

'Really? Me too. Twice now.'

Bert and Cassie gaped.

Mac shrugged, nonchalant. 'Sometimes it's easier to be dead.'

'You both look pretty lively to me.' Bert scratched his head as he also sat. 'Wouldn't the police confirm your status, Ben?'

'It's complicated. I was seconded from ASIO to work for a confidential project team which can legally deny its own existence and my connection to it. I could face criminal charges for even speaking about it.'

'Based on this newspaper article, that's exactly what you'll face if you don't.' Bert folded his arms.

'Has your project endangered Mac?' Cassie asked.

'I don't know. She's certainly connected to it.'

Mac looked mystified. 'I know nothing about it.'

Cassie pursed her lips. 'Ben, I appreciate your dilemma over confidentiality. As Christian ministers, Bert and I are obliged to keep confidences, barring intent to harm. I assure you, we'll consider your information discreetly and responsibly.'

'And then?' Ben held his breath.

'We'll trust the Lord, and our instincts, to decide what happens next,' Bert said.

What choice did he have? 'Mac, can I ask you for similar consideration?'

'Consideration!' Mac's eyes sparked, and her cheeks flamed. 'You want consideration! My family got blown up. My carers were slashed to pieces. My minder left me to drown. I'm dead. You're dead. And, for all I know, Pluto knocked off Jupiter. But alive or dead, Ben, Ben or boogie-man, you'd better blab like a howler monkey or I'll consider you with my fist!'

Hello, Miss Spitfire! Ben reined in a wry smile. 'When you put it that way … So Bro? Dro here. I hope you're getting all of this. Tell HS I've exhausted my options.'

Mac's eyes grew wide. 'You're wearing a recording device?' She scanned the surroundings.

For mythical suits in shades?

'No, Mac.' Ben shook his head. 'You are.'

THREE SCEPTICAL faces eyeballed Ben.

'I write drama but this takes the cake. Hold up a mo.' Cassie pointed to the HOPE team, who were shuffling around the bus. 'I'll send Sarah and Eli to the supermarket for your essentials. The others can take a stroll around the town centre.' She stood. 'Stay put. I'll be back. This is some story.'

'Far-fetched, even to me,' Bert said. 'And I live with Cassie's wild imagination.'

'Essentials?' Ben looked to Mac.

'Toiletries and undies. For me at least.'

If Ben walked the tightrope, Mac was the wind shear. Ironically, her unpredictable responses both challenged and enhanced his credibility as he described the car explosion that had prompted his decision to go AWOL.

He carefully unfolded the newspaper cuttings. The first named Benjamin Alejandro, only son of the late Patriarca Alejandro, as the driver killed in the incident. The next, an obituary, described Pat's 'commitment to the advancement of medical technologies and dedicated service to his country'. The third described the 2006 cartel-bombing of Dr Alastair Maxwell and his family.

The blood drained from Mac's face as she read. 'Only we didn't all die in the explosion. My brother wasn't home. He tried to reach us, but collided with a truck and died from head injuries. I wanted to die too when I found out. Locke's Wit Pro solution's been slowly killing me ever since. So unfair! I'm the one locked up and silenced. The crims got off scot free!'

'Not for long. Not if I can help it.' Ben grimaced. 'But for now we need to remain vigilant, not to mention cautious and discreet. Have you any idea who's behind the latest threat?'

'You, posing as Jake, according to the mugshot Locke showed me. I've no idea how any of this connects me with ASIO.' Mac contemplated Ben. 'I do know your father's name. Patriarca? It's unusual.'

'How do you know it, Mac?' He gently touched her hand.

She withdrew it. 'I had problems with my cochlear implant. He came to the hospital with Dad. When he saw how long it took me to sign Mr Alejandro in Auslan, he suggested I call him Pat, and he patted his shoulder. I'm sad to hear he died. He was nice.'

'Mac, our fathers developed a prototype implant that improves communication for people with aural and oral impairment. Your father designed the medical implant. Mine developed the electronic interface and software that synthesises brain impulses into text. He died before he'd finalised the software. I took over. If we could create text from simulated data, we planned to initiate live trials.'

Bert whistled. 'Are you suggesting this technology might be able to convert brain waves directly into speech one day?'

'Into text. And the technology already works.'

'How do you know?' Cassie asked.

'When I finished the software, I discovered a living person generated our signal samples. I had no idea who. That knowledge died with my father. It was only by the grace of God, I think, that I found him. Her. You, Mac.'

'What!' Mac's stare could have chilled a kiln. 'You lousy, lying con-man son-of-a—'

'Mac!' Bert's interruption activated Mac's dagger look.

'Benson, Benjamin or Jake the Fake. You expect me to believe that hogwash? He's gotta be lying, Cassie. Agent Locke reckoned Jake was grooming me for a paedophile ring.'

'I am not Jake Leicester! Someone hacked my ASIO file for that photo.' Ben clenched his fists. 'I don't know who or why. I can only speculate. Someone wanted to keep tabs on you or keep tabs on the LIES program through you. I'm a victim here too.'

'Lies program!' Mac's eyes flashed fire. 'Lies! You're beyond lies! You're ludicrous!'

'I know it sounds far-fetched, but screaming at me won't change the truth.'

'Maybe this will!' Mac's fist connected full force with Ben's nose. The shock was stunning! Ben's eyes watered.

'Mac!' Bert and Cassie yelled together.

Ben squeezed his nose to staunch the blood. Bert offered him a handkerchief. He wiped the blood away and dabbed another dribble before continuing. 'I'm sorry. I didn't mean to provoke you, Mac, but I'm not lying.'

Mac was fuming. 'Prove it! You reckon you can read my thoughts? Do it. Do it now. Tell me what I'm thinking.'

'You'd like to throttle me, but I don't need software for that. It's written on your face.' He wiped another drip and sighed. 'Your LIES transcripts are in a protected computer file, accessible only via a secure computer connection. I left my laptop in the van when I dived into Pumicestone Passage to save your scrawny hide.'

Mac geared up for a second punch.

'Please, Mac,' Bert said. 'Let Ben finish his explanation. Without provoking the lady please, Ben.'

Mac scowled at Bert. 'Meanwhile, I'm freaking out. What if your thoughts were recorded on a stranger's computer? Wait. If it's in the van, can the police read my mind too? Screeching banshees. This is going from bad to worse. You're killing me here, Ben. Please, please admit you're lying. I won't hit you if you just tell the truth.'

'The police can't access the files. There's only one other person who can.' Ben turned to Bert. 'May I borrow your phone and call him?'

Bert reached for his phone.

'Wait.' Mac narrowed her eyelids. 'How do we know you won't call an accomplice to pull you out of here?'

'I guess you'll have to trust me. Again. How else can I prove that the STIR implant and the LIES transcripts exist?'

'Tell me what I thought about. I remember everything. I'll know if you're lying.'

All eyes locked on Ben. He locked onto Mac's. Despite her obvious displeasure, they were still incredibly beautiful. He cleared his throat. 'You listen to Green Day, songs like *Boulevard of Broken Dreams* that resonate with your experience, your isolation. You thought Brock Bosworth—you called him Bozo, but rarely to his face—looked like a Titicaca Scrotum frog. I had to Google that. Poor bloke.' Ben grimaced. 'You're smart. Cynical. Have an exceptional memory.' He paused.

Mac bounced her legs and jiggled the table. 'I told you I was smart. The Green Day thing? A spy could've hacked my phone's playlist. You said you were Bosworth's backup plan. I told Jake on chat about a frog called Bozo. You could've discovered all that without mind-reading. What do I dream about?'

'The STIR implant doesn't transmit dream impulses. It doesn't record every thought. It requires intent to communicate, either with someone else, or with yourself. Speaking, listening, reading, writing, your reflections, contemplations, prayers.'

Mac folded her arms. 'Not convinced.'

Ben took a deep breath and closed his eyes. 'You like the name Ariel, no, Arianna. You'd rather be a writer than a hairdresser, but you don't want to write ordinary stuff. How'd you put it? You were thinking about trains, how their journey was linear, ordered, like an essay. How you loved stories because they weren't constrained like that, but could transcend time. In your heart of hearts, you want to write— No! You want to *become* a story that can jump tracks—'

'Without derailing.' They said the words together.

Ben opened his eyes and sought Mac's. He held her gaze for several, intense seconds, imploring, longing, till she broke the connection.

Mac looked to Cassie then back again, blanched and morphed through a decorator's crimson colour chart.

'I've never told anyone that.' Her voice trembled as she spoke. 'You really have been inside my head. You ... I ... you ... a total stranger knows my thoughts? Only you're not a stranger. You're right here. In my face.' Her pitch had risen with every phrase. 'Oh, my God! You know! How embarrassing. I'm gonna die. For real.'

She threw up instead.

46. RALLIED
Tuesday 20 November 2012

Queensland, Australia

BEN SWEATED Bert and Cassie's private discussion, incredulous that they were actually considering keeping himself and Mac on board.

'Want to know what they're saying?'

'I would, but I can't read their minds.'

Mac's expression was conspiratorial. 'I can lip read. Enough to get the gist.' She winked and focussed on their faces.

Mac's mood changes were dizzying. Ben's head spun.

'Bert's worried about their travel deadline. Must make a decision. Cass's arguing legal obligation to turn you in.'

Ben groaned.

'Bert reckons you should be presumed innocent. Why, I don't know.'

'I'm dead meat.'

'Maybe. Cass likes that you saved me from drowning. Far-fetched story ... psycho ... innocent by virtue of insanity. Ha! I like the way Cass thinks.'

Ben swallowed billiard balls. Cassie was staring at the sky.

'She said a sign from the Lord would be good about now. She's kidding right?'

'I dunno. They're pretty heavenly minded.'

'Bert's turned side on. Shuffle over so I can see his face.'

Ben obliged.

'He's checking his phone's ... Bible App? Something about Rahab hiding spies in Jericho. Who's Rahab?'

'Not now, Mac. What else is Bert saying?'

'Mary and Joseph carried Jesus to Egypt, away from King Herod's rampage. But Cassie reckons they're no more Mary and Joseph than you are Jesus.'

Cassie was rubbing her temples. Ben shared her headache.

Bert squatted under the tree and buried his face in his hands. Cassie was sky-gazing again.

'Looks like they're praying.'

'Nah. Cassie's talking about a wild platypus.'

'You must have misread.'

'Did not! Cassie said it came and went like a glance ... could have missed it with a blink, but we didn't ... see how Ben and Mac looked at each other ... intense ... You wanted to gaze into ...'

'What, Mac?'

'Nothing.' Mac blushed.

'Nothing?'

Bert stood up and embraced his wife.

'They're being lovey-dovey.'

'Lovey-dovey?'

Mac cleared her throat. 'It's okay. They think we might be—'

'What?' Ben could see they were still talking, but Mac was not sharing. 'Be what, Mac?'

'Be allowed to go with them. Into the desert.'

'Seriously?' Ben couldn't read Mac's enigmatic expression.

Mac shrugged. 'Apparently. But Cassie wants to speak with our mutual Federal Police friend for clarification. Question is, will he acknowledge either of us? Bert wants to get moving, so she'll try now.'

On cue, Bert walked towards them. 'I'll rally the troops. We've miles to cover before midnight.'

Ben had no trouble hearing that.

———

DRIVING HIGHLIGHTED the knot in Ben's neck muscles, but he was thankful for Cassie's diplomacy and relieved he'd avoided a jail cell. She'd spoken to Locke's assistant without divulging delicate information, explaining who HOPE was, that they'd collected two backpackers who lacked Working with Children Blue Card certification, but they both claimed to know Mr Locke.

Apparently the assistant's response had satisfied Cassie. Ben had immediately offered to drive the Gin Gin to Rockhampton leg—he'd caused enough delay—giving Bert time to nap in the rear of the bus.

They stopped for fuel and ablutions at Gracemere and collected a one-meal-fits-all selection from MacDonald's to go.

'If we eat Macca's for six weeks, I'll have to hit the Boxing Day sales for a plus-size wardrobe.' Sarah chomped her Big Mac with relish.

'I could eat your fries,' Eli said.

'You will not.' Sarah tucked them in her lap.

'I'm only thinking of your figure.' Eli blushed when Motto's wolf whistle highlighted his double entendre. 'It is worth thinking about.' He winked at Sarah. She blushed.

'Are Sarah and Eli an item?' Ben asked Bert.

'Not that I know of. But I'm usually the last to know things like that.' Bert chewed and swallowed his last French fry. 'If that's dinner, I've had it, like my nana nap, thanks to you. I'll drive the next leg. After two consecutive La Niña's, the roos are as thick as flies. The road trains litter the road with carcasses. Last trip, road kill was so thick we had to weave in and out and over. A big red on the Barkly busted the luggage trailer's axle. We had to unload the luggage, unhook the trailer, undo the axle, and drive an hour back to Camooweal for a temporary welding fix. Lost half a night and most of the next day.'

With Bert at the helm, Ben moved towards the back. Cassie was sitting with Tully which left a spare seat beside Mac.

'Mind if I join you?'

Mac shrugged her shoulders. 'Suit yourself. I should warn you, I'm not feeling chatty.'

'Then I'll nap, in case I need to drive later.'

Ben stretched his neck, wriggled his shoulders, rested his head, closed his eyes and breathed deeply. He'd read somewhere that breathing in for a count of four, holding for eight and exhaling for seven could induce sleep. Mac nudged him on his fourth breath.

'Are you really an ASIO agent?'

He opened one eye. 'Last time I looked.'

'You're not very James Bond-ish.'

'James Bond is not an ASIO agent. He's a fictional character. You should know that.' Ben closed both eyes again and tried another deep breath.

'So what do you do exactly?'

'I can't tell you exactly.'

'Right. Because then you'd have to kill me.'

Ben smiled. 'That's what my dad used to say.'

'Was Pat a spy too? Wow! That must have been cool growing up.'

'I didn't know he was a spy back then. I only found out later.'

'After you joined ASIO?'

'More or less.'

'But you had a hunch before then.'

'Yeah, I had a hunch.' Ben opened his eyes and gazed out the window. It had been much more than a hunch. He'd imagined a new scenario for every work-related absence, with his dad as the Bond-like liberator of innocents, saving the world from diabolic malefactors. At home, his dad was so gentle and normal and dad-like, Ben would pooh-pooh his idea as ridiculous.

'Can you hint? About what you do, I mean. As a spy project, I deserve some insider goss. Did you have to go to spy school?'

'I thought you were in no mood to chat.'

'I don't want to appear rude.'

'That horse already bolted.' Ben dropped his arm to his side, half expecting a jab.

Mac lifted her nose in the air. 'It is a woman's prerogative to change her mind.' Then she clapped her hands. 'Ha! I've waited a lifetime to say that!'

Ben grinned. 'Fair enough.'

'So did you go to spy school?'

'ASIO recruited me from year twelve via a special program. It was on-the-job training.'

'ASIO spy training must be a snip.'

'Why do you say that?'

'You're twenty-one right?'

'For now.'

'Say you were eighteen when you joined. That's only three years.'

'You're a maths whiz too. Ow!' Ben rubbed the rib Mac elbowed. 'I keep forgetting how touchy— No! I'm sorry. Really.' Ben hugged himself protectively.

'Yeah, you look it. And you can wipe the smirk off your face.'

Ben obediently mimed a face wipe. 'I was fast-tracked because of the LIES Program. Our special team is separate to ASIO.'

'So you're special, huh? Like me.' Mac pulled a horrible funny face.

'No. I'm more special than you.'

'But I'm smaller than you, which means there's less of me to be special in, so I'm more concentrated special.'

Ben guffawed. 'Outsmarted again.'

Mac smirked and smiled smugly.

For several minutes Ben watched dusk silhouette the montage of grass, trees and scattered cattle into nocturnal mystery, enjoying the pace and space as the highway skirted the edge of the Brigalow belt.

Mac stretched and sighed.

'Penny for your thoughts?' Ben asked.

'So you'll pay me for them when you can't steal them.'

'Oh! Low blow, but awesome aim.' Ben doubled up as if in agony, even though Mac hadn't touched him. 'I'm hurting here.'

'You should be.' She poked her tongue at him. 'Experience it from my perspective.'

'If it's any consolation, I made every effort to contact you once I knew you were real.'

Mac burst out laughing.

Ben had not expected that. 'That's funny? I agonised over it. Talk about an ethical dilemma. I lost sleep.'

Mac hauled in her hilarity. 'I'm sorry, Ben. When you knew I was real? See the irony?'

'No.'

'I must be the most unreal person on earth.'

'Oh.' Ben offered a lopsided grin.

Mac folded her arms. 'Considering I'm the social retard, being isolated and all, you're not real good at this banter thing are you? Are you an only child?'

'Yes. And no.'

'You can't be both.'

'I was my parents' only child. My father's ward lived with us. I thought of him as my brother.'

Mac looked thoughtful. 'My brother would have been twenty-one if he'd lived.'

'Do you …' Ben hesitated. 'Do you want to tell me about him? Was he like you?'

'He called himself the Ordinary Mac—' Mac drew her breath

sharply and covered her mouth with her hands. 'Oh, you're good. ASIO interrogations one-oh-one, right?'

'I'm not interrogating you, Mac. I'm happy to listen if you want to talk. You haven't been able to discuss yourself or your family for so long. That's painful. I know.'

'How can you know? You had a real family.'

'Maybe I don't know firsthand. But my brother never talked about his past. His self-imposed silence ate him up. And closed him off. He wouldn't let anyone in.'

'Maybe his silence wasn't self-imposed. I know what that's like.'

'You two should meet one day.'

'I'd like that.'

'Are you any good at gaming, Mac?'

'You mean like computer games and such? Not really. Why?'

'Chris is the most awesome gamer I know. Head and shoulders above the rest.'

'Chris? Whoa! That's like—' Mac bit her thumb knuckle. 'I hate secrets.'

'Forced or self-imposed?'

'Both. I'm sorry, Ben. I want to tell you. But my past life is supposed to be dead and buried.'

'I'm more concerned about your present life. Which has attracted the spurious attention of a murderer. Whether he wants you alive or dead, I doubt his motives are altruistic.'

'And yours are?'

'Well, I'm trying.' Ben surrendered, open palmed.

'You're definitely trying. But I'm learning to tolerate you anyway.'

'Tolerate me? Listen here Miss Smarty-pants. I've lost my phone, computer, money, clothes, means of transport and my identity. I've risked my job, my neck, and my freedom for a cantankerous mystery woman who won't trust me as far as she can throw me. I'm headed for woop woop with a bunch of happy-clappy strangers. I've no clue when or where the next threat will erupt, whether it will kill me first or you, or how high the stakes are. But I've pretty much bet everything I have and am on you, Mac. How can I convince you my motives are honourable, and your secrets are safe with me?' Ben thumped his knees.

Mac exhaled slowly. Her arresting expression begged eye contact. *I could so easily dive right into your eyes, girl, and forget to breathe.*

He crossed his arms instead.

'You know what's weird?' she said.

'What isn't weird right now?'

'Someone's out to kill me. I've been tumble-dried and hung out to dry. My future, should I live so long, is an unknown quantity. Heck, I don't even have a calculator. But here, now, on this bus, going who knows where with who knows who, is the safest I've felt in a very, very long time.'

Ben indulged a slow blink before he answered. 'I think we can trust these people.'

Mac closed one eye and nodded slowly. 'Besides, they bought us clean undies. Gotta be thankful for that.'

'Amen.' He smiled and closed his eyes again.

This time, she let him nap.

47. DUPED

Tuesday 20 November 2012

Canberra, Australia

NEW LIES transmissions converting to text! Chris's relief was palpable. At least Dro had made a decent fist of things.

Chris flexed his knuckles and winced. His funk had departed. The bellyache from his adrenaline rush hadn't—three loo trips in thirty minutes—with no bad prawns or booze to blame. What a mess. What a stuff up.

'And the plumbers are on convention in Coocooboonah.'

'Where's that?'

'Von! Snuff my living daylights!'

She tapped his open door. 'You never learn, do you? I thought you'd gone home.'

'That was your suggestion.'

'So you stayed. Coocooboonah plumbers?'

'Did I say that out loud?' Chris face-palmed. 'It was metaphoric! I need to clear a mess of—'

'Oh. I getcha. Anything I can do to help?'

'You could get me a peppermint double shot affogato from that new coffee place around the corner? I could use a caffeine hit.'

'That's a sugar hit.' Von collected the first aid stuff. 'You've had enough hits for one day. I'll bring you another white-n-one from the lunch room. Say ta!'

'Ta, Von.' Chris locked his door.

For several hours, he glued himself to the computer. The disjointed nature of Mac's transcripts suggested her processor was still cutting in and out, but she was alive and apparently safe. For now.

Ben, on the other hand, was a pickle in vinegar.

Call me, Dro! I'll convince them you're legit.

Screamin' piglets! Ben would call his mobile. The one he'd smashed. He had to replace it. Quickly.

And get a better temper tether. His blowouts had fouled things up again. He added a message to the GRUnGE about getting his phone fixed, in case Ben connected online.

Another LIES transmission arrived.

LIES/MXP2/20121120pm52564

Okay, Ben's bro! I know all about your stinking LIES project. Don't you dare read my mind, you low-down snake-belly eavesdropping [censored]. My thoughts are my business. Capiche? So get your [censored] eyes and nose out of it before I detach them from your face. Transcribe one [censored] [censored] word or comma, I'll sue the knackers off ASIO. Then I'll take yours and—

Chris crossed his legs reflexively. Whoa! Mac had a potty mouth. Or head. No wonder Ben had instigated an auto-censor.

The office phone's sudden jangle pinched a pair of heartbeats before he answered with, 'Darnell here.'

'Mr Darnell, I'm glad I caught you. It's Talbot Locke, NWPP Liaison?'

'Mr Locke. Your PA said you were away.'

'I check in. Wedded to the office, I guess.'

'I booked an appointment for Thursday.'

'I believe someone of the utmost importance to you is in grave danger. Given the confidential nature of my information, I'm reluctant to discuss it by phone. Could we meet tonight? My coffee machine brews an excellent Maxwell House, fairly exploding with flavour.' Locke emphasised the words 'Maxwell', 'House' and 'exploding'.

Chris's heart skipped a beat. 'I haven't enjoyed a Maxwell House for many years, Mr Locke.'

'It's Agent Locke, but please, call me Bud. Shall I collect you from home? Seven-thirty?'

'That works. My address—'

'I'm a Fed, Chris. I know where you live. See you tonight.' The phone beeped Locke's disconnection. Chris contemplated the handset as if it was an alien probe. Locke's implication was astronomical. Seven-thirty seemed light years away.

He dropped the phone into its cradle, trekked yet again to the bathroom and stared at the baffled face—his face—in the mirror. He splashed it with water and watched the droplets drip from his cheeks like a million salt-laden predecessors had done. Perhaps one day his soul would shed pain and grief as easily. Not today.

He ripped paper towels from the dispenser and scrubbed.

———◇———

CHRIS'S DRIVE-THRU double espresso was vile. As Locke followed Mount Ainslie Drive towards the loop at the lookout, Chris hoped his information would prove more reliable than his taste in coffee.

Locke eased the vehicle over to park. 'Behold the sparkling terrestrial galaxy, man-made magic revolving on motes of reverential deliberation; a grand homage to power and politics.'

Chris surveyed the surging swirl of car lights traversing Canberra's radiating layout below them. 'I guess.' He looked at Locke askance.

'Come, come. Is this not the perfect place to ponder the ebb and flow of cabinet and controversy?' Locke punctuated his question with the handbrake's ratchet.

'If you want heartburn.'

'Ha! A true cynic.' Locke's laugh sounded suitably contrived. 'I often come here to watch the weavers or other watchers. Some gaze at the view and move on. Others ponder the mysteries of heaven and earth.' Locke's tone suggested he saw himself among the latter.

A random lightening strobe illuminated a distant heap of clouds. Chris sighed. 'The night lights clearly have you bewitched.' *Quit waxing lyrical and get to the point.*

'Let me share a story, Christopher. A story of two men. One, a brilliant software creator, a veritable god in the industry. The other, a humble physician, eager to bring the music of communication to those denied its pleasure through disability. This humble servant cared for his wife and children and enjoyed their lakeside Eden. He walked and talked with the software creator god who promised they'd lack nothing if they did his bidding.' Locke paused dramatically.

'Mr Locke, I've had a difficult day. I'm in no mood for a sermon.'

'Fast food and instant solutions. Not happy now? Move on! Spoken like a true Gen Xer.'

'I wouldn't know, but as a Gen Y millennial, I'd appreciate specifics before the next millennium, please.' Chris repressed the urge to toe tap.

Locke drained his coffee and licked his lips. 'Couldn't have brewed better myself.'

Chris was glad he'd missed it.

'I speak, of course, of Patriarca Alejandro and Dr Alastair Maxwell, names familiar to you, I believe.' Locke's polished expression was indecipherable.

Was he probing?

'Pat was my legal guardian, of course, but the nature of his work was confidential. I respected that.'

'Confidential, yes. Respectable? Initially perhaps. Dr Maxwell's daughter, Amy, was a prime candidate for the new technology, so their alliance progressed naturally, until Alejandro got greedy. He wanted to increase the purse, fast-track the research, rush recipients into testing. His callous disregard for the privacy, security and ethical ramifications of the project was appalling.'

Chris's heart rate accelerated. 'You damn a man who was very good to me.'

'When it was in his interest to be so. His Machiavellian proclivity for keeping close tabs on friends and enemies alike is as legendary as his ability to manipulate them. Sadly, when Maxwell resisted, Alejandro hired cartel criminals to disguise Amy's kidnapping with a bomb, and obliterate her family.'

Chris's ire flared, but he was uncertain where to direct it. 'If that's true, why wasn't Pat arrested?'

'Insufficient evidence to secure a conviction.'

'Or your story's wild conjecture. Either way, Pat's beyond accusation now, false or otherwise.' Chris breathed deeply and exhaled slowly to stop Locke's torturous tale powering his burn. 'What has this to do with Aidan MacGreggor?'

'Ah, yes. Ben's inquiry, curtailed by his unfortunate accident.'

'Accident! Ben's car was blown to smithereens. Did the cartel do that too?'

'More likely an inside job. Perhaps a higher authority removed the younger Alejandro from the equation to bolster his share of the profits.'

'Perhaps? More flimsy speculation? What higher authority?'

'HS Chassic offered protection and funding long ago. Alejandro milked ASPT to get the project operational, then disappeared to Europe to sell out to the highest bidder. He sent his wife to Spain ahead of him to initiate negotiations, possibly with Basque terrorists looking to revamp hostilities.'

'But I thought—'

'He's a genius at forward thinking, Chris. Did he not prepare his sons to run the family business in his absence?'

'I knew nothing about this project until I came to work for Mr Chassic.'

'As I said, Chris, Patriarca Alejandro is a master planner.'

'You mean was.'

'Was? Not one trace of Ben's body or Pat's was recovered. Ever wonder why? Or why Imee left without a by-your-leave? Why Pat never pursued her? Why Ben was so eager to find Aidan MacGreggor? Why Ben's personal particulars were hacked to befriend Aidan, despite her protected existence?'

Her. Locke had called Mac, 'her'. He *knew*. Chris's innards stormed and surged as the atmosphere inside the vehicle intensified. 'The paedophile ring?' He squeezed the words through his teeth.

'There's not one shred of evidence for paedophilic criminology behind the Leicester profile. We were manipulated, Chris. The reports were red herrings to mask the stink of collusion and conspiracy.'

Manipulated! Red herrings? Chris gagged and gaped like a beached codfish, gulping air. He wrenched the car door open and threw himself out, craving oxygen and clarity. How could he have been so utterly duped? Trusting the very wretches who'd destroyed his family. Destroyed him!

Locke joined Chris and laid a hand on his shoulder. 'Dr Maxwell was a good man. His daughter, Amy, was unique. But you know that, don't you?'

Chris nodded. 'She could have turned this world on its head if she'd lived.'

'She did live, Chris. As did her brother. Is that not so?'

There it was. Confirmation. Amy was alive! The sheer, mind-numbing injustice of Locke's revelations vaporised his joy. But not his outrage—that old familiar friend energised him, fed his determination to cultivate it; nurture it until he could inflict maximum damage. He'd take on Little Benjamin Perfect and win his deadly game. He'd drive the Alejandros into hell itself.

Then he'd stomp on their graves.

Chris locked his gaze on the horizon; still black, but the clouds had dissipated. 'Aidan MacGreggor is Amy, isn't she?'

'Yes, Christian.'

'Please explain.'

'Amy was on the upper level of your allotment at the time of the explosion. The kidnappers couldn't find her, but they bombed the house anyway. Amy was found unconscious but alive in a cubby house. We took her into protective custody and established her deep cover identity. That was my responsibility. If we'd known you were alive, we'd have reunited you. Alejandro got to you first.'

'So how do we set this right?'

'Amy and Ben are on the run. Amy's only chance to escape the Alejandros' devious network is if we can get to her before Ben squirrels her out of the country.'

'And you think I know where they are.'

'Call it a hunch. You and Ben are close, are you not?'

'We were. We drifted apart.'

'A temporary glitch, I'm sure. No doubt he'll use Amy to get to you. Enlist your help to elude capture. You know there's a police alert out. He murdered Amy's carers in front of surveillance cameras.'

'He says otherwise.'

'So he has contacted you.'

'Before they disappeared. I think he lost his phone when he rescued Mac.'

'You mean when he kidnapped Amy. I've no doubt he also sabotaged the scuba equipment to eliminate my man, Brock Bosworth. Brock lost family too. He was a good police officer. Generous enough to sacrifice a well-earned retirement for the sake of a somewhat difficult responsibility.'

'So I've gathered.' Chris smiled at Mac's—Amy's—defiance. Not that he wasn't sorry about Bosworth, but he was beginning to understand what a fighter his little sister had become. He would not let her fighting spirit down.

No way José!

'Then you have current insight into Amy's reactions and whereabouts?'

Caution nudged Chris. Locke knew highly sensitive and confidential information. His question implied he knew LIES was functioning. Had HS told him? 'If I can locate them, what will you do?'

'I have federal police resources at my fingertips, Chris. I can have a private plane ready to lift off the tarmac in under an hour.'

'With me as a passenger?'

'First class.' Locke pulled a notebook from his pocket, penned a telephone number, tore the page out and gave it to Chris. 'Call me on this number, anytime 24/7, with a probable location and I'll move things asap. Now, shall I drop you home?'

As much as Chris wanted to return to the office, that would have to wait till the morning.

———◦○◦———

CHRIS TOSSED and turned, as sleepless as *Sleepless in Seattle,* MPeg's favourite movie, which she'd watched at least fifty times since they'd met. Chris had artfully avoided it and had no clue what it was about. But Talbot Locke's revelations had stripped away all hope of sleep and, like a wood turner's blade, the words, 'Sleepless in Seattle' scored a never-ending groove in his brain. Their trite congeniality irked. He craved words that cut the quick. Blood red words like the numbers on his digital alarm clock. He watched it click over to 1:00am. 1:01am. 1:02am.

Stuff it. He rang office security and told them he'd be in early. Very early. Under a brutal shower, he reminded himself that revenge, if it couldn't be sweet, could at least be savoured. Calm and calculated.

His intensive towel dry amplified the red blaze left by the shower. Chris ran a hand over his sandpaper stubble. Rough. Good. Skip the shave. He ironed sharp creases into his shirt sleeves and trouser legs, dressed, brewed and dispatched strong black coffee, no sugar. Attended to final ablutions and slammed the front door behind him on the way out. He rammed his car into gear, reversed and gouged a racing stripe onto the side panels with the letterbox.

He repeated some of Mac's expletives.

So much for calm. Perhaps it waited for him at the office. Calm. And LIES.

Farting fire ants! Tracking Amy would mean reading the transcripts. She'd consider it a violation of trust. Again.

As siblings, he and Amy had weathered childhood squabbles with remarkable humour. All but one. Chris cringed at the memory. He'd read part of Amy's journal to his mates for a lark. They'd howled with laughter, then teased her about it. The anguish in her face had lacerated his conscience with enduring shame.

Surely he had no choice this time. He'd guard the transcripts with his life. But he must know exactly where she was.

———◦◦◦———

CHRIS SQUINTED at the hotchpotch of text and pulled a face. How could he pinpoint Amy when each transmission was more confusing than its predecessor? Group conversations fractured continuity. Even her private thoughts flickered like a torch with rusty contacts. Perhaps she was exercising control born of awareness. *You're not making this easy, Mac. Ames.* Ugh! Chris couldn't get a handle on what to call her. She was little Amy in his memory and a non-conformist revelation on his screen.

He was not altogether in the dark though, apart from his mood. He knew roughly where Amy was, even if the who had him baffled. He could tell Locke that Mac and Ben had joined HOPE's Central Australian Tour and that their itinerary included Barkly Homestead Wednesday night and Tennant Creek, Northern Territory from Thursday for a couple of days at least. He pulled out his wallet, retrieved Locke's note and rang the phone number.

48. PLAYED

Wednesday 21 November 2012

Canberra, Australia

SINBLED SCOWLED as his phone vibrated. He checked the text message then telephoned another number.

A gruff, age-coarsened voice answered. 'What?'

'You've outdone yourself this time, letting young Alejandro grab the girl. I underestimated your gift for farce, Deabrua.'

'The girl's irrelevant.'

'Unlike the mess you left behind.'

'Two illegals? I doubt they'll be missed.'

'Bosworth was ex-police. Boys in blue hate losing their own. They take it personally. They'd squash an annoying mosquito, if you get my drift.'

'I'm suffocating downwind of it. Meanwhile, the Volcano's itching for software you've yet to provide. An itch makes him irritable.'

'Mozzies have that effect.'

'It's you he'll slap down, you arrogant fool. In his game, you're a pawn. Pawns are expendable.'

'You haven't played much chess, have you, Moz?'

'Meaning what?'

'Of all chess pieces, only a pawn can improve its rank, become a rook, or a knight, or a bishop, or even a queen. Ulvelaik might enjoy a new queen.'

'Don't say that to his face. He's killed people for less. I've killed people for less.'

'You're a grunting warthog and a repetitious bore.' Sinbled faked a yawn.

Deabrua grunted. 'I get the job done, which is more than you can say. Unless you have the software.'

'I have the software. And we can utilise the girl's brother.'

'I thought he was dead.'

'You thought wrong. He's ASPT's new LIES guru.'

'So what?' Deabrua coughed and grunted again.

'He'll help us locate Mac using her thought transcripts. We can bargain with a package deal.'

'The software works?'

'Good grief, Deabrua, did you doubt it? Would Ulvelaik, or ASPT for that matter, waste their resources on anything less than a certainty?'

'The Volcano speculates. He can afford a few misses.'

'Well, he's hit the jackpot with LIES. Exclusive access to foolproof mind-reading technology? Think about it. With an implant in your head, you could be butt naked in a jail cell with your tongue cut out and still communicate with your people across the globe. This is name-your-price technology. So play nice with me, Deabrua, if you want your cut.'

'I'm listening.'

'Go to Brisbane Airport and wait for my instructions. When I've pinpointed Mac and Alejandro, you can secure them for me. I'll arrange safe passage for us all, including the brother, to Ulvelaik.'

'Where's the catch?'

'No catch. I'm feeling magnanimous.'

HORON SINBALLIDH had no intention of telling Deabrua his cloned copy of the contents of Ben's computer was useless, nor that he had tried to enhance its value by eliminating Ben when he'd believed his copy was good. All the administrative and costing files were there, but no software. Just a stack of dummy files and games. Games! Stupid idea, employing kids to do a man's job.

He thought about the tiny transmitter hugging the underside of Chris's keyboard, sensing every sound, indulging every touch, whispering Chris's secrets while Sinbled pleasured himself with their intimate clarity, and smiled. He'd soon have it all—implant technology, interface, functioning software, a hostage or two. He'd play for Ulvelaik's money direct, or cut his own deal with the highest bidder. Using Deabrua to grab Ben and Mac for him was merely expedient.

The latest communication about the wanderers was most helpful. With a few discreet inquiries—church Facebook pages were particularly helpful—Sinbled extrapolated HOPE's itinerary. Their accommodation plans were more elusive, not one single hotel, motel or caravan park booking. Sinbled guessed churches were providing private billets. That made his follow-up call to Deabrua urgent.

'It's me. I forwarded an itinerary.'

'I read it.'

'Our prey will be at Barkly Homestead tonight.'

'Can't get there tonight.'

'There's a commercial flight leaves Brisbane for Mt Isa at ten to nine. Lands before lunch.'

'Still a six-hour drive to Barkly. Let me know when they're near an airport.'

'Get to them tonight, Deabrua. Get Ulvelaik to cop for a private plane and pilot, or get your butt onto Qantas and hit the highway.'

'Lavalake's rampaging over the cost and time blow-out as it is. He has fiscal responsibilities.'

'I suppose he views kidnap and murder as standard business protocol.'

'He also punishes underperforming employees. That should worry us both.'

'So why won't you grab them at Barkly?'

'It's unfamiliar territory with no network infrastructure. Their itinerary includes Alice Springs where I can access a suitable vehicle and plan the grab. The Stuart Highway has plenty of lonely stretches for a hijack. Even better if you can tell me where they're staying in the Alice.'

'I can't. Not yet. We only know Barkly for certain.'

'The only certainty is your lingering, excruciating demise if you fail at your end, and a bloody feast for Lavalake's sadistic appetite.'

Sinbled figured the sadistic appetite belonged to Deabrua. But he didn't say so. No point biting a hand that would kill you for it.

49. DARED

Wednesday 21 November 2012

Outback, Australia

LIES/MXP2/20121121am17722

'ARE YOU asleep, Cassie?'

'Is it my turn to drive?'

'No. Ben just took over from Bert. Everyone else is asleep.'

'Oh. Righto. You okay, Mac?'

'My mind's busy, that's all. I usually trawl my dictionary app to distract me, but I lost my phone. I collect words, memorise them, what they mean, how they're used, play with them. It sounds weird, but putting them into sentences and stories—or poems like we did earlier—relaxes me.'

'I get that. My Roget's Thesaurus is in the luggage trailer. Old school wordplay.'

'I use Thesaurus-dot-com.'

'Me too, at home.'

'So, Bert was singing about God saving a wretch like him. Wretch is a weird word. It can mean the opposite of itself depending on how you use it. Which wretch did he mean?'

'I thought wretch meant miserable or contemptible.'

'Urban Dictionary says it's also an attractive, highly intelligent, witty, humorous person. I guess God would be happy to save that kind of wretch.'

'God longs to save both kinds. We sure can't save ourselves without his help.'

'Mum used to say that. Bert also used the word doctrine. What does doctrine mean?'

'It means teaching. It's mainly used in the context of theology and religion.'

'You mean like catalyst in chemistry, or genre in English, or—'

'A priori and a posteriori in philosophy.'

'Ay what? Sounds like a bum rap!'

'Mac! I'd expect that response from a high school boy. Bum rap indeed.'

'I was impelled to think and act like a boy.'

'That's what I'd call a bum rap!'

'It had some advantages, like getting the inside goss on what boys think about girls from my online mates, rather than having to guess. But tell me about ay-pos-teer-ree-or-eye.'

'At five o'clock in the morning? That's straining my brain.'

'Please?'

'I'll try. A posteriori is knowledge gained through experience or observation. A priori is knowledge achieved through reasoning.'

'Can you give me an example?'

'Let me think … How many married bachelors live in Sydney?'

'How would I—? Oh! They aren't bachelors if they're married. So none.'

'Excellent. You reached a conclusion using reason. That's a priori.'

'And a posteriori reflects experience, like I know that sitting on a hard surface for ages makes my bum sore because I've done it?'

'Good call. And wordplay.'

'So that's philosophy, is it?'

'More like a snapshot of the pimple on its derrière, if you'll pardon my French.'

'I say much worse.'

'Funny thing about words, Mac. Their meaning and usage shifts with context and culture. What is acceptable in one context offends in another. Urban Dictionary reflects that.'

'Urban Dictionary is bizarre. Every word has a double or quadruple meaning. I guess you thought I'd relate to your expression because I swear a lot. I never used to. It sort of happened. I don't mean to offend.'

'Considering your horrendous experiences, I can understand where you're coming from. I … lost close family too, under difficult circumstances. That was most certainly wretched. And not as in smart or witty.'

'Or lost, as in carelessly misplaced.'

'No. Lost is a convenient word that rolls off the tongue in polite company, after it's shredded your soul.'

'So true. Can you tell me about it? I mean, I'm genuinely interested, if you don't mind talking about it.'

'I don't usually talk about. Tends to make people feel awkward.'

'Well, I'm already awkward, so don't let that stop you. Please?'

'I, um … had a half-sister who was much older than me. Our father was with Jenny and her husband when a drug-addled driver hit their vehicle head-on. Dad and Lonzo died instantly. Mum and I spent hours at Jen's hospital bed, trying to talk her out of a coma. She was pregnant. They delivered Sophie by Caesarean section, but Jen suffered a fatal brain haemorrhage.'

'That's way beyond lost.'

'Yes.'

'So Sophie's your niece? That's such a pretty name.'

'She was a darling, a bright and beautiful child. We grew up as sisters and— I get it! Sophie did that very thing you said. Her happy would burst out all over, just because it could. Your expression captured it perfectly.'

'Did it? I'd like to meet her one day.'

'In heaven, perhaps. She died when she was seventeen. I'd moved away from home by then. With the shock of it all, my mum went home to be with the Lord soon after.'

'Oh, Cass! That's … you poor thing. I just want to hug you.'

'I … would love a hug …'

'Cass, how did you find hope again? Because I can't. I don't know how.'

'Neither did I. Eventually, I let hope find me. God's persistent love— that's where hope dares to breathe again.'

'Do you think God would, I mean, I told God I wanted to smack him in the face. Why would he persist with me?'

'Because he loves you unconditionally.'

'How do you know for sure?'

'A posteriori. From experience.'

50. DISARMED

Wednesday 21 November 2012

Outback Australia

BEN HAD to admit he was enjoying himself, despite having to cool it around Tully, whose interest terrorised platonic boundaries. Mac's reaction to Tully's shenanigans bemused him. Guarding a prior claim to his attentions perhaps? Unlikely. Mac's attitude suggested she tolerated him under sufferance.

Either way was problematic. He'd need a working rapport with Mac to fine-tune the LIES system, but he had an uncanny knack for making her snap. It was tough taming a wildcat. Or an abused and neglected puppy. Though Cassie seemed to have nailed it. He could use a leaf from her book.

Ben kept turning pages, hoping to find one that would ease tensions between himself and Mac. They clapped and cheered in unison when Eli and Motto practiced a new script with two cute and furry monster puppets called Egermeier and Forbes, especially when a lolly-laden 'dust storm' blanketed the audience. While Mac consumed the lone Mintie that landed in her lap, Ben scrabbled to fill both hands with Minties, Fantales and Chocolate Eclairs. He emptied a handful into Mac's lap and they chewed and chomped in sync for several minutes.

'I need dental floss.' Mac picked at a rear molar.

'Yeah. I figured you'd be a flosser,' Ben said.

'What's wrong with that? Flossing is good.'

'For you, maybe. When I floss, it's a horror story of wrenched fillings.' Ben shuddered.

'Bad floss experience?'

'You try surviving a dozen lengths of Oral B wrapped around your neck like a strangler fig.'

'Use waxed floss and twist the ends around your fingers.'

'Tried that. Cut off the blood supply to my pinkie. It shrivelled into a mummified witchetty grub.'

'Benjamin Alejandro, are you pulling my leg?'

'Better than pulling my tooth.' He winked and Mac poked her tongue at him. He patted his tum and burped. 'Excuse me. I couldn't eat another lolly if you paid me. Too much of a good thing is not so good.'

'Like my implant.' Mac slipped the remaining lollies into the seat pocket.

Huh? 'How is that like lollies? Or dental floss?'

'A good thing turned bad. It's twisted my life into a horror story.'

Ben drummed his fingers on the arm rest. 'But the implant has such positive potential.'

'Then why is it hush-hush? People don't hide good things.'

'Unless they're selfish and greedy.'

'My father may have been prehensile, but hardly pleonectic.'

Ben opened his mouth. And shut it. How could he answer a walking dictionary? He chose to play it safe, stick to what he knew. 'I think your father, and mine, meant it for good. They kept it secret to prevent it being hijacked.'

'Didn't stop them dying.'

He wanted to argue their deaths were unrelated to the STIR, but even he believed otherwise.

'How can I live with an implant that's tainted with death? I want it out of my head. Destroyed. Software too. Promise you'll help me?' She pressed her fist to her mouth and bit her knuckle.

Destroy the software! When he—and others—had sacrificed so much for it? What could he say? *Sure, Mac. I'll gladly toss my father's STIR baby—my creative legacy—out with the bathwater in a knee-jerk reaction because you've wrapped me around your little finger.*

Mac frowned at him—or at his non-response. 'Well?'

'Surgery's not without risk, Mac. I'll certainly support your informed choice in that regard. Decisions about the LIES program aren't mine alone to make. You're not obligated to participate but—'

'But what? You can't think it's good?'

'The technology's neither good nor bad. It's a thing. People use things for evil, not the other way around.'

'Guns are things, killing things. You can't tell me guns are good.'

'I might if a croc had my foot. A gun might be very good then.'

'Do you have a gun, Ben?'

'Not on me.'

'But you own one?'

'I've been trained in weapons management.'

'Surely someone smart enough to be trusted with a gun wouldn't be stupid enough to cavort with crocodiles.' Mac pursed her lips.

Who could argue with that, other than a *QI* contestant perhaps? Ben tried, unsuccessfully, to keep a straight face.

'You always do that.'

'Do what?'

'Smirk. Like you're laughing at me.'

'Maybe I'm laughing at myself; my failure to outgun your logic.' Ben's face muscles itched with mischief.

'Now you're making fun of me.' Mac folded her arms and huffed.

'I'm admiring your … reasoning.'

'A posteriori or a priori?'

'Ay what?' *Out of the frying pan into the fire?*

'They're philosophical terms. Knowledge gained by experience versus knowledge achieved through reason.'

'And you know this?'

'Cassie told me. Stop it. You're smirking again.'

'Am not'. Ben sucked in his cheeks as an unruly grin tickled his willpower.

'Are too.'

'Am not.'

'Are too.'

'Mmmm not.' *Don't betray me now, straight face. Hold it. Hold it. Hold—*

'Are too. Are too.' Mac poked his ribs.

Ben lost it. His cheek suck collapsed and he and Mac convulsed with laughter, until she got hiccups.

'Sto-hic! Stop-hic! Stop-it-ic!'

'Hold your breath.'

Mac gulped air and clamped her hand over her mouth till her face turned red and her eyes bulged.

Not good. 'Gone?'

Mac nodded, eased her hand away and exhaled. 'I think-hic-so! Aargh!'

Ben cracked up again.

'Now you're defin-hic-ly laugh-hic at me!'

'I am—' A snort gobbled his 'not'. 'You win, kiddo. I humbly concede your superior debating skills. Your verbal crossfire could drop me at fifty paces, any day.'

Mac scowled.

'Twenty paces?'

'You know full well I couldn't not, couldn't never, not—aargh!' Without warning, she was fractious again.

'Oh puh-lease! Shoot me now. End my misery.'

'Jerk!'

Ben corked a rude retort. Saint Job himself would have needed a mobile LIES App to comprehend Mac's mood swings.

'Honestly, Mac, I'm as thick as a Tolkien trilogy when it comes to reading you.'

'Lucky I'm not an audio book. With my diction, you'd have no hope.'

Ben gaped, tongue-tied and mortified. Though he'd noticed her slight speech impediment when he'd hauled her, feisty and sopping wet, out of the water and into the boat, he'd not given it a second thought since. It didn't detract one bit from her vivacity and wit.

'Cat got your tongue too?' Mac sighed as Mordor's fire fizzled and died in her pupils. 'Sorry. Your verbal crossfire comment struck a raw nerve. Li mocked the way I speak to shut me up. I spent way too much time composing defensive comebacks for non-existent conversations.'

'All brilliant ... no doubt.' Probably better he not mention his personal favourites.

'Dumb waste of time, especially now that I have bigger problems to ponder.'

'Such as?'

'I dunno. Life, death, love, loss ... you.'

Ben's breath fled as, yet again, the spark in Mac's eyes completely disarmed him.

51. SOURED

Thursday 22 November 2012

Canberra, Australia

CHRIS CHEWED through the latest transcripts. Some bits were hard to swallow. It sounded like Mac was stuck with a busload of heavy duty religious nuts, doing their whole religious program on the bus. Egermeier and Forbes: Lost in the Desert. The LIES transcript had caught the gist of it, then deteriorated into garbled confusion.

Egermeier. What a blast from the past. Elsie Egermeier's Bible Story Book—their mother's only tangible link to Grandma Arianna—had been a mainstay amongst Maxwell family traditions. They'd taken it in turns to pick and read at least one story from it every evening after dinner.

The memory triggered a smile that defied Chris's mood as he recalled one family meal—roast beef with all the trimmings, followed by lemon delicious pudding and fresh strawberries. Dad had carved the roast, so Chris had volunteered to serve the pudding. He'd tipped a huge spoonful of the custardy, cakey treat onto the table's edge where it slithered over the side into his lap. They'd all gasped. Mum had shaken her head. 'See? No good deed goes unpunished,' she'd said, deadpan. 'Who said that? Was it Luce, Wilde, Wilder or Lemon? No. Mellon.' They'd all ended up in stitches. Thereafter, it had become their 'melon and lemon quote', a sweetener if they were caught in a jam.

Chris's smile went taut and grim. Who'd punished his mother's good deeds?

His desk phone buzzed. 'Yo?'

'How's it going, Chris? Can you spare a minute?' HS was back. 'Grab coffee and join me for a two-way update? My door's open.'

Never had making coffee been such a chore. Chris was so busy being cranky, he scalded himself with steam. He entered Chassic's office with two coffees and a searing burn to complement the scabs on his knuckles.

'With you in two shakes.' HS hoisted a new water colour onto his wall. 'This bright and breezy beauty caught my eye in Pamplona.'

'What happened to the stormy seascape?'

'The oil? Too moody and restless.'

'I quite liked it.'

'Technique was good, just not my taste. It was time to let it go, like the former employee who gave it to me.' Chassic turned to Chris. 'What happened to your hands? They're a mess.'

'Had a fight with a desk and it won.'

'I'll say.' HS sat, nodding his thanks for the cup of coffee. 'Any news from Ben? Has he located our mystery Mac?'

'Nothing recent. Just hints.'

'Hints? From the transcripts? He's been successful?' HS held Chris's gaze.

Chris squirmed. He wanted to scream, *the greedy mongrel has Mac in his clutches. I'll kill him the moment she's safe.* His awkwardness at having kept HS out of the loop tied his tongue. Chris dropped his eyes. 'Have you seen the news reports? Ben's picture was in Tuesday's papers. Police think he murdered Mac's carers.'

'I'm aware the police seek a person matching Ben's description as a possible witness.'

Chris said nothing.

'What's bothering you, Chris?'

Three thousand kilometres between me and revenge. 'It's been an emotional roller coaster, dealing with Ben's death, resurrection, disappearance, fearing for his safety. He contacted me online Monday. Nothing since. The police say he's a murderer.'

'No, they haven't said that.'

'Implied. I haven't slept a wink all week.'

'Why didn't you phone me? I left details with Veronica.'

'Truth is I'm wrecked over this.' Chris fingered his knuckles. 'I could use a few days leave.' For a flight with Locke.

'I did load you with responsibility after precious little preparation. Take leave, certainly. May I suggest you see a doctor? We can access ASIO debriefing specialists.'

'I don't need a shrink. I need time out.'

'To chew, stew and recriminate? Professional assistance can make things more manageable.'

Chris shrugged his shoulders. 'For me or for you?'

HS raised an eyebrow. 'I'll get by. I tracked missing persons long before LIES technology came into play. My sources and instincts tell me Ben is fine. He doesn't want to be found. The car bomb spooked him. Now, with this murder investigation, he's doing what his covert training taught him—staying off grid till he knows the full state of play.'

'Yeah, but whose game is he playing? Maybe he's not the shining star you think he is.' Chris's acrimony swelled like a rogue wave.

HS stood, paced his sea wall twice, and sat again. 'The game plan was always need to know. You've let non-disclosure sour your judgment. People have killed and been killed over this technology. Secrecy's imperative. Awareness equals risk.'

Chris's face contorted. 'I think you're wrong. An open policy from the get-go could have eliminated the threat. Safety in numbers and all that.'

HS sighed. 'Perhaps. It's moot now. But know this. Ben is not now, nor has he ever been, a killer. If he contacts you, I must know. Ben must know I'm on his side. As I am on yours.' HS rose, walked around his desk and put a hand on Chris's shoulder. 'I, too, want to see you and Amy safely reunited.'

'You knew?' He flipped from mad to flabbergasted and back again. 'Why didn't you tell me?'

'I was not free to do so.'

'And now you are. How convenient.' Chris booted the leg of the desk.

HS sighed and returned to his seat. 'When they destroyed your house, we believed Zoe, Alastair and Amy had perished. Pat insisted on caring for you. He refused to rely on the NWPP because it failed to protect your mother.'

'From the drug cartel.'

'From being identified and located. Pat always believed the explosion happened because of the LIES program. Organised crime targets big money from any source—drugs, weapons, people trafficking, industrial espionage.'

'What if Pat was in cahoots with them? What if I was his insurance policy?'

'That's absurd, Chris. What gave you that idea?'

'Can you prove otherwise? Or won't say because it's true? Given your loyalty to Pat and his software.'

'You think I'm involved in a conspiracy?'

Chris steeled his stare.

HS grimaced. 'You've suffered much harm, Chris. I can forgive your accusation because, without doubt, these insidious criminals have inside men, high enough in the hierarchy to wield serious clout. We have our suspicions, but no proof.'

'Exactly who is we?'

'Me and my boss, Patriarca Alejandro.'

'Boss! But I thought—'

'Pat called it a partnership, but he's the instigator and I facilitate. Pat believed the only way he could shake these snakes from their tree and grind them underfoot was by working off the grid. Make them cocky enough to move openly then wring their necks.'

'Enough rope to hang themselves. So the plane crash was a ruse?'

'Sadly, no. People lost their lives. Pat was not among them.'

'So where is he now?'

'Good question. Prior to Ben's departure, I received unconfirmed reports that a man fitting Pat's description was seen in France and Spain. I immediately sent a Field Agent, Raz Karey, to investigate.' HS raised his hand. 'No joy yet, but that's why I went to Spain.'

'For your conference?'

HS nodded. 'Karey's following a fresh lead as we speak.'

'So you still don't know.'

'Pat knows what he's doing. I'm still need to know. I'm confident he'll communicate when he's ready, if he is alive and able to do so.'

'Wow.' Chris shook his head. 'Bosses and underlings, eh?'

HS smiled concurrence.

'Does Ben know?'

'Ben knows he's doing what his father would have done. Of course, if you were in touch, you could pass on the latest intel.'

Why was this so hard? Like nosediving into a mine shaft with no grip on truth or foothold on hope. Chris sighed. 'Let me check the GRUnGE again.'

'Grunge?'

'It's a secure location on the computer. It's got all the LIES stuff—software, transcripts, research—locked away. I broke Ben's encryption ages ago. He left me a message and said he'd send a phone number when it was absolutely necessary.'

HS picked up his handset. 'What's the number?'

'It's useless now. I think his phone's at the bottom of Pumicestone Passage. He saved Mac from drowning then they both went off the grid again.'

'But you think he'll leave a message in this grunge?'

'I hope so.' How he'd respond to Ben's message, should it come, remained to be seen.

52. RELEASED

Thursday 22 November 2012

Outback Australia

TENNANT CREEK: Northern Territory's Golden Heart. That's what the welcome sign said as the HOPE bus arrived mid-morning. Ben failed to see a connection, although the sun blazed hot enough to melt metal.

'They had a gold rush here. Nineteen-thirties, I think. Pity we can't Google it.' Eli shrugged.

'I tried,' Sarah said. 'I had two bars of reception for the first time since Mt Isa. Links crash before they download.'

'Cheap network provider?' Eli asked.

'Non-existent most of the way. I hope my 'we're-fine-don't-worry' text reached the parentals. Mum's such a worry wart.'

Ben shared the frustration of the phoneless. He asked Bert about the chances of picking up a prepaid smartphone.

'HOPE operates on a shoestring. We could stretch to a basic prepaid.'

'I'll reimburse you. I can communicate with my co-worker via Internet.'

'Could you use a desktop computer? Fixed line is more reliable than mobile data out here. Outside Darwin, Katherine and Alice Springs there's not much coverage without a satellite phone. Once we're settled, I'll see what I can arrange.'

The 'settling' involved Cassie and Bert sorting billets and itinerary with the local organiser over morning tea, held under a shady tree. Ben learned that he, Mac, Cassie and Bert were staying with the pastor. His wife would take them home via the op shop when everyone else was sorted. The HOPE team set about separating personal luggage from props.

Ben poured two cups of iced water from a dispenser and wandered over to tell Mac, who sat leaning against a tree trunk, staring into space. She'd developed a strange body tic, repeatedly swiping her right hand across her left thumb and forefinger. The movement reminded him of … sign language. Hearing impaired students had attended Ben's primary school.

'Drink?' He offered.

'Thanks.' She downed the liquid, balanced the cup on the ridge of a tree root, and resumed the repetitious hand movement, as though oblivious to the fact.

Ben shimmied down beside her, thankful for the shade. Perspiration prickled his neck. No wonder HOPE usually travelled this route in winter. He sipped his drink, relishing an equally cool gush of appreciation for the perfect timing of their Good Samaritans. Still, he was antsy for internet access to confirm he could bring Mac in, and that ASPT would cover airfares from Alice Springs. Ben had finally convinced himself that HS Chassic would never condone paedophilia. Or murder. Surely Locke's suspicions were misplaced.

'Ben?'

He jumped as Mac interrupted his reverie.

'Exactly how important is this LIES program? I mean, what's it really worth?'

Ben thought about it. 'Honestly? I don't know. How do you place a value on giving someone who can't communicate the chance to do so? You're better able to answer that than me.'

Mac tilted her head. 'Being able to hear? That's life changing. Life saving even. But there are other ways to speak: sign it, write it, type it, draw it. Most people talk too much anyway. When communication takes effort, you tend to be more careful, more succinct.'

'But you learned how to speak. Verbalise, I mean.'

'Eventually. As a kid, most people couldn't understand me, unless they knew Auslan. I was older when I got my first cochlear implant, so I had to catch up. Now they help children much earlier in the language development process.'

'So this is an Auslan sign.' Ben mimicked Mac's hand tic. 'You were doing it over and over.'

'I was not.'

'I don't think you were aware of it.'

'What's it matter?' Mac stared at her feet.

'It clearly matters to you.'

'That doesn't make it your business. You don't have to know everything I'm thinking do you? Or can't you help yourself now?'

'Hey, I get that it's bizarre, knowing I eavesdropped. In my defence, I argued vehemently for getting your permission as soon as we found you.'

Mac's eyes flashed fire. 'Woo-deludey-hoo! Hey Mac, our mind-reader breaks every privacy law in the book. Please say you're okay with it, or else I'm in deep doo-doo. Sure, mate. No worries. Trawl my brain anytime. Like hell! My thoughts are my business.'

'Yes, they are.' Ben's heart beat faster. He was pretty sure he should shut up, but his heart pummelled words into his throat anyway. 'Truth be told, that beautiful brain of yours is what drew me to you in the first place.' Too late. They'd escaped.

Mac screwed up her nose. Cute as.

Ben offered a half-smile. 'I guess that sounded kinda weird.'

'It did.' Mac twisted her mouth to one side, as if evaluating him. 'Mainly because, well, men aren't usually drawn to a woman's brain, are they? They say that to get something else.'

'Except I thought you were a guy from your LIES transcripts.' *Change feet while you're at it, Ben-man.* Would Mac consider him misogynist or—?

Her eyes went wide then narrowed. 'Uh-huh.' She pinned him to the board of her scrutiny as if he were a sticky maths problem.

Ben squirmed. 'Is that better or worse?'

'X or Y? Who am I to judge?'

Ben balanced his empty cup on the tree root beside Mac's. 'You've got to admit, you are kinda cu—unique.' Was that a quick save or what?

'One of a kind, that's me.'

'An amazing one of a kind. You're inquiring. Clever. Creative. Quick-witted. Spirited. An independent thinker. And you've handled real-life Hollywood drama like an Academy Award winner!'

'Oh, I'm a star, I am.'

'You know how to take a compliment too.'

Mac rearranged herself, folded arms, crossed legs. 'I'm somewhat out of practice from having to hide my light under a bushel, to stop people using me for target practice.'

Ben chose an open-bodied position. 'So, if I hadn't read your thoughts I wouldn't know how extraordinary you are.'

'Extraordinary? That's a bit much.'

'You *are* extraordinary.' Ben nodded for emphasis. 'You know why? Not because you're smart or even because you have that rather unique memory. You're extraordinary because—' Ben leaned so he could look at her face. 'Because, in spite of everything that happened, you kept the main thing the main thing.'

'Oh, that's profound, that is. What are you saying? I got shat on from a great height, so I shat back?'

Ben shook his head. 'You held on to your inner self. That peculiar, determined, glorious inner you. They squirrelled you into obscurity. You dreamed of touching the world. They stole your life, subverted your brilliance, robbed you of all control. You nurtured the things that matter most to you, your passion for language, writing, creative thinking. You thought like the real you, not Mac the decoy, but the person you were born to be. You could've opted out. Many would have. Thrown in the towel, escaped with alcohol or drugs.'

'I might have if I could have. Don't forget, I was a virtual prisoner. As in, not flout the rules and you're grounded, Mac, but ignore the rules and we'll bury you six feet under.' She hugged herself defensively. 'I contemplated ending myself.'

Ben picked up a pebble, cradled it in his hand and caressed it with his thumb. 'I'm glad you didn't. Thank God you kept fighting for the important things.'

Mac relaxed her straitjacket grip and threw a couple of mock punches. 'Comeback Mac, that's me.'

'Yep. You're one gutsy lady. Just sayin'.' Ben dropped the pebble into his lap, curled his hands to his mouth and mimicked a seething fan-crowd roar. 'Comeback Mac has done it again. Wowed the crowd with her—' Ben burst out laughing.

'What? How is that hilarious?'

Ben shook his head and settled. 'Something I remembered from your transcripts.' He held up a hand as a stop sign to ward off a possible punch. 'Did Brock Bosworth really look like a Titicaca Scrotum frog?'

Mac grinned. 'Crossed with a proboscis monkey. He was one ugly mutt.'

A random bird, perched in the tree above them, squawked a rapid-fire tweet.

'Even the wildlife agrees.' Ben smirked.

Mac's grin turned bittersweet. 'I feel kinda bad about the way I treated him. He was only doing his job. He tried to look after me.' Mac's lower lip trembled and she resumed her Auslan tic.

Ben moved to hold her hands, hesitated, retreated, and kneaded his own hands instead, Mac's agonised expression clawing his heart.

She shuddered. 'Don't you see, Ben? Brock's dead because of me. Li and Liss? Both dead because of me!'

Ben sat bolt upright. 'No, Mac, not because of you. No way. The fault lies with the murderous thug who killed them, and with his criminal cohort, assuming there is one.'

'Who got involved because of me and this ... this LIES thing. It *is* my fault.' Mac's tic intensified.

Ben shook his head. 'It is not your fault! Did you know about the implant? Did you ask for it?'

'No.'

'See? You're the victim here, Mac.'

Mac curled her fingers, lacerating her skin with the repetitious tic. Ben couldn't bear it. He scooped her hands into his. 'This sign? I know some Auslan.' He held her eyes with his own. 'It means accusation or blame doesn't it?'

Mac cast her eyes down and tried to pull her hands free. Ben held on, gently but firmly.

'Look at me, Mac!' He poured his soul's conviction through his gaze. 'Whoever you really truly are, believe me when I say, this is absolutely, categorically, no way in heaven or earth or out of hell itself, your fault! Do you understand me?'

Tears dripped down her face. 'I want to believe you, but how can I? Six people are dead over this thing in my head. I have to live with that. Live with LIES. LIES! I don't even know what it stands for!'

Ben cupped Mac's face in his hands and smoothed her tears. 'Your dad called your implant the Sound and Thought Impulse Reader, or STIR. The software project was called LIES. I figured the acronym was the brainchild of some over-zealous spook who saw it as a lie detector. But now I know you, Mac, I think it's the perfect fit.' Ben touched his fingers to Mac's lips to curtail her protest. 'LIES stands for Language Impulse Enhancement and Synthesis. It takes the pure essence of your creative thoughts and converts them into words on a page so that others may feel their intensity, taste their richness, gaze at their beauty and marvel at their brilliance. I think your father knew this is exactly what you were born to do. He dedicated his work, his life, to making it possible.'

With that, Mac buried herself in his embrace, and sobbed.

53. DRAINED

Thursday 22 November 2012

Outback Australia

BEN WAS a racing snail on steroids, pumped and going nowhere. Their 'whirlwind' op shop stop took him ten minutes. It took Mac fifty. She sure shopped like a girl.

As for their 'quick' lunch at the pastor's residence, long-term friends of the Adlers, Ted and Elsie Meyers, had gatecrashed; their endless chatter slowed food consumption considerably.

'So Ben, Mac, how long have you been with HOPE?' Ted placed his knife and fork parallel on his empty plate.

'A couple of days,' Mac said. 'We're hitching a ride.'

'Oh? Where to?' Elsie dabbed her mouth and scrunched her serviette.

'Good question. Ben?' Mac smirked as she put him on the spot. Her alliance remained arbitrary when not downright contrary.

'Alice Springs airport for a flight home, hopefully on Monday night or Tuesday.' Ben offered to take their empty plates.

'You'd miss seeing Uluru, Kata Tjuta and Kings Canyon. If you don't mind roughing it in our five-berth air-conditioned RV, we're returning to the Alice tomorrow. We'd be happy to show you the sights.'

Elsie clarified. 'After a good night's sleep at home first. Maybe an early-morning dip in the pool. Sun's a killer by seven am this time of year. Then a hearty breakfast—Ted's specialty—he's a gourmet chef.'

'It's tempting, thank you, but I promised Bert and Cassie I'd heft luggage in exchange for their kindness.' Ben also needed assurance that HS would supply plane tickets for himself and Mac. For that, he needed to use the pastor's computer. 'Come on Mac. Help me clear the table and stack the dishwasher.'

'No need for that.' The pastor's wife smiled. 'You're our guests.'

'It's the least we can do.' Ben stood. Anything to move things along.

His suggestion that Mac join HOPE's afternoon practice session to 'avoid the appearance of impropriety' evoked eye-rolling huffs of 'don't be ridiculous' and 'Regency protocols belong in Jane Austen novels.' Thankfully, Cassie had intervened and piqued her interest. Mac had pretended to flutter a fan as she left.

Now, finally, he was alone with the pastor's computer.

I hope you have good news for me Chris, like an all clear to bring Mac to Canberra.

Ben found two message files from Chris, one titled 'Mac's Eyes Only Priv & Conf'. Ben suppressed his annoyance. He was effectively Mac's guardian, if not ipso facto then at least in loco parentis. What did Chris have to say to Mac that warranted privacy? But Ben only opened his own message.

Hey Dro!

I feel like a burst appendix here. Useless and hurting like hell! YOU DIDN'T CALL! I thought you and Mac were DEAD!!!!! Mac's dunking drowned the STIR transmissions. They clicked in early today (Tues). Thank God you're both alive.

What can I do? Contact me! I smashed the screen on my mobile. I'm off to get a replacement now (mid-arvo), so NO EXCUSES DRO! Get on the blower, asap!

I know you're hitching home via woop woop. Hope you're headed south. Spooked by the police manhunt, hey? But isn't running more sus? You posted the DVR right? Doesn't that clear you?

Mac sent me a blast that'd make a bullocky blush. Threatened dire consequences if 'Ben's bro' read her thoughts. As I hope to father children one day I promised Mac (other msg) I'll only read transcripts with a code word (Arianna) so I know her message is intentional. I need to add a 'search and flag' command, but I can't crack the software GRUnGE. What are the pass codes?

Meanwhile, I'll check transcripts for signs of trouble. (Read: Risking my privates to save yours!) TALK TO ME DRO!!!!

HS is in Spain. Back Thurs am.

Bro.

Ben replied:

Hey Chris,

Sorry for stressing you out. No phone or internet till now. No money either, but we're safe with a Christian outreach team—real Good Samaritans. They're at Tennant Creek till Monday, then touring Alice Springs and places south for six weeks. We'd rather not be puppeteer wannabes for weeks.

You need to sus HS out for me, Bro. Even confront him. I never doubted Chassic's integrity until Talbot Locke suggested the Leicester profile was a paedophile thing. Maybe he knew about Mac all along (tracked her via Jake?) hence his relaxed approach to locating her. Need to know! Grr!

Doesn't explain the car bomb, unless it was meant for HS. He drove that SUV before assigning it to me. And Mac really was in danger. Coincidence? Sabotage and murder? I think not. But if HS wanted Mac or me silenced, wouldn't he have done it long ago?

Sorry, mate. I'm thinking on the fly here. If you can send an all clear while we're still at Tennant Creek (with GRUnGE access), Mac and I could fly to Canberra from Alice Springs. We'll need ASPT to pay though. I drained my funds when I went AWOL. Otherwise, we'll ride with HOPE and hope for the best.

Over to you, Bro. I can check the GRUnGE till Mon am. Landline 08 8962 1169. Hope to get prepaid mobile tomorrow. Will phone/text number. Reception's lousy here. Thanks Bro.

Dro.
PS: Pat's pass code system click here

54. SKEWED

Thursday 22 November 2012

Outback Australia

MAC SQUATTED at the rear of the marquee, distancing herself from the team's flurry and scowling as she contemplated a dozen despicable ways to repay Ben for shunting her off.

Until Cassie sought her out. 'Want to come for a walk with me while they set up?'

'Sure, although I'd like to watch them practise.'

'We'll be back for that.'

Mac trotted beside Cassie, grateful for the distraction. They discovered a park nearby and settled under a shady tree. 'It's strange how the heat out here shimmers the air. It skews ordinary things into surreal masterpieces.'

'A common trick of perception displacing reality,' Cassie said. 'As though time itself has taken a break so we can step into another dimension, wander through an imagined future, explore a distant memory, or experience an ancient dream.'

'Yes! Like *The Persistence of Memory*. Salvador Dali's melting clocks!'

'You know Dali's work?'

Mac nodded. 'Art assignment research. I was hooked. His double images fascinate me. It's like I'm looking in a mirror, where real me and fake me coexist in a twisted, irrational mess. Dali painted swans on a lake, but their reflections look like elephants. That's me. I had to shove all this grey cumbersome stuff under the surface, but I can't forget it. It clings. Pretending it's not there is unreal. I wish I could tell someone, you know? Or even write it down in a diary, but the only thing I'm allowed to write on is my memory. It's like a swansong I can never sing.'

Cassie looked thoughtful. 'They do say, "where there's a will, there's a way." Dali expressed his hidden world through his art. He pulled ideas from dreams and hallucinations and put rational and irrational thoughts out there in a way that was interesting and fascinating, but still obscure.'

'I'm not much of an artist though.'

'You may not be a visual artist, but you have a phenomenal vocabulary. You want to be a writer, don't you?'

'One day.'

'What's to stop you writing your truth in fiction?'

'Isn't fiction made-up stories?'

'Even fiction writers incorporate universal and personal truths in their stories. Real life experience not only informs our writing, it influences our voice, makes it unique.'

'I hadn't considered that. Truth in fiction. Duh! It's so obvious.'

'If you're worried about privacy, use a pseudonym.'

'I'm living a pseudonym. I'm not sure if I know what's real any more.'

55. TILTED

Thursday 22 November 2012

Canberra, Australia

'YOU AND me both, sis.' Chris was ready to scratch his eyes out, irritated by more than screen fatigue. Mac's transcripts were stuffed with absurdities. Maybe, like Alice in Wonderland, she'd fallen down a rabbit hole. Or he had. But if he wanted to find her …

Here we go again, Alice.

LIES/MXP2/20121122pm54484

'HI, EVERYBODY. I'm Potsherd Pavarotti. Are you ready to watch the show? That's great! Are you ready to meet my friends? Terrific! One of my friends is here, and ready. She's Rilly Truly Reddy.'

'Hi, Pots. Hi everybody. Listen, Pots, ready or not, you have to fire Milly.'

'Fire who?'

'Milly Nilly Reddy, my silly dilly sister, who's never ever ready.'

'Truly, Rilly, I can't fire Milly.'

'Why not, Pots?'

'I didn't hire Milly. She's a volunteer.'

'Then volunteer her outta here.'

'Why would I do that?'

'Because she calls the audience, ewes, like they was sheep.'

'Were sheep.'

'Well, if you insist. All hail Potsherd Pavarotti!'

'What are you doing, Rilly?'

'Following orders. I want you to fire Milly, not me. You said "worship", so I did.'

'Not worship. Were sheep. You said "was sheep". You mixed your singulars and your plurals. "Were sheep" is proper grammar.'

'Try telling that to Milly.'

'Hi, Rilly! Hypotenuse! What's your angle? I'll set youse straight!'

'Aargh! She did it again! Milly doesn't know her proper grammar.'

'I do so too! She lives in a suitcase with our proper Grandpa.'

'Oh, Milly!'

Another puppet play, replete with dad joke humour. Chris groaned and face-palmed. Mac was clearly enamoured with the performance—the transcript was conspicuously devoid of her usual cynical inner commentary.

Curiouser and curiouser.

A new message arrived from Ben, phone number included. Chris picked at his scabs, too drained to sustain anything beyond indifference.

Who's your puppet, Alejandro? Me? Mac?

Chris toyed with his mobile phone. What could he say? He had nothing left to pretend with. Stuff it. HS could ring Ben.

Chris had a higher priority—adding the Arianna flag to the software to protect Mac's privacy.

There was another option … destroy the software. Claim his coding addition corrupted the whole file, leaving it beyond redemption. But who'd believe that? Of course, he could still do it. Own the decision. Stuff the consequences.

Ben's linked message explained Pat's GRUnGE code was disguised as Lukas Nuevo (New) Int +34 912 223157, to be interpreted as: Username: Luke NewTestament; Password: 223157NIV; Sudoku alpha-code: The first two or more letters of each verse from Luke 22:31-57 in the New International Version of the Bible.

Chris sighed. Ben had done it again—rubbed his nose in inadequacy like a pup that had piddled the rug. He'd forgotten Pat's Bible reference method.

He searched for an online NIV and picked a link. A pop-up appeared which offered daily inspiration free to his inbox. No way, José! He hit the X, but a sample took its place, in big, glaring letters:

If an enemy insulted me, I could endure it;
If a foe rose against me, I could hide.
But it is you, a man like myself,

my companion, my close friend,
with whom I enjoyed sweet fellowship
at the house of God.
Psalm 55:12-14

The words challenged him, mocked him, pulsed within him. Enemy. Foe. You. My close friend. Friend against friend. Ben against him? Or he against Ben? If only he could unsee what he'd read as easily as he could unfriend Ben.

They weren't even the verses he needed. He located and copied them intending to delete all but the essential letters. Oddly enough, he felt compelled to read them first. Why, he didn't know. To glimpse Pat's motivations, perhaps?

Simon, Simon, Satan has asked to sift you as wheat … I have prayed for you, Simon, that your faith may not fail.

What did that mean? Did it matter? He'd quit believing years ago.

You will deny me three times.

The hair on Chris's neck played porcupine.

'Judas! Do you betray the Son of Man with a kiss?'

Chris bolted from his seat. 'Holy shhhockamole, HS! I didn't hear you come in.'

'Your door was open. I've been watching a while.' HS pointed to the screen. 'Powerful words.'

Chris swallowed. 'Ben's message included this reference. And a phone number. I haven't called it. I thought you'd want to do that.'

'I do. Jot it down for me please? I'll phone Ben now.'

Chris obliged.

HS nodded at the computer screen. 'That scripture gives you access to the LIES software—is that what the message implies?'

'Apparently.'

'I thought the software worked fine.'

'It does. I need to code a flag word into it.'

'Why?'

'It will allow Mac to say or think a unique word or phrase as permission to transcribe. Otherwise the communication is unintentional and/or private—don't transcribe.'

'Sounds reasonable. But it can wait until Ben's back. He's the software expert. We wouldn't want to corrupt the program by accident, would we?'

Chris choked on spit. 'C-course not.' His eyes watered.

'Print Ben's other message and bring it to me directly please?' HS rapped on Chris's door as he left.

Chris shuddered. Who was reading whose mind?

He printed the message, closed the files and reset secure encryption— never leave files open and unattended. Or doors.

He drifted down the hallway, almost colliding with Von. 'Oh, hey Von.'

'Chris, Talbot Locke is here to see you.'

Now? The building tilted.

HS stood in his doorway. 'Thank you, Veronica. Show Agent Locke to my office, please? We'll both be here.'

'Will do, HS.' Von went to get Locke.

HS nodded to Chris. 'Locke's AFP, NWPP liaison. Please, come.'

Chris's shoe locked on the carpet pile. He skidded against the wall. 'You right?'

His equilibrium didn't think so. Chris handed Ben's message to HS and sat as Von and Locke arrived at the door.

'Locke. We meet at last. We've an uncanny knack for bypassing each other.'

Locke shook Chassic's hand without a word.

HS moved behind his desk. 'Ben said you'd called by prior to his unfortunate Majura Park incident. Take a seat.'

Locke slipped a doubtful glance at Chris. 'I ... er—'

'Chris is our newest tech expert. Bright lad with a great future. How can we assist you, Agent Locke?'

Locke rubbed his mouth before he sat. 'Truth is I've run a gauntlet of false reports spiked with innuendo. I didn't want to bother you without something concrete.'

'Not boots, I hope.' Chassic's lip smile was bereft of humour.

'No. God forbid.'

'Amen!'

Locke recoiled at Chassic's vehemence. 'Fact is, we suspected high level agency, or subsidiary staff, were operating a paedophile ring.'

'Serious accusation.'

'The name Horon Sinballidh came up. Given those initials—HS—I held back until I knew for sure. You understand.' Locke cleared his throat.

'What do I understand, Locke?'

'That I had to ensure this office was beyond suspicion before confirming certain information, requested by Mr Benjamin Alejandro concerning one Aidan MacGreggor's status within the National Witness Protection Program.'

'Go on.' HS folded his arms.

Chris slowly released the lungful of air he'd held.

Locke crossed his legs. 'Until I could ascertain the motive behind Ben's enquiry, I could neither confirm nor deny—'

'But you did both.' Chris's outburst gained Chassic's stare and Locke's glare.

Locke cleared his throat again. 'I can confirm Aidan is one of ours, but we've lost him. Temporarily.'

'How is that our concern?' HS asked.

'We believe Aidan was abducted by a male person fitting the description of one Jake Leicester, a person of interest—'

'In a murder enquiry. I read the newspaper, Locke.'

Locke matched Chassic's condescending expression. 'Did the newspaper explain why Ben's photograph and Leicester's are identical? Or how your supposedly deceased employee managed to abscond with Aidan?' Locke spiced his query with sarcasm.

HS filled the silence with … silence.

'Fortunately, I've tracked them to the Northern Territory. I have a charter plane on standby. I intend to fly to Alice Springs to appre— rescue Aidan.'

'And Ben?' HS raised an eyebrow.

'Ben will be questioned, naturally. He'll have no cause for concern if he's innocent of wrongdoing, assuming Aidan is with him voluntarily.'

'Why come to us with this information?'

Locke unfolded his legs and crossed them the other way. 'My investigation has led me to believe that Mr Darnell may know Aidan personally in which case his presence could alleviate Aidan's fears.' Locke's expression was more cavalier than caring.

HS scrutinised Chris. 'How do you feel about Locke's proposal, Chris?'

'I'm … happy to assist, if you believe that's appropriate.' Chris felt the blood drain from his face.

'I'll need to discuss this with Chris privately, Locke. We also have concerns about Ben's safety. We're aware his travelling companion may be at risk, though I can assure you, not from Ben. You'll have our answer in the morning. Good day, Agent Locke. Chris will show you out.' HS picked up the phone.

—◦�〇◦—

CHRIS WALKED Locke to the car park before he spoke. 'HS didn't give much away, did he?'

Locke opened his car door. 'As a gamer, you know how it works. To overthrow an opponent, a player must gain the advantage—a better position, stronger team, accurate intel and a minimum-risk-for-maximum-impact strategy. It's paramount we ensure your sister's safety without raising Chassic's suspicions. Once you and Amy are united and protected, I can take the kill shot, gamewise. Understand?'

Chris nodded.

'Can I count on you, Chris?'

'I'm in. Ben and Mac will be in Alice Springs on Monday.'

'Then so will we.'

Chris waited while Locke phoned to confirm a plane would be ready that evening.

'Thanks, mate. We'll board at … Hang on.' Locke looked at Chris. 'Can you confirm by seven-thirty tonight?'

Chris nodded.

Locke offered a thumbs up. 'Nine pm. Yeah mate, so long as we're underway before midnight. Cheers.' Locke pocketed his phone and got into his car. 'Call me, Chris.' He raised a telephone hand sign to his ear for emphasis before he drove away.

Chris contemplated his return to Chassic's office and decided a three-block walk to procure a caffeinated peace-offering made excellent sense.

56. SURRENDERED

Thursday 22 November 2012

Outback Australia

BEN JIGGLED his knee eight quavers to each heartbeat. *Come on, Chris. Reply.* He rechecked his watch. It had misted up after his ocean dip, but had dried out by the time he'd moved it back half an hour for Australian Central Standard Time.

Daylight Saving! He'd forgotten Canberra was an hour and a half ahead. He jumped as the phone on the desk rang. Should he answer it? His mind blanked on the pastor's name. He scanned the room for a hint. None was forthcoming. Was it Chris calling?

'Ah, afternoon? Pastor's residence.'

'Hello Ben. It's good to hear your voice.'

'HS!'

Three conversations later, first his with HS—

'I'll have Veronica purchase plane tickets and complete a safety check of the Meyers. If that's good, I'll send Chris to meet you Saturday.'

Then HS spoke with Mac. Her reticence to engage collapsed into screams of delight as she learned Chris was her brother, and he was alive. Ben was still digesting that part himself.

And finally, HS with Cassie—

'We're glad we could help, Mr Chassic. Your man's borne the brunt of suspicion, accusation, and Mac's irascibility from the outset, though I've noticed, of late, when Ben waves a white flag, Mac surrenders ... Oh, I'm sure they'll sort it out. I've even detected a hint of affection brewing ... Ha, ha! Perhaps they just need time and space.'

Ben guessed he wasn't meant to overhear that bit. He kept his smile to himself. He still had to survive Mac's interrogation about Chris.

57. STUNG

Thursday 22 November 2012

Canberra, Australia

'I NEEDED to stretch my legs.' Chris placed a takeaway cappuccino on Chassic's desk. 'Hope it's still hot.' *Not*.

Chassic shuddered after the first tepid sip, though he still nodded thanks. Chris turned to leave.

'Please, Chris, take a seat.'

Where to? He sat.

'Ben's message—the one you printed out—is both interesting and informative.' HS read from the sheet. 'You need to sus HS out for me, Bro. Even confront him. I never doubted Chassic's integrity until Talbot Locke ...' HS raised an eyebrow. 'Locke seems to have arrested Ben's attention and yours.'

Chris studied the scratches on the desk's privacy panel.

'Trust is a wonderful and dangerous thing, you know. By testing our mutual trust with his unsupported theory, Locke misused his positional authority to undermine mine.'

Chris inspected his knees.

HS sighed. 'I'm not angry with you or Ben. I'd be more concerned if you'd ignored Locke's theories. I am disappointed. I've tried to create an atmosphere of mutual responsibility, care and trust. I'm sad to see it so easily shaken.'

Chris brushed fluff off his trousers. 'Locke appeared confident with his accusations.'

'And what do you think?'

Chris kept his head low. 'I don't know what to think, or who to believe. You talk of trust, yet you don't even trust your colleagues with your name. For all I know, you could be Horon Sinballidh. Locke's convinced that Pat, Ben and possibly you conspired to use LIES for personal advantage.' He folded both arms. 'All at the expense of Amy and myself. We have the most to lose if I call it wrong.'

HS folded Ben's printed message, then tapped its edge on the desk. 'Horon Sinballidh is a contemporary rendering of Sanballat the Horonite who opposed Nehemiah's work rebuilding the Jewish temple at Jerusalem in the fifth century BCE. It was an alias adopted by a twentieth century assassin and enemy of Israel who inflicted many deaths, until Hosea Shelomah of *HaMossad leModi'in Ule Tafkidim Meyuhadim* thwarted his reign of terror.'

Chris frowned. 'Ha Mossad? As in Israeli intelligence? Are you telling me—?'

'Hosea Shelomah was himself assassinated soon after. His pregnant wife fled her homeland. She wanted to honour her husband by giving his name to their unborn son, but the risk was too great. She simply named him HS and was granted special permission to register the name.' HS stopped tapping the folded page and eyeballed Chris. 'I've no doubt your search of Australian birth records was as effective as every other employee I've ever had in confirming that.'

Chris deadpanned his guilty-as-charged response.

HS continued. 'All I ask is that you reciprocate the Alejandros' good will, if not mine, based on your experience. You've known Locke, what? A week? Less? Pat, Ben and Imee gathered you into their family six years ago because they wanted to protect you. Care for you. And from my observations, they did that very well.'

'Until now.'

'I would say still. Ben put his neck on the line here. He fought to have you brought in to this program. And no, he did not know your real identity, or Amy's. He only wanted the best for you both. That care and concern comes from who he is, Chris, not from what he would gain.'

'So you say.'

'Bah!' HS flipped the folded page across the desk—a paperweight halted its slide. 'Maybe you'll get it once you're reunited with Amy and Ben.'

'I only want what's best for Amy.'

'A noble response. Take tomorrow to settle your soul and pack a travel bag. Agent Karey flies in tomorrow. Veronica's booked a commercial flight for you and Karey to Alice Springs on Saturday morning. Ben and Amy will meet you there.'

'On Saturday? I thought Ben said Monday.'

'Change of plans. I've spoken with Ben. They'll travel tomorrow and stay with ...' HS checked his notepad. 'Ted and Elsie Meyers, part of the Adlers' network. Veronica's checked their bona fides and booked tickets for you all.'

'What about Locke's offer of a private flight?'

HS drummed his fingers. 'What if Locke is the leak that endangered Amy in the first place?'

'Why would he wait till now? He put Amy in witness protection years ago.'

'Chris, Amy is not now, nor has she ever been included in any official witness protection program. I checked.'

'He said it was an especially deep cover.'

'Did he now? And you believe that such information is not available to Australia's Intelligence Security Organisation?'

'Considering our muddy, ruddy need to know policy, I don't know what we know, let alone who knows it.'

'Well, Chris, I know this and so do you. Murderous felons want Amy. Locke might be one of them. If you join him, you'd be risking life and limb.'

'Or I might expose the truth. If he's behind the crime, we should find out.'

'If he is, he's already fooled a lot of savvy and experienced people.'

'And you think I'm neither savvy nor experienced. Was basic training a waste of time?'

'Three weeks training is better than none, but you'd be a sheep among wolves.'

'Maybe. But I'm one savvy, pissed off sheep! Look, I've knocked off virtual bad guys for years. That experience will help me now, like it did in basic training. Our instructor said as much. HS, I *need* to do this. You have to let me go.'

'I am letting you go, Chris, but not with Locke. End of discussion. Go home and pack. I'll send you the Meyers' contact details by text.'

Chris stood. 'I guess I'll see you some time in the future, if I still have a job.'

'Oh, you won't get away from me that easily, Christian.'

Hearing HS use his real name was unnervingly honest—for a change—but, as Chris drove home, the old gripes gripped him harder than ever, dragging his loyalties to Ben, Pat and HS into a cesspool of disillusionment.

Need to know or not, HS still didn't trust him. He'd treated him like a loser while denying him the chance to win. Locke was a federal bigwig, for cryin' out loud. He could sort Ben out if he was dirty. Or vice versa and Ben could be the big hero.

Frankly, Chris couldn't wait to jettison them all. They could wallow in their stinkin' ASPT. He'd take Amy with him to Melbourne, to MPeg, who at least thought he was worth the invitation. Why wait for Saturday when he could fly to Amy tonight?

Chris rang Locke the moment he reached home.

'Good job, Chris. Meet me at the airport. Eight-thirty. There's a hero's reward for you in this. Guaranteed.'

A hero's reward? Who would pay for that? Chris would soon find out whether his mother's 'melon and lemon jam' haunted him too. No good deed ...

<hr />

CHRIS TROTTED across the tarmac towards Locke's aircraft, relieved it had no blue-and-white checks to trigger that awkward feeling you get when a police car flirts with you in traffic. Locke's small charter craft had no obvious markings at all—for undercover operations perhaps?

The interior was also unremarkable, but comfortable.

'It'll be a kangaroo run I'm afraid,' Locke said. 'We'll jump from one small airstrip to another, as the crow flies.'

Chris's phone chirped a text message.

'You X-ers! Social life in a pocket.' Clearly Locke had forgotten Chris's previous correction of his generational faux pas.

Chris checked the message. 'It's the address where Mac will be staying.'

'Ben and Mac.'

'Yeah.'

'Oh, there we go. Phones off and seatbelts on for take-off.' Locke fiddled with his mobile phone and slipped it into the seat pocket in front of him.

Chris followed suit. No point wrestling it into his jeans pocket while he had the seatbelt on.

Once they were airborne, Locke pulled a blanket and pillow from a storage compartment. They were squished in a vacuum sealed bag which Locke offered to Chris.

'Stretch out. Have a kip. I'll do the same after a word with the pilot.' Locke moved toward the cockpit.

Chris doubted he'd sleep, but he'd appreciate the pillow's comfort. It smelt odd, but hey, it had probably shared the cupboard with … the halter and bridle. Chris mounted his golden-winged Pegasus to fly to Amy's rescue …

The sting when a horsefly bit his neck felt surprisingly real.

———◦◦◦———

THE URGE to pee disturbed Chris's sleep-sodden state. The stench from his pillow was revolting.

'What the—? Eww!' Tethers stymied his recoil from a desiccated camel carcass.

He twisted onto his elbow to prop himself up, head woozy, stomach churning, while his eyes accommodated the darkness in this … shack of sorts—corrugated iron, no windows. A shaft of light sliced through a slit near the door.

'Hey! Anybody? Help!'

A dingo yipped and yawled in the distance as Chris's confusion spun the word 'fail' into another dream.

58. PUNCHED
Friday 23 November 2012

Central Australia

BEN HAD begged a break from Mac's inquisition about Chris around 1:00am—after he'd nodded off mid-sentence. Thankfully, a few hours of deep sleep and a hearty breakfast had bolstered his energy reserves, though his emotional reserves were running low. He braced for a reluctant round of goodbyes, grateful for the friendship and spiritual energy imparted by Bert's enfolding hand-shake.

Cassie drew Ben and Mac into a group hug. 'I'm thrilled you two share a brother. A big God makes the world small, eh?'

Mac squeezed her hand. 'I'm going to miss you, a lot. Maybe I could visit? To talk writing and stuff.'

Cassie nodded, swiping a tear. 'I'd love that.'

'Please visit us, Mac.' Sarah hugged her. 'Tully and I will treat you to the girliest adventures imaginable, won't we Tull?'

'The most frivolous and epically awesome girlfriend dates ever! To make up for your socially-deprived high school experience.'

'While you were shut up like Rapunzel.'

'With my hairdo? Surely you mean Cinderella.'

'Ooh!' Tully squealed. 'We could hire a pumpkin carriage and cruise Coolum Esplanade in style.'

'Sans rodents, please. I hate rodents.' Mac shuddered. 'Thank you George Orwell.'

Tully frowned. 'Who?'

'Big brother, watching you!' Sarah pounced on Tully, who shrieked.

Sarah winked at Mac. 'No rats, I promise. We'll organise a pony.'

'On roller skates?' Before Tully could elaborate, it was time to go.

AUSTRALIA'S RED Centre—red rocks, red dust, red sand—splotched with clumps of grey-green spinifex. The horizon's endless foreverness rewrote Ben's perception of wide open spaces.

Mac's animated response to HOPE's puppet show rewrote his understanding of closeted existence.

'I went to a *Play School* concert once. I was adapting to my cochlear implant and missed heaps of action watching Mum sign dialogue. Seeing and hearing Egermeier and Pots and Milly on stage yesterday was amazing. I could *feel* the experience.' Mac shivered her excitement. Since they'd left Tennant Creek, she'd repeated most of the show verbatim. Insulated life experience or not, she was incredibly savvy.

'How come you know so much, kiddo?'

Mac narrowed her eyelids and scrunched her adorable nose. 'I snuggled into my pillow and bwankey and I read lots and lots and lots of books, Benny. I read picture books and nursery rhymes and chapter books and novels, anthologies, biographies, history books and other texts. I listened to music, researched art, watched documentaries and—'

'Okay, okay. I asked a stupid question.' Ben raised his hands in surrender.

'How did you spend your time?'

'Reading superhero graphic novels and watching spy thrillers. Oh, I also tried to beat my brother—'

'*My* brother.'

'*Our* brother at computer games.' Ben patted himself on the head. 'And sang what a good boy am I.'

'He thrashed you every time, didn't he?'

'Yup. I won when the blue moon rose on Sunday.' Ben winked.

'Sounds like you had an idyllic upbringing.'

He had, compared to hers.

Mac slapped her hand over her mouth. 'I'm so sorry. How could I say that when you lost your parents too? That's the trouble with being a misery guts. You think you're the only one with troubles.'

Ben smiled a little sadly. 'I miss them terribly. But at least I grew up with them around. I have so many wonderful memories.'

'I treasure the good memories too.' She gave a short, puzzled frown. 'Last night you mentioned Chris had moved out. When?'

'About a year ago. After Mum left.'

'It's weird knowing my brother shared your mum. I wish I'd known her. I reckon Chris shoulda stayed with you. Family is everything.'

'Maybe he had to find—' Ben's throat locked. Mac had gathered his hand into hers, leaned over and rested her head against his shoulder. He swallowed. 'Had to find—'

She bolted upright. 'Ben! You found me! You *found* me! I used to wish … I never thought … I mean I prayed, and—' Mac's eyes went wide and she gripped his arm like she was drowning again. 'You found me! When I was drowning—no! Before! When I was so angry with Brock for sabotaging my exams—I heard this voice sort of come into my head. It said, "Don't fight me, Mac. Trust me." Don't you see?'

See what?

Mac shook him. 'That's what you said. "Don't fight me, Mac. Trust me." I thought my brain wanted me to stop fighting and die. But you said it, didn't you?'

'I don't know. I might have. You were thrashing like a hooked fish. I wanted you to—'

'Stop fighting and trust you.' Mac touched his chin, claiming his dedicated gaze. 'I never even thanked you, for finding me.' Mac kissed her finger and touched it to his cheek.

His mind went completely blank.

'Sounds like divine intervention to me.' Ted Meyers made a huffing sound. 'Thank you, Jesus!'

For several kilometres, Mac supplied companionable silence, while Ben's innards juggled cannonballs.

Ted interrupted both. 'Let's get some music happening. Plug your phone in, Elsie?'

'Which playlist?'

'Do you like Newsboys, Mac?'

'I don't know them.'

'The puppets performed some of their songs last night,' Ben said.

'When the audience did the hand-wave-in-sync thing?'

'Yeah. You can do that with a lot of Newsboys' songs.'

'My hearing set-up is attuned to speech more than music. I had special earbuds for music. Oh! Is that them?'

'One of their specials,' Elsie said, 'for a VeggieTales song mix.'

'VeggieTales?'

'Singing, dancing vegetables—with attitude. Once I introduce you to my VeggieTales collection, your life will be complete.' Ben grinned. 'Guaranteed.'

'A likely story. Now shush so I can listen … Jonah and the whale? Clever rhyme scheme. Rap's cool but the words are so quick. Can you play it again?'

Ted obliged.

'Hmm. Catchy.'

'Sounds a bit fishy to me.' Ben winked.

Mac groaned. 'Quit your *belly*aching.'

'Touché.' They high-fived.

'HOPE should use that one.'

'They do,' Elsie said.

'You know, my speech quirks could sound cute coming from a furry monster.'

Ben nodded. 'Egermeier and Mac, Lost in the Desert.'

'Nah. I'd need a pseudonym to keep my identity secret.'

'Egermeier and Slack, Lost in the— Ow!' Mac had thumped him.

'How about Egermeier and Whack?' Mac added another thump.

'You got me already. You're worse than Chris playing punch buggy.'

'Punch buggy?'

'A road trip game. Pick a car type or colour. The first person to see one yells "punch buggy" and thumps the loser.'

'That was fun?' Mac looked dubious.

Ben shrugged. 'Chris thought so. But seriously Mac, you'd be a terrific puppeteer. You'd never forget the script.'

'I'd want to write new skits all the time, so I didn't get bored and resort to playing silly games, like punch buggies.' Mac thumped.

'Ow! Punch buggy. It's singular, not plural. Ow! Ow, ow, ow, ow!'

'It's plural now!' Mac grinned like a puppy.

THE BED in the Meyers' home was deliciously comfortable, but sleep eluded Ben. Mac's banter had filled him with delight, but his thoughts churned in the midnight hush.

Chassic's phone call had been wonderful.

And terrible. With their adversary still at large, Ben's responsibility to keep Mac safe overshadowed his relief at their imminent reunion with

Chris. HS had been frank about the complications Ben faced. 'They'll rap you over the knuckles for interfering with evidence, leaving the crime scene, or both. Video footage shows you were in the house, but Chris said you retrieved footage of the actual murder.'

The actual murder! He relived the ugly horror of it, the race to Pumicestone Passage, the shock of the water, the flesh and blood mortality of Mac as he'd tried to calm her thrashing terror. His body memories of her were so ... vivid!

The skin on his arm tingled as it had when Mac had grabbed it in the car. Ben sucked air and choked on saliva.

Drowning in my own spit—what an ignominious way to die. If nothing else kills me first.

He blew his nose, stuffed an extra pillow under his shoulders, stretched his arms over his head, and reflected on Mac's unrestrained chatter during the day's drive. What a difference from the surly, sour Mac of those early transcripts. Perhaps they really were lies after all. A façade, a shabby veneer tacked over an original beauty. He had glimpsed that original. It was—*oh, Mac, to see your true self liberated would be amazing.*

Ben chided himself. He needed to rein himself in—Mac was only sixteen. He rolled over and winced. Mac's plural punch buggies were still talking. Even that recollection made him smile. Not that he'd appreciated Mac thumping him, albeit in jest, but she'd behaved like ... a kid sister, a joy she'd been denied for so long. She was right. Family was everything. For sure, he could be another big brother for Mac.

And the heaviness returned. This time, he understood its substance. It was not about responsibility, or safety, or legal ramifications.

The ache in his chest was all about losing Mac and Chris. They belonged to each other, but not to him. In truth, he had no legitimate claim on either of them. His parents hadn't adopted Chris. He'd been Dad's ward, a legal responsibility. In the eyes of the law, he'd become his own man at eighteen—quick to exercise his independence, and distance himself from Ben.

True, they'd joined forces to find Mac—after Chris had recognised Amy, though he hadn't trusted Ben with his secret.

Despite his risking all to save her, Mac had shared snippets about herself reluctantly. Their connection held no guarantees, had no strings attached, especially if she chose to lose the implant.

Or him. Tears stung his eyes and burned hot across his face. He'd already lost his family.

Losing Mac as well? He'd rather die.

———✦———

AN HOUR later, Ben woke lathered in sweat and rose to get a drink. He threw a cotton bathrobe, borrowed from Ted, over his boxer shorts and opened the bedroom door.

Rrrrrrrrrump!

The noise sounded like a van door sliding shut. Ben glanced at the hall clock. At midnight? He padded towards the front door. It was locked. A shadow brushed the window and moved on. Ben's heart rate kicked up a notch. He eased the curtain aside and peered through the glass. An eerie disc glowed and hovered above the Meyers' RV.

Beside the RV, a Mitsubishi Delica four-wheel-drive van cast a spooky shadow—in the ambient light of a streetlamp, not a spaceship. Ben relaxed with a chuckle. The Meyers probably had older children, or boarders. They seemed most hospit—

'Ow!' Ben's neck burned as he slumped.

59. TEMPTED
Saturday 24 November 2012

Central Australia

SINBLED SQUATTED in the spindly shade of an anorexic beefwood tree. At least the tree grew upwind of the stink wafting from Deabrua's shack. The only alternative—a scrawny clump of feather duster desert oaks—grew downwind.

Local scuttlebutt claimed a hikikomori-plagued hermit had built the isolated shack in obedience to a 'divine' revelation. He'd hedged himself in by planting a 'crown of thorns' comprised of Euphorbia milii, a spiny succulent. Though Hiki Harry had long since departed his desolate mortal existence, the noxious herbaceous icon had flourished. Its latest victim, a young feral camel, decomposed inside the shack.

How Deabrua had appropriated Harry's shack was anybody's guess, but it was the perfect escape when escape was no option. Deabrua had devised an ingenious, if heinous, assortment of rope and pulley tethers to ensure guests enjoyed an extended stay, under his control.

A recent shower had topped up the corrugated metal rainwater tank built into the shack's structure. The water tasted surprisingly good. Nevertheless, Sinbled had opted for motel comfort overnight and left the swag—spread under a rocky overhang outside the shack—to Deabrua.

The brouhaha emanating from Deabrua's Delica confirmed Ben's sedation had worn off. He was shackled to a bar inside the van's cargo space. No doubt Deabrua planned to hammer out a deal with his usual vile hubris. Hopefully Ben had the sense to cooperate.

No regrets …

Sinbled shifted to the scant apron of shade cast by his own four-wheel-drive and squatted again, out of sight but close enough to listen in.

'I apologise for my unorthodox invitation, young sir, but you're a hard man to nail down.' Deabrua's guttural rasp polluted the desert's torrid hush. 'Zorro De Broker, International Business Consultant and Network Negotiator, at your service.'

Pompous git. Sinbled missed Ben's mumbled response.

'Your young lady friend and her brother are relaxing in a luxurious rustic retreat, awaiting the success of our impending negotiations.'

'Potato bake with a lemon roll? Not in New Delhi!'

Huh? Sinbled cupped his ear.

'Criminal? That's a bit harsh, considering we've only just met.'

'Break and enter! Abduction! Illegal restraint! And hats for farters!'

Sinbled cupped the other ear.

'As you're in no position to argue, I suggest you shut up and listen. I represent a private investor who requires your technological expertise. He's prepared to make a substantial upfront payment for your existing software, and provide an ongoing development retainer. I'm talking big money—billionaire bucks.'

'Blood money, you mean, if your investor condones kidnap.'

Clear enough.

'Everyone's a critic. Or a hypocrite. Technically, you abducted the girl, after your boss tried to kill you.'

Ben's silence shouted.

Deabrua hawked and spat phlegm. 'What can I say? Betrayal's a bitch. Why not stick it to the man? Put yourself in control with our financial backing. It's your legacy, after all.'

'Which makes it my business, not yours.'

'Not entirely. Our Spanish network offered the scheme's originators financial assistance and protection, in exchange for international sales rights to the end product. Regrettably, Dr Maxwell declined our offer and his family suffered the consequences. Your father was wise enough to accept and he reaped the benefits.'

Another hushed hiatus then, 'My father's dead.'

'Sadly. Señor Alejandro suffered an unfortunate accident when he moved beyond our protective net. Your loss is our loss. Nevertheless, we're willing to compensate you with our guaranteed protection, for mutual profit. *El Volcan* is the king of investors in volatile ground-breaking technologies. As his hottest, brightest talent, you would be prince. As his protégé, virtually invincible.'

'My father would never endorse your treachery. Neither will I. You're deranged to think I'd agree.' Thuds echoed as Ben kicked against his prison.

'You sanctimonious turd, insulting my hospitality. Perhaps a taste of my speciality will change your mind.' Deabrua snarled and dished out several thwacks of his 'specialty'—a braided leather whip—till Ben groaned from the blows.

Sinbled stood and shook circulation back into his legs, waving Deabrua over when he paused to catch his breath. 'Sort it, Moz. I'll finalise arrangements for our own and Miss Maxwell's journey to Ulvelaik.'

'What of the Maxwell boy?'

'If you can't extract access codes from Ben, work on Chris.'

'And if that fails?'

'Not an option, despite your usual form.'

'You'd have none of this but for me.'

'It's too hot to bicker.' Sinbled moved to get into his vehicle.

Deabrua pulled a gun. 'I could easily end your part in this now.'

'Why don't you? Extract the codes all for yourself. Get yourself and dear little Amy to Canberra. Waltz into ASPT and help yourself to the software. I assume you know your way around a computer? Then get yourself, the girl, and the software out of the country.' Sinbled's easy smile induced Deabrua's eye tic. 'Sorry, Moz. You need me as much as I need you.'

Deabrua tucked the firearm into the back of his trousers. 'I'll get the codes, don't you worry. I've rigged a persuasive set up inside for this mongrel.'

Sinbled nodded and climbed into the driver's seat. Before he shut the door, he added, 'If not, I'll need Chris alive. *Compos mentis* is optional. Two offspring may provide more leverage over the doctor than one. But you'll pay for the inconvenience.' Sinbled slammed the door.

Deabrua thumped it. Sinbled watched him carry his rage across to Ben.

'I've withdrawn my offer, boy! Give me the access codes, or I'll rip them from your hide.' He dragged Ben from the van and kicked him over and over, bulldozing him into Hiki Harry's thorns.

Sinbled drove off, leaving them to choke on his dust.

60. DENIED

Saturday 24 November 2012

Central Australia

CHRIS'S NEED to pee had passed. He could push wakefulness further into the day, but not his need to—

Breathe! He gasped and gulped putrefied air. It countered his drug-induced apnoea, not the stench. Where on earth was he?

Screamin' piglets! He was still in the shack, lying on a dead camel. Another prone body rested nearby—female, breathing, and familiar!

'Amy? Amy, is that you? Amy! Wake up!' Chris stretched his foot as far as his tethers allowed and nudged Amy's knees with his toes. 'Amy! Wake up.' He nudged harder.

Her eyelids fluttered. 'Five more minutes, Daddy?'

Daddy? What the—? Chris toed her again. 'Amy Maxwell! Wake up. It's not safe.'

No response. Chris wriggled and yanked against his restraints, edging his feet close enough for a firm side swipe.

Amy jerked awake, her face contorting as the camel stink registered. Ropes thwarted her upward lunge. She fell back with a sort of mewing sound before making a calculated effort to sit, tucking her knees and rocking. She stared, wide-eyed. 'Dad?'

Chris shook his head. 'Not Dad. Chris! Big brother. Remember?' He shimmied onto his bottom.

Amy squinted. 'You're backlit. I can't see you very well. Your face is in shadow.' She scanned their odd surroundings. 'What is this place?'

Chris followed her gaze towards a rumpled heap of ... Ben?

'Ben! Ow-ah! Help!' Amy wailed.

'Ben! Wake up! Talk to us, Dro!' Too far for a toe jab.

'Help! Ben's hurt!'

'He's probably been—'

'You! Help him!'

'—drugged, Amy. He'll—'

'Please! Whoever you are. I'm begging you.' Amy babbled right over Chris's reply.

No processor! Without it, she couldn't hear him. He leaned into a shaft of sunlight and touched his mouth. 'Read my lips, Amy.'

She homed in on his face. He spoke carefully, signing as best he could with his wrists zip-tied—spelling worked best.

'Chris! Wow! You're so like Dad now. It's incredible.' A buoyant smile lifted her expression.

A stranger's entrance sank it. 'No point yelling. Nothing but desert and dingoes around here.' He pulled a small box from his shirt pocket and flipped it open. Amy shied as he pressed her implant's sound processor to the medical abutment in her head.

'Don't worry, princess. I have bigger fish than you to gut today.' He sneered at Chris. 'Or skin, as the mood takes me. Have knife. Will cut.'

Chris sat mute as a stunned mullet while Amy turned her processor on, an awkward manoeuvre with her wrists tied. She had plenty to say.

'Who the devil are you? What've you done to Ben?'

'Who the devil am I?' His tone mocked. 'Your mother called me a devil. I am indeed, Mozorrotua Deabrua, devil in the flesh, sent to torment unruly brats.' He raised his arm to strike Amy.

'Leave her alone, you mongrel or I'll—' Chris wrenched himself as far upright as he could.

'What? Cast me out? When you're trussed up like a pig on a spit?' Deabrua laughed. 'Poor little Chrissy's wet his britches.'

Chris's face burned. He'd no idea how long he'd been sedated, but the stain on his jeans confirmed nature had taken its course.

Deabrua placed a metal bucket beside Amy. 'Facilities for your comfort, m'lady. Can't have you following your brother's indelicate example.'

Amy shook her head. 'I don't need to go.'

'Don't be shy, princess.' He cut her ankle ties. 'I'm happy to admire the foliage while you attend to your ablutions.'

'I said I don't—'

'Pee in the bucket! Or else! Oi! You! Pisspants!' He turned and backhanded Chris. 'Make sure she does!' He booted Chris's hip—hard on the bone—and went outside.

'For pity's sake, Amy, go while he's gone. At least you're wearing a nightdress, not jeans.' Chris turned away, brimming with shame. What a fool he'd been to trust Locke, defying HS just to bolster his own pathetic ego.

Deabrua returned and added his own contribution to the bucket in front of them. Vulgar, disgusting philistine. Thankfully, Amy had the sense to close her eyes. The mangy devil hawked and spat phlegm into the bucket before he re-zipped his fly.

'Time to wake Mr Alejandro I think.' Deabrua hefted the bucket—

And tipped its contents over Ben's face. Unbelievable!

Ben grunted and gagged.

'You filthy barbarian!' Amy's eyes blazed.

'You wanted to chat with your friend, didn't you? Would you rather I used your drinking water?' Deabrua tossed the bucket. It clanged against the water tank and bounced off its wooden platform.

Amy shuddered. 'What sort of monster are you?'

'I'm nasty and horrible and I eat brats for breakfast.' Deabrua growled, curling his hands like claws. But he whistled as he unhooked an enamel mug and drizzled water into it, helping himself before handing the mug to Chris. 'Don't forget to share. Must care for the merchandise.'

Chris strained to pass the cup to Amy. 'I can't reach.'

Deabrua tipped his head to the side. 'You see? You are totally dependent upon me.' He adjusted Chris's tether. 'You and me will get along fine, if you cooperate.'

Chris wriggled closer to Amy and helped her drink first. He sipped a couple of mouthfuls and held out the mug. 'We've finished thank you. Please give Ben a drink.'

'Sure, if he coughs up the access code for his software. Or you do.'

A dreadful foreboding seized Chris as the brute used tethers—like his own—to haul Ben upright against a roof support post which intersected a cross-beam about head height. Ben dangled, a puppet in a shredded bathrobe, head slumped forward.

Deabrua tied off the ropes and ripped Ben's robe off him, exposing horrendous welts and lacerations.

Amy gasped.

'Like my handiwork, princess? I'm quite the artist.'

Deabrua threw the robe's bloodied remnants over Amy. She flinched and yelped.

'Shut it! Or your brother joins him.' Deabrua smacked Ben's face, back and forth. 'Wake up, you cur. I want you to feel this.'

Amy signed, 'Do something,' behind Deabrua's back.

'What can I—?' Chris blanked on the sign for 'do'. 'I'm stuck.' Like the king-sized potato lodged in his throat.

'Interrupt!' Amy's glare goaded him.

'Stop!'

Deabrua spun round.

Chris swallowed. 'If you want software access, don't waste your time on Ben.'

'So you can help?'

'Not me. Ben's father encrypted the software. I could use it, but not unlock it. You'll have to talk to Pat.'

'Should I read crash debris like tea leaves?' Deabrua sneered.

'Pat's not dead. He survived.'

'I'm in no mood for fairy tales.'

'But it's true.'

'What is truth but the utterance of a soul in despair? Or pain?' Deabrua spat, backhanded Chris, and went outside again.

Moments later, a diesel generator sputtered into action and Chris heard the explosive *phit* of compressed air being released.

The devil returned with a nail gun attached to an air hose. 'If Pat is alive, no doubt he communicated the code to his son. Or to you.' He aimed the nail gun at the stain on Chris's jeans.

'No! For cryin' out loud, I don't know! I can't help you!'

'We'll see.' Nail gun in one hand, knife in the other, Deabrua sliced Ben's wrist tie and pocketed the knife. He slapped Ben's face to rouse him. 'What's the code, boy?'

Ben mumbled incoherently.

Deabrua turned to Chris. 'What'd he say?'

'He said, "They don't know".'

The maniac grabbed Ben's left arm, held it against the cross-beam and fired a nail through Ben's palm.

Amy screamed.

'No!' Chris yelled. 'For all that's sacred and holy, no!'

Ben's breath scraped and rattled.

Deabrua pushed Ben's right hand to the cross beam. 'Cough up the code, or convince your piss-weak mate to give it up. It's all the same to me.'

'Chris, if you know the code, tell him,' Amy pleaded.

'Don't you think I would if I could, sis?' He'd be signing death warrants for himself and Ben if he did. And God alone knew what horrors awaited Amy if Deabrua gained access.

'Last chance.' Deabrua punched Ben's stomach.

Ben gagged and gasped. 'Let'm go. Chris can't ... help.' His voice rasped. He looked at Chris. 'Look after Mac, Bro. Love ... you.'

Deabrua nailed Ben's right hand.

Amy vomited.

Deabrua's face contorted as he snarled at Chris. 'Feet next! His or yours? Give me what I want.'

'I can't! I got nothing.' Chris's frantic headshake cricked his neck.

Outside, a dingo howled an eerie rebuke.

Deabrua slammed the nail gun against Ben's feet—one, two, three bursts failed. Two didn't. The gun jammed again. Deabrua pelted it at the wall with a curse. The hose clamp fractured on impact, pinging the tank. Pressurised air whooshed as the hose split from the gun and whipped wildly, smacking Deabrua's legs and Chris's chest.

Deabrua yelled and ducked. 'This isn't over!' He fled the shack leaving Chris warding off blows from the snaking hose.

Till Deabrua killed the compressor.

Ironically, Chris's defensive movements had loosened his wrist ties a couple of notches. He'd still have tethers to deal with, but a sudden yank might—

Deabrua returned with an auto-ignition butane blowtorch.

'Perhaps you'll cooperate if I burn pretty patterns into your sister.' He lit it and bent over Amy.

Chris yanked. 'For God's sake, Deabrua! She's a kid! I'll give you what you want. Just ... please don't hurt her. She's suffered enough.'

Deabrua straightened. 'I'll be back with notepad and pencil.'

'I can't—'

Deabrua grabbed Amy's pixie-cut curls, wrenched her head back to expose her face and raised the burner.

'No! Stop! It's not a password. It's an interactive encryption program. Solving one stage generates a key to unlock the next.'

'Can you download the software to a laptop here?'

'Do you have satellite broadband?'

Deabrua released his grip and turned his back on Amy. She thrust her bound fists up between his legs. He doubled over with a yowl. She booted the back of his knees and knocked him sprawling—he dropped the burner. Chris grabbed it, slammed it into Deabrua's head—once, twice! Knocked him out.

'Way to go, sis!' Chris burned through his bindings and released Amy.

'Quick! Free Ben!' Amy scrambled towards him.

'We need to pull the nails out before I burn the ropes. Look for—'

Crack! A bullet whacked the butane burner from his grasp. Deabrua! Up on one elbow! Firing! Chris shoved Amy aside.

Crack! A bullet struck Ben's side. Chris whirled and launched a powerful roundhouse kick at Deabrua's head. Another shot went wild as he collapsed.

'Chris! He shot Ben! We've got to—' A boom and a burst of flames cut Amy off.

'Butane's blown!' Flames licked the base of the tank stand and leapt towards the doorway. 'Run, Amy! Run!' Twenty-seven fire-filled images underscored Chris's scream.

'What about Ben?'

Ben's eyes flickered open and shut. 'Go!' A command. 'I'm done.' He exhaled and his body slumped.

Chris propelled his sister through the door. She fought to turn back, but flames raced outward and upward, devouring the doorposts. Chris grabbed her arm and dragged her. 'There's a van. Amy! Come on!'

She wept as Chris half pulled, half carried her to the van. He wrenched the driver's door open. 'Keys are here! Thank God.' He bundled Amy up and over to the passenger's seat as a bullet smashed into the rear tailgate.

Amy screamed. 'He's coming again!'

Chris gunned the engine and planted his foot, spewing a shower of sand and gravel behind them. The onslaught turned Deabrua, but not the flames. They spat their triumph in the van's mirrors as Chris accelerated.

God forgive me! Chris gritted his teeth and drove as though fleeing the fires of hell itself.

61. MOURNED

Monday 26 November 2012

Central Australia

'WHATEVER HIS justification, your hot-headed recruit inserted himself into the situation. His absurd and preposterous actions created an unmitigated disaster. I agree with Proctor. We should lock him up and throw away the key.'

'Please! I didn't mean to—' Chris rocketed awake. Who the heck was Proctor? As sensibility returned, Chris realised Proctor et al spoke from the television on the wall. 'Where am I?'

'Alice Springs Hospital,' said the middle-aged man sitting nearby.

Chris vaguely remembered asking the question before. His drug-addled brain was still slow on the uptake. 'Where's Amy?'

'Your sister is in the next ward. She's fine, physically.' The man offered his hand. 'I'm Bert. We met Mac and Ben on the road.'

Chris swung his legs over the side of the bed. 'I need to see her.' He stood and his knees buckled.

Bert steadied him. 'Not if you collapse first. Besides, you have a drip in your arm. Back to bed with you.'

Chris had no strength to argue. As he flopped onto his pillow, the whole shack nightmare returned—dead camel, nail gun, fire—backed with the panic of being lost in the desert. Thank God for Amy's good sense to check the glove box for a GPS, and for the welcome relief when they found Santa Teresa.

That only left the soul-wrenching guilt of causing Ben's horrible death. 'What have I done?' Tears of shame and remorse flowed unchecked.

Bert passed him a box of tissues. 'It's a brave thing you did, son, saving your sister. Now, sit up and have a drink. Orange juice, by the looks of it.' Bert helped him sit up, peeled the lid off a small tub of juice and handed it to him.

Chris sipped, then gulped the rest.

A nurse arrived with a trolley. 'Time for obs.'

The phrase stirred painful memories.

Bert stood to leave, but she waved him back.

'You're right. Temp, pulse and blood pressure. Nothing embarrassing.' The nurse winked at Chris. 'Your sister's doing well, mate. Dehydrated, but not as bad as you, and no burns. Can I check the dressings on your ankles?' Chris surveyed his ankles as if they were a foreign attachment. He winced as the nurse's touch proved otherwise. 'Sorry. Still a bit tender? All looks good. Heard you dodged a fire. Outback camp outs are fun till it goes wrong. Try a luxury beach motel next time, eh?' The nurse trundled out.

Chris checked his wrist. Hospital ID band. No watch. 'What time is it, um … Bert is it?'

'Bert Adler.'

'Cassie's Bert?'

'That's me.'

'Weren't you in Tennant Creek till Monday?'

'We left Sunday morning, after we heard about the kidnapping.'

'Sunday! What's today?'

'It's Monday afternoon.'

Chris had trouble processing. 'I left Canberra on Thursday.'

'You must have been sedated over thirty hours. No wonder you were dehydrated. Ben and Mac were taken early Saturday morning.'

Chris scrubbed his eyes with the balls of his hands.

'You and Mac reached Santa Teresa after dusk on Saturday. The priest saw you were in a bad way and brought you both here.'

'Priest … that's right. I wanted him to go back for Ben.'

'He contacted the police, Chris. Apparently, you were caught up in some sort of sting. There was a federal police bigwig in town, an Agent Locke?'

Chris bolted upright. 'No! He's one of them. As crooked and corrupt as—'

'Now you believe me.' HS Chassic entered the room.

'HS! I'm so sorry. I was such a fool.'

'Well, you're safe now, and so is Mac.'

'But not Ben.'

Bert filled the awkward silence by standing and offering his seat to HS. 'I'll check on the ladies.'

HS nodded, then sat beside Chris. 'We found the shack, or rather, what's left of it. And some skeletal remains.'

Chris nodded and teared up again.

'But no human remains. The bones were more like—'

'A camel?' Chris's voice rose.

'A small one, perhaps.'

'Is it possible Ben survived? What if that madman took him elsewhere?'

'On foot? Unlikely. Unless he had another vehicle.'

'They will keep searching?'

HS nodded.

Chris shook his head. 'I feel useless. What about Locke?'

'Possibly escaped by air from the Allambie Airstrip south of Santa Teresa. Destination unknown.'

'But they're looking for him too?'

HS pursed his lips. 'It's not that simple. You willingly boarded an aircraft with Locke, after which you were apparently drugged and abducted. Locke may have left the country, or he may be a victim. At best, all we can hope for is a missing person alert.'

'You mean he could get away with this?' No way José.

'Justice will prevail, I expect. Don't concern yourself now. You'll be asked to give testimony later.'

'Except I can't swear to Locke's guilt. Not in court. He only talked about his intention to help Amy and his suspicions. He's cunning.'

'I could add a few choice descriptions for him.' Chassic's frown intensified before he smiled at Chris. 'But the doctor says you and Mac should be good to go by morning. Ah! Speak of the dev—er, young lady. Here she is. Good timing. I need a word with Cassie and Bert anyway.' HS stood as Amy came in.

She didn't wait for an invitation to clamber onto the bed and snuggle up.

Tuesday 27 November 2012

CHRIS COULD see why Amy had bonded with Cassie so easily.

'Cassie was here when I woke, helping, hovering, praying, mothering. It's been so long.' Amy's tears had triggered his own again.

'I guess that's her job, you know, being a minister and all.'

'Maybe. But I think it's more personal with Cass. She's been through a lot. Pain. Loss. Her father, sister and brother-in-law were killed by a drug-driver.'

'Then she understands grief.' Chris pursed his lips. 'I felt like a dead man walking after the house fire, when I thought you'd all died. Lucky me, sole survivor, but all I wanted to do was die. And I had the Alejandros caring for me. Sis, I would have moved heaven and earth to find you if I'd known.' Chris hugged her fiercely.

'I know.' Amy sighed. 'Liss never understood why I got so crazy angry over movie and book funerals. Those characters got to say goodbye. I didn't.'

'A hundred and one eulogies,' Chris said. 'Imagined. Never spoken.'

'You should give the eulogy at Ben's funeral. One hundred and two. Heartfelt and true.'

Chris disengaged their hug. 'I don't know, Amy, I—'

'Why not?'

'Ben's already had a funeral, after his car blew up.'

'You mean they won't have another? How can I say goodbye?' Dismay flooded Amy's face.

Chris wiped a tear from her cheek. 'I can't ask it of you, but, personally, I'd like to return to the shack. Maybe take flowers and—'

'Say goodbye properly. Absolutely. I'm right there with you.'

———

CHRIS WAS determined to honour Amy's wish—going back to the shack showed serious gumption on her part—but his efforts to persuade HS met solid resistance, until the Adlers mentioned HOPE had a program booked at Ltyentye Apurte, the Arrernte Indigenous Community's name for Santa Teresa.

'You're all welcome to come with,' Bert said. 'We'll need permission to travel to the site. If the Elders decline, we need to respect that.'

HS agreed.

After the puppet show, the local children swarmed Chris and Amy, abuzz about their survival which, apparently, was 'pretty amazing, eh?' Humbled by the community's welcome, Chris was quick to acknowledge that Arrernte Country was no place for an inexperienced whitefella to go walkabout.

'How's it going, mate? Joe's the name. These kids giving you cheek?'

'Not at all. It's amazing what they know.' Chris shook Joe's hand.

'Yeah. Our kids know Country before they can talk, eh? I'm from Amanbidji, m'self. Our mob run the cattle station there. HOPE visit our kids' school too. Hey Bert!' Joe waved him over. 'I saw your Jesus fella, eh? Nailed to a cross orright, but he's not dead.'

Bert smiled. 'You're right, Joe. Jesus rose from the dead—'

'I found him 'long Phi'pson Creek way. Hurt real bad, eh? Fixed him up with water 'n' bush medicine. Tucked him into a cave. Had to build a rock wall to keep ruddy dingoes out. Figured the padre'd want him back in one piece.'

'You told this to the parish priest, Joe?' Cassie asked.

'Tried. Bloke's a ring-in. Thought I was out of it, eh? From this.' Joe touched a wound on his head. 'Prob'ly sounded bonkers. I woulda brought his Jesus back in me ute if that pluddy whitefella hadn't nicked it. Pluddy crook shot me. Bad fella that one. Debil on his back long time.'

'Where'd this happen, Joe?'

'Part way to 'lambie, 'bout half-hour drive. I can show you if you got wheels. Pluddy long walk otherwise.'

'We'll hire four-wheel-drives.' HS had joined them.

'Goodo. Local mob know how to reach me. Oo-roo.'

Chris gripped Amy's arm. Dare they hope?

They located the interim priest—Joe's 'ring-in padre'. 'Now you mention it, I was showing tourists the inside of the church,' he said. 'Joe stumbled in, ranting and raving he'd seen Jesus and the devil together in the desert, then he took off.'

'Joe may have encountered the young folk you took to the hospital at Alice Springs,' Bert said. 'He's offered to show us the exact spot.'

'The police already searched the area.'

'Did Joe tell them where to look?' Chris asked.

'Doubt it. I didn't make the connection. But the official search was thorough.'

'Please, Bert.' Amy tugged his sleeve. 'We've got to try.'

Bert gave her hand a reassuring pat. 'We'll ask the Arrernte Elders for permission,' he said. 'If they have no objection ...'

—◦◦◦—

Wednesday 28 November 2012

JOE WAS unerring in his direction heading back to Hiki Harry's shack—which is what Joe's Uncle had called it. The fire had partially demolished the structure. The tank stand had collapsed, spilling water which had quenched the fire.

Joe pointed. 'Roof fell in. Cross fell out. Jesus fella nailed to it. I pried him loose, eh? Carried him round the hill. This way.'

They followed Joe to a shaded niche in a rocky outcrop. Stones were scattered in front, but the niche was empty.

'Other fella musta took him.' Joe shrugged.

Yet again, the old yo-yo of hope and despair twisted and tugged Chris's heart. But he needed to be strong for Amy. And he was as they laid farewell gifts in the niche, the nearest thing they had to Ben's final resting place.

62. RECKONED

December 2012

New South Wales, Australia

CHRISTMAS AND Canberra might have been a sneeze away, but Chris and Amy were stuck in a safe house just outside the Australian Capital Territory border. Their idyllic retreat was set well back from a rural access road.

The sprawling house boasted three comfortable living rooms, large open-plan kitchen-diner, several bedrooms, each with ensuite, an extensive subdivided office area, two well-provisioned underground storage bunkers, a separate caretaker's residence, and round-the-clock armed security guards roaming the grounds.

Was that to keep criminals out, or them in? He and Amy had only been allowed out twice, to view police line-ups of criminals with known drug syndicate affiliations. No familiar faces among them. No devil in the flesh.

And HS wouldn't hear of Chris returning to work. Yet.

'I need to ensure the investigation ramps up without being worried about your safety,' he'd said. 'Your sister needs you there, and you both need time to grieve and heal. It's hard, but you have to start somewhere.'

Chris wore 'time to grieve and heal' like an ill-fitting bunny onesie in which he pretended to eat, sleep, watch TV, smile for the security cameras, ignore Amy's habitual word fetish and that pestiferous, disconsolate, dipsomaniacal dictionary app she was besotted with. It wasn't normal. Or healthy. And she was at it again.

'Traumatised? Too banal. Outraged? Way past that. Stupefied? Vandalised? Perfunctory. That's you, Chris. Lacking interest, care, or enthusiasm; indifferent or apathetic—'

'Farting fire ants! Stop it, Mames! What else can I do? I'm locked up like a benched loser.' Chris slammed the fridge door shut and banged a bottle of Appletiser on the bench. 'Not that I've ever been anything else.'

'Mames? Mames? What's that?' Amy tossed her brand new, made-to-order smartphone onto the coffee table and stood, hands on hips. 'It's not my name, that's for sure.'

'Mac, Amy, Mames. Why not? You ignore me when I call you Amy. Like you've forgotten your own name.'

'I had to. At least you got to keep Chris, although you ditched Christian without remorse. In name and behaviour!'

Chris winced and bit his tongue. His anger still flared way too easily, but he had no right to burn Amy with it. 'I know. You've every right to castigate me. That maniac crucified Ben, but my anger and ego drove the nails in. I ran away and left him to die.'

'You also saved my life, don't forget. You're not the only one with regrets. I smacked Ben in the face and bloodied his nose. He was only ever kind to me. I'm not angry with you, big brother. Only with Locke and his criminal cronies. Please don't forget that.' Amy walked over and hugged him.

He held his sister tightly and his tears loosely.

She stepped back and pointed to the bottle on the bench. 'Is that the last Appletiser?'

Chris nodded. 'You can have it.'

She walked to the cupboard and pulled out two glasses. 'We can share, so long as you don't ever call me Mames again. Mac is fine. At least it contains a smidgen of the real me.'

January 2013

'IMPOTENT. FRUSTRATED. Stonewalled. Chomping at the bit.' Chris gave a small bow. 'With or without a dictionary app, if I don't get back to my own place soon, I'll go stir crazy. And living 24/7 with minders in tow is such a drag.'

'Tell me about it! Be thankful we haven't killed each other. Yet.' Mac signed, 'How's your Auslan?'

'Rusty,' Chris signed back.

'We can polish it together. What's your place like?' Mac signed.

'Not as spiffy as here but—'

'What happened to signing?'

Chris shrugged and gave a sheepish grin. 'Too out of practice.'

Mac rolled her eyes and signed, 'You're forgiven. Your place?'

'Nothing pretentious.' He took a short bow for using a fancy word which elicited Mac's grin. 'But it has me written all over it, you know? My brand of messy tidy. My gaming stuff and posters. Stuff I can do. Winning stuff. Here, it's all about what I can't do. What I failed to do.'

'You keep thinking like that, you'll end up as sour as—'

'You?' He'd signed that one.

'Ouch!' she said. 'Wow! Two months together and we're fighting like—'

'Siblings?' Chris screwed up his face.

Mac mimicked his expression. 'Yeah! Ain't it awesome? Watch out, Bro!' She chucked a cushion at him.

Chris threw it back. Mac caught it running and crash-tackled him onto the lounge chair. They wrestled, laughed, tickled each other. Hugged.

Chris sat up. 'You sure know how to take the mickey, Mac. MPeg's like that.'

Mac sat up, wide-eyed. 'MPeg? Who, pray tell, is MPeg?'

'A friend. She lives in Melbourne.'

Mac folded her arms. 'Please explain?'

Chris shook his head. 'Nothing to explain.'

'I don't believe you.' Mac drilled Chris with a squint and threatened tickle fingers. 'Fess up or regret it.'

Chris squirmed. 'Margaret Peregrine Blythe. She always used her middle name, shortened to Peggie, at school. We were gaming friends so—MPeg.'

'Cute. And?'

'We were housemates for a while. Not living together. Just friends. Nothing more.'

'Why are you blushing then?'

'I am not! Am I?'

Mac waggled her eyebrows. 'What colour's beetroot?'

Chris's cheeks burned hotter. 'Honestly, Mac. MPeg's a friend, a good friend, who wouldn't put up with my bellyaching. She's the one who convinced me to get a life … on my own.' Chris stood up from the lounge and paced. 'So why am I holed up like a napping bandicoot? Hiding from snake-bellied criminals is not living.'

'Maybe it's time we fixed that.'

'I'd like nothing more. But how? HS won't even have me back at work yet.'

'I don't know, but I'll think of something. And when I do, I will tell your Mr Chassic we're coming to see him, whether he likes it or not.' Mac's face said she meant it.

February 2013

CHRIS WAS debating another of Amy's cockeyed proposals when Chassic phoned.

'Are you and Mac happy to come in today? I have some interesting information to share.'

'We have some ideas to run by you too. Our protection detail changes over in five minutes. We'll come then.'

'Excellent.'

They entered ASPT's reception area forty-five minutes later.

'Hi, Von.' Chris saluted.

'The prodigal has returned. None the worse for wear, by the looks of it.' Von raised an eyebrow.

'I'm hiding it well.' Chris led Mac towards Chassic's office.

'What's with all the closed doors? It's claustrophobic.'

'It's policy. Welcome to my world of secrets, sis.' Chris knocked on Chassic's door. It clicked open.

'Come in, please. Save me from X, Y, Z and other fruitless loops.' HS tapped a pen on his desk pad. 'Did you know the English alphabet once contained twenty-seven letters?'

'Which one did we lose?' Chris asked. 'Or did it defect?'

'Since you asked …' Chassic's eyes twinkled. 'We lost the *and per se*—or ampersand as it's known in modern usage. Perhaps it defected to the symbols array during the Qwerty keyboard uprising, but I have a sneaking suspicion the alphabet song sealed its ignominious demise. C'est la vie.'

Mac leaned over the desk and studied Chassic's doodles.

'X, Y, Z, and. No wonder they dropped it. Nobody likes a loose ending.'

Nailed it, Mac. Chris pulled out a chair for her before he sat.

'I couldn't agree more.' Chassic's smile was warm. 'Sorry, guys. I began with Plan B and scribbled downhill from there.'

'Try the Khmer alphabet. It has seventy-four letters.' Mac stepped closer to Chassic's wall of seascapes and sailing ships. 'That's the wreck on Dicky Beach, isn't it?'

'It is. Do you know it, Mac?'

'Only by reputation. Beach visits were taboo under Li's safety regimen. No exceptions, not even for school assignments. I researched the *SS Dicky* for a feature article based on a local tragedy—seeing as I wasn't allowed to post selfies.'

HS sported a wry smile as Mac sat. 'I see you have your father's brilliance, your mother's spunk, and your own quick wit. If you have Chris's drive to win, I'd say you're far from tragic. More like a force to be reckoned with.'

'I'll say. Ow, Mac! Why'd you whack me?' Chris rubbed his arm.

She offered a look of pure innocence. 'Just practising ... being a force to be reckoned with.'

HS had the look of a teacher who was trying not to laugh at the antics of a mischievous student. 'Perhaps you should leave the exercise of reasonable force to the authorities, although ... you may need to hone your combat skills one day.'

'About that, HS. Mac and I want to be proactive in taking Ben's killer down. We've come up with a plan to flush Deabrua out, or whatever his name is.'

'Police have known about Mozzie Deabrua ever since his brother's murder trial. Your mother testified to his involvement.'

'What! And he's still at large?' *Unbelievable.*

'What murder trial?' Mac looked from HS to Chris.

'I only know what Pat told me, which isn't much,' Chris said.

'According to trial records, your mother said Deabrua was an onlooker, not the shooter, and she described his distinctive tattoos. Police say he's an illegal immigrant who disappears into a criminal snake hole the moment he's spotted. He's as slippery as the tattoos on his neck.'

'But now you have us, as witnesses. We can testify to his rat-shat.' Mac folded her arms.

'We have to catch him first.' HS looked grim.

'You set a trap to catch a rat.' Mac looked determined. 'Use me for bait.'

'No, Mac. It's the software they want. That's my domain. Use me for bait, HS.'

Mac barrelled on. 'Use us both, at a public memorial for Ben. Not only did he save me from drowning, he gave his life to protect Chris and me. He was a true hero.'

'Ben certainly deserves the accolade. But how is that a trap?'

'Make a huge splash in the media—coverage Deabrua can't miss— saying Chris and I will be there.'

'The man's arrogant. Pounds to peanuts, he'll come after us, if only to save face. Fill the place with non-uniformed police and surveillance. Nab him the moment he shows up.'

'Then we can officially identify him.'

HS held their enthusiasm with his eyes. 'It's a dangerous long shot. I think you've been through enough.'

'Sure, if you can call Hell enough. I've grown up in a monster's shadow, not knowing whether to run, or welcome the chance to die. Now I know. I don't want to run. I want to live, but not in fear. Not looking over my shoulder. Chris and I outwitted Deabrua before, when he held the power. This time, we'll have it. You have to let us try.'

Chris added, 'For Ben's sake as well as ours.'

'Amen!' Mac gave a cheesy grin. 'Sorry. Musta caught it from Bert. He's kind of in your face about his faith.'

'I must chat more with Bert.' HS smiled.

'Then we should send Cassie and Bert a special invitation. Ben and Bert really hit it off—once Ben convinced us he wasn't a murderer. I'd love to see Cassie again. I ... miss girl talk and stuff.'

'I'll follow up with the Adlers, in any case. Of course, there's no guarantee Deabrua will take the bait. Regardless, I agree Ben's actions deserve recognition. We'll make an event of it.' HS checked his desktop calendar. 'How about one month from now?'

'Why wait so long?' Chris shuffled his feet.

HS stretched back in his seat. 'To make sure Ben is fit enough to attend.'

'Ben's alive!' Mac's chair crashed to the floor as she leapt up.

'You found him?' Chris grabbed the edge of the desk.

'Yes, and yes.'

'Where is he? Can we see him?' Mac jumped up and down.

'He's recuperating at a private medical facility. It's not in Canberra.'

'Incredible.' Chris rubbed his face in his hands. 'How did—?' A knock interrupted his query.

'That'll be Raz. Admit him please, Chris?'

He obliged.

'HS.' The newcomer nodded deferentially.

'Chris, Mac. I'd like you to meet Agent Raz Karey.'

Chris shook Raz's hand. 'The agent I was supposed to travel with to Alice Springs. Had I not been so pigheaded.'

'You're not the first agent to learn things the hard way.' Raz gave a jaunty salute.

'Your timing is impeccable, my friend. I was about to explain how you located Ben.'

'By the grace of God, I'd say. I happened to be outside the church at Santa Teresa when Amanbidji Joe rocked up.'

'Happened to be?' Mac tipped her head.

'Let's say I possessed directed intel.' Raz winked. He placed his briefcase on the desk, opened it and passed a sealed post-pack to Chassic. 'The Landsborough DVR Ben posted to Anchors, showing Mozzie Deabrua committing murder.'

Mac tapped her fingers on the desk. 'When can we see Ben?'

'If you're up for a road trip, and HS approves, I'm good to go now.' Raz smiled.

'Yes, yes, yes!' Mac jumped up and down. 'HS! Please say yes?'

Chris wondered if she'd kneel and beg.

'I'd hoped you or Chris could identify voices from some phone intercepts. That's why I called you in. But the video should suffice for now. Thanks, Raz. They're all yours, if you can handle them.'

Mac was out the door before Chris could blink, but not before he'd noticed Raz's ear stud—a gold anchor set into black opal.

'Wait! Directed intel? Or GPS locator?'

Raz's nod was barely perceptible.

'Ben's double helix studs!' Chris glared at HS. 'You didn't need me at all.'

'Perhaps not. But Ben wanted you.' HS retrieved a black velvet drawstring pouch and handed it to Chris. 'The tracking function is optional. Ben chose to engage his after I phoned him.'

Chris peered into the pouch and drew a sharp breath. A single stud, like Raz's. 'I assume this means I'm not fired?'

Mac stuck her head around the door. 'Chris, what's taking you so long?'

'I believe he's contemplating his future.' HS smiled.

Chris stood and pocketed the pouch.

63. PRESERVED
February 2013

Anchors Retreat, Lake Macquarie, New South Wales, Australia

Ben FOUND the comfy hammock suspended between a flowering blackbutt tree and a red bloodwood after a nurse directed him to the secluded nook. Even the grounds at Anchors Retreat held secrets.

He'd thought this place belonged to his parents' hippy fishing buddies. He'd never dreamed the casual exterior hid a sophisticated underground medical facility.

He'd hovered beyond dreams since the last time he was here.

Experienced feelings, words, images beyond life's edge …

Racking, thrashing, ravaging pain …

Heaven … his father's face … together at last …

Pain beyond pain where it had no right to exist …

Why? Dad?

I'm here, my son …

Being with his father, riding fire and freedom …

Phoenix and eagle … rising … soaring … edging together …

'Pulse is back! He needs—'

I must go now, Ben-man. Raz will see you home safe.

Ben's eyes blurred. The time with his father had been so brief. So very brief.

Ben swallowed hard. Raz Karey had explained he'd been clinically dead for several minutes before he finally responded to CPR. His father's face, voice, presence, had been so real.

It's behind you now, Ben-man.

Was it? Ben settled into the hammock's cushion-laden cocoon and opened a book. Maybe its distraction would provide him respite.

He read the same page three times and still had no clue what it said. A yellowed leaf, discarded by its tree, landed in his lap.

His gaze wandered to the subdued hues of his forest enclave, muted grey-green eucalyptus leaves, placid red-pink Christmas bush sepals, elusive hints of gold, jade and emeralds where the sunlight kissed the understorey plants. The bloodwood's bark oozed deep red sap from possum-inflicted scars in its cindered tessellations ...

Ben shuddered. Had the tree felt as he had, when thorns ripped and shredded his skin? His attacker had called them euphoria something. 'Inflicting pain is so exhilarating,' he'd gloated.

The torment still invaded Ben's dreams.

A rustling sound from the overgrown pathway caught his attention. He turned the fallen leaf into a bookmark as Mac burst into the opening and threw herself at him. The book and its mark went flying.

'Ben! Ben-Ben-Ben-Ben-Ben! Are you okay? Can I hug you?'

'I think you are!'

Mac squeezed him like there was no tomorrow.

'I'm glad to see you too, kiddo. I just need to breathe a smidgen.'

'Sorry.' Mac eased back and clung to the hammock's edge instead. Concern etched her expression. 'Did I hurt you?'

'No more than punch buggies.' Ben grinned. 'Hey, Chris?'

Chris lagged behind at the edge of the nook, scraping leaf litter into a pile with his foot.

Ben pulled a pillow out from under his head. 'Don't hold back, Bro. I'm not!' He threw the pillow.

Chris caught it, brought it back to Ben, and shook his hand.

'Thanks mate.' Ben pulled him into a hug.

'It's just a pillow, Dro.'

'Thanks for saving Mac from that mongrel, Bro. You're a hero.'

Chris pushed out of the hug and swiped his eyes. 'If you think that, you're more damaged than you look.'

'And how do I look?' Ben opened his arms wide.

Chris surveyed, and clicked his tongue. 'Epic and awesome.'

Ben gave Chris the thumbs up. 'We should go on tour as the Epic Brothers. What do you reckon, Mac?'

'I reckon you already did.' She grinned and hugged him again.

'Deabrua's still at large.' Chris blew a raspberry. 'We've a plan to flush him out.'

'We sure do. And you get to enjoy some well-deserved honour in the process, Benny-boy.' Mac did a happy dance.

Ben swung his legs over the edge of the hammock and rescued the book from the grass. 'No rest for the wicked, eh?'

'Well, you know what they say?' Mac dusted her hands together.

'No doubt you'll tell me.' Ben winked and tucked his arms tight against his ribs.

Mac opened her mouth, shut it again, and blushed. 'I, um …'

Like pointer stars, the freckles on her cheeks drew Ben's eyes towards hers—evening sky glow, a mesmerising universe of infinite possibility. He reached out and gently traced her magnetic freckles with his thumb. 'What do they say, Mac?'

Her eyes opened wider. Ben caught himself from leaning forward, and offered a tender, tentative smile instead, which Mac returned in kind.

'They say, "Only the good die young".' Her smile spread to a grin. 'But since you've already done that—'

'I get to be bad-ass now?'

Mac's jaw dropped. 'Benjamin Alejandro! Did you say …?' She wagged her finger. 'Naughty, naughty, naughty.'

Ben grinned and winked again. 'Must be human after all.'

Chris cleared his throat. 'It's high time we all got back to living. Are you in, Dro?' Chris raised a hand for a high five.

'Absolutely!' Ben smacked it like a winner.

⸺◈⸺

February 2013

Safe House, New South Wales, Australia

'YOU CALLED it grunge? How rude!'

Ben's laptop screen smacked onto his knuckles, courtesy of Mac. He yanked his fingers free.

'It's an acronym, Mac. Guaranteed Retention Under Gridlocked Encryption—wordplay based on the software's format because the contents cling to the bottom of a recycle bin.'

'A garbage bin? You trashed my thoughts? Which is what they're worth, but that's hardly the point.' Mac pursed her lips and folded her arms.

'Maybe that's exactly the point, Mac.' Chris waded into the fray. 'Your thoughts were preserved, not trashed. Thank God they were, otherwise we'd have never found you.'

'Chris is right, Mac. Ironically, the GRUnGE gridlock unlocked your identity for us, and revealed the dangerous criminal grunge you were caught up in.'

'So don't huff at Ben. He risked everything to save you, grunge-head or not.'

'Great. Gang up on me. What would a stupid grunge-head know, anyway?' Mac took off, lickety-split, towards her room.

They hastened after and found her sobbing on the bed.

Chris sat beside her. 'I'm sorry, sis. I shouldn't have said—'

'Grunge-head? Why not? It's true. Grunge-mouth. Grunge-head. Grunge-heart. That's me. And Ben knows it.' She wailed into her pillow.

'I called it a GRUnGE long before I met you, Mac. Believe me, I'm on your side.'

Mac howled louder.

Ben mouthed silently to Chris: *What have I done now?*

Chris shrugged and patted Mac on the back. 'Come on, sis. Want a hug?'

Mac shook her head then nodded, rolled over, sat up, and swiped her tears. 'I'm sorry. You're both right. I don't know why I got so angry. I'm a miserable, horrible, ungrateful wretch. I'm so ashamed.' Mac buried her face in the crook of Chris's shoulder.

Chris rocked Mac gently. 'Well, you've got some competition there, sis. Either way, what's done is done. It can't be undone. Only forgiven. Then we can move on.'

'Sounds like a plan.' Ben reached for a tissue, passed it to Mac and knelt in front of her. 'Besides, I overheard you explain how Urban Dictionary defines 'wretch' as an attractive, witty, highly intelligent person.' Ben smiled at Mac. 'In your case, I heartily concur.'

Mac took the tissue and blew her nose. Chris ruffled her curls.

She managed a weak smile. 'Some dictionary entry we'd make, hey Bro?'

Chris nodded. 'Maxwell Kids: Grunge Incorporated. That's us.'

Mac's eyes went wide. 'We could write a book. All three of us. A collaboration. I'll write my part. You guys write yours.' Mac grinned then frowned. 'What? Don't look at me like that. Have I turned green and grown antennae?'

Ben snorted a laugh. 'Maybe! Your talent and imagination are cosmic enough.'

'And I love you too, Benny-boy.' The hint of a grin undermined Mac's dagger glare.

'We can't write a book. Chris and I are bound by confidentiality agreements—in order to preserve your privacy and safety.'

'And our necks.'

'We could use pseudonyms. Write it as fiction. Let's at least discuss it.' Mac's face glowed with enthusiasm.

'It's your story, Mac. You run with it.' Ben had no desire to trash her passion on his account.

'But I'll need details from you guys, to be authentic.'

'Nah! Fudge it.' Chris stood up.

'Hey Chris, you could design an interactive gaming version.' Ben waggled his thumbs.

Chris grinned. 'Guess Mac's thoughts or die.'

Ben winked. 'Good luck with that.'

Mac poked her tongue at him. 'S'not fair. LIES let you guys inside my head. It's only fair you let me into yours.'

'Use your imagination, Mac.' Ben also stood and patted her head. 'Be creative.'

'But—'

'End of discussion!' Ben and Chris spoke in unison.

'Sheesh! What are you guys? Two-fifths of a boy band?'

Chris pulled a pose, spun around and moon-walked out the door.

'Face it, kiddo. Writing is your thing, not ours. Except for writing code.' Ben smiled. 'Speaking of which, I'd like to code a flag word into the software so it will only transcribe your thoughts and conversations if you want it to. Think of a word you'd like to use. Better still, a phrase. Okay?'

'How about, "Chris and Ben are pikers"?'

Ben shrugged his shoulders. 'It's your call.' Ben walked to the door, paused and looked back. 'But I'd rather code, "Mac is an amazing woman." If you want it, that is.'

64. DISCOMBOBULATED

March 2013

Canberra, Australia

So MUCH for baiting a trap. Chris kicked over the car's ignition, gripped the steering wheel, and squeezed. Pity it wasn't Deabrua's grubby neck. Their tightly orchestrated media whirlwind had failed to produce one whiff of that stinking sewer rat. Spooked, no doubt, by the unexpected contingent of uniformed police who'd rocked up to give Brock Bosworth a posthumous salute.

Mac's concession that Bozo had 'tried his best, as one pain-in-the-neck to another' was ... Mac's, not his. She'd have drowned if not for Ben's heroics.

Standing beside Mac, watching Ben receive his commendation and bravery medal—without Pat and Mim there to see it—had loosed a tumbling avalanche of joy, pride, brotherly love, and heartache. He'd landed feeling ...

Discombobulated!

2010 People's Choice Word of the Year.

Thank you, Mac.

Still, things weren't all bad. Chris glanced at his passenger. MPeg *had* flown up from Melbourne. And HS *had* invited her to join them for lunch at a swanky restaurant. 'Well, so much for pomp and circumstance—a brobdingnagian brouhaha, for sweet fanny all!'

'Brobding what?'

'Big fuss. No result. Mac's been edu-macating me on the finer points of literature and language. Impressed?'

'With Mac, yes.' MPeg tapped ba-dum tish on the dashboard with her long fingernails. 'I thought the ceremony went well.'

'Hmph.' Chris edged their vehicle, the fourth in a cavalcade of five, towards the exit. A uniformed constable chauffeured Mac and Cassie in the third vehicle. HS drove Ben and Bert in the vehicle second from the front, and security agents drove the first and last vehicles.

A couple of Bosworth's uniform buddies stopped the traffic flow on the main road so their convoy could exit as one.

'Preferential treatment. I could get used to this.' MPeg's tone was soothing.

Chris shrugged, loath to surrender his frustration, and triggered a dry windscreen wipe instead of a turn signal. 'Bah! European fleet car with reversed levers.' *Mind on the job, Bro*. Which, at that moment, meant *safely* driving MPeg to lunch.

'Who's Joe? From Amma-something-or-other? You had a long chat with the Indigenous Elders who stood up on his behalf.'

'Amanbidji Joe. He's the bloke who found Ben, still alive. Thank God he did. His bush medicine helped Ben survive until reinforcements arrived.' Chris grinned in spite of himself. 'You should've heard Joe's response when I rang him about coming today. "Me," he says, "visit talk-too-much-and-do-nuttin gov'ment fellas? Nah. Can't stand their tripe. You come visit Amanbidji, eh? Bring that straight-up puppet mob wit'ya, Milly Nilly Rilly an' all."'

MPeg frowned. 'Triplets?'

'Puppets. Bert and Cassie's Arts outreach crew.'

'Good excuse to road trip through the Territory.'

'Maybe … one day.' He'd eaten enough outback Territory bulldust to last two lifetimes. 'Bugwhumps!' Another wiper-scraping left turn. 'Think I left my brain in the desert.'

'Maybe the bugwhumps ate it.' MPeg laughed. 'Thank your lucky stars you missed my driving debut with Melbourne's hook turns and trams. Totally blew my comfort zone.'

'Canberra's concentric layout and endless roundabouts totally blew my sense of direction when I moved here. So different to Sydney, where all roads lead to bridges—if you want to go anywhere, that is.'

'You never told me you'd lived in Sydney.'

'Didn't I?' Chris was shocked at his faux pas. Had he undermined years of silence with one lapse of concentration?

'Don't sweat it. I suspected you had a secret past life. A man of mystery and intrigue. Perhaps that's why I find you interesting.'

'Interesting? And?'

'I'll give you curiously fascinating.'

Chris grinned again.

'Kind of like a mongrel puppy—really cute and so-o-o adorable, but I don't know whether to pat you or send you to the dog pound.'

'Oh.' Chris's face dropped. 'I was hoping for dashing and debonair.'

'Mmm. Me too.' No mistaking her come hither vibe. 'Especially since you received a citation for bravery.'

Chris's ear suddenly itched. 'Honestly, Peg, I had no idea that was coming.' Beyond being a trap for murderers, the reason for the award ceremony was to honour Ben.

'You've really turned your life around since I left.' MPeg sighed. 'Seems you're better off without me.'

'Don't say that.' Chris studied her odd expression.

'Oi! Look out. Brake!'

He did.

MPeg exhaled. 'Nice reflexes!'

'Thanks. Looks like a collision on the roundabout, third exit.' It had blocked both lanes interrupting traffic flow. 'Must have happened a while back.' Police and paramedics were already on site.

A uniformed policeman diverted several oncoming vehicles through before directing Security Agent One and HS into their left turns. He halted Mac and Cassie's vehicle.

'Not the fairest cop, hey?' Chris pursed his lips. 'We'll be late for lunch.'

'We'll get there.' MPeg pointed. 'Second ambulance coming in.'

It stopped midway, obstructing all traffic and rendering the traffic cop temporarily jobless. He walked over and spoke to Mac and Cassie's driver who got out and followed him past the second ambulance and out of sight.

'He shouldn't leave Mac and Cassie unattended like that.' Chris drummed his agitation on the steering wheel.

'Stop stressing. He'll come back.' MPeg patted his leg. 'See? There he is. Back where he should be.'

Mac's car trembled as the constable started the engine.

'Still no sign of the traffic cop though. This is ridiculous. Come on, mate.'

'Ambo's on the move.'

Strain and concentration tightened the ambulance driver's face as he reversed his vehicle. Chris wouldn't like his job. Too many bad—

Memories! Chris's neck hairs snapped to attention. Xbox; anticipation; thrumming bicycle spokes; and that face! Driving the ambulance for Elias Spinnaze's dialysis!

And Mac's driver was executing a U-turn!

Chris yanked the steering wheel to the right, floored the accelerator and charged at Mac's vehicle, ramming the driver's door and front wheel arch.

MPeg screamed, 'What the hell?' as he bulldozed Mac's vehicle sideways, sandwiching the front passenger door against a lamppost.

Chris wrestled airbags. 'You okay, Peg?'

'Think so. Why on earth—?'

'It's a setup! Ambo's fake. Get to the escort car.' Chris released seatbelts—his and MPeg's, shoved his door open, and raced to Mac.

'Banshees, Chris! What—?'

'Deabrua! Second ambulance. You hurt?'

'No, but—'

'Help Cass to the escort car and call Ben.'

Chris bounded for the fake ambulance. A 'medic' shoved a stretcher at him. He dodged it and crash-tackled the pusher. A sickening crunch disabled his opponent as they hit the bitumen. Chris rolled to his feet, adrenaline surging. A second assailant lunged, syringe in hand, arm raised to jab his neck.

Chris ducked, tucked, twisted and elbowed his attacker's solar plexus. He grappled the man's arm and wrenched it down, plunging the needle into his opponent's thigh. With a curse and a grunt, the man sank to the ground and passed out.

The ambulance raced away, tyres screeching.

'What have you done, man?'

Chris spun around ready to tackle another assailant. Mac's original driver pulled himself to his feet, blood dribbling down his cheek.

'Are you mad?' The constable staggered sideways.

Chris stepped up to steady him. 'Deabrua's in that ambulance. The crash was staged to stop us. You should take it easy, mate. You've got a head wound.'

'It's mostly gravel rash. I'm good. I'm also betting that was no traffic cop. Blighter caught me from behind.'

'I've pinned him in your vehicle. Are you steady enough to sort him out? I need to check the others.'

'Go mate.'

The escort vehicle pulled up beside them.

Chris slid in beside MPeg. 'You ladies okay?'

'Apart from a split lip.' MPeg dabbed it with a tissue.

'Shaken but safe.' Cassie nodded from the front seat.

'I'm fine, but you're bleeding.' Mac pointed to the gravel rash on his arm.

'I'll live. We need to stop that ambulance.' Chris buckled his seatbelt.

'Your boss is on it, plus backup. I'm taking you to the safe house.'

'But—'

'They'll get him.' The driver triggered the windscreen wipers and pulled out. 'Bah! Flippin' fleet cars.'

MPeg nudged Chris. He wrapped his good arm around her, smiling as she snuggled in.

They heard the chase progress over police radio as extra squad cars channelled the ambulance into a bottleneck.

Ben phoned Chris. 'We got them. Found Deabrua hunkered down inside, smelling like a sewer rat.'

'In Deabrua's case,' Chris said, 'the odour's way beyond skin deep.'

March 2013

Safe House, New South Wales, Australia

CHRIS STARED through the window, contemplating the surrounding bushland. Four eastern grey kangaroos grazed less than fifty metres away. Regular visitors, the roos meandered through the grounds, reacting instantly if startled. He'd seen them flip a U-turn in a single leap. Strong, quick-witted creatures graced with placid natures.

Chris shivered, though not from cold. Was it actually possible? Had he executed a back flip, a life-defining U-turn away from uselessness? The roundabout encounter could have gone terribly, horribly wrong. It hadn't. Thanks, in part, to his split-second recognition of a face from the past.

He'd spent years regretting his survival; years keeping a mental tally, an internal whiteboard with God on one side, the devil on the other. The God side had always tallied nil, the devil's side had tallied one black mark after another. Chris's eyes blurred as, for the first time ever, he could imagine a hand with a duster erasing all those black marks.

'So this is a safe house?' MPeg's question pulled Chris out of his reverie and his attention back to her. 'What exactly have you dragged me into, Darnell? Should I check your closet for a Halle Berry lookalike? Because she needs to know I've got first dibs.'

Mac grinned and wagged a finger at Chris, rubbed it on her palm then over her mouth in a circular fashion—her signed equivalent of 'What colour's red?'

He answered Mac's silent question with a blush and a surreptitious middle finger movement which was not an Auslan sign. Fortunately, the pizza they'd ordered for lunch arrived.

Thai takeaway was on its way for dinner before HS, Ben and Bert finally arrived. They wanted to hear all about Chris's heroics.

'I thought he'd lost his marbles, crashing headlong into Mac's car like that.' MPeg rolled her eyes.

'Thank God we were moving slowly.'

'Thank God for airbags.' Cassie rubbed her shoulder.

'Thank God for Chris's quick reaction.' Ben slapped Chris on the back. 'Must've been those finely tuned gaming reflexes, Bro. Of course, I taught him everything he knows.' Ben huffed on his knuckles and scrubbed his chest.

'Excuse me.' MPeg faced Ben with friendly familiarity. 'Chris was *my* gaming protégé, Benny-bear. We slaughtered you and Cokecan.'

Mac folded her arms and gave MPeg a hard stare.

Here was trouble. MPeg's familiarity with him was apparently fine, but not with Ben. Was Mac being protective or staking her claim?

'Extreme punch buggies!' Mac stepped closer to Ben.

'Say what?' MPeg tilted her head.

'The jolt when your car hit ours punched me into Cassie.' Mac bristled.

Uh-oh. Chris's gaming sense kicked in. Diversion required.

'Good thing I'm well padded.' Cassie smiled. 'Poor MPeg suffered the brunt of it with her split lip.'

'Don't worry. I'll kiss it better.' *Double uh-oh.*

MPeg and Mac both grinned. Chris's cheeks burned.

'It would have been far worse if you hadn't stopped our car, Chris,' Cassie said. 'Mac and I owe you our thanks and possibly our lives for making a brave decision at the crucial moment.'

'More like a gaming fluke. A split second judgement re friend or foe. I'd be a pickle in vinegar if I'd called it wrong.'

Mac hugged him and squeezed. 'You were extraordinary, big brother.'

'You mean I finally made the club?' Chris patted her head.

'No.' HS deadpanned. Mac tossed him a withering glare. HS caught it with a wink. 'Club extraordinaire welcomed you long ago, Chris.'

The doorbell buzzed. 'Ah! I suspect our dinner is here.' HS headed for the door.

'Great. I'm starving.' Chris rubbed his hands together.

'Me too. You get plates. I'll get cutlery.' Ben grinned.

MPeg and Mac ferried the glasses.

With the table set, HS asked if Bert would offer a blessing before they ate.

'I'd be honoured,' he said. 'Let's join hands, shall we?'

Chris smiled as first MPeg, then Mac, squeezed his hands.

'According to the prophet Isaiah,' Bert said, 'This blessing is from the Lord, who created and formed you. This is what the good Lord says.

Fear not, for I have redeemed you.
I have called you by your name; you are mine.
When you pass through the waters, I will be with you.
When you walk through the fire, you shall not be burned.
You are precious in my sight, and I love you.
Do not be afraid, for I am with you.
I will gather my sons and daughters from the ends of the earth.
Amen.'

65. UNEARTHED
March 2013

Safe House, New South Wales, Australia

IT WAS the morning after the night before. Ben supposed he'd slept as well as any of them, judging by the yawns from Mac and Chris. The three of them played UNO at the dining table while HS debriefed MPeg in the office. Bert relaxed in the lounge room. Cassie brewed a round of coffee in the kitchen.

Chris threw a card onto the pile.

'It's a pick up four, Chris. Match it, or pick up, Bro.' Mac kissed the single card she held. She'd already called 'Uno' after her last turn.

Chris retrieved his card and added four more to his overflowing handful. 'Sorry. My mind's elsewhere.' He gazed longingly at the office door.

Ben glanced at his watch. MPeg would have to leave soon, to catch her flight. 'She'll be back, Bro. I'm sure of that.'

'Does water flow downhill?' Mac put her card down and grinned. 'I win. Pick up eight, Ben.'

Ben fumbled and dropped the swag of cards he held. 'Call it a draw for second, Bro?'

The office door opened. Chris stood as MPeg came out. She offered a rueful smile. 'I hope you're happy, Darnell. I've just signed my life away on your account, and you haven't even tried to put a ring on it.' MPeg waggled the empty fingers of her left hand.

Chris entwined his fingers with hers. 'Is that what you want, Peg'ms?'

MPeg tilted her head. 'Maybe.' She kissed his cheek. 'Stay safe, just in case, okay?'

'I'll try.'

'You guys keep safe too.' MPeg smiled and waved to Ben and Mac. She took Chris's hand. 'Walk me to the car?'

———

'COFFEE'S UP.'

Ben carried Cassie's tray of coffee makings to the table and set it—and himself—down as Bert wandered in from the lounge. Mac poured percolated coffee into each mug. HS was adding milk when Chris returned, face downcast.

'Peregrine's a delightful young lady. Understanding too, given the secrets and complexities of your situation and employment. Not easy to find.' HS sipped his coffee.

'I'll say.' Chris sighed and sat. 'Need to know sucks.' He reached for the sugar.

'You're going to ship Cassie and Bert off too, aren't you?' Mac looked miserable.

'Actually, that depends on you.'

'Me? Why?'

'Because the Adlers have offered to become your new carers.'

Chris froze, spoon suspended, sugar granules cascading. 'Mac has me.'

'Their role won't usurp your relationship, Chris. But Mac's only sixteen and we have her future to consider.' HS raised a hand against Chris's protest. 'Please hear me out.'

Chris dropped the spoon into his mug with a clang and a splash.

'S'okay, Chris. Listening's not deciding.' Mac rested her hands, prayer like, against her lips.

Ben watched her face, wondering what curious contemplations, insights, or prayers shaped her expressions. Would she ever knowingly, willingly, share them with him?

'Cassie? Bert? Would you like to explain your situation?' HS asked.

Cassie nodded. 'Sure. Bert and I have loved our role with HOPE, but towards the end of last year, we felt God was preparing us for something new. We just didn't know what. Three weeks ago, Eli and Sarah announced their engagement. They plan to marry prior to HOPE's winter school program and have offered to lead the team this year.'

Bert winked at Ben. 'You were right about them.'

Mac dropped her hands. 'But you guys live in Queensland. I won't leave Chris again.'

Bert smiled. 'We wouldn't ask you to. A colleague of mine offered me a chaplaincy position in Canberra. Given the cost of relocating, we'd planned to decline, but HS has a workable proposition.'

'ASPT will fund the Adlers' relocation and provide safe housing for you and them, as your carers, here.'

'What's wrong with my place?' Chris sounded defensive.

'It's listed in the phone book for starters. I'm sorry, Chris, but Deabrua's one link in a criminal chain.'

'Don't forget, Locke's still out there, Bro.'

'Your sister's safety must take priority. Yes, I plan to escalate your training as a covert operative, but that requires extended periods of Australian and overseas fieldwork.'

'Spy school, big brother!' Mac's face filled with mischief. 'Will he get a pay rise?'

'I'm willing to negotiate.'

'Good, because Chris needs to consider his future with MPeg—without me complicating things.'

'Mac!' Chris blushed.

'Cassie cared more for me in six days than Liss did in six years. I feel safe with the Adlers, and loved. Relationships are important, Chris.'

'Exactly! My relationship with you trumps career. I can go back to my old job.'

'No way! That's compromise thinking—Locke, Brock and loaded barrel! They sabotaged my dreams for their own stinking convenience. I fought to keep my options open and so should you.'

'ASPT needs you, Bro, and so do I.' Ben couldn't help himself. He didn't want to lose either of them.

Mac smiled at Ben. 'My brother *and* my best friend, both spies. How cool is that?'

'You can't divulge that information, young lady.' Chassic's tone was kindly, but stern.

'Bert and Cassie will know.' Mac smiled at Ben, her eyes glowing with delight. 'I've decided to enrol in a Bachelor of Arts, Creative Writing. That way, I can study *and* advance the LIES program.'

Ben caught an exultant yes with the tip of his tongue before he grinned at Mac's pun.

Chris rolled his eyes. 'Are you sure, sis? You don't have to decide today. We can think about this.'

'Nup. Time is precious. I've lost too much of it already. I want to live now. And I want you to do the same, okay?' Mac gave Chris a squeeze. 'I love you, Bro.'

He smiled as he ruffled her rapidly growing shock of red curls.

'Good. That's settled.' HS rubbed his hands together. 'Now, I need a private confab with my employees. Ben? Chris?'

They followed him to the office.

HS passed a USB to Ben. 'Audio files. I'd like your response.'

Ben sat, plugged the USB into the laptop, and played the first file.

> The mosquitoes are bad this time of year. You don't want to get bitten.

Chris sucked a sharp, noisy breath. 'That's Deabrua's voice.'

Ben ground his teeth. 'Locke showed me partial transcripts of these, modified to suit his own manipulative purposes.'

HS nodded. 'We've a plethora of similar conversations, thanks to Judy's brother.'

'2PD Judy?'

'Who?' Chris sat beside Ben.

'Judy Callahan. Past ASPT employee.'

'Now deceased. Suicide, according to the coroner.' HS pursed his lips. 'Only someone jammed a USB drive down her throat post-mortem and dumped her body at the Lower Molonglo Sewerage Treatment Works in a manner reminiscent of some cold cases.'

'Why would they do that?' Chris asked.

'To send a message. The USB contained files from Ben's ASPT computer, presumably copied by Judy the night she left.'

Ben frowned. 'I'm sure I locked my door.'

'Tampered with by someone in the know. Security firm's on notice.'

'I kept the critical files on an external drive, secured in my wall safe overnight, until the day I left.' Ben omitted to explain his doubts about HS had prompted his caution.

'Good thing you did. Although ... if Judy had succeeded, your suffering may have been avoided.' HS glanced at Ben's hands.

'But not Mac's.' Ben tucked his hands under the table. 'Was Judy's brother in cahoots with Deabrua or Locke?'

'Neither, I believe, despite Judy's involvement. Her brother worked for Locke at one stage. Locke kept surreptitious records of phone conversations. When Stephen Callahan challenged his methods, Locke accused him of sexual misconduct with a minor—unproven, but the mud stuck. AFP ousted Callahan, but not before he'd acquired Locke's questionable material. Judy's death prompted him to come forward.'

'Will it help convict Locke?' Chris looked hopeful.

'Got to catch him first.' Ben gritted his teeth. 'How can we help?'

'Leave the Locke hunt to experts. You two need to hone your field agent skills.'

Chris blushed. 'Like how to follow orders and avoid abduction.'

Ben mirrored Chris's contrite expression. 'So being a software guru doesn't quite cut it in the field?'

'No, but that's fixable, and my best field agent couldn't access this.' HS passed Ben another USB drive. 'Can you?'

'I'll give it a go.' The USB contained a Word Document and GRUnGE Sudoku. 'Dad's program! I …' Ben struggled to focus. 'It sounds crazy but—I thought I saw him, before Raz revived me. No! My father revived me! With CPR. Dad's still alive, isn't he?' Ben glared at HS. 'Why didn't you tell me? And don't you dare say, 'need to know' because this I needed to know.'

HS raised open palms. 'I'm sorry, Ben. I assumed you did.'

'Where is he now?'

'Perhaps his GRUnGE will enlighten us both.'

Ben sucked in a ragged breath and opened the Word document. It contained one line of text:

Phone Hechos Nuevo (New) Int +34 912 222247

'What's Hechos?' Chris asked. 'Bert has an NIV.'

'Acts. Chapter 2, Verses 22 to 47.' Ben solved the Sudoku while Chris borrowed Bert's Bible and worked out the Alpha code. 'We're in. Two photos and a video.'

The first photo showed a classified advertisement.

Attn: PA. Item in reasonable condition. Will exchange for software. Disposal imminent. Details: 43:267720 – 1:441649

'Looks like a geographical reference, longitude and latitude,' HS said. 'Easy to follow up.'

Ben opened the other photo. 'That's my grandparents' home in Spain. Mim went there when she left us.'

HS tapped the desk. 'Play the video.'

Ben obliged.

'Hey! That's Deabrua's shack! Before it burned.' Chris wrung his hands.

The footage zoomed in on a blanket-covered body. Someone off-camera yanked the blanket away to reveal a female body.

'Mu—!' Ben's voice choked but his mind screamed her name. 'I thought she left us willingly.'

HS rested his hand on Ben's shoulder. 'It certainly seemed that way, though your father had his doubts.'

'Dad must have recognised the shack when he found me. That explains why he left. But where'd he go?'

'I'm right here, my son.' Patriarca Alejandro stood in the doorway. 'I let myself in.'

'Dad!' Ben ran to his father's arms.

POST-MORTEM

Some months later ...

Unknown Location

LOCKE HEARD the light aircraft circle overhead. Not a hint of engine splutter, unlike ... He shuddered, roused himself from bed and felt his way to the chair which, by his reckoning, faced the cabin's door. If the door opened, if it was daylight, if the darkness belonged to his prison and not his vision, if the hint of ambient light wasn't a figment of his imagination ...

His sweat beaded and trickled.

He eased his hand across the rough, upturned crate that served as a table, knocking the radio off it before he located his water bottle. Its tepid contents quenched his thirst, but not his satisfaction. Caffeine cravings had dogged him like a hound on a hunt. He resisted the urge to snarl, and waited.

The scratch of a key, the click of a bolt, the creak of a hinge. A rectangular, light-filled haze surrounded a murky silhouette.

Locke exhaled, slowly, deliberately. 'Long time, no see, Ron. Or did you ditch the Sinballidh alias along with the plane?'

'Sadly, both had reached their use by date. But hey, I got us down, didn't I?'

'Just.'

'Be thankful I didn't bail out and leave you to meet your maker.' Zèf Kayif unlocked a metal cabinet, retrieved a light bulb, screwed it into the empty socket and flipped the light switch on before he closed the door. 'Your vision loss was temporary, I take it? Maxwell said a vitreous haemorrhage is not unusual following head trauma. Given his highfalutin medical background, he should know. Sorry for leaving you in the dark. It was a necessary precaution.'

'A necessary precaution … is that how you justified sanctioning Ben's murder?'

'Murder? That's a bit harsh. Martyrdom, perhaps. His choice. One man's noble sacrifice to safeguard our nation's intellectual assets and pecuniary interests.'

'Impressive game plan. Sugar-coat your stuff-up with dubious semantics while the hero lives on to die another day. I nearly puked when I heard all and sundry sing Ben's praises on national radio.'

'Pure propaganda. Chassic's shindig was a sham. Ben's as dead as the nails in Deabrua's shed. Coroner's report verified every gruesome detail. They awarded a medal to a lookalike. Relax, mate. Neither father nor son can trouble us now.' Kayif's nonchalant indifference was masterful. 'And … I have Pat's pretty little filly safely corralled where I can ride her at my leisure. All's well that ends well.'

Locke's attempt to digest that thought gave him heartburn. 'And how will it end for me?'

'That, my friend, remains to be seen.'

Locke stood, defiant. 'I could kill for a decent cup of coffee.'

'You might have to.' Kayif turned, opened the door, and walked through it.

Locke followed.

Meet the Puppets

The puppets were crestfallen after I culled
their moment of glory. So, if you'd like to know
how their performance ended, read on!

xx Mazzy

PS: If you loved this book, why not
share the love by posting a review?

LOST & FOUND

Bonus Scene

'HI, EVERYBODY. I'm Potsherd Pavarotti. Are you ready to watch the show? That's great! Are you ready to meet my friends? Terrific! One of my friends is here, and ready. She's Rilly Truly Reddy.'

'Hi, Pots. Hi everybody. Listen, Pots, ready or not, you have to fire Milly.'

'Fire who?'

'Milly Nilly Reddy, my silly dilly sister, who's never ever ready.'

'Truly, Rilly, I can't fire Milly.'

'Why not, Pots?'

'I didn't hire Milly. She's a volunteer.'

'Then volunteer her outta here.'

'Why would I do that?'

'Because she calls the audience, ewes, like they was sheep.'

'Were sheep.'

'Well, if you insist. All hail Potsherd Pavarotti!'

'What are you doing, Rilly?'

'Following orders. I want you to fire Milly, not me. You said "worship", so I did.'

'Not worship. Were sheep. You said "was sheep". You mixed your singulars and your plurals. "Were sheep" is proper grammar.'

'Try telling that to Milly.'

'Hi, Rilly! Hypotenuse! What's your angle? I'll set youse straight!'

'Aargh! She did it again! Milly doesn't know her proper grammar.'

'I do so too! She lives in a suitcase with our proper Grandpa.'

'Oh, Milly!'

'Look, everybody! Egermeier's here. Hello, Eggie.'

'Hi, Milly. You're in fine form today.'

'She is not! Milly's rilly truly cranky. Worse than a bear with a sore head.'

'I am not cranky! I'm sad. I've lost my favourite teddy bear. I've searched here and I've searched there and I can't find him anywhere.'

'Serves you right for being rilly truly cranky.'

'I was not rilly truly cranky! I was milly nilly cranky.'

'Rill and Mill, you need to chill! I get rilly confused when you two argue!'

'Sorry, Eggie.'

'I'm sorry, too, Eggie. Will you please help me find my teddy? I rilly truly miss him.'

'Sure, Milly. In fact, I've already found your bear. He's hiding here, in Rilly's hair! Go the fro, Rill!'

'Teddy! Teddy! Thank you, Eggie! You've made me so happy I could sing for joy.'

'Really truly?'

'Absolutely!'

'Do you girls remember Jesus' story about the woman who lost her silver coin?'

'I do! She searched everywhere, just like Milly did. When she found her lost coin, she invited all her friends to celebrate with her.'

'That's right! Our favourite Christmas beetles, Jon Lemming and Paw McCassie, wrote a song about it. *Hey, Youse!* We could sing it now.'

'Oh, Milly!'

'Join in and sing if you know the tune. Cue the music, maestro!'

Hey youse, I feel so sad,
Dropped my bag full of coins all over the place,
I've checked ev'ry space I thought they could go,
Searched high and low, and swept ev'ry surface.

Hey youse, I'm so dismayed,
Got to pay all my rent by Saturday,
My landlord has said that he'll throw me out,
Without a doubt, if I cannot pay him.

But can it be? Is this my coin? It is! What joy!
The treasure I lost has been restored to me,
It's safe and sound where it belongs, no longer gone,
How can I contain this joy I'm feeling?
Come and rejoice with me everyone, yeah!

Hey youse, in the same way,
All of heaven will sing and celebrate,
Whenever somebody opens their heart,
Gets a fresh start, there's wild jubilation.

And can it be my long-lost child's now reconciled?
My wandering treasure's been located,
She's in my arms, where she belongs, no longer gone,
Her value has been accentuated,
Come and rejoice with me everyone, yeah!

Hey youse, in the same way,
All of heaven will sing and celebrate,
Whenever somebody opens their heart,
Gets a fresh start, there's wild jubilation.

And can it be? My long-lost child's now reconciled,
My wandering treasure's been restored to me,
She's in my arms where she belongs, no longer alone,
I cannot contain this joy I'm feeling.
Come and rejoice with me everyone, yeah!

Hey youse, in the same way,
All of heaven will sing and celebrate,
Whenever somebody opens their heart,
Gets a fresh start, there's wild jubilation,
Bells are ringin', angels singin' Yo!

Sing hal-le-lu-u-u yah, hallelujah, hey youse,
Sing hal-le-lu-u-u yah, hallelujah, hey youse,
Sing hal-le-lu-u-u yah, hallelujah, hey youse,
Sing hal-le-lu-u-u yah, hallelujah, hey youse,
Sing hal-le-lu-u-u yah, hallelujah, hey youse,
Sing hal-le-lu-u-u yah, hallelujah, hey youse,
Sing hal-le-lu-u-u yah, hallelujah, hey youse …

Acknowledgements

My muse fired the starter's gun for the idea that became *Licence to Die (GRUNGE.001)* in 2012. Provoked by an image of a despondent youth riding a train, I leapt from the creative starting blocks with Mac's wry critique of '*the industrial backside of Brisbane, the bums of shops and the private parts of houses, places you're not supposed to see, full of junk, debris and dirty secrets*'.

For years her desperate, cynical cry pestered the dim recesses of my mind, begging a decent hearing. Giving Mac her voice (and saviour) became my privilege and my marathon. It's my delight to acknowledge the loyal cheer squad who urged me toward the finish line.

Gary Sercombe, my beloved forever-friend and husband, thank you for believing in me, for backing my creative streak and subsequent endeavours with your unwavering, unconditional support (emotional, physical, spiritual and financial) and for devising regular random road trips that blow away the cobwebs and nurture our life-long communion.

My beautiful daughter, Ruth Taylor, thank you for triggering my re-entry into the world of study so I'd explore and develop my passion for writing. Thank you for bolstering my sagging spirits during the eleventy-seventh edit of my 'final' draft with this Facebook post:

'I'm so proud of my Mumma B. I have seen the hours and hours you have put in to this amazing story and I have had such fun brain storming and defending my favourite characters (so you don't kill them off). I am truly amazing [sic—yes you are!] *by your creativity and dedication and I hope that maybe I will possess a smidgen of that!! You are my best friend, my partner in adventures (literal and literary) and my inspiration xo'*

Bless your compassionate heart for defending Bozo, thus provoking my desire to unearth his powerful background story and give meaning to his broken life—before I bumped him off. (Sorry about that.)

Thank you David and Peter Sercombe, my wonderful sons, for eagerly developing your own God-given creative talents, for aiding and abetting mine as willing Thespians and musicians, for embracing the challenges of Distance Education and enduring the wilds of the Australian outback with smiles on your faces and guitars or puppets in hand.

I praise God for Gary and Kerrie Armstrong who instigated that outback adventure in 1999, helped us safely negotiate 13000 kilometres of blacktop, bulldust, and roadkill with prayers on our lips and God's love in our hearts and introduced us to so many amazing Indigenous Australians along the way.

Special thanks to Dr James Cooper, Tabor, Adelaide lecturer and mentor, whose genuine encouragement fuelled my genre rebel tendencies and cemented my desire to write and keep on writing. And also to Dr Jo Wurst for appreciating and nurturing my unique (and somewhat quirky) way of seeing and interpreting all things literary.

Thank you to my treasured friend, Nola Passmore, for lovingly drawing me into the Quirky Quills sisterhood and for persuading me to submit my poetry, devotions, creative non-fiction and short stories to various anthologies, knowing that success in publishing, once tasted, is a powerful motivator to persist through the long haul of writing and publishing a novel. Thank you for your insightful beta-reader feedback and for your unceasing encouragement and belief in my abilities as a writer.

I'm incredibly blessed by the depth of friendship, fellowship, and love I receive from my Quirky Quills writing sisters, Nola Passmore, Janelle Moore, Pamela Heemskerk, Kirsten Hart, Adele Jones, and Sandra Troedson. To quote a certain Pooh Bear, it's great to have friends who use words like, 'How about lunch?' Even better when you can chat about writing (and its frustrations) while feasting.

Many thanks also to Iola Goulton, a brilliant editor with heart, skill, and a discerning eye for both big picture and detail. I hope I've done justice to your wise and welcome input.

I include among the many who inspire and encourage me personally, my precious sister, Thelma Atwell, who totally made my day when she apologised for being so engrossed in the story, she'd forgotten to proofread. Also Jeanette O'Hagan, Sue Jeffrey, Paula Vince, Anusha Atukorala, and Anne Hamilton for boldly cheering the writer's cause (including my own) with wisdom, good humour, happy mischief, and touches of wonder.

Most importantly, I'm eternally grateful to the Triune God for loving me, wanting me, seeking me, finding me, saving me, guiding me and inspiring me. To Him be all the glory, now and forever.

About the Author

Once upon a lifetime, Mazzy Adams tumbled into a melting pot of creativity, crafting (and performing) songs, Aussie bush poetry, puppet plays and drama sketches before adding a Creative Writing Degree through Tabor College, Adelaide, to the mix. She met fascinating and perceptive people in the process.

She subjected hoards of drafts to soul-destroying slash and burn edits and raised short fiction, poetry, creative non-fiction, blog posts, and this—her debut novel, *Licence to Die (GRUnGE.OOl)*—from the ashes.

With a growing portfolio of published works in multiple anthologies and formats, Mazzy happily identifies as a bona fide genre rebel. Her picturesque, tongue-in-cheek writing style injects a quirky Down Under vibe to intrigue and inspiration alike.

Mazzy also employs her think-outside-the-box neural pathways and passion for words, pictures, and the positive potential in people to guide students through the perplexities of English written expression.

Best of all, her wonderful husband, amazing children and delightful grandchildren make Mazzy's otherwise ordinary life most extraordinary. For that, she is eternally grateful.

Discover more and connect via https://mazzyadams.com

www.ingramcontent.com/pod-product-compliance
Lightning Source LLC
Chambersburg PA
CBHW020336120726
47904CB00002B/426